LOVE A MAN OUT OF UNIFORM

VOLUME 1

SEALS UNDONE

ZOE YORK

PROPERTY OF:

BY THE AUTHORITY OF ZOE YORK

FOREWORD

This collection contains the first five (of ten) books in the SEALs Undone series. The first story, Fall Out, was written for the first SEALS OF SUMMER military romance superbundle in early 2014. It was my first foray into military romance, and that collection hit the New York Times list (#6 combined) and rode the USA Today bestseller list for four weeks. It was an honour to be a part of something that exciting.

I named this series *SEALs Undone* because that's exactly what happens. Big, tough Navy SEALs are undone by the women they fall hard for. These stories are light on conflict, full of sexy heat, and short enough to read in a single night.

There are ten stories out in this complete series. Each can be read as a standalone romance. If you enjoy small town military romance as well, check out my Pine Harbour series.

And if you like to keep up to date on new releases and sales, I recommend you join my VIP reader email list, my Facebook reader group, and follow me on Instagram!

I hope you enjoy!

~ Zoe

FALL OUT

ABOUT THIS BOOK

Drew Castle is a Navy SEAL with a bad case of indifference. Until
Annie Martin shows up on his doorstep, scared out of her mind, and
all of a sudden, keeping her safe becomes the most important
mission of his life.
And this time, he's on his own.

CHAPTER
ONE

TRAINING AT DAWN was easier on the east coast. The slap of sand under his feet, the salt in the air, men all around him...that was the same. But Drew missed the sunrise. Eventually it would make an appearance, climbing over San Diego, lazily providing absolutely no inspiration to drive hard at the end of the run.

He missed Virginia. Early to bed, early to rise. That was the east coast way. But after completing his time at the Senior Enlisted Academy in Newport, he'd been given the choice, and for reasons he still couldn't understand, he'd chosen the west coast.

It wasn't that he hated California. Drew was far too disciplined to spend that kind of energy on what was just a place. Places held no meaning. It was what you did there. Who you saved. Sometimes, who you killed.

Maybe he was getting too old for this shit. All around him, young hotheads made it look easy. Novak and Dumbrowski, third-generation Americans who still got saddled with the Polish jokes, were at the front of the pack. He saw a lot of himself in Novak. A lot of Kevin in Dumbrowski. Coming out here didn't get him away from any ghosts. If anything, breathing in the Pacific Ocean every morning kept a part of his best friend alive inside him.

Kevin. Losing a team member was an understood risk of the job, and over the years, everyone had experienced it. But he hadn't been the same since he dragged Kevin onto that helo thirteen months ago, knowing that it was too late to save anything other than his body. They'd been more than team members. They survived BUD/S together. Brothers from another mother, they used to joke, even though it hit a little close to the truth. Kevin had been the closest thing to a family Drew had.

Sixteen years. That motherfucker stayed alive through firefights, infiltrations, recon missions and more than one long weekend in Miami. And got shot in the back when they thought they were done the job. Fucking fate.

Drew didn't have PTSD. He'd passed his psych eval with flying colors, and he'd been pretty honest with the docs. Not completely honest. There were some dark corners of every SEAL's mind that one learned never to share. But compared to some of the bullshitting that happened in that chair...he was mentally fit for the job. But did he still have the necessary drive?

He just didn't care about *anything*. And if it was anyone else, he'd counsel them to think about walking away. Because without that fiery urge to conquer, he wasn't useful to the team.

That was a terrifying thought.

Not just for himself, although he really had no idea what he'd do if he retired early. But also for the mission. Missions. They were at war, quietly and unendingly, and leaving that fight to others just didn't seem right, especially when he was still physically able.

In front of him, Novak kicked it into high gear. The pull-up bars, their informal finish line, were in sight and Drew shook off his thoughts. He'd missed the moment when he could have left the younger guys in his dust, but he was going to stay with them. At least for today.

"Hoo-ya." One by one, they pushed hard to the end. Dumbrowski launched himself into the air and held himself from the horizontal rail for a moment, then lowered his body in a controlled fashion.

"Show off," Drew muttered.

"Shut up, Castle, you can kick my ass if you want to."

"Fucking right, and don't you forget it."

"We're hitting a club tonight, you wanna come with?"

He could. He probably should, he didn't socialize enough with his men. But he wouldn't. "Nah, but thanks. Maybe another time."

Fun was something he'd also left behind in Virginia. Kevin had always raved about the girls out here, and Drew couldn't deny there was something about the sun-washed hair and bikini-ready bodies that revved a guy up. He'd even enjoyed a bit of casual revving with a bartender he'd met while being surly. But he'd just bring the party down, and his guys didn't need that.

They hit the showers and changed into uniform. Just another day at work, with meetings and managing officers. What Drew wouldn't do for a deployment right about now. Nothing like a well-planned attack to take your mind off meaningless shit like feelings.

By the end of the day, he was ready for an omelet, a video game and bed. He stopped at the grocery store—he was constantly running out of eggs. In Virginia, he'd lived with two other guys. Apparently, the only thing he missed about having roommates was their quiet support of his omelet addiction. On the other hand, no one groused if he played Metal Gear Solid for three hours straight, which was a win in his books.

He let himself into his apartment building and set his bag of groceries down on the floor so he could check the mail. His phone chirped in his pocket—Dana, the bartender, wanted to know if he'd be up for a late night visit when she finished work. His dick twitched yes, so he responded affirmatively, and jogged up the stairs.

Grub, game, girl.

It was what passed as a rollicking good time in Castleland lately, and he wasn't too twisted not to appreciate that he still had it pretty good. If Kevin were alive, he'd kick Drew's ass for not living every day to the fullest.

I'm trying, asshole.

Try harder, dickhead.

In the shower, he leisurely stroked his cock, looking forward to the midnight booty call. Dana liked guys in uniform. She was a part-time student, with plans to move to Europe the following year. Zero questions about commitment, and a wicked mouth. Given that he had absolutely no emotional ability to be a boyfriend right now, their occasional arrangement was perfect.

You should go to Europe with her.

It really annoyed him that Kevin talked to him.

I'm not really talking to you. It's your misplaced guilt or something.

"Tell me something I don't know, asshole." He pulled on a pair of workout shorts, turned on the TV for some background noise, and made quick work of a mushroom and cheese omelet.

When a knock sounded at the door two hours later Drew winced at the timing, and hit pause on his game. Maybe she'd cuddle up with him while he finished the level.

Okay, maybe she's not the girl to throw your career away over. Definitely not if he wasn't sure who he wanted more, Dana or the big boss.

But it wasn't the pretty bartender on his doorstep. A beautiful brunette stood in her place, a woman with whom he shared a special and tragic connection. All other thoughts fled his mind as he tried to process why she was in front of him. "Andrea?"

Kevin's younger sister stared back at him as he stood there, blinking, and he realized he was being rude. "Come in. How did you..."

"Some guy held the door for me." She followed him into the apartment, her arms twisted together in front of her body. "I'm sorry for showing up unannounced. I took a chance that you were around."

He took in her jeans and blazer, her polished boots and careful jewelry. She hadn't made the drive south from L.A. for a casual visit. He grabbed a hoodie he'd left on a barstool at the kitchen counter and tossed it on, all of a sudden feeling underdressed for whatever conversation they were about to have. "It's no trouble, I'm glad you caught me. What's going on?"

She let out a nervous laugh. "You're going to think I'm nuts."

He shook his head. "Promise I won't."

She pulled out her phone, pressed a few buttons, and passed it over, her hand shaking. "Press the star button to listen to this message."

Kevin's voice filled his ear, for real this time. "Andrea, it's me. It's really me, and I need your help. It's about—" his voice broke up in a rough electronic crackle, then warbled back to life "—so I've set up a private email address we can use to communicate back and forth. The password is our first pet's name. You'll remember that, won't you? I miss you so much."

Drew fisted the phone tightly in his hand, the urge to pitch it against the wall almost overwhelming. He took a deep breath and turned his back to Andrea for a moment.

Her voice was watery and small as she spoke behind him. "It's not him."

His shoulders sagged with relief that he wouldn't have to explain that to her. He turned around. He didn't know her very well. They'd only met a handful of times. Easter one year, when she was still a teenager. Her parents' funeral, an overnight stay with Kevin a year later on their way to Hawaii, and then again at Kevin's funeral. But his best friend had talked about her enough that he had a picture of who she was. Smart, analytical, but also a dreamer. A romantic and an optimist, with a tidy, uncomplicated life.

Drew's total opposite. He was glad he didn't need to drag her into the dark recesses of his mind where he could too easily imagine where that kind of twisted message came from, but he hated that she figured it out on her own. Clever girl.

But right now, standing in front of him, she just looked scared, and he was reminded that her uncomplicated world was built on a foundation of loss. And now her cage had been rattled. *Fuckers.* He wanted to make that go away for her, protect whatever was left of her innocence. "No, it's not. Andrea..."

"It's Annie," she whispered. "No one in my family called me Andrea. Ever."

The cruelty of that mistake in the faked message twisted his gut. "I'm sorry you had to hear his voice like that, in a sick joke."

"Is it just a joke?" She cleared her throat. "I have some money. Life insurance from my parents, Kevin. The house."

"Whoever did this didn't ask for money."

She furrowed her brow, her eyes still wide and scared. "Don't you think that's the next step? A fake ransom demand?"

Yeah, probably. "Have you called the police?"

"No, I heard the message, got in my car and drove here. I don't know what I would have done if you weren't home. Maybe gone to the base? I'm terrified to make a wrong move here." She looked at the phone in his hand. "That didn't feel like a joke. Or a fake kidnapping, to be honest. It felt like a threat, but I can't imagine to what end."

His first instinct was to call his CO, his commanding officer, and take Annie into work, hand the phone over to the Intel guys and let them figure this out while she had a nap behind the secure gates of a United States naval base. But there was something in her expression, a slight tremor in her pinched brow that gave him pause. "Annie, are you telling me everything?"

She swallowed hard and nodded.

"Because you came here for a reason."

Her big blue eyes searched his face, and he willed her to see whatever she was looking for. After a minute, she dropped her gaze to the floor and sighed. "Kevin always told me that if anything happened to him, I could trust you."

"You *can* trust me. Kevin trusted me, and I'll do everything in my power to honor his memory and protect his family. But I need to know everything that you know." He ducked his head, grabbing her attention. "No secrets."

A flutter at the base of her neck gave her away, and she groaned. "I don't know how anyone could know this, because I'm guessing you don't, and I wasn't supposed to, but Kevin...has a child. A secret son, being raised by his mother. And her husband."

Drew reared back on his heels, like she'd just tossed ice water in his face. No way. *Dude, what the fuck?* But Kevin didn't answer, because this time, Drew couldn't fill in what his best friend would say.

"It was a short affair, while he was in Washington ten years ago. Nobody should know. The husband doesn't know. I was a teenager when it happened..." Annie kept talking, and Drew sorted through what she was saying, but most of his mind was trapped in a flashback to ten years earlier. Kevin had come back from the capital decidedly cagey about his recreational activities. Uncharacteristically so. All he'd said was that he'd gotten involved with someone he shouldn't have.

"Do you know the couple's identity?" Drew's mind was whirling a mile a minute, sorting out the possible outcomes. He didn't like the threat assessments he was coming up with. "Is there anyone else who might, a cousin or something?"

She shook her head. Annie and Kevin's parents had been killed in a car accident a few years earlier. Drew had been at their funeral. Well attended, but little in the way of extended family.

"And you didn't tell anyone else about this call?"

"No."

He'd seen a lot of awful shit over the years, and while this barely scraped the surface of gross human behavior, he couldn't imagine Annie would share his jaded outlook. Or appreciate it. "Okay. There's not much we can do before the morning, given that it might just be a prank."

She nodded and took a deep breath. "And then we'll call the police?"

"Probably start with the Navy, since that's what I know. They might punt it to the civilian investigators. I don't know." He splayed his hands wide, unsure of what to say next. "Hell, Annie, I'm sorry this happened to you."

"It's okay." She let out a watery laugh. "Probably this time tomorrow I'll be back at work and some teenager with aspirations of being a hacker will be having an uncomfortable conversation with the LAPD."

He stepped closer and touched his knuckle to her chin, lifting her face so she could see the confirmation in his own that she'd done the right thing. "This might be just that. But if it's not, then I'm glad you reached out to me."

"Kevin always said..." She bit her lip, her teeth pressing into the plump skin to hold back the rest of the sentiment. A crease formed between her eyes, and he wanted to reach up and rub it smooth, ease that ache.

He wasn't the only one struggling with loss. He felt like an ass for not acknowledging that sooner. "He was right. It's good that you came."

She tilted her head to the side with a wry smile, and he cupped her cheek in his palm for a moment before reluctantly letting go. "Well. Then, I'll just go find a hotel, and first thing in the morning—"

"No." He surprised them both by interjecting. "Stay here."

"I couldn't impose, really."

"This probably isn't about you, but if it is, you should stay here. I'll find you some clothes to sleep in and a toothbrush—"

Another knock at the door interrupted him, and he cursed. "Okay, so that's, uhm...That's a friend. I'm just going to explain to her that my plans have changed for the night—"

"Oh, god. No. I'll go."

The knocking resumed, this time in a playful pattern, and they jockeyed around each other to get to the door first. Drew won, and pressed his hand flat against Annie's chest. "Seriously, stay." He took a peek through the peephole. *Shit*. Dana was wearing a trench coat. That could only mean one thing.

He took a deep breath and opened the door. "Dana, before you open that coat, you should know I've got a guest."

The bouncy blonde grinned and sashayed in. "Isn't that the kind of thing you should ask a girl if she's into first?"

"It's not like that. We'll—"

Annie cleared her throat and stepped into the open doorway. "I'll head out so you can continue with your plans."

Dana looked Annie up and down and spun back to Drew. "What's going on here?"

Drew sighed. "It's a long story. Annie, please don't leave." He braced his arm across the doorway, blocking her exit. "Dana, this is Annie, the sister of an old friend, and she's going to be staying with me for a few days. Maybe I'll call you next week."

Dana pursed her lips. "Maybe?"

What the hell? Yes, maybe. That was their deal. In the three months they'd known each other, they'd hooked up seven or eight times. There was no guarantee of more sex. No dating. Just...easy. And if it wasn't easy, he didn't need any drama. "Or not. Up to you, okay?"

She hitched her shoulders and tightened her belt. "Or not sounds about right. Have fun on your sleepover, Drew."

Annie stepped out of the way and Drew lifted his arm, and as quickly as Dana had swirled into their conversation she was gone again. He pressed the door shut and threw the deadbolt and safety latch. "Okay, so I'll get you—"

"No." Annie shook her head. She'd crossed her arms at some point, and from the firm set of her shoulders, wasn't planning to uncross them any time soon. *Shit.* Was this a girl code thing?

"That was just a misunderstanding."

"Like, where you misunderstood how to be a human being?"

Jesus Christ. "Pardon?"

"You really hurt her feelings!"

"So? Feelings weren't supposed to enter into it! Not my problem she saw you and got catty. Maybe she was jealous." Drew tamped down his annoyance. They had bigger things to worry about than Dana and her temper tantrum.

"That's ridiculous. She didn't get upset until you said," Annie cleared her throat and dropped her voice a register. "*Or not. Up to you, babe.*"

"I didn't say babe. She's not my babe." He rolled his eyes and stalked off to his bedroom. He yanked open his top drawer and pulled out a black t-shirt and the smallest, lightest pair of running shorts he owned. She'd still be swimming in them, but they had a drawstring waist. He'd changed his sheets earlier, in anticipation of the ill-fated hookup, so he tossed the clothes on the bed and stalked back to the living room.

Annie had shrugged out of her blazer and was laying her jewelry carefully on the raised kitchen counter. Chunky necklace, matching bracelet, sparkly earrings. It all looked good, but without it she looked nice in a different way. Pretty. Young. He searched his memory. She was ten years younger than Kevin, who was a year

Drew's junior. Twenty-five, and she dressed like a school principal. Acted like one, too.

She was going to make some guy's life hell. Drew chuckled to himself. With good sparring might come angry sex, though, and that would be fun.

Dude, that's my fucking sister.

He took a step back into the hallway and scrubbed his palm against his jaw. Shit. Where had that thought come from?

I don't know, asshole, but lock it down.

Consider it locked, bro. Drew cleared his throat and moved forward to try again. "The bedroom is yours for the night, I'll take the couch."

She swung past him, avoiding his gaze. When she reached the doorway to his room, she paused, then glanced up. "I'm sorry about commenting on your private life. It's none of my business."

He shrugged. "Sort of was, given it played out like that in front of you."

"If you want me to talk to her, tell her there's nothing to be jealous about..." She waved her hand. "Once all of this is sorted out, if you want her to be your babe after all. She seemed..." Annie cleared her throat. The obvious choice there would be *nice*, but Dana wasn't really that. "Fun."

Yeah, she was fun.

But as he turned off his PlayStation and grabbed a blanket from the hall closet, it wasn't images of Dana sliding all over his body that he had to push away. And when he woke up to screams in the middle of the night, it wasn't worry about Dana that made his heart leap into his throat.

CHAPTER
TWO

ANNIE CLAWED her way to full consciousness, desperate to escape the awful noises in her dream. As she blinked awake, she realized she was the source, moaning and groaning under her breath. Drenched in sweat and shaking like a leaf, she gulped for air and took what little she could see in the strange room around her. Clean sheets, big bed. *That belonged to Drew Castle.* Douchebag extraordinaire and real-life hero.

And then he was in the doorway, his large body tense and at the ready. "Annie?" Light flooded into the room from the hall behind him, and instead of moving directly to her, he looped the long way around the bed and flicked on a lamp.

She opened her mouth but nothing came out. Fear squeezed around her neck and across her chest, and she couldn't prevent tears from welling up and spilling down her cheeks.

"Jesus, Annie." He came around to her side and crouched, his gaze darting from her face to her phone, which sat untouched on the bedside table, then back to her face and finally down her body. "Nightmare?"

Must have been, she thought silently. *Holy fuck.*

"You didn't get another call? You aren't hurt?"

She shook her head.

He glanced at the alarm clock next to the lamp. "It's the middle of the night. Any chance you're going to get more sleep?"

Another shake. Not a chance in hell. She cleared her throat, tentatively testing her vocal cords. "Is—" Her voice cracked. "Is there anything we could do about the message right now?"

"Most of the Intel guys won't be in until 0800, but I think we should go grab some breakfast and then head to the base. If only to help you feel safe." He hung his head. "We shouldn't have stayed here last night."

His regret was palpable, and she scrambled onto her knees, shaking her head. "I do feel safe with you." The simple truth of the words made her feel better. She shook her head again, ridding herself of the creepy feeling she'd woken up with. "No, I wasn't scared last night. I'm not sure what my dream was about, it was too abstract to explain, but that's all I'm freaked out about."

He lifted his head and cocked one eyebrow. "Would diner breakfast make it better?"

She couldn't help but laugh. He was a grown man, but crouched beside the bed he looked like an eager kid, and his smile warmed her from the inside out. "Absolutely."

It didn't take her long to wash up and get dressed in yesterday's clothes. What had she been thinking, hopping in her car and driving south from L.A. without a bag of stuff?

She hadn't been thinking. Driven by adrenaline and fear, she'd tunnel-visioned on the fact that Drew Castle was the only person in the world she could trust when it came to her brother's memory. And even now, knowing that he was an overgrown teenager, that didn't change anything. Kevin had been the same way, chasing anything in a skirt and kicking back with boy toys at every opportunity.

And it didn't matter what or who Drew did in his spare time if he could help her. A tremor of something suspiciously pride-like niggled at the back of mind as she reflected on the fact that he'd dropped both his video game and his booty call to help her, and she pushed that thought away. She wasn't a teenager anymore, in awe of the sex-on-a-stick SEAL lounging in her family room after a big Easter dinner.

Ten years ago she'd have given anything for Kevin and Drew to look at her as more than a kid. But as it got dark, they'd gone out without a backwards glance, and Annie had drifted off to sleep wondering what it would be like to be sexy enough to capture the attention of a grown man.

Ha, she snickered. They were barely older than she was now. How much her perspective had changed in that near decade.

But her big brother had taken his job seriously, and his family as well. More than one holiday had been spent perfecting "What to do in a Zombie Apocalypse" plans. Annie understood Kevin was making sure she knew how to protect herself. He'd taught her to shoot, to fight dirty, what to yell at the top of her lungs to grab maximum attention and how to be stealthy.

The last tips came in very handy in her last year of high school.

The first time she got drunk with Kevin, on the Christmas Eve of her twentieth year, she shared how helpful he'd been to her teenage social life. And he told her about some epic drives down the Eastern Seaboard with Drew for crazy weekend leaves. It had been a rare moment of sibling bonding, almost as equals. The following year, their parents were gone, killed in a head-on collision with a minivan. No more Christmas Eves with her brother.

He'd offered to come home, but she had friends with large families. With no shortage of holiday feasts for her to attend, it didn't make sense for him to travel at peak time when it was just the two of them. They'd have time for that in the future when they had families of their own.

Annie blinked back unexpected tears and shook off the melancholy memories. No time to get lost in what might have been. Some asshole was messing with her brother's memory, and that couldn't stand. She straightened her shirt and joined Drew in the living room, just in time to see him tuck a handgun into a concealed holster at his hip.

"Is that really necessary?"

He turned and smirked as she reached for the jewelry she'd left on the counter the night before. "I could ask you the same about that stuff."

"My *stuff* can't kill someone." She kept her tone playful, because she had no doubt that his was the safest concealed carry around, but did people really just *do* that?

Had Kevin? Due to their age difference and his career choice, she hadn't known her brother as well as she'd have liked. There was supposed to have been time for that later as well.

Of course, that meant she didn't really know Drew, either. How much of her opinion of him was colored by her memories of a brash older brother who played hard and resisted taming?

As if he could read her mind, he patted the gun. "I don't wear it all the time. I just..."

Yeah. There was something about having a stranger show up on your doorstep worried about boogeymen that brought out the paranoia. "No worries."

"Besides," he muttered as he pulled on a sweater over his snug black t-shirt. "Your stuff is pointy. I'm surprised Kevin didn't teach you a thing or two about using whatever's on hand."

She laughed. "He did." She took a sobering deep breath. "I was just thinking about that, actually."

He opened the door and gestured for her to move into the hall. As they made their way to the elevator, Drew regarded her with quiet curiosity, but he refrained from asking just which Kevin memory she'd gotten lost in. She was just about to offer something to keep the conversation going when he made a gruff noise in his throat and changed the subject. "We can take my car. I park underground."

She bobbed her head in agreement, and before too long they were buckled into a sports car that seemed way too small for his oversized frame. But he drove it with ease, his long, lean fingers dancing around on the gear shift, his right knee bopping against the center console panel whenever he wasn't accelerating. She found herself following the long curve of his arm up to his shoulders, round with working muscles, and then down the front of his body. She wondered idly if he looked larger than life when naked as well, and as that thought twirled around in her head, she turned and looked out the window, afraid the pink of embarrassment would give her away. What was wrong with her? From panic to pervert in less than five minutes.

Her friends would protest that looking was just fine, but it really wasn't when it was your dead brother's best friend who was trying to help you figure out why you'd been creep-stalked. Besides, looking at Drew probably got women in trouble. Women like Dana. God, he might be the world's nicest friend, but Drew Castle had shown the night before that he could be a first-class dog when it came to women, and no good would come of imagining him in his underwear.

Or out of it.

He drove northeast out of downtown, and before too long they pulled up in front of an old-school diner lit up with blue neon lights. They seated themselves in a booth and a waitress showed up a moment later with a steaming pot of coffee and two menus.

"Hey, honey." She smiled at Drew, a friendly middle-of-the-night grin. "Where are your friends?"

"Pushed 'em off the boat." He slid his mug forward and turned to Annie. "Coffee?"

"God, yes." She offered them both a weak smile. Breakfast at four in the morning, in the middle of drama...*sure, everyone just act like it's just another day at the office.* But for Drew and Sarah, if her nametag could be trusted, it was exactly that.

They ordered—two eggs with ham for Annie, three with steak for Drew—and after Sarah whirled away with a pop of her gum, Drew leaned back in the booth and notched his head to the side, regarding her with unvarnished curiosity.

"What?"

"You're handling this well."

"Doesn't feel like it on the inside, trust me. I'm a fish out of water."

He lifted his mug and sipped slowly, his eyes trained on her the whole time. "So what is your water?"

"UCLA. I'm a graduate student there."

He stilled for a moment, his mug in mid-air, then he set it down and eased forward over the table. "Really? That's great."

She laughed. "I'm not sure how great it will be when I'm looking for a job at the end of my studies. I'm in the History Department."

"Ancient History?"

"Nope. The exact opposite actually. Modern American History."

"Fascinating." From the way his eyes had lit up, and the keen interest all over his face, she actually believed him. A warm flush started in the middle of her chest and radiated up and out. "Kevin said that you were smart, but he never—" He cut himself off and reached across the table to touch her hand. "I'm sorry. He talked about you all the time. I just wasn't the greatest listener."

It wouldn't have occurred to Annie that Drew, or anyone else, would find her studies anything other than boring. But with his warm, strong fingers branding themselves on her skin, she was having trouble thinking of a way to reassure him it was fine. "Uhm..."

He shifted his grip, slipping down and around her hand so his fingers cupped hers and his thumb traced over the round pad of flesh on her palm. "I'm listening now, Annie. I'm glad you came to me last night. I'm going to help you." She glanced up, reluctant to look away from the hypnotic pattern he was tracing on her skin, but something in his voice snapped through her silliness. She looked at him, and he looked at her, something heady and tempting on his face, but then he licked his lips and shuttered his gaze. "I'm going to be there for you because Kevin can't. Think of me as his surrogate, okay?"

No, she wanted to shout. *You can't sit there like sex-on-a-stick and ask me to think of you like a brother!* There was no way she'd be stupid enough to actually sleep with the man, but if he kept invoking her brother's name, it would make her future filthy fantasies incredibly awkward. "Sure."

They both retreated to coffee and private thoughts until Sarah returned with plates piled high with food. As the scent of buttered sourdough bread, perfectly cooked ham and heavily seasoned hash browns filled her nose, Annie's mouth started watering and her stomach growled loud enough to grab Drew's attention. He glanced up from his plate with a smirk and she blushed. "I didn't eat dinner last night."

"This is dinner and breakfast all rolled into one." He pointed with the back end of his fork. "Dig in. You're not going to offend me."

That hadn't been on her mind. She wrinkled her brow and shook her head.

"What?" He washed down his mouthful of food with a big gulp of coffee.

"Do women usually eat like dainty flowers around you?"

"No." He laughed. "I don't usually eat with the women I...hang out with."

Wow. That was even less sexy than the surrogate brother comment. "That's...nice."

He cocked one eyebrow, but didn't respond again.

She started to slow down as her plate emptied, and when he looked up again, his smirky tone had shifted back to the keen interest of before. "So, history. What's your specific area of interest?"

"Economics. One of my advisors specializes in modern world capitalism, the other in American political history. My interest is the financing of grassroots political activism, but it'll be a while before I get to my own research. For now I'm taking classes and working as a research assistant on other projects."

"Shoot, that's pretty cool. And your dad was a professor, right?"

She nodded. "Yep. Public Policy at USC. That's where I did my undergraduate studies. I had to have a special course schedule in my third year because his class was a required component." She knew her voice was wistful, but this was Drew. She might not know him very well, but instinctively she understood she didn't need to hide her pain from him. "Him teaching me would have been a conflict of interest, so I took an equivalent course online. That was probably harder, having him grill me to see if I was learning everything I needed to know from *some other teacher*."

Drew nodded and chewed, then swallowed some coffee. He took

his time looking at her and rolling that over before pushing the conversation again. "Kevin didn't talk about your dad a lot."

She quirked her lips to the side. That didn't surprise her. "They didn't get along, really. My father worried Kevin wasn't interested in academia. Kevin didn't like that Dad questioned the government's use of military action from time to time."

Drew snorted. "What an asshole."

"Hey!"

"Not your dad. Kevin. He probably shared the exact same opinions. We just don't have the luxury of voicing them."

Annie picked up her coffee, buying herself a second to think. "Kev? Critical of...anything?"

"Hell ya. Between you, me and the toast, most of us get frustrated when we're sent in like an expensive Band-Aid when the real solutions are longer, more complicated—"

"And probably even more expensive." She sighed. "Wow."

"Hey, it's okay."

She curled a small smile for his sake. "Sure, I know. It's just... you knew him better than me."

"While you're here, I'll share what I know, okay?" She nodded and he grinned. "But first, tell me about the boring research they're making you do while you jump through hoops to do your own." He took a huge bite of his steak and chewed.

"How did you know?" This time, the smile was bigger, and very real. "Uhm, let's see. I get to tag along on some interesting research trips. We're going to Washington next month to interview a few senators. Muriel Castillo, Lawrence Lassiter and Rob Harris."

Drew's fork clattered on his plate. He finished chewing, slowly, while his eyes burned a hole in her head.

"What?"

"Rob Harris?"

"Do you know him?"

"Do you?"

"What? No. I know he's on the Senate Committee on Armed Service. Is he one of the ones you and Kevin aren't fans of?"

"First, I said that Kevin had opinions. Lots of guys do. I don't. Not really. I do what my commanding officer orders me to do, because I trust he's thinking about that shit so I don't have to. Second, when these interviews were set up, who made the arrangements?"

"I did. Being an RA is a lot like being a lackey."

"You called Rob Harris's office and set up an appointment? What did you say the interview was about?"

"Civilian leadership, military connections, rise to power...that's the scope of my advisor's research." His probing gaze was completely freaking her out. "Drew, are you thinking that has something to do with the message?"

It definitely did, but how much could he tell her? A little bit of knowledge was a dangerous thing, and she was already on the verge of panic.

Now wasn't the time for talking anyway. He slid a glance at her cell phone, sitting quietly on the table beside their mostly empty plates. A rapid-fire burst of curse words slid through his mind as he realized they'd probably said too much. He couldn't tell her everything he knew about the dark underbelly of Washington, even if there wasn't a probable bug in front of them. Frustration rolled through his gut that he was operating on the fly. He was a team player. Sure, he was trained to deal with any variability, but his operations were analysed, planned and executed based on a lot more intel than an ugly gut feeling.

Waiting for the other shoe to drop was an option, but not one that sat well with him. An alternate plan started to crystalize in his mind. He grabbed his backpack, threw some money on the table, and without another word reached across and tugged Annie out of her seat. With a yelp, she snatched her stuff with her free hand and stumbled along in his wake as he tugged her out of the diner.

"Drew, what the hell is going on?" She slammed her hand on the car door as he moved to open it. "Hang on a second!"

"Sugar, we might not have a second. Get in, and I'll explain as soon as I can."

He waited just long enough for her to do up her seatbelt then he peeled out of the lot and tore off into the darkness. His destination was just on the other side of the next main thoroughfare. Annie kept glancing at him, and he willed her not to say anything until they got there. He turned again, this time in the dark pre-dawn shadow of a hospital. He quickly navigated around the building branded with a glowing H and pulled into a parking garage.

Annie gave up any pretense of not staring at him as he quickly wound his way up to an upper level and pulled into one of many vacant spots. Her gaze was hot on his skin and a small part of his mind started to process why that didn't make him uncomfortable.

He grabbed her phone, stuck it in the glove box along with his, and silently indicated for her to get out of the car.

"Why are we here?" she asked as he started walking toward the stairwell, the hollow echo of his footsteps the only sound bouncing off the bare concrete.

"Because if anyone calls asking about you here, they'll hit a wall of privacy protection. At least temporarily. Let's go find a bus."

"This is crazy," she muttered, but she trundled after him. "We don't want my phone in case they call again?"

"No."

"No?"

"No."

"Well, that clears that up." She ducked past him as he held open the door to the stairwell.

He sighed. She was right. She deserved at least a partial explanation.

The blaze in her dark brown eyes told him taking a second to think about what information he could offer was a mistake. "Hey, if this is annoying for you—"

"Annie, this isn't—" He barked out a short laugh. "Annoying? Hell, no. This is better than a regular day at the office for me. But I'm not used to explaining myself."

"And I'm not used to ditching my phone in a parking garage and going on the lam!"

He ducked his head and propped his hands firmly on his hips, willing himself not to laugh. When she put it like that...it was a miracle she'd let him drag her out the restaurant.

When he looked up, prepared to defend his wild and crazy and totally random plan, the look on her face surprised him, and not just because the fiery spark had softened. He swallowed hard at the bare trust staring back at him. *Jesus*. He was on her side and he'd keep her safe but he wasn't a fucking hero.

Something dark and possessive clenched hard in his chest. He *wanted* to be her hero, probably for all the wrong reasons. How could he know that he was making the right call here?

She stepped forward and pressed her hand to his arm. Her touch, cool and smooth, slithered under his skin and took root. He stared down at her, wanting more of her touch. A lot more, and as if she sensed his desire, she stroked her palm up to his shoulder. "Drew, I appreciate all of your assistance. But if you think this is truly some sort of spy-game, then we need to go to the authorities."

It was time to share. His heart thudded in his chest. The uncommon reaction bothered him more than he wanted to admit.

"Senator Rob Harris, senior ranking Democrat on the Armed Forces Committee," he said quietly, his muscles shifting with each word as he chose them carefully. "He's a good friend of the Director of the CIA. There are other connections that I'm not sure I can tell you about right now, but let's just say I'm aware of him and his colleagues." Harris had never meddled directly in any operation Drew had been involved in, but others had. "The senator also has a 9 year old son and a beautiful wife."

CHAPTER
THREE

DREW SAID the last sentence slowly and carefully, his eyes tracking over her face as the words sank in, but his measured delivery didn't stop the point from knocking her for a loop. She gasped out loud, then slapped one hand over her mouth to keep the sobs inside and pressed the other hard against his chest. *Oh my god.*

Even as the pieces slid together, she didn't want to believe it. "You can't know—"

"Not for sure." He held her gaze, his own strong and confident, and she blinked hard to keep the tears at bay. "All I'm saying right now is I'm not sure going to the authorities is a good idea. I have a friend I can call, who was in Washington at the same time as your brother, but I can't do it from the phones we had. The main bus lines will start running soon, and we'll head back downtown. Then we'll get some more information and make a new plan."

"You think that Kevin...and Senator Harris's wife..."

"I think someone knows Kevin's secret, and misunderstood your request for a meeting." He glanced down at her hand, still pressed against his chest, and groaned under his breath. He tugged her hard against him and ran one large hand over the back of her head. "You okay?"

"No?" She let out a watery groan of her own. This was crazy. "Then what was the phone call about?"

"Testing the water? Hell if I know. But we can't...fuck. We can't just walk onto the base and open a can of worms without knowing more."

He made a good point. She sagged against him, letting his strength seep into her bones. It felt...right, and she didn't pull away until he reminded her they needed to keep moving. They found the bus stop, noted the next arrival time, and waited.

———

Drew didn't know if he was anywhere in the vicinity of making the right decision. Frankly, other than getting as far as possible away from what was guaranteed to be a tracking device, he hadn't *made* any decisions. And for the first time in seventeen years, he didn't have orders or a plan. Sure, he'd run into unexpected situations. He had to make snap decisions all the time, with lives on the line.

But this time, the situation had knocked on his front door, and he didn't have any back up. No team. Just his gut instincts warning him that Annie had accidentally wandered into something ugly.

Drew paid cash to the driver of the first bus to come along, and Annie led the way to seats in the very back. Under the hum of the fan overhead and the dull noise of the engine, Annie asked him the question he was just asking himself. "Where are we going?"

"I have no idea," he answered honestly, looking out the window. "We're heading downtown. Might as well loop back to my place and grab some stuff, then..." He trailed off. He needed a new phone. There was a convenience store two blocks east of his apartment, and he could have Annie wait there while he dodged home for supplies. "Will you be offended if I hide you somewhere while I do that?"

Her eyes got really wide and her lips parted. Dark pink lips, soft pillows on an otherwise lean face. Fuck. She was scared and he was lusting after her. Asshole.

"Uhm, I guess not. Do you think that's necessary?"

"The odds of you actually being in danger are pretty low. But if you are, for whatever reason, the odds that they've tracked you to me are pretty high."

"With my phone?" She closed her eyes and rubbed the tiny crease between her eyebrows. "Damnit. I should have just gone to the police in L.A."

"And let me miss all this fun?" He rubbed a knuckle against her jaw. "Annie, you can put the weight of the world on my shoulders, okay?"

She let him lift her face, and she blinked up at him, but doubt and confusion still warred in her eyes. "Why?"

Because it was his job.

But this didn't feel like work. For the first time in ages, he felt that tug from the inside out, a sense of right and wrong and he knew what side he was on. But it was more than that. It was personal, too, and not just because of Kevin.

Dude...

Sorry, bro. Just being honest with myself. And he'd keep it to himself, too. No good could come of admitting he was motivated by her pretty face and pouting lips. *Focus.* "Because it's my job. I mean, *you* aren't a job, but this is what I'm trained to do."

"Why do I get the feeling you're going to tell me that a lot?"

"It's the only answer I've got, sugar." The only one he could voice out loud, anyway.

She stretched her legs out in front of her, rotating her ankles left and then right, then lifted her chin and pinned him with another look. "Do you call everyone that?"

"No." She wasn't mad, but he couldn't read her expression. "It just slips out. I'll stop."

"It's okay." She cleared her throat. "I don't mind..." She held his gaze for a minute, her eyes crinkling at the corners before a smile split across her face. "Brotherly affection is better than nothing, I guess."

If that's how she read it, he wasn't going to correct her. He looped his arm around her shoulder and tugged her close. "You're not alone, Annie. I can't give you much, but I can give you this."

"Wow, an early morning escape from a deadly cell phone, by city bus no less. It's the stuff of action movies." She snickered and tossed her head back, letting it rock against his bicep, and he fought an urge to pull her even closer, until there was no space left between their bodies, and his hand could slip off her shoulder and down to the delicate curve of her high, round breast. He'd just graze it with his fingertips, the barest of touches, and she'd tip her face toward his. The laughter in her eyes would fade, replaced with heat and then they'd kiss...

Instead, she slapped his thigh and stood up. The bus was waiting at a red light, and Annie pointed out the window at a twenty-four hour discount store. There was a bin of baseball hats in the entrance, and a rack of sweatshirts. He nodded. Smart girl. He tapped the signal strip, indicating to the driver they wanted off, and ten minutes later he was paying cash for a burner phone, two hats, two hooded sweatshirts, and a spare outfit for Annie, who'd apparently leapt in her car without packing an overnight bag.

While they waited for the next bus, he sent an international text to one of the few numbers he had memorized. **Rik, it's Drew. When you've got a chance, call this number. Soon, if possible. Have some questions about your time in DC with KM.**

The phone rang three minutes later, his friend's slight accent barely noticeable in the three short words he spit out. "What is it?"

"Kevin's sister came to visit me last night." He spelled out the details of the message, and what he'd learned over breakfast. He could hear Rik's smirk as he described their current mode of transit, but it didn't last long.

"You're such a law-abiding citizen, Drew. It didn't occur to you to steal a car?"

"Some of us still work within the law. I know it's a novel concept."

"Your mistake is working, period." Rik had gotten married the year before, and was officially retired from the Norwegian FSK. Unofficially...well, Drew didn't want to know how his friend could afford to live on a private Caribbean island. "Give me her phone number."

Drew realized he didn't have that information. He covered the handset and turned his attention back to Annie, who was staring at him with unabashed curiosity. "What's your number?"

He relayed the information to Rik, who said he'd call back in a few minutes. "And Castle...you know enough to stay clear of security cameras, right?"

"We've got baseball hats and a plan to get back into my building underground, yes."

When he disconnected, it took Annie all of five seconds to let the questions fly. "Underground? Within the law? Who did you just tell my life story to?"

"Rik Amundson, a total son of a bitch and the only other person in the world who might know about your brother's child. He was stationed at the Norwegian Embassy in Washington when Kevin was at the Pentagon. They got pretty tight, and two years later, we spent time with him overseas. We've kept in touch." He paused before sharing the next piece of information. "Kevin saved his life once."

"In Afghanistan?" Big eyes, small voice. Annie's knowledge of what they did was probably limited to whatever was on TV.

"No..."

"Never mind, I know about operational security, I shouldn't have asked." She waved her hand and turned around, looking down the increasingly busy street for their bus. Her long brown hair swung loose to the middle of her back, and he swallowed against the temptation to gather it into a handful and tug her back against him. He shoved his hands into his pockets, not trusting his will power, and once again wondered where this attraction was coming from. She was pretty, but she'd been pretty before. He'd noticed her beauty when he'd visited with Kevin on their way to Hawaii, and the three of them stayed up late in her kitchen, but it didn't affect him then like it was now. It should have... she'd made them cookies and teased him about being a bikini snob, and now that he was thinking about it, he couldn't understand why he hadn't been attracted to her then. But there'd been some sort of block. Even last night...it wasn't like he opened the door and saw her as a woman for the first time.

So what had shifted? Was it having her in his bed, even if he'd been on the other side of the wall? He must have conflated her with some fantasy and if he wasn't careful he might act on it. Which would be stupid, because easy come, easy go. He'd wake up tomorrow and she'd just be Annie again. For today...he needed to spend more time talking about Kevin and less time wondering if she'd tremble when he kissed her neck.

If, not when, asshole.

"It was in the Artic," he blurted out. "Rik got on the wrong side of a polar bear and Kevin took the beast out at five hundred meters."

Her head lifted, paused, and then started bobbing with silent laughter. She slowly turned back, her hands held up in disbelief. "Please tell me it wasn't a cute little one like on the Coke commercials."

"Nah. Although that would have made for excellent ribbing, this was a big motherfucker, definitely scary and planning to tear Rik limb from limb."

"A bear!" She took a deep, steadying breath and let out one more giggle. "I didn't realize SEALs operated in the Arctic."

He shrugged. "Training exercise."

"Mmm-hmm." They both heard the hiss of bus brakes at the same time, and the conversation faded as they stepped onto the next bus. Forty-five minutes made a huge difference, and this time they weren't alone. They stood near the back door, holding onto opposite sides of the same pole, and before he knew it they were disembarking a few blocks east of his apartment.

"I don't need to buy a phone anymore, but I'd still like you to stay somewhere safe while I go home and grab my stuff. There's a coffee shop over there. Can you go read a paper for twenty minutes?" He wrote down two numbers on a receipt and pressed it into her free hand. "If I'm not back in half an hour, call my CO. I'd rather not involve him until we know what's going on, but you say my name and he'll come and get you. Then call Rik. He'll find a way to keep you safe."

Another nod, and she sprinted across the road, ball cap firmly in place, their shopping bag dancing in her hand. He faded into the shadow of the building behind him, watching for a few moments, then turned and headed for the building behind his. A rarely locked door connected the underground parking garages. He took the stairs up, listening for shifting movements above and below, but there was nothing. He eased the stairwell door open, reassured himself his hallway was empty, then let himself into his apartment. He went first to the small safe in his bedroom, removing his emergency stash of cash. Then he retrieved his loaded FN57, the spare magazines for that as well as for the Glock 29 on his hip. He grabbed a backpack, stuffed some clothes in it, and since he was standing at his dresser, the box of condoms he kept in his top drawer.

Don't even think about it.

I'm not.

You're a douche—

The burner phone vibrated in his pocket, cutting off his inner quarrel. He glanced at the time and headed for the door. He'd have to talk on the run. He checked the peephole before shouldering his way into the hall. "What did you discover?"

"Not a lot yet, but what I did, I don't like. Where are you?"

"Leaving my apartment now."

"Is she with you?"

"No. Heading back that way now."

"So, that message..."

Drew didn't want to know how Rik had accessed it. "Can we figure out who sent it?"

"Yes, in time. Why would someone want to have access to her phone?"

"What kind of access?"

"The message was a Trojan horse. It delivered a tracking app that connected with the GPS in the handset, but also gave the receiver access to the camera and internal memory."

Drew punched his way into the stairwell and took the steps down two at a time. "Can you tell if it's still in my car?"

"It hasn't moved."

"Just a matter of time, though, right?"

Rik was silent at the other end of the line for a moment, then exhaled slowly. "If a senator is involved, I'd imagine yes."

"I need to keep her safe, man."

"I can help with that. You have passports?"

"I do. I think she does."

"They're not necessary to get here, just to get home again. I'll text you details."

"Got it. Hey, and Rik?"

"Yeah?"

The thought of Annie losing any memories of Kevin... "Can you back up her phone? Photos, text messages, that sort of thing?"

"Already on it."

"Thanks." He emerged back into the early morning brightness. "Don't look at any of it."

"See you soon."

———

Her booth provided a clear sight line to the front door and a quick exit out the kitchen. She'd paid the waitress for a cup of coffee she hadn't touched and now flipped through pages of day old newsprint she wasn't reading. Drew would be back any second, she had no doubt. This was all a complete misunderstanding, and there was no reason for panic to be winding its way around her chest and up her throat. Stripping her mouth of all moisture and making her so light-headed she could barely think straight.

The deep breathing exercises her grief counselor suggested were hard to harness, but she focused on counting each breath, in and out, and slowly logic found traction. Drew was the only person who knew where she was, exactly. If someone wanted to find her, a prank phone call would be a bizarre and convoluted way to do that when her office hours were posted on the university website and her home address was listed probably everywhere. Unless they didn't want to find her, but test her. Had running to Drew been a mistake? No. Call from Kevin, go to his best friend. That made sense, and didn't make her look suspicious.

She *wasn't* suspicious, for heaven's sake. She'd put together a dossier on Rob Harris and not once had she made the possible connection that Drew pieced together in a matter of moments. Now that he had, it seemed pretty obvious, but stranger coincidences surely existed.

The junior senator from Texas, Robert Harris III was no Machiavellian character. Maybe ten years away from the White House, but more likely a strong Vice Presidential candidate at some point—ambitious but not cut-throat. Annie hadn't needed to do any research on his son, but like Drew she vaguely knew he was nine years old. There'd been some coverage of the family on the campaign trail.

Her pulse picked up. Oh, what she'd give for her iPhone right now. Now that this boy was more than an abstract reality, she ached to know more about him.

When Drew strolled in, a backpack slung over his arm, she almost surged out of the booth. He slid in across from her, shaking his head at the waitress to decline a cup of coffee.

"I need to find a computer—" she started.

"We need to leave the city," he interrupted. "Wait, what? No, you can't."

"Drew, hang on. I want to…" Be a creepy Google stalker? "I just want to know a bit more about the boy. He might be my flesh and blood, for goodness sake."

"No. We can find out more when we get to a secure location."

"Maybe we could go to an Internet cafe. Just for a few minutes."

"Not going to happen, sugar. I need to get you locked down and off-grid for a couple of days while we sort this out." He wiggled the burner phone. "I spoke to Rik again. He's got a plan. Let's go."

Locked down and off-grid? Hell no. "Excuse me?"

Drew leaned forward over the table, looming large over her. The brim of his matching baseball hat shadowed his eyes but she didn't miss the serious glint. "We have a plan. Let's go."

She matched his pose, the brim of her hat bumping his. "Go where?"

"Not sure yet. Do you have your passport?"

"I don't need a passport to go to the base."

"I told you--can of worms."

"But we can't just...what about you? Aren't they expecting you today?"

"I called in sick."

"Why?" She shook her head. Could SEALs even do that? It was Friday, wouldn't that be suspicious?

"Keeping our options open. We've got the weekend to deal with this now."

"I don't think the..." She glanced around and lowered her voice. "I don't think the senator is a threat to me. I need to find out more about his son."

"Sure, we can do that. Once we get away from here." He curled his hand over hers, the warm reassuring slide of skin on skin wicking away the top layer of her resistance. "Annie, I only have my gut to go on here, so I can't tell you why I think we need to lay low for a bit...you're just going to need to trust me."

She did. Even if it was a wild goose chase—or a wild goose run—Drew wouldn't let anything bad happen to her. Worst case scenario, she'd spend a day or two in a quiet location with an overprotective, super good-looking bodyguard. Maybe there'd be a swimming pool and she could ogle him from afar.

"This is crazy," she whispered. "Where are we going?"

He grinned. "I have no idea."

CHAPTER
FOUR

"WHAT THE HELL do you mean, you have no idea?" Annie stared across the table at him and he resisted the urge to grin again.

"Rik's making arrangements. Do you have your passport in your purse?"

Shock rolled over her face, her eyes going big and wide for a second before she closed them with a sigh. "I thought you were joking! This is ridiculous. Seriously, your solution is that we skip the country?"

"It would be easier to secure you offshore, yes." He resisted the urge to touch her again. "Look, I get that this is bizarre for you, but it would just be for the weekend. Long enough for Rik to work his connections and figure out what's going on. Because something *is* going on. Your cell phone was hacked to use the camera to spy on you."

"I don't understand…someone's been watching me?"

Drew didn't blame Annie for looking at him like he was certifiable. He needed to work on his sales pitch, although he hoped he'd never have this conversation again.

"Drew, this is insane. You can't…Hell, I don't even know what your plan is, but we're not getting on a plane and running away."

"We're not running away."

"Then what are we doing? We need to get to the bottom of this!"

"Sugar, that's not what I do."

"It's what I do!"

He gave her his best hairy side-eye.

"I'm a researcher."

"You're a historian."

She pursed her lips and sniffed sharply. "Look, before we go all random commando, maybe we should just do a little more digging—"

"You're not an investigative reporter or a federal agent." He held up his hand. "I'm not saying that you shouldn't be involved in sorting this shit out, but staying here runs contrary to what I do."

"Which is what?"

"I keep you safe, sugar. With my life, if it comes down to it."

"That's really not—" This time, Annie cut herself off. The blood drained from her face and he felt the air around them still as she froze for a second, then leapt up. Without looking over his shoulder, he snatched his backpack and followed her as she ran through the kitchen past a surprised line cook. "Back door?" she yelled at the man flipping eggs, and he pointed to her right.

Drew managed to grab her arm just before she launched herself out the door. "Annie!"

She spun around, landing hard against his chest. Her words spilled out in a breathless rush. "Two guys in suits talking to a cop at the front of the diner. I can't be certain, but I think I saw them on campus yesterday. Might be nothing, but now I'm okay with fleeing."

"Really?"

"Who knows?" Panic edged into her voice.

"I do. Let me go first." He cracked the door, grateful to see it emptied onto a side street, not an alley. Across the way was a clothing shop, and down the block sat an idling cab. "Come on."

He grabbed her hand and they took off for the taxi. He resisted the urge to just pick her up and sprint. Behind them, the door slammed shut, and he didn't hear it open again before they reached the car. He whipped open the door, surprising the driver mid-bite. "Sorry to interrupt your breakfast, bub, but I'll make it worth your while. Go in any direction."

The man hesitated, and Drew was tempted to pull out a gun, but knew a fifty would be more convincing—and less likely to get him arrested. Annie gasped beside him as he dug out his wallet, and a quick glance over his shoulder told him they had company. He flipped two bills over the front seat. "Take us ten blocks away from here and pretend you dropped us somewhere else, okay?"

The car jerked forward, turned right, and headed east for a few blocks before turning suddenly into a parking garage. "There's a stand of cabs up one level, in front of a hotel side entrance."

Drew clapped the driver on the shoulder and muttered a quick thanks under his breath. They tumbled out and ran for the stairs, not stopping until they were secure in another backseat, this time heading to a small airstrip northeast of the city. Annie glanced at him nervously when he gave that direction to the driver, but Drew just eased back on the seat and pulled her close against him. She gasped almost inaudibly but didn't resist the tug. He laced one hand into her hair, ignoring how the slide of the dark brown strands against his fingers made his dick take notice, and brushed his lips against her ear. He kept his voice low, a whisper just for her. "This'll be easier if we act like we're on a spontaneous weekend getaway."

She twisted in his arms, bringing her face in line with his. Her lower lip trembled almost imperceptibly, but steely conviction pulsed through her gaze. "You're crazy." Her tongue darted out of her mouth and left a glistening trail along the heart-shaped curve of her upper lip. He stared at that spot a beat longer than he should, and when he glanced back at her eyes, the heat there surprised him.

"We don't need to..." he muttered gruffly, but his protest trailed off as she wiggled closer.

"It's a good thing you're cute," she whispered against his mouth as she pressed her lips against his. She held the simple kiss long enough to make it look good, and it took all of his restraint not to take over, to open up and make her breathless for a whole other reason. She hummed a happy little noise and slid her lips along his jaw, taking her turn at the secretive whisper. "Because this would be a total chore otherwise."

Her cheekiness in the face of potential danger completely undid him, and laughter boiled up and bubbled over as he held her against him. "Key take-away from that, sugar, is that you think I'm cute." The snort in response set him in his place more clearly than a cold shower, and after that little exchange, he needed both. Annie Martin was far too sexy when she wanted to be.

He did a subtle sweep of both the driver and the available mirrors, but nothing caught his attention. He pulled out his phone and texted Rik, letting him know they were headed to his first directed location.

———

Annie watched in disbelief as Drew spoke quietly with the man at the counter, then grabbed her hand and pulled her through the glass doors to a small jet waiting on the runway. The clock on the wall told her it was ten minutes to eight, and she dwelled momentarily on the fact that she had office hours later in the morning. Skipping work was not in her nature. Of course, neither was running from the authorities or kissing someone like Drew.

Kissing Drew.

It had been the adrenaline rush—there was no other explanation. When he said they needed to act like they were going away for the weekend, she'd gotten caught up in the role play, and it was exhilarating. The playacting, not the kiss. No, there was nothing to like about kissing Drew, who'd probably tongued his way through more than a couple Tijuana weekends. Not the delicious scrape of stubble against her lips, or the hissed intake of air as she moved along his jaw. Definitely not the way his hand tightened in her hair, his fingertips stroking her scalp with erotic promise. Her body's pitiful reaction to the brief caress was simply a sign of her weakened defenses, given all that was going on.

At least he hadn't read anything into it. He'd just laughed and settled back against the seat, and damned if curling up into his hard warmth hadn't been just as nice. She really did feel safe with him.

Safe from outside threats, at least.

On the plane, he pressed her into a leather seat and stowed his backpack above them before stripping off his sweatshirt and filling the space between her and the aisle with way too much flexing muscle and yummy soap smell for her to handle without breakfast. Or a reality check.

"Do you want a drink? We won't be leaving for a little bit yet."

"Where are we going?" Her voice cracked. "And yes, water or maybe Coke would be awesome."

"I'll raid the kitchen. Be right back." He slipped away and returned with two of each. He cracked open his can of cola and she did the same. "We're hitching a ride to New Orleans, because that's where this plane was already going. From there, we'll fly to Miami if the pilot has time, or maybe rent a car if he doesn't."

She glanced around. They were alone on the plane, but she couldn't bring herself to raise her voice above a whisper. "Whose plane is this?"

"It's a charter. Rik knows the owner of the company."

"I'm starting to think I'm going to owe this guy an awful lot at the end of this adventure."

Drew ducked his face, grabbing her gaze and holding it. "This is nothing for you to worry about. Rik doesn't offer anything with strings attached. He'd move mountains for Kevin's sister, you hear me?"

A sentiment that should make her feel better, but it didn't.

There was no comfort in the sad reality of being an orphan. Having two real-life superheroes rescuing her from the jaws of some unseen danger only underlined the fact that she didn't have a big brother anymore. That her parents were gone and she was on her own when the chips were down.

She winced at herself for drifting into maudlin territory. Besides, she could handle—

"Hey, what's that face all about?"

She blinked at him, embarrassed that her thoughts had played out so obviously. "Nothing."

"Don't buy that, sugar. No secrets, remember?"

Who was he to ask that of her? She bristled. "No secrets about Kevin, or the mysterious phone call, sure. I really doubt you want me to unload my feelings on you."

He lifted one eyebrow ever so slightly and quirked his lips. "Don't be so sure."

Maybe if his response wasn't so cocky, so casual, she'd believe him. But his smirk left too much room for him to walk away after she'd unburdened herself of her deepest, darkest fears. A harsh laugh burbled out. "You're a grown man who plays video games and flicks away fuck buddies like they're nothing. Now I'm supposed to believe you're sensitive?"

She regretted the words as soon as they spilled out. Drew's face closed up tight, and he took a long drag of cola before nodding. "Fair enough."

"Drew—" But her apology was cut off by heavy footsteps on the stairs, and they were joined by a burly man in a suit carrying an overstuffed briefcase. He nodded to them, unperturbed by other passengers on his flight, and took a seat toward the back.

"We'll be leaving soon, Annie. You should have a nap." And with that, Drew Castle tipped his head back and closed his eyes.

———

They stopped briefly in New Orleans to drop off their travel companion, refueled, then took off again. Drew made a mental note to thank Rik for helping him avoid a ten hour car ride with the disapproving woman next to him. It was bound to happen, the crash of adrenaline and reality of what was happening to her setting in. But he didn't think that was the real reason she was mad.

It was *him*. Annie didn't want him.

And he didn't mean sexually, although he probably didn't have a chance in hell of scoring with her, either, but she didn't want *him* to be her hero in an emergency. He was a poor stand-in for Kevin. That he was a stand-in at all, that she didn't have anyone else...he'd be pissed off in her shoes as well.

It wasn't fair that she was all alone in this.

But life wasn't fair. Drew had learned that lesson early on, and as a result, committed himself to never needing anyone. Kevin had been the closest thing to family he had. His mother had left when he was seven. His dad drank himself to death sometime during Drew's basic training. He'd been on his own for twenty years and he'd never minded the solitude. It made leaving easy, and he left all the time. His life was based in San Diego but he lived around the world, in helicopters and sand pits. On constant stand-by.

Her crack about fuck buddies had landed with unnerving accuracy. He loved women, and he was clear on his limitations up front, but there was no denying that sex changed things. Added complications, even in the early stages of flirting. An uncommon feeling of guilt wormed its way into his head.

You're not feeling badly about Dana.

No. Maybe he should, but he hadn't been lying the night before. Dana had only reacted badly because she thought Annie was competition. The prize could have been anyone, and he wouldn't be surprised to find out she'd found another bed to warm.

But Annie...Jesus, he shouldn't have suggested they pretend to be lovers in the cab. What the fuck had that been? There was no need, except his desperate desire to hold her against his body, feel the lean stretch of her in his arms and smell the sweet scent of her skin as she pressed her lips to his. And now he was paying the price. Guilt, desire and confusion warred inside him for the first leg of their trip, and he couldn't work out why.

What did he care?

When it came to affection, Drew could take it or leave it. He wasn't dead inside—he enjoyed an evening spent with a woman as much as the next man. More than most when everything clicked. But despite what Annie thought of him, it wasn't an everyday occurrence.

And he was fine with weeks, even months, of solitude. Would

trade that for any inkling of possession or emotional entanglement, because he couldn't return it in kind. Particularly in the last six months. Since Kevin's death, he'd been adrift, but not once had he thought the solution lay in the arms of a woman. Dana had helped him scratch an itch, and he'd returned the favour, but she didn't smooth over the ache in his heart. Nothing could.

Except the last fourteen hours, he hadn't felt alone, not once. Not even with Annie closed off and grumpy beside him on the plane, unable to say anything further because of their companion three rows back. The truth was, he'd spent the flight worrying about how to reconnect with her rather than how to escape her needy clutches.

And Kevin had been completely silent, which unsettled him more than he'd like to admit.

He needed that voice of conscience telling him to back off, or he might not.

Who was he kidding? They were heading to paradise with nothing to do but fight and make up. Over and over again. There would be no backing off, not until it was too late. And for the first time ever, Drew was walking straight into an entanglement with eyes wide open.

"What are you thinking about?" Annie muttered under her breath.

"Your brother." It wasn't a complete lie.

"I miss him," she sighed. "I listened to the message over and over again on the drive to your place, even though I knew it wasn't real."

"I hear his voice all the time," he admitted. "He's become my...moral compass."

She laughed. "I'd love that...for a day or two. I can't imagine it's easy to constantly have another opinion rattling around in your head."

Especially when your thoughts are running dirty with regard to his sister. "It's unusual for me, that's for sure. Took some getting used to."

"And then I leap into your life...Martins making you crazy all over the place, huh?" She twisted slightly in her seat and glanced toward him under her lashes. Shy and brave at the same time. "I'm sorry about what I said earlier. It's none of my business."

His response stuck on the first try, and he cleared his throat. "I told you last night. It played out in front of you, it's your business. But for what it's worth, the video games...yeah, that's me. The girl in the trench coat is a bit more unusual."

"Okay." Her tone sounded like she still wasn't sure of that, but then it softened. "I wasn't judging, I just didn't want to talk about..." Her jaw clenched as she swallowed back the rest of the sentence, and he couldn't resist turning fully toward her and stroking that spot of tension on her face. Her lips parted ever so slightly, and he slowly drifted his thumb to the corner of her mouth.

"I'm sorry I asked. I don't want to make you uncomfortable." Her skin was soft to the touch, and he wanted his turn to press kisses there. Taste her as she'd tasted him, however briefly.

"Not uncomfortable. Weak." Her voice wafted between them on a thready whisper, and he shook his head.

"You're so strong, Annie. More than most, I promise you."

"You're just saying that because you're saddled with me until this gets resolved."

He jerked his head back. Had he really given her that impression? "Hell no. The thought of you being yanked between power players, not knowing what's going on, maybe getting hurt...sugar, that kills me." He stroked his palm down her neck and along her arm, finding her fingers. "We're in this together, got it?"

She glanced down at their entwined hands, then back up at him, the shock on her face feeling very familiar. "Together?"

One word, loaded with meaning.

A word he'd always avoided in the past, but this was different. And it wasn't because he wanted her, although he did, something fierce. This was different. They were bonded together, he and Annie, and she wasn't a burden. Her problems were his problems, no ques-tions asked.

She tipped her head back, feelings tripping across her face as she processed her thoughts. He waited, letting her have a moment. The tug of arousal was hard to ignore, but she had to want it too. Her clear gaze when she faced him again, promising a matching response if he did something, decimated any lingering restraint. He reached between them and unbuckled her seat belt, the rub of his knuckles against her abdomen eliciting a hungry noise he wanted to hear again and again. "You and me, sugar," he whispered as he elbowed the armrest between them out of the way and hauled her into his lap.

CHAPTER
FIVE

"WHAT ARE YOU DOING?" A stupid question, given the glassy look in Drew's eyes as he stared at her mouth. She should know better than to like it. *Should.* Totally didn't. At his touch, her heart leapt into her throat, and instead of worrying about who he'd touched before, and when the affection would be taken away again, she just wanted to revel in it. Let the thrill of being wanted wash away the fear.

"You kissed me earlier." The rough need in his voice worked its way into her chest and blossomed into an itchy heat.

"You told me to," she whispered, not trusting her voice to hold. "And then you laughed."

"You took me by surprise." His unexpected admission made her squirm. "I'm happy to clarify my position on you kissing me. I'm a fan."

"And what if I don't plan to kiss you again?"

His heavy-lidded gaze jerked up, finding her eyes. Searching for permission, which, damn him, she'd give. Soon. "Then I'd want to kiss you."

"And you think I'd let you?" Like the fact she was vibrating against him wasn't proof of that.

"You shouldn't."

"Maybe I won't." Their faces were close enough now that her breath puffed off his skin, warming the small space left between them.

Instead of closing the gap and taking her mouth, he wove his hand deeper into her hair and tugged gently. "This isn't the time or place, is it?"

Confusion and sadness traced through her veins and landed heavy in her chest. She contemplated throwing good sense out the window and pushing herself on him, but if he didn't want her... "Probably not."

His other hand crossed her lap and squeezed her hip. "I'm not sure what's going to happen when we land."

"I'll be cool," she promised with what felt like an unconvincing nod.

"Just follow my lead, okay?" That she could agree to with more assuredness. They were in this together.

That word again. *Together*. It was for the best if they didn't entertain the new spark of attraction between them. Barely a taste and she was ascribing feelings and values to it that didn't belong. She nodded one last time, with firm resolution, and shifted her legs to get off his lap. His grip on her hip tightened and the fingers in her hair slowly pulsed against her scalp.

"Annie..." Her name dripped like honey off his tongue, the single word warming her from the inside out. "If things were different..."

She smiled weakly, willing herself to look cool and unaffected. "We probably would have never met. It's fine, Drew, don't worry about it."

A moment later the pilot's voice crackled over the intercom, advising them they would soon begin their descent, and she scrambled into her seat.

Drew watched her buckle up, then stood and grabbed his backpack before sitting again.

"Give me that shopping bag," he muttered gruffly, and consolidated the results of her discount shopping spree into his bag. He paused almost imperceptibly when he reached the three-pack of black bikini panties, and she willed herself not to blush. *Everyone wears underwear*. Which of course sent her thoughts in the direction of wondering what Drew looked like without his cargo pants. *Maybe not everyone*. A girl could dream.

The pressure change in the cabin as the plane dipped back toward earth snapped her back to reality. As far as she knew, there was no record of their cross-country adventure, but she was quickly learning that ordinary people were incredibly transparent to those keeping an eye on the unsuspecting population. A shiver wracked her as she once again considered the horrifying invasion of privacy —someone had hacked her phone. Watched her through it as she drove to San Diego, listening to the fake Kevin message over and over again. As she told Drew what she knew and then slept in his bed. Bile rose in her throat, not for the first time, as she processed just how stupid she'd been.

Until Drew took over. Now she wasn't with an ordinary person, and once they got wherever the hell they were going, she'd be able to get some answers.

When Kevin had been alive, she'd kept his secret because it was his choice to make. She didn't understand why he felt he couldn't be a father, but that was his call to make, not his teenage sister's. Guilt gnawed at her gut as it had from time to time that her parents never knew their grandchild. No, not their grandchild. Kevin had essentially given his child up for adoption. Annie had to accept that—and she had, until Drew put a name in her head.

She closed her eyes as the small jet made quick work of the landing. When Drew squeezed her hand, she cracked her eyelids just a slit, heart thumping, and watched as they taxied toward a waiting black SUV.

After what felt like a lifetime as the lights flickered and the engine noises cut out, the pilot came out of the cockpit, nodded to them and opened the door. A ground crew was waiting with a mobile set of stairs, but Drew didn't move to the exit, he just stood there, arms casually braced against the seat, watching the vehicle. Waiting. When the door opened, and a blond man stepped out, Drew cracked a wide smile. "Come on, sugar, let's go."

They met in the middle of the tarmac, two Greek gods reuniting in common purpose. A rough handshake turned into a back-slapping hug, but their expressions remained stony.

"Annie, this is Rik. Man, I wasn't expecting you to personally meet us here."

"I was already in the city last night. My wife, Calli, likes to dance." Their host turned his gaze toward Annie, his eyes softening. A soft accent cut into his fluent English. "Come, we must hurry. But it's lovely to meet you, Ms. Martin."

"Annie, please," she murmured as he guided her to the car.

Drew shifted closer, his hand in her back. "She'll ride in the back with me."

Rik nodded. "Of course."

They didn't talk as they sped away from the airport. It wasn't until they pulled into a marina that Annie asked about their destination.

"It's...well, I'll let Calli explain." The other man parked, then twisted in his seat to glance at them. "Ready?"

Hell no, Annie thought, but she'd come this far. What was a little adventure at sea?

Rik led them down a wooden dock, past sailboats and small yachts, stopping in front of a smaller power boat. Small being relative, she realized as they stepped down the thin walkway alongside the motor craft. At the back, there was seating for at least eight, and in the middle of the gleaming white and polished wood space stood a beautiful woman with mahogany hair and a beaming smile.

"You found them!" she exclaimed, clapping her hands.

"Calli, I'd like to introduce you to Drew Castle and Annie Martin." Rik offered his hand to Annie as she stepped into the boat.

The heels of her boots clattered on the deck, and she winced. "Nice to meet you, Calli. I'm sorry I'm not dressed appropriately."

The other woman shushed her and pointed to the small cabin door beside her. "Don't worry about it. I've got some things laid out for you in there, if you'd like to change."

Annie glanced at Drew who nodded. Not like she needed his permission to get dressed, but just to check in. He offered her a quick half-smile. "Go ahead. I'll help Rik push off."

She ducked below, again surprised to find more space than she was expecting. A small kitchen space, a bathroom and cozy sleeping nook. Hanging on a hook was a long sundress that wrapped around in the middle—and would easily fit most women, a thoughtful touch from her hostess. On the shelf beside that was a basket overflowing with flip flops of varying colors and sizes. Annie shucked her boots, jeans, and blouse, stacked them in a neat pile, and pulled on the lighter outfit. She felt the engine fire up, then a bit of a jerk as they slipped away from the dock. A turn, then they picked up speed. Bracing herself on the bathroom counter, she freshened up, and as she re-emerged onto the open deck, they were pulling out into the open sea.

She paused, breathing in the salty air. Hard to wrap her head around hurtling into the Atlantic Ocean when just last night she'd been driving south along the Pacific. And she hadn't needed to buy a ticket on Expedia or pack a suitcase...any minute now she was going to wake up and go to work. She wiggled her shoulders, trying to shake her disquiet. Kevin had gotten all the adventurous genes.

"You okay, sugar?" Drew's voice slid over her skin at the same moment his body pressed into hers and one hand wrapped around her waist. She wanted to melt into him, but she couldn't walk that same line he could. Be all touchy-feely without wanting more. She could feel the hot branding of his palm on her hip. One of his fingers rested on the elastic edge of her underwear, easily felt through the lightweight fabric of the dress, and that hot, itchy feeling returned.

"We're heading out to sea," she whispered.

"Rik has an island." His voice was thick and rough, and she wondered if it was fatigue. Or if his mind drifted to the same place hers did. Would a few hot Caribbean nights lead to more of what almost happened on the plane? She'd never done anything like that before, and the thrill of a time-limited affair made all her nerve endings stand up and take notice.

On the other hand, Drew probably slept with all the damsels in distress he rescued. Maybe this air of resistance was part of his playbook. She didn't really believe either of those thoughts, but layered on top of her innate wariness they spilled enough doubt into her otherwise molten core to give her the strength to push away. "Right. Calli was going to tell us about that." Without looking over her shoulder, she wiggled out of his grasp and carefully moved across the open space to join the other woman on one of the bench seats.

"Annie," Calli reached out and touched her hand. "I understand this is an unexpected trip for you."

She didn't know how much to share, so she simply nodded and smiled politely. "Thank you so much for the dress."

"I'm sure I can scrounge up anything else you need once we get home."

"Which is where, exactly?"

Calli laughed, a rich peal that Annie couldn't help but find infectious. "I call it Camo Cay, although that's not its original name. Rik claims to have retired, but we have enough hulking men around most of the time for it to be confused with a military base." She took a sobering breath. "It's a private island on the far side of the Bahamas. Well protected and completely anonymous."

"And you just come and go like this? What about Customs?"

"We sometimes go through the official channels. Today isn't one of those days."

Because of her. "If I get you in trouble..."

"Oh honey, have you seen my husband? There won't be any trouble." Calli tipped her head back, soaking up the late-afternoon sun. "And your shadow looks pretty formidable as well."

"He's not my...I just showed up on his doorstep last night and made my problems his problems."

Calli looked over at Drew, who'd procured sunglasses from a pocket in his backpack, and was leaning lazily against the opposite railing. But his attention seemed trained on them, reflective mask notwithstanding. "He doesn't look like he wants to be anywhere else."

"I guess." Annie rubbed a fresh crop of goose bumps off her arms. This adventure was entirely his idea. She didn't need to worry about his motivation to help her. And the sooner they got to the bottom of the call, the quicker she'd be out of his hair. A yawn took her by surprise, then another, and before Calli noticed, Drew was standing.

"Come on," he said quietly, his hand outstretched.

Her head ached, heavy with fatigue just now catching up to her. They'd been on the move all day and she hadn't rested at all on the plane. Too tired to resist, she took his hand and let him lead her back into the cabin.

"It'll probably be a couple of hours before we get there and Rik can give us his full attention." His voice filled the small space even though he spoke quietly. A gruff edge caught her attention, but the need to sleep pushed that observation to the side. "Are you hungry, or would you rather have a nap?"

"Nap," she whispered.

He pulled her toward the bunk, and for a second she thought he was going to lie down with her. Her heart leapt into her throat as he cupped her chin in his hand, but he just brushed a soft kiss to her forehead. "Lie down."

Stay with me, she wanted to say. *Keep me warm and safe*. A terrible, wonderful idea that she knew better than to voice. Asking opened the door to rejection, and she wanted him too much to hear he didn't want her. She closed her eyes as he draped a soft blanket over her body, and gave in to the muzzy weakness, letting a dreamless sleep carry her away before he even left the cabin.

———

He couldn't bring himself to leave her alone. He should head up top and talk to Rik, but instead he sat on the tiny bench in the kitchenette, watching Annie sleep. Worried she'd have another nightmare, he told himself, but it felt like something more base. Something selfish.

He waited for Kevin's voice to interject, but his buddy wasn't going to cut him off this time.

Because he didn't need to be cock-blocked. He could do that all by himself.

He wasn't noble. Fuck, no. He wanted to strip Annie down to her birthday suit and feast on her body. It wouldn't be one-sided and he'd feed her soul in the only way he knew how. But making it good in the moment wouldn't be worth anything in the cold light of morning.

And after a few nights? It would be too damn easy to pretend their connection wasn't a cruel combination of chemistry and adrenaline and nostalgia.

For a few minutes on the plane, Drew had lost sight of that reality.

But he just didn't have the capacity to love inside him. To serve? Absolutely. To protect? With his life. To love? He didn't even know what that would look like. But he was pretty sure it wasn't possible with a guy who could get on a plane and disappear for six months without a backward glance.

He knew what it was like to be abandoned. He'd never want to do that to someone he cared about. And since leaving wasn't optional--that was his life--attachment couldn't happen.

He'd keep her safe until she could return to her life of innocent scholarship. And until then...it was time for some distance. Polite boundaries. And a cold shower or three. Because he couldn't—wouldn't—be this mopey guy.

Not even if being with Annie made him feel bigger, stronger than he had in months. He wouldn't use her like that, and he couldn't risk the flip side of that attachment. Emotional entanglement and Drew Castle didn't mix.

Twenty minutes passed by the time he joined Rik, who wisely kept the conversation focused on the threat.

"While you were in the air, I transferred what I'd already discovered this morning to our secure servers. I have a guy--"

"Rik, I trust *you*. I don't know your guys."

"I'd trust Trent McTavish with my life. With Calli's life. He was SAS for ten years. Has a younger brother with significant medical expenses, so he went private. But he's one of the good guys. He and Jackson Sutter make up the--" He raised his voice to grab his wife's attention. "Calli! What do you call Jackson and Trent?"

A trill of laughter carried toward them. Instead of yelling back, the dark haired beauty stood and sashayed over. Drew watched as she wound her limbs around her husband. She was warm and gracious toward Drew, but her voice took on a unique huskiness when she answered Rik. "The dynamic duo. They're like oil and water, a Scotsman and a Texan, but they've bonded like brothers."

Drew couldn't keep the surprise out of his voice. "You know them, too?"

"Sure do. My living room is command central." She stroked Rik's jaw. "I'm the chief sandwich-maker."

"And she mediates disagreements about sporting events and whiskey superiority." Drew watched with increasing discomfort as Rik patted his wife on the ass, their casual and open intimacy making him unexpectedly uncomfortable. *These people need a room.* "As I was saying, Trent will have a full portfolio on Rob Harris when we arrive, and Jackson and my brother Mats will have started to work up some action plans."

"Whoa there, Rik. We're not taking action against an American senator."

"The nice thing about working with me, Drew, is that I'm happy to take all the glory. Or blame, as needed. But in this case your patriotism is not misplaced. My initial research suggests Annie's being used by an international force as a pawn to somehow hurt Harris. Would his campaign really be derailed by a paternity scandal?"

Drew shrugged. Probably. Not his area of concern.

Rik shook his head and made a disappointed sound. "How ridiculous. In my country—in most countries—it would be a non-issue."

On that point they were in agreement. "I don't care about any of that. We just need to neutralize however this involves Annie."

"Then that is what we shall do."

CHAPTER
SIX

THE SUN WAS SETTING as Rik changed direction, steering toward a small island like many they'd already passed. He maneuvered the Donzi into a covered boat house at the edge of a protected bay. From the landmarks they'd passed and Drew's estimation of their speed, he was pretty sure they were somewhere in the Exuma island chain. A canopy of dark green, a mix of leafy trees and scrub brush, masked the space between the beach and the buildings in the near distance, but the raw beauty of Camo Cay still made itself evident. White sand, a craggy bluff to the south, and a quiet stillness that promised the small island was in fact a private paradise.

Annie had woken thirty minutes earlier, but after a glance in his direction as she stepped into the open, she'd taken a seat next to Calli. Drew had resisted the urge to join them. Now he leapt onto the walkway and helped secure the craft before extending a hand to the women, helping them out.

Calli first, then Annie, who maintained the innocent contact as she joined him on the wooden decking.

"Thank you," she whispered, her simple words digging into his chest.

"Nothing to thank me for yet."

She smiled slightly. "No? First class travel to the tropics is pretty sweet."

"Rumor has it other people come here on vacation. You've got low standards if a hideaway with Rik and his gang does it for you."

"There's a gang?"

"Apparently so. You ready for this?"

She laced her fingers into his and squeezed. "We still in this together?"

Fuckity fuck. "As long as you need me, sugar."

So much for boundaries. He wanted to lean into her, needed to feel the rub of her bare arm against his. A hot, fizzy awareness tingled all of his nerve endings like his own private Annie alarm system. Warning, too close. But also, warning, too far away when she stepped back to let Rik pass.

As they followed a long, winding boardwalk path with occasional stairs to accommodate slight changes in elevation, dusk now rapidly descending on them, he could feel her glancing at him in the dark shadows thrown by the surrounding greenery. Each look thrilled and terrified him, and he found himself wrapped in a nervous energy vaguely reminiscent of his first high school dance. Ahead of them, Rik and Calli led the way. Dim solar lights lit the path every few feet, but they just underlined the private moment they were sharing as they slowed in tandem at the edge of the overgrowth.

Annie swallowed hard as she looked up at the three-story main villa rising in front of them. A combination of modern glass and traditional Colonial architecture, it was gorgeous. And imposing. Obviously not a vacation resort, but a private space renovated with serious purpose. If there was any doubt about that, an armed guard stood in front of the main doors.

"Hey, I'm with you every step of the way." As if watching himself have an out of body experience, Drew felt the tug toward her at the same moment as he tried to tell himself to keep moving forward. But her lower lip trembled, and she needed to be comforted. He dropped his backpack to the ground and wrapped one arm around her shoulders, just meaning to pull her close enough to kiss her temple.

But when she tipped her head at the last minute, and looked him straight in the eye, lips parted and eyes shiny...he was lost. He swept her into his arms, one hand around her tiny waist, the other at the top of her spine. Covering her mouth with his, he swallowed her gentle moan as she opened to his probing tongue.

This didn't feel like high school. It was an adult kiss, unhesitant and hungry, but there was something else. A chemical bond, a desperate transfer of need and promise, and when they broke apart, Drew knew he was in a world of trouble, because attachment? No longer optional or avoidable. A done deal he hadn't seen coming. So much for protecting her and walking away.

"Wow," she said, and he laughed weakly, still holding her against his body. "You really know how to distract a girl. All that practice, huh? Whew! Good thing I know the real Drew."

Ice water wouldn't have been as effective. "Sure do," he muttered. "Come on, let's get this thing resolved."

———

He really needed to stop turning her on and then changing his mind.

Annie chased after Drew as he stalked toward the main entrance, her previous shock and awe at the scale of the structure forgotten. "Hey!" she hissed, yanking on his arm. "What the hell was that?"

It wasn't in her nature to lash out, but she'd been pushed too far. Not by Drew, but the situation, and even as she tugged him toward her, she knew she was about to unfairly unload twenty-four hours of stress onto his massive shoulders. All because she said something stupid and he stopped kissing her.

He spun around, the garden lights bouncing off the hard planes of his face. "This really something you want to do in front of an audience?"

"Apparently privacy is just a myth anyway, so sure, why the hell not." She ducked around his brick wall of a body and waved at Rik and the similarly gorilla-sized man standing next to him. She'd never cheekily flipped off a man with a machine gun before, but this trip was proving to be all about firsts. Her first international spy adventure. Her first ill-advised infatuation. How had she managed to go twenty-five years without acting like a giggling school girl? And why, oh why, did it have to be over Drew Castle?

"I shouldn't have kissed you. I apologize."

"Shut up about that! If you don't want to kiss me, just don't do it. I'll survive, you big ape. You've got a talented tongue, but it's not made of stardust. That guard over there probably has just as much international tonsil hockey experience as you do and if I need distraction--"

"You can't kiss him." Drew crossed his arms and scowled.

A gleeful tremor rippled through her lower belly at his possessive stance. Not that it would do her any good if he didn't get over his hang-ups about her. That annoyed her enough to needle him again. "Let me get this straight. I can't kiss you--not that I want to anymore--and you think you get to decide I can't kiss *him*...how about Calli? She's cute."

From behind them, Rik cleared his throat. "We'll head inside, you'll join us soon?"

Drew ground his teeth together. "Yep, in a minute."

She waited, mostly because she wasn't really sure what they were fighting about. He laid a zero-to-sixty kiss on her then dropped her like a hot potato because she made light of it. Drew Castle, it appeared, had some issues. Totally not her problem.

Except for the nagging desire to sooth his stupid warrior soul. A misguided urge she should know better than to entertain. He was practically her brother's long-lost twin, which should be reason enough to dislodge her interest, even before the itemized list of reasons he couldn't be anything more than a fantasy. Unavailable in every sense of the word. Uninterested in politics or nuance. Unrelentingly boyish. But also unbelievably kind and generous. Unable to turn his back on someone in need. And most importantly, unlike anyone she'd ever met before.

Including Kevin.

But Drew wasn't Kevin's twin. He was his own person, flawed and wonderful, and for however long they had together on this island, she wasn't letting him run hot and cold anymore. She wanted to get to know the real Drew better, and there was only one way to do that.

"Listen, Annie..." The temptation to interrupt him was almost irresistible, but she bit back a snarky retort and let him finish. "I've found myself tipped sideways. Over you, about Kevin, all of this...this isn't how I normally do my job. But you aren't a mission, and I'm having trouble figuring out if I need to keep you at arm's length because it's the right thing to do for you, or if I need to do it for me."

Oh, Drew...her heart melted a smidge for him. "But you're sure you need to keep me at arm's length, huh?"

"Nothing good can come of this getting complicated."

She twisted her lips, trying to remain soft and understanding, but the laughter burbled out. "Oh, I think something good can come of it..."

He genuinely looked confused, and she wondered if his twelve-year-old boy tendencies had transferred to her on the boat, like some Freaky Friday scenario.

"Sex, you big oaf!" Understanding dawned on his face, and one eyebrow notched in response. "You need to let go of this idea that satisfying this attraction between us would be a bad thing. I don't think you've ever had that concern in the past."

He squirmed as she made a direct hit. "This isn't about my history. You can't tell me it's not going to be weird between us if we get involved."

"I don't care." She surprised them both with the truth of that statement. "First of all, I haven't seen you in a year. I'm pretty sure the opportunities for total awkwardness will be few and far between. And second...life is short, right? I don't want any regrets."

"I walk away, sugar. That's my life." He scrubbed a hand over his face and cleared his throat, pushing away the hoarse edge that made her insides squish happily. "You might not regret that, but I sure as fuck will."

He didn't want to leave her? That was both heavy and sweet at the same time. God, there was so much there to unpack, but they didn't have time. Behind him, the door thunked open. "We need to get inside, but this isn't over, Drew Castle."

She brushed past him, her arm glancing off his brick wall midsection, and for a second she thought he was going to grab her and kiss her again, but he shuttered the wild look in his eyes and stepped in behind her. First they would figure out the mystery of the creepy message. Then they both needed more sleep. But tomorrow? She wasn't sure what her next move would be, but it might need to include borrowing a bikini from Calli.

Inside, they found a large and empty tiled foyer. Annie blinked hard at the larger-than-life double staircase that rose in front of them, veering at the midpoint left and right to the balcony running the length of the second floor. Rik led them down the hallway to the left that opened onto a sunken living space. Padded benches and modern couches delineated a seating area, and behind that, three men were standing in a large empty space featuring only an over-sized dining table that would easily accommodate twenty people. To the right was an archway to what looked like a kitchen, and from the clanging and banging, that might be where Calli had disappeared.

Drew squeezed her shoulder, and she took a deep, fortifying breath before striding across the room to join the group. Rik made quick introductions. His younger clone was Mats, the guard from the front door turned out to be a friendly Texan named Jackson, and the shorter, wiry man with the serious face and rusty colored hair was Trent, who proceeded to lead them through a lightning fast briefing in his clipped Scottish accent.

"It seems an effort was made to trick Annie into contacting Senator Harris, possibly to get Harris to reveal the true paternity of his son. If the voice mail hadn't been garbled, it might have been a more successful endeavor."

"No, it wouldn't." Annie sighed. "I wish I could speak to my brother again, of course, but I knew from the first second that it was a prank. Or something more sinister."

"To be honest, we think prank is a good characterization. I need a bit more time to run the data, but I think the call originated locally to you."

"Someone I know?" Shock rippled through her. Her circle was small and tight-knit. High school girlfriends and some academic colleagues.

"No. You share a zip code with a large population of paparazzi. Tabloid TV shows would have a field day with a Republican politician hiding a paternity scandal. Particularly one that involved a member of the special forces."

She could feel Drew drawing himself up to the full extent of his height and weight. "How could they have figured that out? Annie didn't even know who the parents were."

"But *they* did. And ten years is a long time to keep a secret. Who knows who they told?"

"So why involve her?"

Trent shrugged. "Maybe she seemed like an easy mark? Accessible, unguarded, unaware of the scandal potential. They probably just wanted to get her to lure out Harris. Or write something in an email...anything that could be flashed beneath a headline as proof."

Heat flooded Annie's cheeks as she realized she'd fled across the country and out into international waters, dragging Drew along with her, because she was running from the press. "Oh god," she moaned. "What a mess!" She turned to Rik and shook her head. "I'm so sorry that I got you involved in all of this...we'll leave tomorrow, and I'll find a way to reimburse you for the expense of all of this." *Somehow*. She had her inheritance. Just how much did a private jet ride from New Orleans to Miami cost, anyway?

"Don't think of that right now, Ms. Martin." She didn't bother to correct him. Maybe formalities were a good thing when so much effort had been put on the line for...for...for...

———

Drew felt her start ever so slightly before she turned white and her eyes rolled back in her head. He braced his arm around her back as she crumpled in a dead faint. His arm snapped tight around her waist, his other hand holding her head close to his chest. "Jesus," he spit out, then scooped her up and carried her to one of the benches.

"Not enough food or sleep, and far too much excitement," Rik muttered, and Drew waved him back. He needed a minute to think. Wanted a minute alone with Annie, even if she wasn't conscious, to process what they'd just heard and figure out their next step.

What's this "we" business, asshole?

Kevin's voice rocketed through his brain. He made a good point. Drew was no basic bodyguard. If he wanted that life, he'd retire and let Rik pay him handsomely for doing shit fuck all. He should probably think hard about getting back to San Diego before the end of the weekend. One sick day he could get away with. If he wasn't there on Monday, there'd be hell to pay. And not just because he didn't file a memo.

You can't ignore me. Mitts off my sister.

Non-issue, dick-head. It was over before it had even started, and the realization slid into his gut like a trickle of ice water.

Before he could move away, let Calli or someone else take over, Annie moaned and blinked twice. "Whaaa--"

"Don't get up," he admonished, pressing her back against the bench when she tried to push up on her elbows. "You fainted."

"Great." She groaned under breath. "Could this night get any worse?"

"This is worse than when we thought your life was in danger?"

"More embarrassing, anyway." She lifted a shaking hand to her forehead. "Everything is spinning."

"Give yourself a minute to get your bearings." In his peripheral vision he saw Calli slip into the room carrying a tray. "And then you *need* to eat something."

"I can't," she whispered.

"You can and you will. And there's nothing to be embarrassed about."

"I ran away from a weenie wannabe reporter!"

"*I* dragged you away from a potentially dangerous situation where someone was spying on you," he reminded her. "You wanted to stay and play Woodward and Bernstein."

She laughed weakly.

As two pale pink spots reappeared on her cheeks, he eased away and held out his hand. "Up."

"Jeez, you're bossy. I can do it my--" She batted away his hand and pushed herself up, swaying unsteadily. "Myself."

"Mmm-hmm."

"Shut up." She leaned her forearms on her knees and shivered.

"Eat, then bed."

"No, I need to apologize to Rik. All this effort--"

Behind him, his friend cleared his throat. "It's what we do. We can consider this a training exercise."

Annie furrowed her brow, and Drew cut her off. "We can argue about that more in the morning before I leave. Calli's brought some food."

"You're leaving?" She frowned and waved off Calli. "Drew, you can't dump me on this island and then abandon me!"

"You're in good hands here." It sounded weak to his own ears, and from the narrow set of her mouth and the difficulty she was having looking him in the eye, even weaker to her.

"I *thought* I was in *your* hands," she muttered.

"Sugar, I made it really clear..."

"You know what? You need to stop calling me that." She stood and addressed Calli. "Is there a private room where I could..."

Rik's wife didn't even glance in Drew's direction. "Of course. Follow me." She picked up the tray of food for Annie and headed back to the foyer. Drew tensed, holding himself back from following like a lost puppy.

He clenched and released his fists a few times at his side, then turned back to the group of men. "What else do you know?"

"If you want to go to her, Drew, we can do this in the morning." Rik lifted one shoulder and made a *doesn't matter* face.

"No."

"Because I get it...they get under your skin...the fighting is good for a relationship, though." Rik grinned. "Making up is, too."

"It's not like that."

"Hmm. Maybe it should be."

Drew narrowed his eyes. "We're not talking about this."

Maybe you should be.

We're *not talking about it either.*

The only person he wanted to talk to was Annie, and every time he did that he ended up with his tongue down her throat and his hand practically in her pants.

Trent cleared his throat and redirected the conversation back to the primary topic. "Jackson has some suggested next steps."

The Texan nodded. "First plan. Get a message to the senator. If Annie's faced this type of mining mission, chances are so has he--or maybe someone in his family. He'd have express service from the FBI. Let them neutralize this so Annie can get back to her life as soon as possible."

"How do we know we can trust him?" Operating in the dark made Drew edgy. He pulled his shoulders up to his ears and rolled them forward, then back. What he wouldn't do for a fist-fight right now. An opponent he could see right in front of him. A chance to pummel. Conquer. Vanquish.

"We don't. Which brings us to option number two. Go to Washington, do some on the ground surveillance."

Not a real option. Time, information, location...none of that was on their side.

"Third idea. Since you're heading back to California anyway, you could execute this. Trent narrows down who sent the message and you pay them a visit."

That appealed to the brute in him, but it would just expose Annie further if the chain of command went higher than the hacker himself. As much as it pained him, the answer was obvious. "Set up a secure call to the senator tomorrow. Annie will want to be in the room."

Rik nodded, eyes narrowed. "And you?"

"Make it early. Then I'm heading..." Home wasn't the right word. "Then I have to leave."

CHAPTER
SEVEN

DREW FOUND Calli in the foyer, coming down the right hand staircase. She pointed behind her. "There are two bedrooms up there. Annie's in the closer one, you can take the one just beyond that. Do you need anything? It's not quite a hotel, but there are towels and some toiletries in each bathroom."

"Do you mind if I raid your kitchen in a bit? I want to grab a shower first."

"*Mi casa es tu casa.* I'm going to bed myself, but one of the boys will be up all night if you need any help." She came down the last few steps and stopped in front of him. "If you're able to stay a bit longer, that would be lovely."

He nodded, though the look on her face said they both knew it was an empty acknowledgment.

Upstairs, he paused in front of Annie's door. What would he say? If only everything was different? He'd already tried that. And she was right. Then they wouldn't have reconnected at all. They occupied two different worlds and his was a deliberate cocoon.

It was for the best that she be disappointed in him now. Reinforce her earlier impression and drift away.

Better than her leaving you after you fall in love?

Out of bounds, dude.

I'm you. There are no boundaries.

I'm not afraid of anything.

You're not afraid of heights, bombing attacks or bad guys. You're totally afraid of a chick that might get under your skin. You know what would be really brave?

Drew shoved his door open, not wanting to entertain that train of thought any longer, but he didn't get far into the room before the sound of running water pulled him up short. Two slices of light cut across the bedroom floor, intersecting in front of him. One from the hall behind him, the other from the bathroom, where someone was showering.

Someone who had left the door ajar.

Ignoring the thump of his heart in his chest, he exhaled deliberately and raised his voice. "Annie?"

When silence was the response, he tried to convince himself to pull the door shut and get changed.

Tried.

Failed.

He pushed open the bathroom door, impervious to the wave of steam that greeted him. He was too focused on the woman on the other side of the foggy glass. She was leaning against the tile, letting the water beat against her chest, head tilted back. Gorgeous. Tired. Done.

"You should join me," she murmured, eyes still closed. Maybe not done after all.

"What are you doing in my shower?" he asked instead of answering her invitation. He was incapable of turning it down. His only option was buying some time. Maybe hoping to piss her off again before things got out of hand.

That's a terrible strategy.

You need to get the fuck out of my head right now. There was no way he could do this with Kevin—

I'm not hanging around, chill. Just…be straight with her.

"It's our shower," she said as she turned lazily under the water, and his gaze lingered on the curve of her hip. The flare of her bottom ratcheted up his pulse. "Shared bathroom, two doors."

"I thought you were mad at me." He swallowed hard.

"I am. Take your shirt off."

"Don't you think we should talk?"

She sighed. "Actually, that's the last thing I think we should do. Come wash my back."

Be straight with her. *Fuck.* "If I get in the shower, I'm going to do a hell of a lot more than wash you."

"Good."

"Annie..."

"Drew..." Her mocking tone made him see red, and he pulled off his clothes, shoving them under the floating counter. He might be emotionally conflicted, but his dick sure wasn't—bobbing in front of him, reminding him he needed a condom. Goddamnit. He rifled through his pockets and palmed the foil packet he'd tucked away earlier. He yanked open the door and flicked it on to the small ledge that held a shampoo bottle before curving himself around her back. Wet. Hot. Trembling.

He slid his hands up her arms and braced his hands on the tile beside hers, present but not pushing. "You talk a good game, sugar, but are you sure..."

"Shut up." She arched her back, lifting her head up and into his neck, her ass pressing a sensuous welcome to his cock. He rocked gently into her, and she moaned. "I need you tonight."

"Turn around." His instruction wrenched out in a guttural bark, but she did it without question or retort, spinning slowly in the bracket of his arms. His whole world narrowed to the current pulsing between them as her taunting, turned-on gaze slammed into his. He leaned in, holding her attention as he pressed their naked fronts together for the first time. Around them the quiet, steady sound of dripping water bounced off glass and tile, enveloping them in a private cloud of desire. "You want me?"

"Need, not want," she panted. "You're a jackass."

"Ah, but I'm a jackass you think is cute." He smirked. "Turning the tables on me, sugar?"

"You sleep with women you don't like?" She rolled her eyes. "Why am I not surprised?"

He didn't, but she could think that. It would make leaving easier. But she couldn't think it about herself, not even for a second. "I like you, Annie. A lot. More than is good for either of us."

"And do you want me?" She whispered the question across parted lips, her eyes hungry as she watched him, waiting for the answer.

Instead of responding, he pressed his erection into her belly. Jesus, he wanted inside her. *Want* seemed a shallow, weak word for how much he desired her.

She growled and looped one long leg over his thigh, trying to lift her core, clearly after the same thing. If they did that, this would be over before it even began, and if they only had one night, he was going to make it fucking last. But even as he palmed her breast and stroked her side, he knew this wouldn't be over in the morning. It couldn't be neat and tidy, either, but he was done pretending he didn't care.

"Not so fast, sugar." He chuckled and caught her knee, pressing her leg up and away from him. Spreading her open. "I want to look at you."

She shook her head and twisted her hips. "Don't make this pretty, Drew. I just want you to fuck me."

He knew he had zero right to disagree, but again the needling got under his skin and he growled right back at her. "Oh, I'm going to, sugar. But I'm looking at a six-month long deployment soon, and this shower's got to fuel a hell of a lot of fantasies."

At the momentary deer-in-the-headlights look she gave him, he realized he'd said too much. The fact he was heading overseas worried her, and he felt like an ass for dragging something that couldn't matter into this step outside reality. But just as quickly as it appeared, she shuttered that reaction and lifted her chin defiantly.

He ducked his head and laid a line of light open-mouth kisses along her jaw, ending at her ear. "I need you too, Annie."

———

She wanted to call him all sorts of names. Punch him, and push him away. Yell and throw things, make him apologize, but with his mouth on her neck and his hands holding her against the tile, one on her inner thigh and the other pinning her left hand above her head… she couldn't remember exactly why.

Right. He was leaving her.

She'd only had him for twenty-four hours. A single day of soaking up Drew's attention, and she'd stumbled head long into a sucker's trap. And it was all because of some fictional drama. He was an adrenaline junkie with a thing for long legs.

Her anger re-focused, she jerked herself away from his mouth. "No, you need thrills."

"This is pretty thrilling, I've never made love to a hissing cat before." He pressed closer, glancing the hard ridge of his erection against her wetness.

"You don't make love, remember? Just easy breezy fucking in Castleland?"

"This feel easy breezy to you, sugar?" Another rock against her, another test of her anger. Why did his body have to feel so good? So perfectly big against her, filling all the sad, empty spaces. "I know I've been running hot and cold. But you invited me in, and I'm not leaving until morning. Now, do you want me to wash your back or not?"

"Not." She ground against him. She wanted relief, that exhilarating high that would come from riding him headlong into an orgasm. She didn't need foreplay.

"Tough." One arm spun her so fast she nearly toppled over. The other disappeared for a moment, only to return with a slippery bar of soap, which he proceeded to trail down her spine and then over her bottom. "Spread your legs for me."

She expected him to push the soap over her sex, but instead he skimmed his hand down one thigh to her knee, then up the outside of her leg and over to the other, across her hips. She wiggled for his attention, but he ignored her, moving next to her arms and shoulders. Again he looped around her erogenous zones, and she wanted to scream as her breasts ached for his touch. She stretched again, pressing her nipples into the cool tile, and he shifted to her side, his erection straining against her hip.

"Tell me what you want." His voice was rough and warm in her ear, and she glanced toward him. His eyes were hooded, but he wasn't trying to hide the emotions brimming there. Drew was in control of their bodies, but he'd given up fighting the feelings between them. Damn him.

"I want to come," she whispered. Just sex. That's all it could be. What she needed to keep this to. She closed her eyes as he cupped one breast, his thumb teasing the nipple. Pure pleasure rolled through her body, wave after wave triggered by his gentle play. Yes. She dragged a ragged breath into her lungs and bumped her hips toward him, wanting more, and he gave it to her, sliding his other hand over her hip and into the cleft of her bottom.

A dark tremor danced through her core as he drifted over her tight anus, and her response didn't go unnoticed.

"Have you ever…?" She shook her head and he swore under his breath. "If we had more time, sugar."

"I don't know—"

He pressed his face into her temple. "No. But that's definitely going in the fantasy vault."

She shivered and nodded. "Mine, too."

He curved his palm lower, finding proof of how much she liked the idea. "Jesus. You feel good."

She couldn't respond, a weak cry the only sound she could form as her mouth gaped open, because as he said that, he'd slid two fingers around her clitoris and begun spiraling lazy circles up and around, spreading her slippery moisture all over. And with each pass over that bundle of nerves, he pushed her closer and closer to the release she craved. The blinding crash of sex hormones and physical tension. But just as she felt everything start to fall away, as she shifted into that muzzy altered headspace, he pulled back, still touching her, but slow enough that she lingered on the cusp. Floating. Wanting. Happy.

"You're so beautiful," he whispered. "I can't wait to be inside you."

She whimpered in agreement, and he moved his mouth to her neck, pressing the barest of bites to her skin there. Then he dropped to his knees behind her, and she grabbed her chest, desperate to replace his touch with her own. He nibbled at the base of her spine, making her squirm against his hand still steadily teasing her folds. And then lower, he kissed one cheek and then the other, and she thought she'd die for sure, of either embarrassment or pleasure or both. When he bit the back of her thigh, she knew it was the latter because she lifted her leg in wanton offer, not caring in the slightest what she looked like, just needing his mouth there. There. And as he kissed her core, the very heart of her, sucking her clitoris into his mouth with greedy abandon, she flew apart, clutching the wall and then his head as she rocketed to oblivion.

———

Drew caught Annie as she tumbled into his lap. His kitten might have claws, but she was sated for the moment. He reached up and turned off the shower, snagging the condom at the same time.

"You've got crazy ape arms, you know that?" She peered up at him through half-closed eyelids and licked her lips. "And crazy other things, too."

"And one of them isn't done with you." He ground against her ass. Oh, to take her there…but that needed time. And trust. Maybe one day they'd have another chance…

No. He couldn't go there. Wouldn't ask her to wait for him. "Come on, let's move this to the bed."

She unfolded to a stand, then smoothed her hands over his abs as he bounced after her, humming appreciatively when his muscles clenched under her touch. Like he could control it. Ha. He was barely staving off an embarrassing explosion a few inches south, he wasn't showing off his physique. As if finally sensing his urgency, she flicked her gaze up to his and licked her lips. "I was thinking of something else." She wove her fingers through his and tugged them together toward the counter.

Bending Annie over, watching them together in the mirror…that would be an awesome fuck, no doubt about it. But he wanted more. Needed more, and so did she, even if he hadn't given her any reason to trust he could deliver. "You want to keep me out of your bed, sugar?"

She froze, and his erection lost some of its vigor, but he wasn't giving up. He crowded her against the counter, caging her in with his arms.

"I wasn't thinking like that." She licked her lips and tossed her hair, the gentle action making her breasts bounce in a perfectly distracting way.

"The hell you weren't, and that's my fault. I've said a lot of bull-shit things about keeping us arm's length, blah, blah, blah. But the truth is we can't fight what's between us. So denying it is a bit point-less." He ducked his head and kissed the curve of her ear, working his way lower to the delicate skin on her neck. The urge to mark her there was overwhelming, and his cock once again rose to full attention.

"What's between us?" she whispered.

"An unbreakable bond." The words spilled out strong and true, and she melted against him. Her breasts rubbed against his chest, high and tight, and the soft, swaying skin undid him. He nudged her backward, tipping her against the mirror so he could capture one of her nipples in his mouth.

She keened his name as he sucked and swirled, and a savage pride ripped through his chest. He slid his hands down either side of her body, blindly seeking her hips, and when he found them he curved his palms around her ass and lifted her onto the cool stone counter. Her muscles twitched and flexed under his touch as he continued his worship of her breasts, back and forth, while sheathing himself. Only when he was ready to slide into her warmth did he pull his mouth back up to hers.

He'd never been a huge fan of kissing before, not during sex, but with Annie he wanted to be joined to her in every way possible as they finally coupled. Maybe he was greedy, but he couldn't get enough of her taste or the way she eagerly gave back as he thrust into her again and again.

Her legs gripped around his waist, and he lost a bit of leverage. "Hang on, baby," he whispered, cupping his hands around her back and bottom as he lifted her. "We're going to do this right."

Still buried deep inside her tight, wet sex, he carefully maneuvered back into the bedroom and navigated them to the bed. Instead of trying to lay down, he climbed on and knelt in the middle, sinking back to sit on his heels. Annie rose above him, riding his lap, and in the dim light he could make out a tremulous smile spreading across her face.

"Hi," she whispered, lowering her forehead to press against his. Her hair fell like curtains around them, and in the darkness her breath against his mouth was heaven.

"Hi," he rasped.

"I think it's your turn to come." She'd found her attitude again, and the cheekiness made him growl.

"It doesn't have to be a turn thing, sugar. Ride me, and I'll make sure we both get there." He flexed inside her and she sucked in a breath before lifting up half his length and sliding back down again. "Ahhhh, yes. You're such a good girl."

"Mmmm." She hummed in pleasure and did it again, then again, and on the fourth grind he bucked up to meet her, ratcheting up the tempo. The hitch in her breath told him that worked for her, so he slid a hand between them, finding her clit, because he wasn't going to last long. Not with her tits bobbing in his face and her pussy clenching him like a custom-fit glove. Her voice ringing in his head like a clarion call.

His balls drew tighter against his body as Annie's delicious little breathy sounds came faster and more desperate, as their bodies slammed together in carnal repetition, speeding them both toward blissful release. She came first, spasming around him, and with a roar he surged into her, toppling them both to the side.

One hand went automatically to his dick, grabbing the condom, and the other snagged her around the waist and hauled her into his side. He needed to get cleaned up, but a leg cramp and not seeing properly just yet were pretty damn good excuses to hold on to her a little while longer.

Being with Annie was right. The logistics were going to be complicated and would take time, but he couldn't let her go. Couldn't go back to the automaton routine he'd sleepwalked through for the last year.

He'd figure something out, and pray like hell that she still wanted him when he was finally free to be hers.

CHAPTER
EIGHT

THEY SLEPT FITFULLY, each reaching for the other multiple times through the night, and when dawn broke, Annie gave up trying. But she didn't get out of bed, because she knew as soon as she did, it would be over.

Instead she lay there watching her sleeping giant, committing the hard planes and sculpted ridges of his body to memory. He'd seared his brand on her soul last night and she couldn't imagine how she'd ever get over him. Wouldn't try for a long time, hence trying to absorb every last detail of his magnificent body.

She traced a finger over an inked bird in flight on his rib cage and he stirred.

"Good morning," she whispered, her voice cracking.

His eyes snapped open and he gave her a long, assessing look. "This isn't the end of us, Annie."

Why did he have to go there? She moved to roll away but he gently cuffed her wrist with one of his large hands, holding her palm to his side.

"You know what this tattoo is?"

She shook her head, not trusting her voice.

"It's a martin. I got it two weeks after Kevin died. He'd fucking hate it, call me a bunch of names for getting it, but he was the closest thing to family I've ever had."

"Your parents?" She knew they were both gone, but with a sinking feeling in her gut, she realized she'd never known the details of that.

"Not a story for this morning, but let's just say they were that in name only."

Her heart broke for a child-version of this hulking man. Salty tears slid down her face, hooking off her nose and lips, and he reached out to push them away, but she grabbed his hand and pressed her mouth to his palm. "I'm so sorry. Here I've been feeling so sad for myself that my family is gone—"

"That's the thing, sugar. I don't feel that sadness about them. I can't miss what I never had."

Understanding dawned and she wrapped the sheet more securely around her body, all of a sudden far too naked for this conversation. "Easy breezy makes a lot of sense now."

He nodded. "It did."

She pasted on an understanding smile and shifted her gaze somewhere

"Did, past tense. Annie, you make me want things I've never considered before."

"Like a second date?" Her nerves were pulled tight and totally raw, the joke was the only response she could muster.

He seemed to get that and laughed gently. "Something like that." He pulled her in close, sliding one heavily muscled leg between hers. "Maybe some visiting back and forth between L.A. and San Diego."

Could he hear her heart pounding in her chest? "Uhm, that sounds nice." A nervous giggle escaped. "Really nice."

He squeezed the back of her neck. "I'm still looking at a bit more time in, though, so I won't ask more of you than that. Not because I don't want to, but it wouldn't be fair."

Service. Deployment. Operations. Fear sliced through her giddy happiness. She couldn't lose Drew, not when she'd just found him. She burrowed into the safe haven of his arms and closed her eyes. "When do you leave on your next operation?"

"Probably five months from now, but the timing can change." His hand wound up into her hair and he tugged her head back to look her in the eyes. "You remember the deal from Kevin, right? No news is good news?"

The lump in her throat was getting bigger by the second. "I shouldn't expect to hear from you." She nodded. "I remember."

"And when I get back…there's a period of adjustment. I won't be a lot of fun to be around."

"You're really selling this, Castle." She tried to push a playful tone back into her voice, failing miserably. She'd take him however she could get him. Broken, grumpy, tired. It didn't matter.

He leaned in and laid a bruising kiss across her mouth. "I don't have much to sell, sugar. But I've got you tattooed on my body. I didn't know it was you when I did it, I thought I was marking a memory. It wasn't about the past, though…it was my future. It was you."

"This is crazy," she whispered, snuggling into his neck.

"You liked crazy last night," he rumbled, his voice all around her.

She pressed a kiss to his bare skin, blushing at the memory of Drew filling her, stretching her from the inside out, making her hot and achy all over again. "Do we have time to get a little crazy again before breakfast?"

"We'll make time. I'm a Navy SEAL, sugar, we're resourceful."

———

Two orgasms and a shower later they made their way downstairs. On the dining room table they found a tray of orange juice, croissants, and fresh fruit. The smell of frying bacon wafted from the kitchen.

Annie didn't think she was hungry, with her stomach twisted in knots at the possibility of talking to the man who was raising her brother's child. Drew had given her a quick briefing from the night before while he washed her hair, which helped mollify her when she realized how much he'd kept secret while they were sorting out their relationship issues.

Relationship. The details of which were still up in the air, but there was no doubt that was what they'd tumbled into. And last night she hadn't been in a headspace to think about anything, and there wasn't any action to be had on the Harris front, not until Rik's people in DC had made contact.

Which had left Drew free to…she blushed as another X-rated moment replayed itself in her mind.

"Thinking of something naughty, sugar?" Drew twisted his body in front of hers, blocking her from the room. His voice was low, for her ears only, and she nodded as she buried her face in his chest. "Good. Want coffee?"

"Mmm-hmmm."

From the kitchen, Calli hollered that more food was up, so Annie left Drew pouring steaming coffee and warm milk into mugs and went to help carry trays of bacon, scrambled eggs, and fried tomatoes.

Rik and Mats joined them next, and finally Trent and Jackson silently entered the room from a hallway Annie hadn't noticed the night before. Trent looked like he hadn't slept—or shaved—since she'd seen him last. But he didn't seem bothered by that at all, flashing her an unexpected smile.

"We're all set for half past nine, Ms. Martin. Rik and Drew can take the call if you'd rather, but the senator has expressed an interest in talking with you."

She slid a quick look in Drew's direction, and her wave of anxiety was dissipated a bit by the comical sight of Drew tucking into a mountain of food. He paused for a moment and gave her a wink as if to say, *got your back.*

She thanked Trent and took the seat next to Drew. "Hungry?"

"I got distracted by a beautiful woman on my way to dinner last night," he murmured. "And then she put me through my paces."

She grinned. "Well, eat up. Maybe we'll have time for another private training session before you leave."

He finished chewing and put down his fork. "I'm sorry I said that yesterday. We came together, we'll leave together."

"I don't want you to get in trouble at work."

"I've got more than thirty-six hours before anyone will be expecting me. We've got some time to enjoy the beach." He nudged her leg under the table. "And talk more."

"Talk?"

"Yeah, you know. String words together, form sentences. Share information. Converse." He grinned. "I'll tell you about the time we locked Kevin out of the showers, buck naked."

"Oh good lord. Deal. And I'll tell you about him dressing up in my Mom's hat and gloves for a tea party."

He lifted her hand to kiss her knuckles and her heart just about exploded from happiness. This couldn't be real, the other shoe would drop any second and she'd go back to being alone. As if he could read her thoughts, he leaned over and whispered in her ear. "Keep breathing, sugar."

"You aren't God's gift to women, you know." She mock scowled.

"Nope, just to you." And with a self-satisfied smile, he dug back into his breakfast.

And that really was the truth. They were a gift to each other, and she wasn't going to over-think it any further than that.

———

After breakfast, Trent led them down the hallway from where he appeared earlier, and Annie realized there was a heavy sliding panel fully recessed into the wall at the entrance. As they stepped into what looked like a NASA control room, she understood the need for secrecy.

She knew better than to say anything, but when Drew leaned in and asked Rik just how top-secret the bodyguarding business was these days, she couldn't help but crane to hear the answer. Which of course didn't come.

Instead, Rik chuckled and waved for Trent to begin. On one of the screens in front of them a black command prompt window opened up, and Trent typed, waited, then typed again. A few more windows flitted by, full of code, then after a minute Trent clicked on a shortcut to a program from his desktop.

"Skype?" All the heads in the room swiveled to look at Annie and she realized she'd asked the incredulous question out loud. In for a penny… "Seriously? We fled the country to a high-tech spy base, and we're going to call him on Skype?"

Trent winked. "Sure thing. And the FBI or whoever is listening thinks we're located in the Mediterranean. If they're even looking anymore."

"Anymore?"

Trent and Rik exchanged a quick look. "You don't seem to be a person of interest to them any longer."

"But I was."

"Briefly, yes." Trent winced. "Possibly because you ran from the police."

Drew snorted. "And why were they looking for her in the first place?"

"Because, wise guy, the senator had identified her the night before as someone who might be at risk."

Annie groaned. With all that had happened with Drew in the interim, she'd forgotten how embarrassing it was being the center of all of this drama.

"All's well that ends well?" Drew gave her one of his patented eager kid faces, and she rolled her eyes.

"It's a good thing you're cute, Castle."

Trent cleared his throat. "We good to place this call?"

"Yep, go ahead." Annie ignored the looks of surprise from Rik and Drew. Yeah, she was in charge now. She didn't love the feeling, but there were times when a girl needed to step up and push the boys out of the way, and this was one of those times. "Where's our web cam?"

On the screen there was just a black box where the return video feed would display. Trent shook his head. "Let's wait and see what happens at their end before turning it on. But it's up there, at the top of the screen. Takes in most of the room."

And everyone in it. Annie's heart rate picked up. She glanced at Drew, who was already stepping into a dead spot in the corner.

The call connected, and the video feed flickered a few times before a comfortably handsome face filled the screen, his brows creased more than Annie remembered from media coverage. Rob Harris was in a richly appointed office, and he appeared to be alone.

"Ms. Martin?"

"Yes. Nice to meet you, Senator Harris." Her voice warbled and she clenched her hands into fists at her side.

"I'm sorry it's not under different circumstances." He paused and glanced at something beside his computer. "I'm sorry it wasn't much sooner."

Annie decided to dive right in. "I understand we have something of a connection?"

He nodded. "And I understand you received an awful phone call the other day. My wife had a similar message left for her as well, and then I received a follow up call yesterday."

She couldn't read his face and stepped closer to the screen, desperate for more. More clues. More straight up information. More connection.

On the screen, the father of her biological nephew rubbed his face and sighed. "I hoped to connect with you before…but that wasn't to be. I think it's time I tell you a bit about my son."

She nodded. "I'd like that."

"His name is Bobby, and he loves dragons and baseball. He's more athletic than I ever was, which makes his grandfather happy, and he's left-handed, unlike my wife and myself." Annie could feel Drew react to that from across the room. *Just like Kevin.* "When he was six months old, he was small for his age and wasn't gaining weight as well as he should. We ended up doing genetics testing for cystic fibrosis. It was at that point that I met your brother."

Annie couldn't help the gasp that slipped out. The overheard conversation between Kevin and the mysterious woman at the other end of the line now made sense.

"Something you need to understand, Ms. Martin, is that I love my wife very much. I always have, and I always will. But there was a period of time when we were new in Washington that I didn't give her as much attention as I should. I was too focused on laying the foundation for a leadership run or some such nonsense, and I neglected our relationship. It was in that time period that she befriended your brother." A wistful look crossed the senator's face. "When she realized she was pregnant, she knew there was only one possible father. I spent a week in the ICU following an untreated strep infection in college that made it impossible for me to have children of my own."

She could fill in the rest. "And Kevin's job didn't allow him to take on shared custody of a child."

Harris leaned forward, his face filling the screen. "We would have, if he wanted. He did visit, in the role of a family friend, once or twice a year. Beth-Anne sent him pictures from time to time, and email updates."

"They stayed in touch?"

He nodded. "Not regularly, but from time to time. We don't have any secrets between us. A lot of sad history, maybe, but no secrets. I was the first person she told when she took the test. First she told me, then she told him. And she would have shared custody with him, but she wouldn't leave me. I didn't deserve that loyalty, but she gave it to me anyway, and I've never let her down since. My wife and my son…they are my world. Your brother gave me that, as hard as that may be to imagine."

———

Drew couldn't watch from the shadows any longer, not when Annie's shoulders started to shake almost imperceptibly. He was at her side as the first tear fell, careful to keep his back to the camera. Trent cut their video feed momentarily, and Drew gave her a quick squeeze.

"You okay?" he whispered.

She nodded and he brushed a quick kiss against her lips. He glanced at Rik and jerked his chin. He didn't have anything to hide.

As the pixels re-formed their moving image, Harris didn't show any surprise to see Drew. Either he hadn't made a briefing book, or Harris wasn't interested in a SEAL's presence. Both possibilities were reassuring.

Harris chewed on his bottom lip for a minute then leaned back in his chair. "Annie, part of why this came up is probably because I've been approached by different people to consider running for higher office. Beth-Anne and I have talked about it. I won't deny I've been swayed, but I'm not interested if it risks my family. And I know we haven't met, but I include you in that. If you're still planning to come here for that research trip, I hope you'll come to dinner."

"Dinner?" Her eyes were big and suspiciously wet still.

"We think it's time you meet your nephew, don't you?"

She swallowed hard. "Does he…"

"Know? No. But he knew Kevin as a friend of the family, and we'd introduce you as his sister." Harris tightened his lips for a moment, and Drew couldn't read his expression. "We've visited his grave in Arlington. When he's older, we'll tell him. I hope that's enough for you."

A sob wracked through her body, and Annie twisted toward him, burying her face in his chest. Drew cleared his throat, drawing the attention of the senator and the other men in the room. "That sounds like it would be enough for Kevin."

Annie nodded into his shirt, and he pulled her tighter. A sharp realization sliced through his gut as he processed that with anyone else, he'd have made the same decision as Kevin. Walk away, watch from afar. But if Annie were carrying his child? He'd slay dragons to be at her side.

Unaware that Drew's entire sense of being had been permanently altered, Rik stepped into the center of the shot.

The senator nodded. "Amundson."

"Harris."

Drew wasn't surprised there was a history there. Rik had always been more than an average special operator.

"There are people who aren't going to like your meddling in this."

Rik shrugged. "Can't be helped."

"There was supposed to be egg on my face here. I'm glad there isn't, but that's probably disrupted someone's plan for something else."

Drew tightened his grip on Annie, not wanting to let her go. Not liking the tone of their veiled back and forth statements. "I thought you said last night this was about a paparazzi thing."

Trent spoke from the corner, the burr in his voice more pronounced than usual. "That's definitely who was interested in Annie, and now that there's no story there, she's probably not a person of interest to anyone. But there's a money trail, and it runs dark in a way that tells us it didn't originate in a good place."

Drew knew some of the options there. Could imagine the others, and didn't like any of the thoughts running through his head. "And what about Harris? And his son?"

On the screen, the senator shrugged. "This is probably bigger than me as well. I have a feeling that we haven't seen the last of each other, though."

"All due respect, sir, but I've got retirement plans in my future. The next time you see me it had better be at a family picnic."

Annie's lips quirked and he glanced down at her. "What? I like picnics."

"Yeah? Me too." She grinned. "I'm just shocked you used the word family without shuddering."

EPILOGUE

9 MONTHS LATER

HER MAN WAS COMING HOME. His flight had left Dubai fifteen hours and forty-seven minutes ago, and now she paced in the arrivals hall at LAX willing herself to play it cool when he walked through the gate. Not to cry. Jeez, no crying. He'd survived a six month deployment, and while she knew he couldn't tell her much—anything—about it, he was all in one piece. When they Skyped the night before, he'd even seemed relaxed and happy.

Really happy. And horny. That had to be a good sign.

Her arms ached to hold him and her heart felt like it might just thump out of her chest. It had only been fifteen seconds since the last time she checked the arrivals board, but she glanced up again anyway, and let out a too-loud whoop when she realized the status had changed from *Expected* to *Arrived*. *Hot damn.* Somewhere on the other side of the sliding doors, Drew Castle was back on American soil.

She wanted to announce to the crowd around her that a hero was about to walk amongst them, but rule number one of dating a SEAL…no glorification of the job. And keeping this reunion private was part of why Drew flew into LAX a few days before the rest of his men came home. Even though she was happy to socialize with the other girlfriends and family members in San Diego, Drew resisted mixing their lives together more than was strictly necessary.

He cited security reasons, but Annie knew better. As much as she loved him, Drew was still an overgrown man-child in many ways, and commitment sat front and centre on that list. It was okay. She likely had two more years of research before she finished her doctoral thesis, and she'd give him that long to sort out what he wanted.

No, that wasn't fair. He definitely wanted her. A shiver wracked her body at the heated words he'd whispered across their computer connection the night before. He wanted her mind, body and soul, and she didn't need to worry about the details. When the time was right, they'd take their relationship to the next level.

She smoothed her hands over the flat front of her cherry-red dress, then tucked her small handbag securely under one arm. How much time would it take him to move through customs and security? He didn't need to wait for any luggage, he just had a carry-on bag as most of his gear was being shipped directly to Coronado. The opaque glass doors on the other side of the barricade slid open as other international travellers passed through, and she craned her neck for a glimpse of her tall mountain of a man.

Five minutes, then ten, passed by, and the few butterflies in her stomach filled the void by procreating and turning into a full on swarm.

Then the doors slid open once more, and Drew was ten feet on the other side. He flashed a wide grin as they made eye contact, but before he got close enough to the sensor, the doors closed, and she leaned hard against the yellow metal barrier. *One...two...three.* And then with a whoosh the glass parted again and he was in front of her and then around her, his strong arms hauling her against his body, the metal bars between them fading away.

"You're home," she breathed into his neck. "Oh my god, I've missed you so much."

He pulled back just enough to press a hard kiss against her lips, then shifted her out of the way so he could leap over the barricade.

"You could have gone around," she whispered, pressing her entire body against his.

"And let go of you? Not a chance in hell, sugar." He slid his hand behind her neck and covered her mouth with hot demands and hungry promises. As his tongue worked its magic, his hands familiarized themselves with her body, and Annie wanted more.

"Come on, let me take you home." She tugged him toward the exit, wanting to get someplace private so they wouldn't need to hold back.

"Wait," he said, reaching for his bag. "I got you something."

She spun around, nerves and relief both making her antsy. Her skirt flared a bit, the fabric dancing against her fingertips, and it occurred to her that was an odd thing to notice. Also odd was how her pulse picked up and how loud all of a sudden her breathing sounded to her own ears.

Drew stared at her for a moment, a secret smile on his face, and the realization of what was about to happen fully dawned just as he dropped to one knee.

Don't pass out, her brother's voice rang through her head, and the tears started to fall in big, wet, embarrassing plops. *He doesn't deserve you, but he'll love you forever.*

"Annie Martin, you are the light of my life. I didn't know what love was before I met you, and—" he broke off and swallowed hard.

"You can cry, all the cool kids do." She laughed and wiped her own face, then touched his.

"Hell no. Okay, I can do this." He cleared his throat. "I love you, sugar. There are fancier words to describe what we have, but I want us to be together forever. I want to be yours forever, and you be mine."

"I'm yours," she whispered, willing her knees to not give out before he finished.

"And I'm yours. Forever, sugar. Will you marry me?" He held up a platinum band, split in the middle around a channel-set diamond solitaire, and she wasn't sure she could take it from him without dropping it because her hands were shaking too much. She nodded enthusiastically and threw herself against him instead, and somehow in between standing up and kissing her again, Drew managed to slide the ring on her finger.

———

"It's a perfect fit," Annie exclaimed a few minutes later as they stopped at a red light. She wiggled her fingers in the sunlight. "I never thought I'd be that girl, but holy crap, look at my ring."

Drew grinned. Hitting a jewelry store was his first and only priority when he landed in Dubai. The unique setting had grabbed his attention and he'd paid for it on the spot.

"How did you know my size?"

"I measured you one night while you were sleeping," he admitted.

She twisted in her seat. "Before you left?" Her lips parted for a second before she took a deep breath. "I had no idea…"

He squeezed her knee. He was thankful her sedan was an automatic and he didn't have to break contact with her. The red flouncy fabric of her skirt sat on top of his hand and in its shadow he stroked bare, smooth skin. "I've been serious about you—about us—since that first weekend, sugar."

"Me too." She bit her lip, and he knew she wanted to ask about future deployments, her schooling, what this meant for their future and where they might live, but there would be time for all of that later. She pushed a bright look onto her face. "Are you hungry?"

Only for her. "I just want to get you home and into bed, sugar."

She smiled, all the way to her eyes this time. "Yeah. Me too."

A few hours later, Drew pulled on black gym shorts from the drawer he'd established months earlier and padded to the apartment door to pay the Chinese food delivery guy. Humming, he dumped the cartons of food on the kitchen table and pulled out plates and chopsticks. From the bathroom, he heard the shower turn off, and a minute later Annie was in the doorway watching him. She wore one of his t-shirts and her damp hair hung loose around her shoulders.

"Come here," he instructed.

"I like to watch you."

"And I like to touch you. Come. Here." He wasn't kidding. Feeling the warmth of her skin under his hand soothed him in a way he'd never appreciated before.

She smiled but did as requested, sliding between him and the kitchen counter. He caged her in with his arms and pressed his forehead against hers.

"It's different than I expected," he whispered. "Leaving someone behind."

She stroked his cheek. "How so?"

"I worried I'd feel conflicted. Want to play it safe, that sort of thing." He squeezed her hip. "But knowing you were here…that just motivated me that much harder."

Her eyes flared wide and he knew he'd surprised her. She cupped his neck and pulled his lips against hers, sliding her tongue against the seam of his mouth. He opened readily for her, and within seconds was ready in another way.

"Are you sore?" He growled the question against her jaw as he worked his way down to lick the spot on her neck that drove her crazy.

"A little." Her creamy skin turned pink at the admission.

"I'll be gentle." He lifted her onto the counter with ease, relishing the feel of her slim hips in his hands. Her bare hips, he discovered as he parted her thighs and dropped to his knees.

"Not too gentle." She moaned as he licked his way to her core. He wanted to greedily feast on her, but he'd already done that earlier. This time he took care to tease and caress, stoking her desire until she was slippery and just as ready as he was to join together.

Together. It was the perfect word for them. Despite their separate lives and sad history, they were building toward a solid future. It was a freakin' miracle that Drew Castle had been given such beauty, and he was going to appreciate it—and her—for the rest of his life.

He surged to his feet and nudged his cock into her wet folds. His eyes rolled back in his head at the warm welcome. *Jesus.* He'd never get enough of her. With gentle pressure he slid into her, groaning as his hips pressed into the backs of her thighs. Her legs wrapped tight around his waist, her heels dug into his back, and against his chest her breaths came hard and fast in moist little puffs that drove him crazy.

"Give me your mouth, sugar." He shouldn't act like a caveman but he couldn't help himself. Being inside Annie reduced him to grunting need. God, he was glad Kevin wasn't in his head anymore.

"I'm so close," she whispered, and the urge to thump his chest swelled again. He starting moving, rocketing them both toward the release they craved. She tipped over the edge first, and the soft, rhythmic clenching of her pussy did him in as well. She sagged against him, pressing hot little kisses against his arm, and then started laughing.

"Hey, that's not good for the ego." He grinned down at her.

"I was just thinking I'm going to need another shower now."

"I've got a better idea." He pulled out and pressed her legs together. "Be right back."

Two warm washcloths later, they were snuggled on the couch trading bites of orange chicken and black bean shrimp.

"Is it too soon to start planning a wedding?"

Annie looked at him with surprise. "Isn't that supposed to be my line?"

"I don't know. I've never done this before." He took advantage of her being distracted and stole her spring roll. "I was thinking the fall." He took a bite, enjoying the curious reaction playing out on Annie's face. "After I retire."

In hindsight, telling her while she had a plate of messy food in her hands was a mistake. Fried rice hopped into the air as she jerked in surprise. "Are you serious?"

A slow grin took over his entire face. "As a heart attack, sugar."

She bounced up and down and squealed. "I thought you'd have a few more years in still."

He shrugged. "Priorities change. Technically I won't retire for another two years, I'll be a reservist. But my life is with you now, wherever you are. I'm committed until the end of the summer, but I've started the process to switch at that point. And then I'll find security work here in L.A. until you're ready to go...wherever you want to go next."

Her eyes lit up. "Then yes, we should start planning a wedding. How does the Caribbean sound?"

"Perfect. I just happen to know a guy..."

FALL HARD

ABOUT THIS BOOK

Jared Sutter has a simple rule when it comes to women: keep 'em happy and keep 'em at a distance. He's got his reasons, and they all make sense until he falls for his neighbor and Cassie Bronson makes him want things he's always kept off-limits.

CHAPTER
ONE

JUST ONCE, he'd like to spend Christmas bundled up in a sweater. Preferably with a ski bunny tucked into his side.

Jared Sutter looked at the text message from his brother Jackson again. Something's come up. We'll do Colorado in the new year.

"Something" would be a mission. His brother was an ex-Navy SEAL turned mercenary who lived in the Caribbean and did the jobs Jared and his SEAL teammates couldn't be asked to do.

Jared could go to Colorado on his own, but that would get complicated. He preferred to play wingman—help his brother or a buddy sweeten up their target, and then pay some attention to her less eager friend who was always relieved to find out that Jared didn't want to get in her pants.

At least, not all the way. Every girl liked an orgasm or two courtesy of his fingers, and if they got to the naked stage, his tongue. He'd gotten pretty talented in both areas over the last eight years.

But it didn't look like there'd be snow, skiing, or ski bunny hookups for his holiday break this year. Oh well. Staying home would give him a chance to finally furnish his apartment. He'd lived in California for almost two years, had rented his own place in Coronado Beach for almost one, and all he had to show for it was a bed, a big-ass TV, and the world's most comfortable couch. The couch was a hand-me-down from Drew Castle, a friend of Jackson's and former senior enlisted SEAL who'd recently switched to reservist duty to move to Los Angeles with his fiancée.

Drew had come home from overseas just in time to teach some courses on Jared's SEAL Qualification Training course, and while Jared had to put up with some extra ribbing for being Jackson's little brother, he'd gotten a couch out of it in the end, so he couldn't complain.

No, his only complaint as a Texas-born, California-trained Navy SEAL who was living the dream was that he once again wouldn't have a white fucking Christmas. Boo-fucking-hoo. Time to go to IKEA and get over himself.

He lived on the third floor of a walk-up apartment complex in the heart of Coronado Beach, close enough to base that he could get there quickly, far enough away that he wasn't entirely surrounded by uniforms when he stepped out his door. A few guys he knew lived in the complex, but his next-door neighbors were civvies and that suited him just fine. His door opened onto a balcony of sorts that ran around an interior courtyard with a pool. He usually swam in the ocean, but when the girls from the apartment to his right decided to lay out by the pool, he could be convinced to join them.

Something that Cassie Bronson—the *woman* in the apartment to his left—gave him no small amount of grief over.

Unlike Jemma and Brittany, Cassie wasn't one to parade around in a bikini. Damn shame, because under her suits and silk shirts he had no doubt she was rocking an awesome body. No, Cassie was a grown-up, through and through, right down to the gourmet dinners she cooked and the fancy wine she drank.

And even though they were like night and day in so many ways, they'd struck up an odd friendship. It had started with a very reluctant tap on his door a few months earlier.

"You're strong, right?" she'd asked, hanging back from his doorway like she wasn't sure what might come snapping out at her.

"Why yes, ma'am, I guess I am," he'd offered back, laying on the polite Texan-smooth in a way that would make his mama proud.

"I need your muscles, if you don't mind."

And he hadn't—not for carrying that desk up to her apartment, or for opening a ridiculously sealed jar of pickles a few weeks later. Each time she'd paid him back with a few containers of the most delicious leftovers.

Then he'd gone away for a fourteen-day training mission, and when he returned she gave him a weird look and said she was glad to see he was all in one piece. The next night she invited him over for dinner. He'd graduated up from leftovers, and before he could worry about whatever strings might be attached, she whipped out the proverbial scissors and assured him there weren't any. She was recently divorced and her rebound relationship had fallen apart in a big way. She was in a man-free period in her life and happy for it.

"Men and women can just be friends, right?" She'd held out her hand like a challenge she didn't expect him to take, but the joke was on her. Jared had never been anything more than friends with all the women in his life, except one. And his mama didn't count.

"Abso-fucking-lutely," he'd drawled, enjoying the way her cheeks pinked up. They'd shook on it, and the odd-couple friendship was born.

So it wasn't strange that he took just three steps away from his door before turning around to knock on hers. She'd do a better job of picking stuff out anyway.

"Ikea?" Cassie stared at him after he repeated the invitation again. She'd answered the door wearing jean cut-offs, an oversized T-shirt that fell off one shoulder to reveal a matching tank-top underneath, and flip-flops. An uncharacteristically casual look for her, but it had been warm the last couple of days. *Fucking Christmas in southern California, man.* Well, at least the view was nice.

"What's so crazy about that?"

"You're not exactly a throw cushion kind of guy."

"I'm a bachelor. I need a swinging bachelor pad."

She snorted. "Right. You're not the entertaining type. When was the last time you invited someone back to your place?"

Well, never. But that might change at some point. And when it did, he'd probably do better if he had some damn throw cushions.

She searched his face for a punch line that wasn't coming, then shrugged. "Sure, I like IKEA. Come on in. I'll grab my purse." He followed her into her apartment, which probably was a mirror image of his, but looked completely different because, unlike him, she *had* decorated.

———

Cassie watched Jared try to navigate his cart around a family of six picking out curtains and bit back a laugh. She should have directed him to the IKEA website instead, but he had muscles and she'd wanted to go to Costco, so having some company for a big box store run sounded like fun. Even on a Saturday, five days before Christmas.

It *was* fun, even if he was cursing under his breath about rules of the road and needing to be aware of one's surroundings.

Her phone rang and she dug it out of her purse. *Melissa.*

"What are you up to? I have a mad craving for dim sum."

Cassie smiled at the sound of her best friend's voice ringing loud and clear through the phone line. "Just at Ikea with Jared, actually."

"Bring him. He's hot. We'll go to that place with the cute gay waiter and get better service."

Jared gave her a funny look, like he could make out part of the conversation and wasn't sure what to think of it.

Mel was the type of woman Jared usually went for. Beautiful, fun, and totally uninterested in commitment. The type of woman Cassie had watched him flirt with, sometimes make out with, and once-in-a-blue-moon get dragged home by. But at some point over the last few weeks, his easy playboy attitude had started to grate on her.

"Can't, sorry. We're stuck in box-store hell. Costco's next. Call you later?" She hung up before Mel could protest further. Cassie wasn't in the mood to share Jared.

Her impulse to keep Jared to herself wasn't fair. They were friends, nothing more, and they'd even shook on it. Who he wanted to play with was none of her business.

Except at some point in the fall, she'd started to want him to play with *her*.

The shift in how she saw him had snuck up on her. She'd thought she was done falling hard. She'd done that with her ex-husband, Mitch, and look where that had gotten her. Then she'd had a whirlwind affair with Craig the dentist that had fallen apart as quickly as it started.

It turned out her being barren was a real turn-off for guys. What a joke. She'd spent her teenage and early adult years using two or three kinds of birth control at once, terrified of getting knocked up, when all along getting pregnant hadn't been possible.

And she was fine with it—when she met someone who she wanted to have a family with, and when they were ready, they'd adopt. Or maybe look into the advanced fertility treatment options like IVF or surrogacy.

But all the guys she was attracted to seemed keen on having a family the old-fashioned way. Didn't that just make her feel special— and kind of stupid, because obviously she'd trained herself to fall for the wrong kind of guy.

Her gaze fell back to Jared. His cart was tucked neatly out of the way, and he stood there, arms crossed and legs planted wide, looking at some rugs like they were topographic maps of a battlefield. Jeepers, the man turned shopping into a serious mission.

He had a chameleon face. Boyishly handsome one minute, fierce and determined the next. No one should get between him and his goal.

Fair enough if it was part of his job in the Navy or buying a rug. But his goal of only having uncomplicated hook-ups with women he didn't know? She had a feeling she was about to get in his way on that front, big-time.

A tiny twinge of guilt made itself known in her tummy. *You had a deal*, her conscience reminded her. *Yeah, but that was before he proved himself to be completely irresistible.* And something told her he wasn't actually a player. He made all the right noncommittal noises and flirted his way through all encounters with the female sex, but there was something noble about him.

Not that having casual sex wasn't noble.

No, with the right person, it might practically be a civic duty.

Her, for example. And that twinge of guilt faded away, a hurricane of butterflies taking centre stage in her midsection instead. Yes, Jared turning his sexy bedroom eyes on her would be good for everyone involved.

He strode decisively toward a black woven rug that she really liked and hefted it over his shoulder with one hand. She smiled to herself and moved to catch up.

Two hours later, they were hauling that rug, a new armchair, a lamp, four oversized cushions, some art, and three giant bags of groceries from Costco up to their apartments. Or rather, Jared was hauling. Cassie carried the lamp up first, setting it down outside his door. Then he gave her the bag of cold groceries, and by the time she'd made room for the turkey in her fridge, he had everything else carried up.

He'd thrown the latch so she could just walk in to his apartment. She found him already assembling the lamp.

"Did you run down the stairs?"

"Down and up, yes."

"Carrying furniture."

He frowned. "The chair is disassembled and in a box with a handle. I wouldn't call it furniture yet."

"I'll stop feeling guilty for not helping more, then. Listen, Mel called earlier today and I blew her off, so I'm going to meet her at the Coronado Brewing Company for beers later. Do you want to come?"

He shrugged, which she understood to mean yes because he had a screwdriver gripped between his teeth.

She left him to the assembly and went back to her place to make a giant salad for dinner. She tossed some garlic toast in the oven, even though she wouldn't eat it, and pulled three servings of sliced steak from the fridge. One for her bowl, two for Jared's.

She picked up her phone to text him that dinner was ready just as he gave a quick double tap on the door and let himself in. How had she ever thought she *wouldn't* be attracted to this man? He was almost over-the-top masculine, all rugged and raw and rough, until he smiled his boyish grin and then his looks took a hard right into gorgeous territory. She liked both sides of his exterior, but what had really awakened her interest was getting to know the Jared on the inside.

Because the man was *nice*. In an age when selfishness seemed to be elevated to an art form—figuring out what was in it for you before doing *anything*—Jared was the good-guy exception. Wrapped in a delightfully sinful package.

"Dinner's ready," she said weakly. He smoothed his hand down the outside of her arm as he passed her. How could he do that without feeling a zap of sexual energy? His casual touch on her elbow made her think of his hands on her knees, spreading her open. Gripping her ankles…

"Smells great. Are you okay?"

She blinked away the dirty fantasies in her head and nodded. "Yeppers. Let's eat."

"Should I call a bunch of the guys, make it a big group thing tonight?"

She shrugged. "You could."

"Groups are more fun," he said as he forked up some salad. "This is good. I like the seeds in it."

There it was—the nugget she needed to hang on to if she had any hope in hell of not falling head over heels for Jared Sutter. He was a man-child of the highest order. All of his maturity was channeled into his job, where she had no doubt he was a leader among men.

But if life was high school, and in so many ways she'd learned it totally was, Jared was a perpetual grade-niner, his voice cracking at the thought of a one-on-one date with a girl.

Which was ridiculous, because he was so damn smooth with women. She'd seen him disappear to dark corners of bars and come back a little while later with a very satisfied looking woman trailing in his wake. But when she picked apart the memories, she realized it was a rare time that he actually *left* with that woman. And when he did, he almost always came home not long after.

She should know. She always left the bar right after he did.

Cassie sighed into her salad. She needed to get laid.

"Everything okay?" Jared put his fork down and flashed her a helpful smile. "Do you need anything?"

Even as her face warmed, Cassie couldn't help smiling back. "Yep. I just might."

CHAPTER
TWO

JARED GLANCED AT HIS WATCH. Cassie had said she needed a few minutes to get changed before they headed out and twenty had passed. He didn't care, but he had shit he could be doing instead of sitting on her couch reading *Real Simple*.

"Hey, Cass," he said, walking toward her bedroom door. "I'm just going to pop back to my place until you're ready."

Her response was muffled, so he asked her to repeat it.

"No, I'm almost done," she said breathlessly, whipping open the door. "Can you zip me up?"

Jared wasn't immune to temptation, but he'd learned to avoid facing it in the first place. And Cassie was just Cassie, his pretty neighbor who didn't want anything to do with men. So he didn't think twice about approaching her bedroom door, didn't think to blink or turn away when she opened the door—and she completely blindsided him.

He was *fucked*. Cassie had poured herself into a tiny black dress. Her left arm held the silky fabric against her tits. *Fuck*. His dick was already thick and rising, and his tongue felt like it was made of lead. He blinked hard and looked down, but that just led to her legs. All of her legs. Even though the dress was longer than the pair of shorts she'd had on before, there was something completely different about her legs sliding out from beneath that short, fluttery skirt.

Something hot and forbidden and utterly appealing. Something dangerous.

And when she turned around, showing him a deep triangle of skin bisected by the prettiest spine he'd ever seen and a narrow band of a bra, he knew *fucked* barely scraped the surface of his current situation.

"Zip?" she asked helpfully, tossing her hair out of her eyes as she blinked back at him. An innocent blink that made reality click back into place. Cassie wasn't flirting. She didn't do the Bambi eye thing. She was smart and sassy and sarcastic.

He ground his back teeth together and gripped the zipper pull in one hand and a pinch of the dress fabric in the other. "Going on the prowl tonight, Cass?"

She gave him a weird look. "Maybe."

"Good," he said, stepping back. He needed space to ensure he didn't just bodily toss her onto the bed and grind against her. *That would feel so good*, his dick protested. *Those tits in your hand, that neck under your mouth.*

Those tits and that neck belonged to his friend. His neighbor. His off-limits-for-real-no-exceptions Cassie. Whatever game she was playing, she could play with someone else. Because there's no way she'd still be having fun at the end of the night if he gave in. No, she'd hate him, or be embarrassed for him, and either way their friendship would be over.

"Will you be my wingman, Sutter?" She bent down, way down, to do up the straps on a pair of heels that he hadn't noticed before and now he couldn't un-notice. He glowered at the backside of the woman who was going to be his undoing tonight. One way or another, this wasn't going to go well.

"Maybe we should let Melanie handle that," he grunted, turning and heading for the door. She followed him, somehow surrounding him with a delicate perfume that defied the laws of physics and bounced around him like an invisible cloak of seduction. "I've got an early morning tomorrow, I can't stay out late."

Strictly speaking, that was true. He was leading PT the next day. But it wasn't different than any other day, and Cassie wasn't one to stay out late. She was usually in her flannel pajama shorts by the ten o'clock news.

He knew, because just the other night they'd watched the news together, curled up on her couch with hot chocolate.

Where the fuck had that dress come from? It wasn't Cassie. She was sexy, sure, but in a cute-librarian kind of way. This vixen was playing tricks on his eyes and messing everything up.

"I've got cash for a cab to come home. It's okay," she murmured as she locked up.

She'd slipped on a jean jacket over her dress, which helped him cage his inner caveman, but just barely. There was no way he was going to leave her anywhere in public looking like that. *Wait, what?* He thought about that reaction as they waited out front for their cab. *Man, you need to get right with the idea that she's looking for something you can't give her tonight. Or ever. And if she wants to go home with someone else...*

His stomach twisted in a new and disconcerting way. It wouldn't be the first time he walked away from a woman he was attracted to. He'd get over the grating regret of letting Cassie go, too.

But when they arrived at the brewpub, and Novak, Steyner, and Dumbrowski arrived at the same time, he kept his hand floating behind her back in a not-so-subtle, *back-the-fuck-off* sign to the guys. Which they all respected because they weren't dicks.

And so he was left holding that bag. *Fuck.* There weren't enough expletives in the universe to properly express how thoroughly screwed he felt. All because of a little black dress and his evolutionary compulsion to explore all the curves it barely covered.

———

She was totally chickening out. After the "good God, get me the hell away from her" reaction Jared had to zipping up her dress, Cassie wished she'd worn something else. Something more head-to-toe covering. Like pajamas. And maybe worn them to her couch instead of a popular pub.

He hadn't said more than two words to her since they arrived, although he stayed close because he was still a nice guy. But his usual easygoing flirtation had left the building. So much for making him see her as a woman.

And his cute friends weren't giving her any interested vibes, either. She felt like a soccer mom at a table full of frat boys. Big, strong, defending-their-country type frat boys, but still…she wasn't their type. Her attempt to channel her inner cougar had been a failure.

Puh-lease, she lectured herself. She was twenty-seven, not thirty-seven, and probably if she was thirty-seven, she'd have the confidence to tell one of these fine young men just exactly what she wanted him to do to her. Instead, she sat like a wallflower, wrapping herself in an invisibility cloak.

Melissa joined them, full of apologies, almost an hour after they'd arrived. She'd gotten caught up at work. And shortly after she arrived, she saw someone she knew across the room and excused herself for a minute.

Cassie shook her head and smiled into her drink. Mel wouldn't have any problem asking a man for what she wanted.

"Your friend is cute," Jared's friend Miles said. Dumbrowski, as Jared called him, leaned in a bit closer. "Is she single?"

Mel was always single. Happily so. "Yep," Cassie said carefully.

Miles bit his lip and looked past Cassie's shoulder. She knew that look. Not that it was ever pointed at her, not by men like Miles and Jared. "Is she a long-walks-on-the-beach kind of girl?"

Cassie laughed. That wasn't what she'd expected him to ask. "She likes to have fun, if that's what you're looking for. Nothing serious, though. She's got a lot on the go."

"Shame." He gave her a hangdog face, and she patted him on the chest.

His phone beeped and as he read it, he perked up again.

"You've got another option?" Cassie teased, and he laughed.

"Excuse me, Cassie. Nice to meet you. Be gentle on Jared, ya hear?" And with that mystifying comment, he was up and off, thumping his friends on the shoulders as he made his exit.

Jared bumped shoulders with her as he sat down—the man took up a ridiculous amount of space. Taller than his friends and broader too, with legs that stretched on forever under the table and bounced restlessly next to her, he was a mountain among men. A mountain she wanted to climb.

"Beer?" Jared asked, pointing at the pitcher he'd brought back from the bar.

She nodded, more glumly than she intended.

"Dumbrowski left, huh? It looked like you guys were hitting it off." His words came out quickly—a tight little bundle of a question.

"He was asking about Mel. And then he got a booty call, I think."

Jared pulled his lips together in a small frown. His perfectly sculpted lips that matched his carved-from-granite jaw, which even at this hour didn't have much stubble on it. She knew from ogling him at the pool that he didn't have much body hair, either—just a blond treasure trail that made her want to rip open his board shorts and fall to her knees.

"Anyway, he's too young for me," she said blithely, blindly casting about for any conversation change that didn't have her thinking about giving Jared a blow job.

He laughed. "That's thin, but yeah, he's not the guy for you."

She cleared her throat. "Well, let me think it's because he doesn't want to date an older woman and not because I don't stack up, okay?"

"You stack up just fine, Cassie," Jared said quietly, dropping his gaze. "And your age is... Jesus, no man worth his salt cares about shit like that."

And yet you don't want to see me as a sexual being, she wanted to point out. Wanted to be brave. But a brutal divorce and her rebound guy dumping her by text message had just about stripped her of all courage. Temporarily. She'd get it back. She was a fighter. Just not tonight.

She sipped her beer just to have something to do with her hands and mouth that didn't involve Jared. When her glass and the pitcher were both empty, she excused herself and went to the bar, needing a break from being so close to Jared and not being able to touch him.

The man was way too touchable. She wanted to rub her fingertips through the blond hair on his forearms and stroke her palms over his biceps. His biceps had biceps, and she wanted to stroke those, too.

She'd just ordered a lime and soda when she heard an unfortunately familiar voice behind her. "On the prowl tonight, Cassandra?"

When Jared asked her that, it felt hot. Intimate and daring. When Mitch said the same words, she felt like she needed a shower. She spun slowly, not missing the slow, gross gaze he dropped to her toes and dragged back up. He lingered on her breasts, but he didn't look pleased with any of it.

"What are you doing in Coronado, Mitch?" She loved the little community, but he preferred living and partying in San Diego. He was all slick suit and smooth lines, and that didn't fly with the girls here—they were more interested in the strong, silent type in black t-shirts and fitted cargo pants. A look Cassie was quite partial to now herself, she thought as she let her gaze slip past her ex-husband and settle on Jared. As if he could feel her attention landing on him, he looked up and without missing a beat he was out of his chair and heading her way.

"I'm on a date," her ex said blandly. Cassie looked around, and her doubt must have been obvious, because he carried on. "Cara is in the ladies' room."

"Well, have fun," Cassie said, lifting her glass as if to say, *got my drink, need to go.* He didn't take the hint and stayed right in her path.

"That dress is a bit desperate, don't you think? It's not really husband bait, is it? It might have worked a few years ago, but you've put on some pounds since then."

"Wow, that's random and mean." She awkwardly crossed her arms. Her glass was cold against her bare arm, and she desperately wanted her jean jacket for more reasons than warmth.

"I'm just trying to help you out. Slutty isn't sexy."

"You got that backwards, asshole," Jared said, stopping right behind Mitch. *Right* behind. "Sexy isn't slutty. It's just sexy and, in this case, it's none of your business. Now back the fuck away from the lady."

Mitch gave her a slow blink, the look she'd dubbed *lizard stare* during their divorce proceedings. She wanted to be immune to it now. She wasn't. "She's my wife. Back off, jarhead," he tossed back over his shoulder.

Jared laughed, and it wasn't a mean laugh. Cassie bit back a grin as he stepped back, giving Mitch room to turn around before stepping right back into his personal space. His smile was knowing and totally awesome. "Actually, she's Cassie. She's nobody's wife, because the loser she *was* married to wasn't smart enough to know just how awesome his wife was when he had her. So if that's you, I'm sorry, bud. And I'm guessing it is, because only a moron who's never served in uniform would call someone a jarhead. You gotta be a Marine to use that term, and only to another Marine. You fail on both points, but try harder next time."

Mitch shifted his way awkwardly around Jared's solid bulk. Her savior stood there, grinning the whole time.

"That was a lot of words for you," she said under her breath when they were finally alone—or as alone as they could be in a crowded brewpub.

"There was a lot that needed to be said." He wrapped his arm around her shoulders and guided her back to the table.

As soon as she set down her glass, she pulled on her jacket. Jared gave her a surprised look. "Ready to go?"

She shook her head, then nodded. "Yes, maybe." She craned her head, looking for Mel. She'd drifted a few tables down and looked well-occupied. "I should tell her…" Cassie said absently. She pulled out her phone only to discover a text from none other than Mel. Think I've found a winner—for the night. Talk to you tomorrow.

Well, that made the decision easy. "Take me home, Jared."

It wasn't quite how she wanted to say those words tonight, but it was better than nothing.

They stepped outside onto Orange Ave. and, without needing to discuss it, headed west on foot.

"You okay in those heels?" Jared asked. As he looked down, their arms brushed, and even through her jacket the contact affected her. Too bad that awareness was painfully one-sided.

"Yeah, I wear them every day."

"You don't wear shoes like that every day," he muttered.

Heels were heels. These were just strappier than her usual pumps. And, apparently, too sexy for her.

"Look," she burst out. "I know that I tried too hard tonight, okay? Let it go. I'll be back to the asexual girl next door tomorrow and the awkwardness will eventually fade away."

She picked up speed, proving exactly how capable she was in her heels, but his long legs quickly ate any distance she'd succeeded in putting between them.

"Hey," he said quietly, not bothering to try and stop her. They were just a few blocks from home now, and she was grateful that he let her little legs churn up the pavement.

"I'm not mad at you, Jared. I'm just feeling a little foolish, okay? Sorry I yelled."

"It's okay. You can take out your aggravation on me. I've got big shoulders. I can take it."

She let out a combination laugh and cry and slowed down. "Can I ask you a question as a friend?"

He hesitated for a minute, then out of the corner of her eye she saw him nod. "Sure."

"What's sexy? I swear, if Mel had worn this dress, guys would have been all over her."

"You're sexy, Cassie," he ground out, his words strained, like he couldn't believe he'd accidentally stumbled into such an awkward conversation.

She snorted, unable to keep herself from oversharing. "Sure. Pour myself into a little black dress and look what happens. No one notices, except my idiot ex-husband and only then to point out that I've gained some weight."

He reared back as if she'd slapped him. "Please don't tell me you believe that shit."

She pulled her jean jacket tighter around her. "I'm not saying I'm fat. I like how I look most of the time. It's just this dress that was a mistake."

"Why do you think that?" He shook his head, looking like he might add more, but he didn't.

They turned onto the walk leading up to their building, and a sad relief washed over Cassie. One last overshare and she'd call herself done like dinner. "None of your friends even looked at me. Not that I wanted to pick up one of them, because that would be weird, but from the second we got there, I felt silly in…"—she waved her hands down her body—"well, in this dress. It's not me. Anyway, never mind," she said quietly. "I'm being silly."

He stopped at the bottom of the staircase that criss-crossed around the interior courtyard of their complex. She started to climb the stairs, but realized halfway up that he wasn't following her. Maybe that was for the best. She slid her key out of her pocket as she hit the landing.

But before she could get it into the lock, Jared's hand slid over her shoulder. Slow and hot like crawling lava, he trailed his fingers down to her elbow and turned her around. The look in his eyes—warring and unsure, but also blazing with want—made her melt.

"You're sexy," he repeated, and this time the strain in his voice was more obvious. He might not want to, but he desired her. And his gaze kept dropping to her mouth.

CHAPTER
THREE

TOUCHING HER WAS A MISTAKE, but he couldn't let her go to bed thinking she hadn't been wanted tonight. If he hadn't been playing guard bulldog, every one of his teammates would have made a play for her.

And her stupid-as-fuck ex-husband obviously still carried a torch for her.

But none of them had seen her half-naked earlier and none of them were going to kiss her good night.

"Here's the thing, Cass," he muttered, trying not to be too distracted by her pink lips. God, she smelled good, that perfume rising subtly from her warm skin with each shaky lift of her chest. And now he was distracted by her boobs. Jeez. He took a deep breath and looked back at her eyes. "This is a terrible idea for a lot of reasons, but you deserve to know just how much that dress affected me tonight. No, screw that. How much *you* affected me tonight. You're the prettiest thing I've ever seen, any day of the week, but tonight you pulled out all the stops and you were easily the most gorgeous woman in that bar."

She parted her lips and he shook his head.

"The reason none of my friends hit on you tonight is because they thought you were my date."

Her eyes flared wide and dark. "Why would they think that?" she whispered.

He shifted uncomfortably. "I might have given them that subtle impression."

"Why?" She searched his face.

"Because I wanted to be the one to do this," he said, lowering his head to kiss the corner of her mouth. "And this." He skated his lips across hers and pressed them against the other corner. She sucked in a quick breath, parting her lips, and his self-control cracked. He pulled her close, bending his oversized body over and around her petite one as he slid their mouths together. Her mouth was warm and wet, and he was lost.

Jared had kissed his first girl at fourteen, and in the intervening ten years he'd mastered the act, but this kiss had him shaking. And he hadn't even licked into her mouth yet, because she was sucking on his lower lip and making this little mewling sound that completely undid him. He traced the lower border of her upper lip— that line where the skin turned even softer and impossibly wet. Like the inside of her pussy would feel against his tongue.

Or the head of his cock.

With a gasp, he jerked back. "No," he said, the word almost strangled by all the other parts of him that wanted to keeping kissing her. "I'm sorry. So sorry. God, that felt good. But I can't."

He covered his mouth with his hand, lest he dive back into her sweet softness again, and braced himself for the tears of rejection that would surely come.

Except they didn't.

Cassie sighed, a heavy acknowledgement, and leaned back against her door. "Yeah, that wouldn't be wise."

He blinked at her, looking for some sign of game playing, but she only gave him a regretful smile. Damn, his chest ached at that acceptance. "You agree?"

"We've got a good friendship, Jared. Any infatuation between us would eventually pass, and I don't know if I could watch you move on to someone else after we sleep together."

God, that image. He'd trained himself not to think about being with Cassie, but now the vision floated unbidden through his mind. Cassie on her back, legs spread. He could imagine the scent of her, the glistening moisture there. He'd make her come with his fingers and then his mouth, so it wouldn't matter if he didn't last long. She'd be flushed and warm, all languid and welcome. Smiling for him as he found her entrance and slid inside. Her legs rocking up against his hips—

"Jared?"

He shook his head. Shit. "It's not you. It's not that I don't want you."

She glanced down and giggled, and when he followed her gaze he realized it was fucking obvious that he wanted her. He'd been so inside his own head he hadn't noticed his dick was practically inviting her to reach out and stroke him. He groaned, and she covered her eyes.

"I'm sorry," she whispered, still laughing.

"That makes two of us."

"I'm going to go inside now. Put on jammies, something flannel and baggy, and eat a pint of ice cream."

That only gave him the image of undoing a loose pajama top, button by button, then slowly licking ice cream from between her breasts. "Good. That's good. You should do that."

"We're okay?"

He nodded. They would be just fine.

"You're going to Colorado with your brother for the holidays, right? When are you back?" She stared at a spot on his shoulder.

"Oh. No. Actually, Jackson has to work. So I'm around."

"Oh." Her voice fell. "I mean, good. Great. So you've got some time off."

"Tomorrow's my last day. Unless there's a national emergency, I've got leave until after New Year's Day." Now he was hoping for something to come up, some last-minute rescue of a diplomat's kid or something. He could go be a hero instead of a sex-avoiding loser.

"I still need to buy some presents for my family. Maybe you could help me."

"Sure." He backed up, heading for his door. "Not tomorrow."

"No, not tomorrow. Too soon."

"I meant because I have to work."

"Oh."

"Cass?"

"Yeah?" Her voice sounded small all of a sudden, and he wanted to pull her in for a hug. But if he did that, he'd kiss her again, and if *that* happened, he'd probably Hulk his way through her door and toss her on the nearest flat surface.

And that wasn't how he wanted to lose his virginity.

But fuck if he could remember what his plan had ever actually been in that regard.

"Tomorrow wouldn't be too soon for me. If you have a pipe burst in the middle of the night tonight or something like that, you pound on the wall, okay? Nothing's changed between us. I'm still your go-to guy."

She nodded, but they both knew he was lying.

Everything had changed between them.

And deep down inside, something significant had changed for him.

———

Half a pint of Cherry Jubilee ice cream had not cooled her feverish libido. Neither had an all-too-quick date with her shower head when she'd first gotten home. Now she was curled up in bed watching *Three Men and a Baby* and silently thanking the apartment gods that her bedroom didn't share a wall with Jared's place. Because she was pretty sure she was going to fall asleep with his name on her lips and her fingers buried deep between her legs.

And tomorrow, they'd go back to being just friends. Neighbors. Secret crushes.

Well, that cat was out of the bag. Not-so-secret crushes that they'd pretend didn't exist.

She thought about how hard he'd fought for control after pulling himself away from her. His very impressive bulge had done wonders for her ego, as had the look in his eyes when his mind had wandered —she'd give all the pennies in her bank account to know what he'd been picturing in that moment. She was pretty sure the heat of it would set her on fire.

One kiss with Jared—now officially the hottest sexual encounter she'd ever had. A few mediocre screws in high school had set her up to think sex wasn't her thing. And it had always been kind of clinical with her husband, even before they started trying to get pregnant, although he'd been fairly giving. Craig the dentist had been more lusty, but she got the feeling he could take it or leave it some of the time. Football or fuck? No telling which way Craig would go.

But Jared... The man was practically vibrating with sexual energy. She didn't want to think about how many women he'd kissed like that, practically picking them up in his giant arms. And how many of those lucky bitches got to keep kissing him as the clothing disappeared?

She gasped at herself. *Bitches?* She groaned, but jealousy was a nasty mistress. *Nothing personal, ladies, but I want a piece of what you've had and I don't think I'm ever going to be so lucky.*

The next morning, Cassie woke up late. It was a slow, heavy drag back to consciousness, and she didn't want to let go of her dreams because they'd been rich with naked Jareds—and naked Cassies. Over and over again, he'd done wicked things to her in her sleep, and for a minute as she lay there blinking at her ceiling, she was excited. Their chemistry the night before had been off-the-charts. So what if he'd put the brakes on it after the barest of kisses? He wanted her the same way she wanted him.

But then doubt crept in. He'd said no for a reason. A pretty strong one. And she knew his track record. She supposed it was sort of noble that he didn't want to screw around with her and then hurt her, but damn... She'd been hoping that player façade had been just that—a cover for a truly nice guy deep down inside.

All the warm fuzzies from her night of erotic fantasies faded away. Right. He might want her, but not enough to change his dirty boy ways. Fine. It would be pretty easy to just be his friend if that was the case.

Her phone beeped with calendar reminders for the day. She had an open house that afternoon, and she needed to swing past the office first. It was pretty quiet in the days leading up to the holiday break, but real estate deals had been inked on Christmas before, so she always liked to be prepared. She also liked that the realty storefront wasn't a place she had to go to every day. Her briefcase and smartphone were all the working space she really needed most of the time, and the printer/scanner/fax machine on her bookcase in the living room was handy as well.

Sometime sooner than later she'd buy a house. She had the funds for a good-sized down payment, but after leaving the condo she shared with Mitch, she'd wanted to be back in Coronado without making a rash purchase decision. The modest one-bedroom apartment had come available at exactly the right time in her life. And now she was reluctant to move on even though her father railed at her about the foolishness of paying rent every month when she could be making an investment in a property of her own.

When real estate was the family business, *renting* was a four-letter word.

But her parents did like that the complex had a few Navy SEALs living in it. And so did she—most of the time. She would again. But as she showered and pulled on pressed black pants and a light blue cotton sweater, she was just angry. Pissed at herself for falling for someone she'd known was off-limits. Mad at Jared for not being the perfect fantasy guy next door. And angry with the rest of the male population of Coronado and the larger San Diego area for not conveniently providing her with more dating candidates.

Of course…there had been the FedEx delivery guy with the cute smile. He'd hinted at offering his number if she needed anything. But at the time, she hadn't needed what he'd been offering. And the same with that chef who'd started working out at the gym at the same time she did. If she went to the ten a.m. spin class tomorrow, he'd probably be there. And when she walked in, he'd finally stop taking his time putting his gear away and snag the bike next to hers.

Okay. So there'd been options, and she'd ignored them. Because she'd wanted Jared.

But he was now confirmed as off-limits, so she was done being foolish.

The next cute guy to smile at her, she'd smile back. And if she got a number, or was asked for her number—no more head in the sand.

————

So much for going back to how they were before the kiss. It was like they'd taken a cosmic jump back to before they *met*, which wasn't at all what he wanted. Cassie in his life wasn't optional, even though she was doing her darnedest to pretend it was. Three days had passed since she'd blown his mind with a few whimpers, and Jared hadn't seen her since. In reality. In his fantasies, she was still front and center, a constant drug in his bloodstream distracting him both night and day.

At night he'd wake up on his stomach, grinding against the bed in a way that was more mortifying than hot. During the day all he could do was *think* about her. Not dirty fantasies, but real-life scenarios about what she'd be like in a relationship and whether he could trust her. His secret was buried so deeply if he revealed it to her she'd be the only other person in the world to know it. She was avoiding him for a reason—she didn't want to be just friends. And deep down neither did he. So if he could get in front of her and admit how he felt, they'd hopefully get back on track. Sharing would be the next step, but imagining his confession had him breaking out in a cold sweat.

It was Tuesday, so she'd go to the gym mid-morning and pick up her Community Share vegetable box in the afternoon. He'd gone with her at Thanksgiving when she'd requested a double order, and he knew she'd put in the same order for Christmas. Even though she hadn't asked him for help this week, he planned to meet her at the parking lot where the farmer did his weekly meet-and-greet drops. It was better than sitting outside her apartment from seven a.m. on, waiting for her to open the door. Not that he'd considered that—for long. He didn't want a restraining order to interfere with his decision to woo her.

And any courting of her would have to be pretty significant given how pissed she was at him. Her silence and total avoidance proved that point.

He set out on foot, trusting that if he was sweet enough, she'd give him a ride back. At the very least so he could help carry the boxes up the stairs. And maybe—if he was lucky—because she hadn't been able to stop thinking about their kiss, either.

His confidence took a big hit when he reached the parking lot ten blocks away and found her fluttering her eyelashes over a Starbucks latte. At a guy holding a matching latte and standing way too close to Cassie for Jared's comfort.

He took a deep breath and observed the scene unfolding in front of him. No point in operating without intel. She was flirting, but it was casual. Her arms were crossed in front of her body and two canvas shopping bags were clutched in one hand. That plus the latte made a pretty clear barrier. He resumed his approach, slower this time.

Mr. Starbucks leaned in and murmured something Jared wasn't close enough to hear. Cassie shook her head.

"Are you sure?" Jared read on Mr. Starbucks' lips as he moved back into view.

Cassie laughed. "Maybe another time."

Their voices carried through the air. "Sure," Mr. Starbucks was saying. "We'll be at the picnic area at the north end of Sunset Park tonight around seven if you change your mind."

A night-before-Christmas-Eve barbecue? Oh, hell no. Jared lifted his voice before he could stop himself. "I was hoping she might have other plans."

Cassie jerked her head toward him. She was wearing sunglasses, like him, so it was hard to read her expression. "Is that right?" Her voice was bland and impersonal. Not a great sign.

He slid his glasses to the top of his head. "Sorry to interrupt. I figured you'd need help with the extra order."

Chalk one up for honesty. She allowed him a small smile before glancing back at Mr. Starbucks. "It was nice to meet you. Welcome to the food co-op. I'll see you around."

With each short, clipped sentence, his hope returned. By the time she'd swiveled her attention back to him, he was grinning like the cocky bastard he usually was.

"You look happy," she said dryly as she stepped past him. The farmer had a table under a pop-up canopy beside his truck, and there was a short line of people waiting to collect their boxes of locally sourced produce. Jared didn't really get why she didn't just go to the grocery store, but buying veggies this way obviously made her happy. Like a nice glass of wine or a perfect sunset, Cassie appreciated the process of choosing and preparing her foodstuffs as much as eating the end result.

And even though he didn't get it, it made him happy to be there with her. Plus she looked *good*. She was wearing jeans today, and the faded blue denim highlighted her sweet curves in a way that made his mouth water. Her long-sleeved t-shirt hugged her in all the right places, too, and he couldn't be sad that the temperature had dipped a bit in the last few days. It wasn't quite the white Christmas he'd hoped for, but something about seeing Cassie a bit bundled up made him think of mistletoe and hot apple cider. And more mistletoe.

"Yeah, I'm happy," he finally responded. "Now that I've caught up with you. You've been…busy." Busy avoiding him, but he didn't add that.

She raised her brow in a non-response and stepped forward in line.

Once she'd signed for her boxes, he helped carry them the short distance to her car. She looked around for his truck and he grinned sheepishly. "I walked. Thought I might catch a ride back with you."

"Sure…" she said, reluctantly.

"Is that okay? I can walk back if you'd rather."

She laughed. "No, it's fine."

They didn't talk again on the short drive home. When they got upstairs, she hesitated on the balcony between their doors.

"Can I carry this inside for you?" he asked, not caring if he sounded hopeful. His box was bigger and heavier, but for a second she looked like she might ask him to just hand it over. He wouldn't, but she could ask.

Instead, she nodded and juggled her own box as she unlocked the door. He followed her, relieved to be allowed back in—first step her home, second step her heart.

CHAPTER
FOUR

JARED SET his box of produce on her counter, then backed up, giving her some space to put stuff away.

But he didn't leave.

"So…" Cassie said, uncomfortable with the silence. "How's leave going?"

He nodded. "Decent. I went shopping yesterday. Bought you a Christmas present."

Her breath caught in her throat. It wasn't that she was surprised —she'd picked up his gift a few weeks earlier, a nice GPS unit because he'd said his was broken and the one in his phone was a "total piece of shit." But yesterday…she hadn't given him any reason to think they'd be exchanging gifts.

"I like presents." She smiled behind the safe cover of the fridge door.

"Are you doing family stuff tomorrow? Maybe I could take you out for lunch first?"

Argh. All of a sudden, spending time with her parents and sisters was the last thing she wanted to do. Unless… "Do you want to come with me? As a friend," she hastened to add.

He frowned.

"My parents have a big party tomorrow night, lots of champagne and appetizers, that kind of thing. My mom has a bunch of brothers and sisters, and they all have kids. So it's basically her family. But it's not…close. More formal. We wouldn't need to stay very long, just an hour or two."

"Sure. I only have one suit."

"It'll be fine." She grinned. "And then I have to go back for lunch on Christmas Day and exchange gifts, but if you don't mind watching the turkey roast for me, I'm happy to share my dinner."

He frowned again, looking at the giant bag of multicolored potatoes on her counter. "You aren't cooking all this for your family?"

She wrinkled her nose. That *had* been the plan, until her mother and sister decided they were going on a diet after she'd put in the food-box order. "They've decided to do a salad and grilled meat buffet thing instead. That's okay. It means more leftovers for us."

"You were going to have Christmas dinner all alone?"

Well, her first plan had been to invite him over, but then her grumpiness intruded. The anger had quickly evaporated at the sight of him in that parking lot, however. A few Jared-free days had been good for her perspective on the situation. He was right to protect their friendship. And by acting pissy, she'd been the one to damage it, not him.

"Not anymore, though, right? That's all that matters. Stop frowning, you're going to crease your forehead permanently."

He scowled. She moved across the kitchen without thinking and pressed her fingertips to his brow. She had to reach up—way up—to do it, which meant she had to stand close to him. Way close.

He closed his hand around her wrist, but instead of moving her hand away from his face, he held it in place. "I've missed you," he said gruffly.

She swallowed hard. "I…I've missed you too. I'm sorry I went quiet."

He shook his head, and his nose brushed the inside of her wrist. Then he kissed her there, a sweet press of his firm lips against her arm.

And her heart started thumping double time.

"We should've talked," he said, his voice a delicious rasp against her skin. He kept his eyes down, trained somewhere in the vicinity of her elbow. "We need to talk now."

"In a minute," she breathed, gliding her palms to the back of his neck. His hair was almost shaved back there, and she teased her fingertips over the neatly trimmed line, exploring the contrast between the soft brush of hair and hot, tight skin. She pressed her cheek against his chest, reassured by the sound of his heartbeat, a quick thump that mirrored her own.

This hug wasn't anything like the kiss they shared Saturday night. It was sweet instead of passionate, tentative instead of hard-charging. But it was hopeful, not scary, and from the way her nipples were throbbing inside her bra and the rough hitch in Jared's breath against her hair... She knew it wasn't chaste.

They were standing on the precipice of something fiery hot, and they wanted to be sure before they dove in.

"I have a three-date rule—" Cassie blurted out at the same as Jared said, "I want to take things a bit slow."

They both laughed, and he eased back just enough to lift her by her waist and deposit her on the kitchen counter. Now she could stare into his hazel eyes, flecked with gold, and what she saw there made her heart sing. He was so damned earnest. Sweet. Not a player at all, unless this was the play of all plays. She frowned. "That's not just a line, is it?"

He blinked at her, then laughed wryly and scrubbed his hand over his face. "You don't know the half of it. Hell, no, that's not a line." He leaned in, nudged her nose with his, then slid their faces together until everything blurred and the only thing she could feel was his lips parting hers.

Don't you dare stop, she thought as his tongue teased its way into her mouth, nudging hers when she started a sweet, sensual exploration of her own. She spread her legs enough to welcome his body into the cradle of her thighs and then squeezed, holding him there as he deepened the kiss, stealing all of her breath. She didn't care. He could have it.

"Mmmm," she moaned as one of his hands slid under her shirt and played with the bare skin at her waist. "Higher," she whispered, pulling back enough to make it clear what she wanted. He groaned against her lips as she pressed little, hungry kisses across his mouth and down to his jaw. "Seriously, Jared, I don't put out on the first date, but you're cleared for second base. Please…"

He made a rough noise in the back of his throat as he cupped her breast, his fingers pressing into the bare flesh spilling over the top of her bra. "Three dates, huh?"

"I'd break that rule for you in a heartbeat, actually." She panted as he wiggled his thick fingers under the lace and started to nudge her nipple free.

"No, it's a good rule. Makes me happy when I think about how few guys have gotten to that third date with you." He sucked her lower earlobe into his mouth and pulled, sending a current of electricity straight to her clit. "And we have to talk."

"You keep saying that," she gasped, wrapping her legs around his butt. "But then your fingers do *that*, and I'm about ten seconds from shamelessly dry-humping you in my kitchen."

"Okay," he said, dragging out the syllables as he jerked his hips away from hers just as she found that magical ridge she'd been looking for. She pouted up at him and he laughed as he kissed her mouth. "Come on. Couch."

She brightened at the thought of getting horizontal for some more making-out time, but even though he laced his fingers through hers, when they got to her living room he sat them down with a throw pillow between them.

Then he swore under his breath and tossed the pillow across the room. She wiggled closer and pressed her face into his neck.

"What's going on?" she asked softly. His Adam's apple bobbed against her nose and his knee bounced up and down as if it was a perpetual motion device.

"I guess I should say up front that I don't have any weird issues or anything. But being with you would be different than how I've been with women in the past. And I want it to be good for you."

She nodded silently. She wasn't sure where he was going, but given his track record for one-night stands, *different* sounded good.

"I had a girlfriend in high school. Hannah. We broke up senior year and I haven't dated anyone else." More bobbing and bouncing. She wanted to reach out and still his knee, but she didn't dare do anything that might derail his sharing. "This isn't about her. Shit, sorry. This is weird for me."

She laughed gently when he didn't continue. "This is weird for me, too, in a good way. Guys usually hate talking."

He nodded vigorously and she squeezed his fingers in reassurance.

"Tell you what. I'll tell you one of my secrets and then you can tell me one of yours."

"I only have one secret. Except State secrets, but I can't share those." He said it so dryly she wasn't sure if he was kidding, but when she looked up, he grinned. "I really can't."

"Okay." She took a deep breath. "My ex-husband left me because I couldn't get pregnant."

Jared tensed up, then made that noise in the back of his throat again. So weird, how the same growly grunt could have two obviously different meanings. "I should've punched him."

"No." She sighed. "Karma will get him in the end. He'll probably knock up a hooker or something. Not that I'd wish a child to have to call him Daddy for any reason." She shuddered. "I really dodged a bullet there."

Jared pulled her close and kissed her forehead, but he didn't say anything. Should she push him? Hadn't the tit-for-tat sharing been clear?

She felt awkward, like he hadn't wanted to hear that from her, and fuck, wasn't that the story of her life… But just as she thought about pulling away, he tangled his hand into her hair, his fingers finding the back of her neck. He squeezed there and pressed his cheek to her forehead, letting out a big sigh. "Well, now I feel like a fucking teenager."

"Why?" She tried to pull back to look at him but he tightened his still gentle hold on her.

"Because my thing is really selfish compared to that."

"It's okay. You don't need to tell me." She gave up trying to put distance between them and melted into his big, warm upper body.

He was both hard and comfy at the same time, like a really firm mattress. She slid her hand under his shirt, loving the way he tensed his already tight abs under her touch.

He coughed and made a painful groaning noise. "Oh, no, I do. Only now I'm not sure how it's going to be received."

"And now you're freaking me out."

"Really?" He tensed again, and she shook her head against his chest.

"No, not really. You're one of the best guys I've ever met, Jared. It would take a lot to freak me out."

He took a deep breath. "Okay. So, I think we have something between us. Something like a relationship, or the start of one. And that's new for me. I haven't done that as an adult. And I want to have sex with you."

She grinned. Good. She wanted to have sex with him, too.

"And I haven't done that before."

He'd said it really fast, and the words all ran together, but she was still pretty sure he'd just said—

"What?" She jerked up, the top of her head colliding with the bottom of his jaw, and he swore as she bounced backwards. "Oh God, I'm sorry."

He groaned as he rubbed his jaw. "I'm fine."

She spun onto her knees and grabbed his arm. "What do you mean you haven't done that before?"

He winced. "The sex part."

"But you're a horndog!" She was yelling, which wasn't cool. "Wait. Aren't you?" She took a deep breath and rubbed his arm where she'd probably pinched off the circulation for a moment. "I'm sorry."

"It's okay."

"Why?"

He sighed. "It's a long story."

"Like, change into jammies and bust out the box of chocolates kind of long? Or just put on coffee kind of long?"

He gave her a seriously weirded-out look. "Is that a girl measurement of drama?"

She nodded. He held out his hand and she slid her fingers over his. "Up until the minute I kissed you last week, choosing not to have sex wasn't a drama for me at all. It was just something that hadn't happened because I hadn't found the person I wanted to do it with yet."

Oh, wow. She could feel her eyes get really big and wide. Despite her previous promise, she knew she was riding a fine line between normal reaction and totally freaking out.

He dropped his voice into a practiced calm-making tone. "This isn't about soul mates, or anything like that. I've never thought I was keeping myself for marriage, although I don't think that's a bad idea." He stroked his thumb over her knuckles. "Maybe we should make some coffee."

"I'll do it," she whispered, but when she clambered off the couch, he followed. "You don't need to—"

"I want to," he interrupted. "I want to pick you up and carry you to the kitchen, but I'm trying not to be grabby."

She stopped abruptly and turned, letting him bump into her. "You want to be grabby with me?"

"Angel, you don't know the half of what I want to do to you. With you. Against you and inside of you."

She whimpered and he wrapped his arms around her, doing that fabulous almost-lift thing as he lowered his head to kiss her. Right. As she melted from the inside out, all the panic faded away. He wasn't a virginal teenager. The man could *kiss*. And talk dirty. He hadn't seemed fazed by her dry-humping reference earlier. He was an adult. A capable, sexy—Oh!

"Stop thinking and kiss me," he growled against her mouth, and she squeaked as he pushed more ruthlessly against her mouth, as if his tongue had a point to make.

"You're good at that," she breathed when he pulled back.

His eyes danced as he gazed down at her. "I'm good at a lot of things. And I think when we do the one thing I haven't done, I'm going to be a quick study on how to make that amazing for you, too."

Her legs quivered beneath her, a wiggly, jiggly feeling that matched how she felt on the inside, too. She dragged in a breath, then another, as he lazily wrapped his big, capable hands around her waist and resumed their course to the kitchen.

"How about I make the coffee?"

She nodded dumbly.

———

The good news was that he was still in her apartment and she still liked him. The bad news was that he hadn't told her everything yet. And he had a sinking feeling that when he did, her ardor would dim in a significant way. Screw the coffee, he needed handcuffs and more than twenty-four hours to convince Cassie they'd be good together—great, even—despite their differences.

Because in twenty-four hours, she was heading to her family's Christmas Eve celebration. Alone, because some jackass broke her heart.

He wasn't going to be the second jackass to do that if he had any say in the matter. She wasn't going to spend the holidays alone, not if he had anything to say about it.

As they waited on the coffee, he tugged Cassie close for a quiet hug. When the pot finished brewing, he carried their full mugs back to the living room.

He sat first, in a laid-back, arms-and-legs-splayed-wide kind of way that invited her to join him however she was most comfortable. But if he was being honest with himself, wherever she sat he was probably going to try and tug her into his lap. Luckily she saved him that caveman embarrassment by curling up against his bent thigh, facing him as she tucked her toes under his other leg. Close enough for now.

She took a deep breath and launched into it. "So…I've seen you. With women. At the pub and at clubs a couple of times."

He nodded. He didn't want to hide anything from her, no matter how awkward the conversation. But he wanted to be respectful, too. Of her and those women. "I've rounded some of the bases, as you put it earlier."

She wrinkled her brow. "I don't get it. None of them…"

He shrugged. "I didn't want to. I'm pretty good at setting boundaries up front." And he liked to watch women come, but he wasn't going to tell her *that*. It had always been easier when he made it about them.

"So, have you ever…" She trailed off, biting her lip.

"Do you want to know what I've done?"

She wrinkled her nose. "Could I ask what you haven't done, instead?"

He swallowed. Yeah, that was better. "I've never been fully naked with a woman—both of us at the same time. I've never spent the night sleeping with a woman, and you know that I've never brought a woman back to my place." He reached for her hand, wiggling his fingers. She took it and the sweet, cool slide of her fingers settled him. "I've never had intercour—I've never made love to a woman."

She smiled.

"What?"

"You're blushing. But you're also saying all of this…in such a mature way. And I don't say that like you're not a grown-up, because just look at you. But I stammer when I talk about sex and I've—" She cut herself off.

He didn't really want to hear about what she'd done with others, either, but she'd been married. They weren't in this virgin boat together.

Cassie pressed her fingers to her lips for a second, then brought her hand to his face, stroking his jaw as she smiled. "Let's just say that I've got some variety of experience, and I'm still shy about it."

He wanted to leave the conversation there and go back to kissing, but he needed to dig deep and lay himself bare for her no matter the consequences. It would be way worse if he didn't and she fell for him. *Like he'd fallen for her.* "How much more can you handle today?"

CHAPTER
FIVE

SHE'D LET his hand go to pick up her coffee, but now she reached for him again, her palm warmed from her mug. She squeezed hard. "No promises there won't be more accidental head butts, but I want to hear anything and everything you have to share."

"Maybe I should ask you a bit more about your… You said you couldn't get pregnant?" Damn, he needed to tread carefully here. But he didn't want to say the wrong thing, either. He knew nothing about infertility. His family had the fertile bit down pat, not that it was something to crow about.

She licked her lips, a nervous tick that he paid careful attention to. He wouldn't push her at all, but if she freely shared something that helped him navigate this conversation better, he'd take it. "Mitch has a trust fund. Part of it unlocked at marriage. Subsequent parts unlock with each child born."

Punching was too good for the jerk. Jared blinked away the seriously thick layer of red he was seeing. "Please tell me he's shooting blanks."

She shook her head. "I have some medical conditions. Nothing serious, but getting pregnant would take significant medical intervention. And neither of us had health insurance that would cover the full cost. I was willing to pay for it, but Mitch…" Her lips turned down at a private, sad memory, and Jared couldn't process how Cassie—sweet, giving, smart, funny Cassie—had ended up married to such a self-absorbed jerk.

He sat a bit more upright, and settled her against his chest.

"What are you thinking?" she asked. He was glad she couldn't see his face anymore—he was clenching his jaw so hard he was worried he might crack a tooth.

"A lot of things that I probably don't know the whole story about. None of them reflect well on your ex, though."

She sighed. "I know. It was a bitter divorce, so my view of him now is pretty pathetic. But he was charming, and we made sense at the time. He liked the idea of us being a power couple, with a nanny to watch our three well-behaved blond children. And I'm ashamed to admit that I once wanted that, too."

He chuckled softly. "That's a bit far from reality, though, isn't it?"

She stiffened in his arms, but her hand curled around his thigh at the same time. What he'd said must have struck a chord, but he didn't think he'd offended her. "Wait until you meet my family tomorrow…you'll understand why I thought that was a perfectly acceptable future when I was twenty-one."

"And now?" He wasn't sure what he was asking. *Are you looking for another husband? Babies? Because I'm practically a baby still myself.*

She sagged back against him. "I'm still trying to figure that out." She twisted her head to look at him. "I can tell you that the last few months, hanging out with you and figuring out who my true friends are…has been amazing." She chewed on her lip for a minute. "I've been thinking a lot about buying a house. My lease on this apartment is up in May and the space here is not really practical. I need a home office. But that's all that I can think about right now—getting back on my feet and living some of my adulthood as an individual. You know I never did that? I moved from my parents' house into Mitch's condo."

It was the right answer. Checked all the boxes. She wasn't looking for a serious relationship. But the idea left him hollow inside. He wished he were older. At twenty-four, he still had fourteen years of Naval service until his earliest possible retirement date—if he lived that long, which he had every intention of doing. And between now and then, there would be literally years of overseas service, in one-, three-, and six-month tours, plus missions of indeterminate length as well. Being a SEAL didn't preclude a family life, but it sure made it damned difficult. He closed his eyes and kissed her forehead again.

"Hey," she said softly. "Do you want to come over to my place and watch a movie?"

He laughed. They were at her place. "You mean like on a date?"

She nodded slowly. "The first of three."

"There's more to talk about."

"There always will be." Smiling, she twisted her body to press fully against his. She straddled his lap for a second, and his dick perked up at the thought of holding her there, but she just gave him a sweet nose nuzzle before slipping off. "I'll make popcorn."

He watched her pert, round behind bounce toward the kitchen and again he was tempted to follow. It was like a switch had flipped inside him and now he wanted all of Cassie, all the time. He let out a slow, controlled sigh and looked at her DVD collection. *Quigley Down Under. Her Alibi. Mr. Baseball. High Road to China.* The complete *Magnum P.I.* series. He leaned in closer. That one was autographed. He was tempted to pick something *not* from the top shelf, but if his girl had a bit of a Tom Selleck thing, who was he to deny her? He picked *Quigley Down Under* and set it on the coffee table.

———

Cassie paced in the kitchen, waiting for the microwave popcorn to finish. Her hands were sweating and her mouth was dry. She pulled a bottle of sparkling water out of the fridge and set it on a tray with two glasses and a big bowl for the popcorn. From the living room, she heard Jared chuckling to himself, and she smiled.

Holy shit. He'd never had sex before. This was going to be so much fun.

Sure, there was a touch of pressure. She wanted to be a good Mrs. Robinson.

Except…that wasn't what this was. The man in her living room was a warrior, noble and proud, and he'd had his reasons for waiting. Now she'd somehow given him reason to take a leap, but could she be worthy of that choice? Plus he wasn't going to need a lot of teaching, although when she thought about being the first woman to see that look on his face when he was all the way inside her...

"Are you okay?" Jared's teasing words made her jump. His lips twitched. "The popcorn's done. You're just standing there, staring into space." He pressed close behind her, reaching for the microwave. "Thinking about something good?"

She blushed—again, apparently, because it felt like her cheeks were already on fire. "Yes..." she murmured, pointing at the bowl for the popcorn. He emptied the bag, then stashed it in the garbage and lifted the tray. She stepped out of his way, then grabbed a bag of almond M&Ms from her secret hiding spot and followed him back to the couch.

Light streamed in the windows. She drew the curtains shut, acutely aware of Jared watching her the whole time. When she turned back to the couch, she was pretty sure her nipples led a painfully obvious advance party.

"Hi," she said, all breathy and girly—she couldn't help it.

He didn't seem to mind. "I noticed you have a thing for Selleck," he said with a grin as he patted the spot on the couch next to him.

She glanced at the DVD. "And you're indulging me. Nice first date move." She got the movie started, then curled up next to him. Warm, cozy heat emanated from his side, and she sank into the comfortable wrap of his arm over her shoulders. He smelled faintly of shaving cream and the ocean, but those were in the distance, and in the intervening hours since he'd gone for a run on the beach and shaved his cheeks clean, his own unique scent had taken over. Like dry, bright sunshine, and she wanted to rub up against him and soak it up.

It turned out she wasn't the only Selleck fan. Jared knew some of the lines by heart.

"Do you have a secret Magnum crush, too?" she asked, tipping her face up to his.

He gave her that big, sloppy, boy-in-a-man's-body grin. "More like I wanted to be a gunslinger growing up."

She realized she didn't have any idea of what Jared's childhood was like. He had a brother—the one who was going to meet him in Vail but had to cancel because of work. She was pretty sure he was ex-military. But that was it. Questions danced around at the back of her head through most of the movie, but as the last few scenes played out, Jared's fingers started moving more on her arm. She liked that move. A subtle test and one he'd pass with flying colors. She slid her leg against his, he dropped his knee, and all of a sudden their lower limbs were entwined. Any questions she might have wanted to ask faded away, masked by a hot, heady muzziness brought on by the growing awareness that they were about to kiss again.

No kiss in the history of this apartment had ever been more anticipated, or as slowly and deliciously stoked by a perfect first-date movie cuddle. It helped that no man in the history of her apartment —or her life—had ever been quite as hot as Jared Sutter. Or as kind. Or as…unsullied.

"Wherever your thoughts just went there, I like it," he muttered, his lips brushing against her temple. She was still watching the credits, pretending she didn't know what was about to happen. He was watching her. And she was panting like a poodle in heat.

"I was thinking that if I play my cards right, I might get to do some naughty things with you," she murmured, staring straight ahead. Her pulse pounded. She'd never been one for dirty talk, but Jared had a way of turning her on with just a few words. She thought it was only fair to try and give him some of his own medicine.

Hot breath puffed against her skin. "What kind of things?"

She leaned into him, aching for more of his warmth. Maybe his entire body stretched out on top of her. "How about half-naked, shirts-off, touching kinds of things?"

On the other side of the room, the credits ended and the TV turned blue. But all she could see was Jared's face moving toward hers, his eyelids heavy and his lips barely parted.

His mouth found hers, hungry and waiting. His hands, rough

and freaking huge, circled her waist, and he tugged her into his lap. He groaned as she shifted in place, rubbing against his straining erection. It didn't take him long to find her bra again, but this time he only cupped her breasts for a teasing moment before sliding his fingers to the clasp in the back.

As soon as he unhooked her bra, she broke away from him, gasping, and in silent agreement they pulled their shirts off in a simultaneous tangle of arms and cotton.

"God, let me look at you," Jared rasped as he gently lifted her breasts and pressed them together. Cassie had never felt more beautiful than in that moment. She stretched her arms up through her hair and arched her back, feeling curvy and desirable and wanted. He lowered his head and kissed first one swell, then the other, before licking his way through the valley between them. She gasped at the unexpected wet brand, and he chuckled before repeating the swipe over her nipples. With a groan, he pressed her breasts tighter together, moving back and forth between her nipples faster and faster until he gave up and picked one.

She lurched off his lap with a cry as he sucked her left nipple deep into his mouth, and he palmed her ass with his free hand, pulling her back against him. He made a guttural noise as their cores re-aligned. She wanted their jeans off. She wanted him inside her, right there and then, but they couldn't do that.

"I want you so much, Cassie," he said as he shifted his attention to her other breast. The first one felt swollen and achy, but as if he knew she still needed him there, his fingers found her nipple and started teasing her again. "What do you want?"

"You," she whispered, holding his head against her chest, rocking shamelessly in his lap. "I've wanted you for so long."

Her breath caught in her throat as he groaned and slid her onto her back on the couch. He fit himself between her thighs, impossibly big and ridiculously gentle at the same time.

"I didn't know." His words were pebbled with regret.

She shook her head. "I told you I just wanted to be friends. My fault."

"Maybe you weren't ready." He kissed her jaw, then opened his mouth and sucked gently on her neck. How did he know all these spots on her body? *She* hadn't known that spot had a direct line to her clit, but apparently it did.

"I'm ready now." Ready, wet, aching. He rocked against her and she lifted her hips, wanting more. She wanted everything, but that would need to wait a bit. And this was delicious too, fooling around on her couch.

"Can you come like this?" He was so earnest. She wanted to give him a gold star. She nodded. "Because I want that, angel. You're so pretty, with your lips all swollen and wet from kissing. And if you keep looking at me like that, I might just come, too."

Oh God. "Wouldn't that be messy?" she whispered, and he laughed. Not chuckled, not a little rumble, but a full-on belly laugh. "What?"

"Isn't it all messy?" He licked up her neck and nipped at her ear, and with his lips right there, he took a breath and undid her from the inside out. "I've never done this, either. Never trusted a woman to understand my limits. But I trust you. And I want you. I want to grind against you until you see fireworks and then I want to have a little explosion of my own. Between your legs. Because I trust you."

Cassie took a slow inhale and let out a soft moan as she slid her hands across his broad shoulders and down his sculpted sides. She tucked her fingers under the waistband of his jeans, loving the flex of his ass against her palms as she held him close. Staring up at him, nothing between them now but breath and desire, she ground herself against him. With each quiet, ragged exhale she floated higher and higher towards bliss. Something deep in her belly clenched as Jared stroked his hand up and down her side, whispering over and over again how beautiful she was.

When she came, she did see fireworks, and before the white spots disappeared from her eyes, Jared came too. He froze over her, then slid down her torso, pressing his face into her chest. "You were right," he mumbled into her boob. "That was messy."

She laughed. "Do you want to take a shower?"

He nodded. "But at my place." She ran her hands through his hair, trying to figure out what to say next. If he went back to his apartment she was okay with it, of course. He didn't have any clothes at her place, and he would need to step outside to get back into his apartment. Better to do that in his jeans than a towel. But she could have gone over and got him—

"Hey, I'm coming back," he said softly.

Right. Of course he was. Cold relief swept over her, and she hated that she'd doubted that the half-naked man between her legs wanted to return to her. Didn't that speak volumes about her sad history with men?

"Good," she whispered.

He gingerly climbed off the couch, then offered her his hand. When she was standing, he pulled her in for a hug. "I figure if I go and then come back, whatever we do next will be the second date."

CHAPTER
SIX

JARED FELT Cassie smile into his chest. God, she was cute. Gorgeous on the outside, and so fucking fragile and sweet on the inside. It was hard to feel self-conscious around her, even with sticky boxers. She blinked up at him. "What are you thinking for this second date?"

"Dinner, definitely. We worked up an appetite." Jared glanced down at the bowl of barely touched popcorn. "Although another movie would be fun."

She slapped his chest lightly. "We should probably leave the apartment."

He nodded. "I have an idea, but I need to make a couple calls first before I tell you what it is. I don't want to promise something I can't deliver."

"Oooh, a mystery!" She gently shoved him backwards, her palms lingering on his abs, and he couldn't resist flexing for her. "Or we could just stay here and I could touch your muscles all night."

He snagged her hands in his and kissed her knuckles. "I think we're going to spend a good part of the holiday break doing that. Tonight we're going out and I'm making up for Saturday night."

She glanced back at the couch, her lips curling into a private smile. "You've already done that in spades."

It was hard to leave a topless Cassie to shower alone, but it had to be done. He walked backwards to the door, pulling on his own shirt before stepping outside. The sun had set, reminding him if he was going to pull off a miracle he had to get a move on. He dialed Dombrowski as he let himself into his apartment.

"What are the chances you're still on speaking terms with that cute event coordinator from The Del?"

His friend chuckled in his ear. "Emma? I just saw her on the weekend. She was pretty happy when I left her place Sunday morning. *Late* on Sunday morning."

"Could I ask for a massive favor? Is there any way she could get me a pair of skating tickets for tonight?"

Dumbrowski whistled. "I'll ask. This for your pretty neighbor?"

"Yep. She's worth whatever it costs me, man."

"I've been dinged to go to that sensitivity training thing next month. You'll volunteer instead."

Even though no one ever wanted to sit through that nonsense, the offer was a gift. Jared took it. "Thanks. I'm hopping in the shower, text me if it's a go."

He dumped his clothes in the laundry basket in his room and walked naked to the bathroom. If he couldn't get the tickets, they could still go to the beach and have a fire. He could make a thermos of hot chocolate—Cassie's favorite hot beverage—and bring a blanket.

And then he'd tell her why he'd held off on having sex for so long.

Before they did anything else.

Definitely before they spent any more time alone in her apartment. Or his.

And at some point in the next few hours, he needed to buy condoms.

He thought about what she'd said about her infertility. That sucked donkey balls for her. Cassie would be a great mom, if—no, when—she wanted to be. She'd dodged a bullet, as she'd said, and she'd find someone else to have a family with. She deserved someone who'd support her in her journey—medical, or adoption, whatever path she wanted to take. And she *would* find someone. She'd buy a house in the spring and meet someone—not like Mr. Starbucks, someone more her speed, like a carpenter or a firefighter. A nice guy who'd love her inside and out, and want to give her the moon.

Jared knew just how easy it was for a guy to want that for Cassie. *Fuck.* He slapped his palm against the wall and tipped his head back, letting the steamy water slide down his torso. He wasn't going to be able to let her go. He didn't even have her yet, and the thought of saying goodbye had him twisted up in knots.

But that's what SEALs did. They said goodbye, over and over again.

And it was way too early in their not-even-a-relationship to ask her to understand that she'd only ever have half of him. The other half belonged to Uncle Sam.

There was a big part of him that wanted to pretend it didn't matter. SEALs dated. They had casual hook-ups and serious relationships. Got married. *Got divorced, at a dizzying rate*. None of it should matter just yet. Second dates should be about chemistry and conversation. No need to put the cart before the horse.

He still found himself bounding ahead in his thoughts. His next extended tour overseas would probably start at the end of May, right as Cassie would be getting settled in her new place. They'd have until the summer. And then when he got back, she'd be on the other side of town. He ignored the hot, burning bubble rising in his chest. No, it was a good thing that she'd be out of sight when she moved on.

Because she would move on.

He wasn't going to be enough for her, not in the long run.

And if he was truly a good guy, he'd walk away right now. But he was selfish enough that he couldn't do that.

He finished washing up, checked his phone, gave Cassie instructions to dress warmly, and made a quick dash to the drug store for condoms.

———

Jeans, long-sleeve tee, belted sweater. See-through black lace panties and a matching bra. A teensy dab of perfume in all the right places. Dangly earrings? Sparkly? Cassie bounced in front of her dresser and tried to tell herself to chill out. She didn't listen.

Condoms. She had an unopened box somewhere from the tail end of her brief fling with Craig the dentist. She found it and stashed it in the top drawer of her bedside table. Then she jerked the drawer open, ripped off the box's plastic wrapping, and shoved a strip in her purse. Just in case.

When Jared knocked, she practically tripped over her toes sprinting to the door. He was dressed in cargo pants and a thick, black, unbuttoned henley stretched tight over a black t-shirt. He held a thermos. "Ready?"

"Absolutely."

As soon as he parked at the Hotel Del Coronado, Cassie guessed what their mystery activity was. "Skating?"

He nodded and grinned, his dimples deep and proud in his handsome face. "Miles knows someone who works here and made a miracle happen for me."

She clapped her hands together. She'd been once before, the year it opened. She'd wanted to return ever since, but hadn't been able to convince Mitch it was fun. "Let's go through the old lobby and look at the tree, too!"

"Whatever you want." Jared laughed as she grabbed his hand and practically dragged him into the historic hotel.

"You look like you know what you're doing there," he said a few minutes later as she carefully laced up her rental skates.

"I took lessons when I was little, but all that I've retained is the ability to glide with style."

"You've got me beat, then."

But even though Jared insisted he'd only been skating once as a child, he quickly caught on. Before long he was confidently weaving around slower skaters and staying close to her side. On the longer stretches, he reached out and took her hand. Around and around they went to the soundtrack of Christmas music. Cassie couldn't remember ever feeling quite so much in the holiday spirit. And the way Jared kept looking at her thrilled her down to her toes. December 23rd was going down in her personal history books as the best day of the year.

When two skaters collided in their path, spilling harmlessly to the ice, he snagged her hand and tugged her to the side of the rink.

"Kiss break." He glided his lips over her fingertips, then pulled her closer, looping her arms around his neck. She tightened her grip, fully supportive of this plan. In the near distance, waves crashed on the beach.

"This is pretty amazing," she whispered.

"You deserve amazing." He pressed his mouth against hers, and she parted her lips just enough to have a tiny taste before they pulled apart. "You also deserve dinner."

Right on cue, her tummy growled. But she wasn't ready to leave yet. She laced her fingers through his and tugged. "One more lap."

He'd thought about taking her to the hotel restaurant for dinner, but a fancy meal didn't seem to go with skating. Instead he headed into San Diego to a Japanese *izakaya* he'd been to a few times. It was quiet and the booths were private.

They dove for their menus right away, and even in the simple act of ordering he found her fascinating. Cassie was shocked that he'd never had *edamame*. She insisted they order a bowl to share, and described the act of eating the salted soybeans in such detail that he found his mouth watering before they even arrived. Of course, they ended up being exactly what he thought they would be—fine but nothing to write home about.

Cassie was momentarily crushed, but bounced right back when the house salads arrived and the ginger dressing was "totally perfect."

"You're such a California girl, aren't you?"

She fluttered her eyelashes and tossed her blonde hair over her shoulder. "Born and bred."

"Ever think about living anywhere else?"

"Not really." She pointed vaguely west. "The whole Pacific Ocean at my doorstep thing."

That made sense. He nodded.

She wiggled a soy bean at him. "Why? I thought you said you'd be here for a while?"

Was the second date too soon to talk about career progression? "I will be."

"But not forever."

"No, possibly not."

"Hmmm." She pursed her lips and dropped her gaze, but before she could say whatever was on her mind, the waitress arrived with the next wave of bar food they'd ordered. *Gyoza* dumplings and *yakitori* chicken skewers.

"Is that a good hmmm or a bad hmmm?" he asked after the waitress left.

"It's more like an 'I don't want to move too fast and say the wrong thing to scare off the cute boy' kind of hmmm."

He laughed. "I was worried that it was too soon to talk about future questions as well."

She looked across the table at him, her smile dropping away. "Does it feel too soon?"

He shook his head. "Really, I have no idea. But I think we should know where we stand. Set some parameters." A delicate line appeared in the middle of her forehead. "No?"

She shrugged. "Like what kind of parameters?"

God, was this a test? He'd fail if it was. All of a sudden he felt like a fish out of water. "I'm going on tour in five months. I'll be somewhere else in the world until this time next year."

"Ah." She reached across the table and traced her index finger down his. "I knew that. Are you saying you'd like whatever happens between us to be over by then?"

This was why he floundered. He *couldn't* say that. But hell, he didn't know if they'd make it to New Year's, let alone May. "I just want you to be aware," he said gruffly.

"Duly noted. What else?"

"Uhm, I can't talk about work most of the time. But you already know that." What else did one warn a potential girlfriend about? "I snore."

Her eyes sparkled. "Okay."

"What about you? Anything you want to tell me?"

"I don't like getting dressed and going home after sex." He choked on his sip of tea and she giggled. "Too much information?"

"Jesus, no. Please tell me no one has ever kicked you out of bed." She winced. "Damn. No, I'm never going to do that to you. I might leave before you wake up, but it's only because I go to work at dark o'clock."

"So you're thinking…yes for sleepovers?"

The thought of *not* sleeping with her already pained him. "Pretty sure I'm going to be in favor. I bet you're adorable in the morning." His confidence hadn't gone far, apparently, because it slid back into place. "I do have a side of the bed, though. You'll have to accommodate it."

"Oh yeah? What's that?"

"The middle."

She giggled. "You're beyond charming."

The waitress arrived with more food, and they tucked in. Cassie leaned back against the booth. "I don't understand why someone hasn't snapped you up. You're perfect boyfriend material."

"That comes with expectations."

"Ah, right." She darted her tongue across her lower lip. "Have I been reading the signals wrong? If you're going to be in the middle of my bed all night…"

This he had no doubt about at all. Like a panther on the prowl, he stretched one arm across the back of his side of the booth and hooded his gaze. "I want to have sex with you, Cassie."

She flushed a pretty pink and nibbled her lower lip. "Why me?"

He shrugged. "You snuck up on me. That whole friends-to-lovers thing, I guess. I like you. A lot. And now that I've seen you in a different light, I can't *unsee* you, if that makes sense."

"You mentioned a high school girlfriend. You didn't see her that way? Or anyone else?"

"Yeah. Hannah. We dated from the middle of junior year to the middle of senior year, and then she dumped me when I wouldn't put out." He'd gotten over Hannah in a week and a half. Exactly the length of time it took her to find a new boyfriend, and for him to learn the lesson that desperately wanting to make love to that one special person was an ideal full of holes—because he'd thought Hannah was more special than he'd evidently been to her.

"And then after that?"

"I joined the Navy."

"Right out of high school?" She blinked. "How did I not know that about you? I thought you just finished your training a year ago."

"That was my SEAL qualification." He gave her a quick rundown of his career progression to date. "And we're never really done training, it just becomes an ongoing cycle of deployment and courses."

"So you've been busy." He nodded. "But not too busy to learn how to kiss."

His gaze dropped to her mouth. He liked her smile. "I'm not a monk."

"But you were never tempted to just…do it? Like a hook-up?"

He dragged his eyes up to hers with a sigh. "Never. I'm the product of a one-night stand. And I never knew my father."

CHAPTER
SEVEN

THAT WASN'T what Cassie expected Jared to say at all. But when she thought about it, she didn't know much about his family life. Her chest ached for him, but she didn't know how expressing her pain for him would go over—if he wanted her sympathy, he would have told her about his family sooner, right? He must be telling her now for another reason.

She swallowed hard and nodded. "Wow."

He held her gaze. "I grew up in a two-bedroom apartment on the wrong side of town. Could have been worse. Could have been one bedroom, or I could've bounced in and out of the system. My mom did the best she could, but I wasn't her first oops, and by the time I came around, she was old and tired before her time."

Cassie tried to desperately do the math. Jackson was, what, five years older than Jared?

"My mom is forty-four." *Holy sugar…* "She had Jackson when she was fourteen. She lived with my grandparents until she finished high school, and then she got a job as a receptionist. She never went out. Never dated. But when Jackson was five, my grandparents took him camping for the weekend, and some of her friends talked her into going out to a bar. Nine months later…"

Cassie checked to make sure her mouth wasn't hanging open. "Did your grandmother help raise you, too?"

He nodded. "Without her, my mother would have been in a world of trouble."

"So that's… I can see why…" She offered a weak smile. "I don't want to say the wrong thing here."

He made a face, but took her hand at the same time. "You couldn't. It's kind of a lot of heavy shit to dump on you. You can react however you want." He looked down at their hands. "There's more, if you're willing to hear it."

How did she explain that she wanted to know everything about him without seeming voyeuristic? "Of course. Up to you."

"By the time I was in school, my mom had added part-time book-keeping on the side, and she finally started to get ahead. We drove to Disney World one year, and rented a house in Galveston a different summer. I actually had a pretty great childhood, the parts I remember. But then my brother started dating girls, and my mom hated it. They'd have the worst fights about it. She didn't want him to get into trouble."

All of a sudden, Cassie realized what was coming next, and her heart broke—for Jared's brother and his mother. And Jared, too.

"Jackson's girlfriend got pregnant in their junior year of high school. Her parents were horrified. My mother lost her mind. And his girlfriend wasn't ready to be a mom. She wanted to put the baby up for adoption."

"What did Jackson want?" Cassie's voice was barely above a whisper.

Jared tugged his lips into a half-hearted smile. "It didn't matter."

"Oh, your poor brother." Hot tears threatened behind her eyelids and she took a deep breath. "Does he know anything about the child?"

Jared shook his head. "It was a closed adoption. And he's never forgiven my mom for not supporting him. But she couldn't do the baby thing again."

"Wow. How old were you at the time?"

"Ten."

Now it was her turn to shake her head. "Hell of an education."

No shit. Any innocence he'd enjoyed up to that point had been stripped away. By the time he hit puberty, he'd heard more conversations about how stupid and dangerous sex was than most people heard their whole lives. And it had scarred him. Not deeply. Just enough to be self-conscious. Self-limiting. Just enough that he hadn't wanted to share that part of himself, because he wasn't sure that his family wasn't cursed.

"I'm not messed up," he said, realizing he was repeating something he'd said to her earlier.

She blinked at him. "I would be." She laughed softly. "I am, in different ways. Aren't we all?"

"I mean, I'm not too messed up to have sex now. And you're perfect."

"Hardly," she said quietly, reaching for the last *edamame*.

"You're perfect to me." She really was. Even if she did like to eat soybeans.

"But…" She slowly squared her chopsticks to the edge of her plate, then pushed all of her dishes away from her a bit. Like she wanted something to do with her hands. "I guess I'm a pretty safe bet for you to jump off the cliff with, then," she said quickly and didn't look up at him.

Damn. "That's not a factor for me."

"You wanted to take things slowly earlier today."

"You did, too. I still should. The problem is I can't keep my hands off of you. That was true before you said you couldn't have kids, by the way." He drained his teacup. "I can see how you'd wonder and worry, but my attraction to you didn't change at that point. Didn't increase, didn't decrease."

"I believe you." Her voice said otherwise and she looked up, making an apologetic face. "I do. It's just…are you sure this is a good idea?"

"I bought condoms," he blurted out. She blinked at him.

"Tonight. I ran out while you were getting ready. Because I honestly didn't even think about your fertility. Doesn't that show that I want to get in your pants because it's time? Because you're perfect and sexy and while I thought I was waiting for other reasons, maybe I was just waiting for you?"

"I have condoms, too," she said, finally smiling, but the sparkle hadn't returned to her eyes.

"We have one more date before we can use them. How about breakfast tomorrow?"

Her eyes crinkled at the corners and her smile turned into a grin. "Perfect."

After paying the bill, he offered her his hand and she slid out of the booth. He pulled her close, sliding his hand around her waist and keeping it there as they walked slowly back to his truck. He got her door, then jogged around to his side. She turned on the radio as soon as he started the engine, but took his hand when he offered it. They sat like that, fingers entwined, not talking, until they were over the bridge and almost home.

"You've never told anyone that, have you?" she asked quietly.

He could feel her eyes on him, even though he was staring ahead. He shook his head slowly.

"Thank you for trusting me." Her voice cracked. "And thank you for tonight. It was a great second date."

He squeezed her hand, then let go as he steered into his parking spot. "It doesn't need to be over just yet." He wanted more time. He didn't want this to be how the night ended. "Let me come in for a drink."

She pressed her lips together, suppressing a smile—sort of. "A drink?"

"And maybe some making out." He twisted in his seat and stroked his fingers over her cheek. "Shake off the heavy talk with a little spark."

She leaned into his touch and closed her eyes. He didn't mind. It gave him a minute to look at her, soak in all the soft planes and delicate peaks of her face. The bow of her lip and the point of her nose.

Her freckles. Even in the dim light from the street lamps he could probably count them if he got close enough.

He was almost there when she blinked her eyes open. "Hey there," she said softly, smiling.

"I was about to count your freckles." He eased his hand back into her hair and down to her neck.

"You know…" He brushed his lips against her jaw and she sighed. "There's no rush. The three-date thing. That was a minimum. Which is kind of silly, too. It's all so…" She gasped as he kissed her neck. "I mean, this is nice. And earlier. That was amazing. We can do other stuff. Maybe it might be—"

"Cassie?" His dick had a lot to say to that, but really, it was simple.

"Hmm?"

"I'm done talking for tonight." They'd sort it out. They'd have sex, and probably soon. Or not, if she changed her mind. But right now he just wanted to kiss her in his truck for a minute. Then against the side of his truck. And definitely on her couch again.

"Oh."

He took her mouth before she was done with her squeaky acknowledgement, and she moaned against him. God, she tasted good. Like the orange candy they'd been given with the bill at the restaurant and a sweet warmth that was uniquely Cassie. She moaned again, softer and longer this time, and he broke away reluctantly.

"Upstairs," he whispered.

"You're bossy."

"Yep."

She held her position just a few inches from his face and gave him a curious look. "Is that important to you?"

"What?"

"Is being bossy how you've managed to avoid being tempted over to the dark side so far?"

He hadn't thought about it like that, but… "Yeah, I guess. It's an easy way to impose limits." He grinned. "I've never had any complaints."

She sank her front teeth into her plump lower lip and stared at him. "Tell me about it."

"Upstairs."

"Tell me about it now and I'll do whatever you say when we get upstairs," she whispered. "I promise."

Jesus. She'd just taken the night from some sweet kisses to filthy promises in a heartbeat. "You want me to tell you…"

"Yes." She laughed, a nervous trill. "No. God."

His pulse pounded in his head. And his cock. There was something irresistible about showing her his experience, but he didn't want to cross the line and offend her—they were from two very different worlds. Hers probably didn't include finger banging in dark corners of bars.

He swallowed hard and tried to guess what she wanted. "When I was nineteen, I went to New York on leave with some friends. We went to a club that had these private alcoves. I was dancing with this girl and she kept saying, 'take me home, sailor.' Well, I knew better than to do that. But I wasn't a boy anymore. I wanted to touch her. And I thought…maybe, if I tell her she can't touch me, I could make it work…and it did."

"So you just…for her?" Her lips curled into a surprised O.

"That time. I told her to show me what she liked and where to touch her."

"And since then?" Her question floated in the truck's quiet cab, her quiet disbelief of the first question bleeding into more obvious breathless arousal.

"You really want to hear how I told other women to suck me off?"

Her eyes narrowed, but then she licked her lips, like now she wanted to do that herself. Every bit of him strained at the seams. "I'm going to get parts of you that no one else has had, right?"

He nodded. More than she knew. He'd give her everything without thinking twice. "I don't need limits with you, Cassie."

"Maybe it isn't about limits. Maybe it's about trust and control."

He rubbed his thumb across her lip, slick and wet, and she swiped her tongue at his digit.

"Is that something you like to do, angel? Give up control?" He never would have pegged her for that.

She frowned. Maybe he wasn't the only one surprised by the conversation. "I've never thought about it like that."

"That makes two of us." He'd done all sorts of things to keep himself on the straight and narrow. Learned that stating up front what would and wouldn't happen kept the focus where he wanted it.

Complete control wasn't something he needed to get off, though. When he thought of having sex with Cassie, it wasn't orchestrated. But the thought of trading control back and forth turned him on in new and unexpected ways. He cupped her cheek and kissed her, hard and deep. "Maybe we should take turns being in charge. Pretty soon we're going to be out of my arena of experience."

She kissed him then, her hands eager and grabby, and he let her have her fill before easing back.

"Now. Upstairs."

In her apartment, she paced ahead of him, slowly sliding off her sweater before unzipping her boots. He grinned and followed her example, taking off his boots and his shirt, leaving his t-shirt on.

"Do you want that drink?" she teased, backing away from the kitchen where any drink would be found.

He shook his head. "And you can lose that shirt, too."

She spun around, showing him her back as she peeled off her top. His erection strained against his fly at the sight of her bare skin curving down to her ass in those jeans. "What next?"

"Take your pants off."

She looked back at him over her shoulder. "Really?"

"You asked me what I wanted next. Pants. Off."

This wasn't new territory for him, and he had a burning desire to prove to her just how good he could make her feel. That he wasn't some boy with whom she had to be careful.

She kept her gaze on him as her hands wiggled over her hips, pushing the denim down to reveal black, barely there panties. When she paused, he crossed his arms to keep from taking over. Then ever so slowly, she leaned forward, all the way forward, and gracefully stepped out of her pants. She picked them up by a belt loop and just as gracefully unfolded her body, spinning around.

"Off," she said with a teasing whisper, holding the jeans out from her body for a minute before tossing them aside.

"I like the look of you bent over like that," he said, his voice thick.

She gave a nervous laugh and swung her hands in front of her body, her confidence wavering a bit. "Oh good. I wasn't sure if that was hot, or just like, whoa, a lot of ass."

"Hot." He cleared his throat. "You're gorgeous, Cassie. I love looking at every part of you, especially the curvy parts. The...*whoa* parts."

"Well that's good, because I've got a lot of those."

If Jared ever saw her ex-husband, he was going to do some damage to that man's face. "You sure do. And they make me crazy." He strode toward her, grabbing her hand. "Feel this?" He pressed her fingers against his cock. "That's what your little strip tease did to me. Hard enough to pound nails." He dropped to his knees and pressed his face into her belly. Her scent and the silky feel of her skin intoxicated him.

"I thought you were being bossy," she murmured, running her hands over his hair.

"You don't think I can be in control from down here?" He licked along the waistband of her panties. "Take your bra off."

Jared held her hips as Cassie bared even more of herself, her breasts swinging free as she gazed down at him. *Oh yeah, he was in charge.* And it gave her such a crazy thrill. Her hands hovered in the air after she dropped the bra—should she touch him again? Touch herself? Wait for a command?

He laughed—a slow, sexy rumble. "Do whatever you want," he said, his gaze solidly on her face.

"I want to take my panties off," she admitted. She wanted to be bare for him.

Another laugh and he rocked back on his heels. "Be my guest. That would make me *very* happy."

She rocked her hips, swiveling them under his touch, then turned around slowly. Her heart raced. It hadn't stopped racing since their conversation turned erotic in Jared's truck. And she didn't know which feeling was bigger or scarier—her need to be sexy for Jared or her fear that she'd fall short of his fantasy.

It was terrifying how much he meant to her. How much she wanted *this* to mean between them. Maybe it was just the season. Or because she knew he was a SEAL. He'd already come and gone in secret, with no clue when she'd see him again.

She didn't know how she'd handle those feelings once she gave him her heart. So it would be foolish to fall in love.

Totally foolish.

But the way he made her feel, all light and beautiful and desirable…with and without her clothes on. Maybe her heart wasn't hers to give anymore. Maybe it was already his.

Maybe by the time he had to leave again, he'd be able to leave his heart with her for safekeeping.

So many maybes. Too many to talk about on a second date.

She pushed the last scrap of lace off her body and shook off her thoughts. Naked, she gave herself over to Jared, trusting that he'd take care of her.

He swept his hands up her legs, sliding over her hips' curves. His big, callused hands left a trail of goose bumps in their wake as his surprisingly delicate touch lit all her senses on fire. He leaned in and kissed the top of her mound. "Spread your legs for me, angel."

She took a deep breath and splayed her legs wide, tipping her pelvis and arching her back at the same time. She could feel how wet she was for him, but instead of worrying, she hummed with anticipation for his touch.

When it came, it wasn't the blunt tip of his fingers. He glided his palm over her folds, cupping her entire sex.

"You feel amazing," he groaned. "So hot and wet. I want to eat you up, Cassie. Can I do that? Can I lick your sweet little pussy until you come on my face?"

"I might fall." Her words hitched as he licked the soft, indented line her underwear had left on her skin.

"I'll catch you." He stood—a giant rising from her feet to tower above her in one fluid motion. "But I'm going to take my time feasting on you, so which would you rather—the couch or your bed?"

CHAPTER
EIGHT

"BED," Cassie said softly, looking intently at his face like she wanted to make sure that was okay by him.

It was more than okay. "Perfect," he grunted, sweeping her off her feet. An armful of naked Cassie and a big soft bed to spread out on—he couldn't think of anything better.

She nestled her cheek against his shoulder and he carried her like she weighed nothing. His strength had been put to more urgent uses in the past, but never a better one. He lowered her gently into the middle of her bed, barely pausing to shove the decorative pillows out of the way.

He'd always avoided this—the fully naked woman spread out on a bed. And now he was glad he'd stuck to couches and dark corners, because the flushed skin, eager little noises, and inviting looks made for an irresistible package. His hands went to his belt.

"No."

He froze. He found her eyes, looking for the sign she was shutting this down before they even got started. He didn't find it.

"Let me," she purred, and his dick swelled in his pants. His balls drew tight, and he willed himself not to come before she did.

One big drawback of letting her in and waiving his usual limits—

he was that nineteen–year-old kid again, shaking like a leaf at the thought of getting his fingers wet.

If she touched him, she'd be the one getting a handful of come, not him. "I'm just getting comfortable, angel. But if you touch me, I'll lose my mind."

She pressed up on her elbows, her breasts bouncing softly. "I really want to see you lose your mind."

"You first." He shoved his pants to the ground and crawled between her legs, flipping one of her knees over his shoulder and gently pressing the other up and away from him, against the bed. He seated his body right where he wanted to be—just above her beautiful, pink sex framed in neat blond curls. She was soaking wet, glistening for him, and his mouth watered.

He was so fucking glad he wasn't new to this. That the heady awesomeness of worshiping her like this wasn't overwhelming like it had been the first time he'd dropped to his knees in front of a woman to get her off. He nosed his way up the outside of her sex, then down again on the other side, breathing her in. Showing her he appreciated her beauty.

Her legs tensed against him in anticipation, then relaxed as he touched her, first with his fingers and then with his tongue. He gathered her moisture and spread it up to her clit, holding himself back from licking it all up.

He spread his legs wide behind him, ignoring the pull toward her that all his muscles wanted to obey. No matter how much she writhed beneath his fingers and his mouth tonight, he wasn't going to fuck her.

His dick was staying in his boxers until she was boneless and out of breath, and then he'd find a way to climb in next to her and wait for the damned third date. Breakfast could be just six hours away. He'd survive.

As if taunting him, his cock pulsed and let loose a few drops of pre-come. *Jesus.* Wet and dripping like a girl.

Cassie lifted her hips against his face, and he grinned to himself. Maybe not quite the same. He snaked his tongue through her folds in a lazy figure eight that made her moan. A fresh flood of sweet honey coated his fingers, and he took that as an invitation to slide inside her.

She was tight as fuck—a hot, silky squeeze that had him grinding his hips against the bed. He wanted inside her. *This is why you stay out of bedrooms.*

But it didn't matter anymore. He'd waited long enough. This wasn't a foolish decision, and he had brand new condoms. It was almost time.

Almost. First she needed to come on his face. Then sleep. *Then* he'd let the most beautiful woman in the world screw his brains out.

He nipped the inside of her thigh and her eyelids snapped open. "What the hell?"

"What time is your parents' party tomorrow night?"

She let out a shaky breath. "Why are we talking about this now?"

He palmed her pussy gently again, rocking the heel of his hand up and over all the sizzling nerve endings he'd just been up close and personal with. "Because, angel…I need to plan out our day of non-stop sex. Breakfast will be served at six. Eggs and toast, for stamina. Orange juice for energy. And me, over and over again for your special Christmas treat."

She gulped. "We need to work on this crazy one-eighty direction change thing, baby."

He grinned. "Baby?"

She pressed against his hand. "Just trying it on for size."

"I like it." He nuzzled his way back into her folds.

She gasped and stretched out on the bed, arching her back. "I like that."

"That makes two of us. You taste so good. I'm going to wake you up like this." He gave her an exaggerated lick, then slid his hands under her bottom and lifted her into just the right position to dive deeper with his tongue. Inside.

She bucked in his hands and he held her more firmly, slowly fucking his tongue in and out of her body. A chant of his name and some colorful vocabulary additions swirled around them as her entire body throbbed beneath him. Because of him.

For him.

"Come on, angel," he crooned as he exchanged his tongue for his fingers. He licked around her clit, testing her sensitivity there before latching on and sucking gently. He worked her inside and out until she gripped his head between her thighs and ground herself against his face, finding that perfect edge for herself and exploding.

———

Oh God, she thought as she fluttered back to earth. *No.* That wasn't quite the right adjective. *Twitched* back to earth. Hot-mess style. She'd wrapped her legs around his head like a professional wrestler and...and...

"That was awesome," Jared said as he pressed a kiss against her belly. A really wet kiss. How many times could she think the phrase *oh God* before it got to be overkill? His face was wet from *her*. *His face.*

Her cheeks were burning up, she knew it. And any second he'd discover that, which wasn't the way it was supposed to be at all. He was the virgin. She was the sophisticated older woman who...who...

Jared rolled her onto her side and tucked in behind her, not bothering to hide the raging erection that made itself known against her ass cheeks. "I said, that was awesome."

"Mmm-hmm." She nodded vigorously. She couldn't disagree. It had been awesome.

"Are you okay?" He brushed her hair to the side and kissed her neck, then her ear.

She was. That crazy, fluttery, twitchy feeling actually felt *good* when she stopped thinking about it and just let it be.

"Do you want to come again?" His words yanked on something deep inside her and made her breathless all over again.

She turned toward him, moving slow like molasses. He was quiet and still, waiting for her. She thought about what he'd shared. They were a t-shirt and a pair of boxer briefs away from something he'd never done before.

Both of them naked. She snaked her arms around his neck and pulled him in for a long, slow, appreciative kiss. "I want you to come next."

His erection strained against her belly. She glanced down and he groaned.

"Blow jobs are fair game on the second date." She licked her lips. "Do you want me to put some clothes on first?"

"Don't you dare." He palmed her butt and pulled her close, dragging his hand down her thigh and lifting it so he could fit his leg between hers. "We should talk about a couple of things first. I'm clean—my risk is pretty low, but I get tested regularly anyway. And I'm okay if you want to use condoms for everything."

God, she hadn't even thought about that when he'd gone down on her. She was a horrible person. *No, just less experienced than he might think.* "I just had a physical last month. And I haven't been with anyone since the spring." She took a deep breath. "I'm not on any birth control, because my chances of getting pregnant are so low. It'll have to be condoms for sex."

"I figured." His voice rumbled in his chest as he tugged her even closer. "I stocked up."

She bit her lip and smiled into his t-shirt. "This is a lot of talking…"

"Something I learned in health class in grade nine that's stuck with me all these years. If you can't talk about it, you shouldn't be doin' it."

"You sure can talk about it." She slid her hands under his t-shirt, looking for more of his warm skin and hard muscles to ground her, remind her this was really happening. She was naked in her bed with Jared, talking about sex. Like responsible adults. What a novel concept.

"Give it a go," he said roughly. She glanced up at him and the look in his eyes took her breath away. He was staring at her like he wanted to eat her up. Or have her eat him up while he lazily spanked her bottom or something similarly filthy. "That. Whatever just made you take that adorable-as-hell little breath. Tell me that."

"Maybe I should give you a blow job," she said slowly, placing each word carefully in front of the one before. This was new territory for her. "I want you in my mouth. I want to lick you all over." He groaned and guided her hand to his waistband. Pride flooded her body and spurred more words. "Do you want me between your legs, looking up at you?"

She slipped her hand inside his shorts and wrapped her hand around him. His hand joined hers, and she let him take over, fisting his erection up and down as she slid down his body. She pressed a kiss to the bare skin at the top of his sculpted hip, ignoring the almost irresistible cock a few inches to her left. He needed to be naked first. She moved lower still, kneeling between his legs. His thighs were long and heavily muscled, and he was tan all over.

"What are you thinking?"

She skimmed her palms up his legs and grabbed the bottom of his boxer-briefs. "I'm wondering if you have any tan lines."

"You should definitely investigate further." Electricity crackled between them as she tugged his underwear off. His erection, still wrapped loosely in his fist, bobbed free, thick and heavy. Her own sex swelled at the sight. She wanted that inside her, and she wanted it now. But she wanted to taste him, too—that hadn't just been dirty talk. She wanted to rub herself all over him and tug on him, kiss and lick him…there was no end to the list of ways she wanted to enjoy his magnificent body.

He was tan all over, but lighter right in the middle. "You have the most gorgeous skin tone," she breathed, crawling toward him on all fours. "I could look at you all night, but it's getting late, and I'm…hungry."

He spread his legs wide as she slid her hands toward his core again, and when she glanced toward him his gaze was almost entirely hooded. Almost. She could still feel the heat in his eyes, and it felt *good*. She let out a long, slow breath as she watched drops of pre-come form at his tip. With one hand, she cupped his sac and with the other she gently circled the head of his shaft, using her thumb to spread that moisture around before lowering her mouth and sucking him in. Just the tip at first, then deeper with each bob, her hand moving up and down as if an extension of her lips. Almost immediately he started groaning and bucking, but then his hands fell away from his hips and he clenched his fists into her bedding. Just like that he found his control again.

Well, that wouldn't do.

"This is a first for you, isn't it?" she asked after swirling around his thick crown with her tongue. "I'm naked. You're naked. On a bed."

"Twist this way, angel, and I'll spank your ass for teasing me," he groaned.

"Maybe I want you to," she taunted, sliding her wet mouth back down his length.

He groaned again, and oh boy, did she love rendering him speechless. On either side of her body, his legs flexed and bowed. She bobbed her head again, then pulled back and took over with her hand, jerking him off as she watched, her head bowed, her hair falling around her. Jared's breathing picked up, and he lifted his hands off the bed, touching her hair and her shoulders, before reaching for her breasts. His touch was needy and searching.

Just as Cassie recognized the move, Jared hauled her up onto his body. She kept her hold on his cock as she straddled his lap, slowing the motion of her hand as her clit made contact with the base of his shaft.

"Do we need a condom?" she asked quietly, watching his face.

He shook his head. "We're going to wait. I just want to feel you like this." He reached for a pillow and jammed it behind his head, his gaze stuck on her the whole time.

"Look down," Cassie whispered.

He laughed, a nervous, strained sound that seemed so out of character compared to his usual confidence. "If I look, I might blow."

She loved him for admitting that. "Then blow," she crooned, arching her back and cupping her breasts. That dragged his attention to her chest, and with a growly moan, she slid her hands down her torso, pulling his gaze with them. To his engorged erection, shiny again with the proof of how close he was, and the soft cushion of her sex underneath it. "Are you gonna come for me, baby? Come on my hand?"

She stroked him lazily as he gripped her thighs and thrust into her hand. The rock of his pelvis under her rubbed through her slick folds and she had the vague idea that she could come again, too, but not as quickly as he was going to. He'd made her come twice today already. This was just for him.

Cassie didn't know a lot about hand jobs. Five years of sex with her ex-husband and never once had she jerked him to completion. She hadn't wanted to give Craig the dentist a blow job on their second date, so she'd started something like this, but he'd taken over and finished himself. She didn't have any lube around—she and Mitch had never used it much.

Natural lubricant, though, she had a ridiculous amount of at the moment. She reared up on her knees and Jared gasped, but she wasn't about to violate his trust like that. She shook her head. "I just need a little help."

She slid her hand between her legs, getting her fingers all slippery before settling back in his lap. Now his cock worked more easily inside the tight ring of her fingers. Her hand couldn't quite encircle his girth so she twisted her wrist as she pumped up and down, relishing his sighs and groans as she hit all the right parts of him with her fingers. He was watching her, but with each squeeze at the base of his cock, his head tipped further and further back until he was staring at the ceiling. He made a noise in the back of his throat, something totally primal and unbelievably hot, and then he jerked, sending a splash of hot, white fluid onto her fingers.

"God, keep going," he muttered, his hand covering hers when she stopped. Slowly she milked the rest of his release, enjoying the mess. *Isn't it all messy?* His earlier question bounced through her head. Yeah. When it was good, it was messy. She hadn't had enough of that in her life. Without a worry about the stickiness—because that was what showers were for—she folded forward and slid against his body until she was nestled in the curve of his arm.

"Damn, Cassie."

She peeked up at him. He was still breathing hard, but his ability to pull himself together was impressive. Jared-in-charge was back in the building. That was fine by her—bossy Jared turned her on. "You told me to say what was on my mind."

"That was the single most hottest thing I've ever seen," he said slowly before kissing her soft and deep. "You touching yourself. I want to see you get yourself off. I want you to touch yourself when I'm inside you. I want you to—"

She pressed their lips together to silence him, then shook her head. "Baby, I want a shower. And then sleep."

"Together, right? I can stay over?"

He took her breath away. "Yes. I want you here when I wake up."

He grinned. "For breakfast. And then sex."

"You're insatiable." She rolled off the bed and he let out a long, low whistle at the sight of her bottom.

"You're the prettiest girl I've ever seen, Cassie Bronson."

Damn, that did nice things to her insides. "I could fall so hard for you, Jared Sutter."

He stood to follow her, a strange look on his face.

"Too much too soon?" she asked.

He shook his head. "Hardly. I might already be there."

CHAPTER
NINE

AFTER SHOWERING and pulling on a basic layer of clothing—Jared in his boxer-briefs, Cassie in a t-shirt and panties—they crawled back into bed. As promised, Jared sprawled in the middle, pulling her on top of him. One hand possessively cupped her hip, his long fingers curving around her butt cheek. The other stroked her hair. It took him a while to speak and when he did, she let him.

"I meant what I said, Cass. You're the type of woman to make a man want everything he can't have in life."

She should have known there'd be an asterisk on his declaration of falling for her. "This feels a lot like you have me in your life," she countered lightly. It was already technically Christmas Eve. No way was she letting him break up with her before they spent the holidays together. Or ever.

"Until I go on tour. I just don't want to hurt you."

"Maybe we should talk about this in a couple of weeks. Go on a few more dates. Actually have sex. Maybe it's a moot point and we'll lose interest in each other." She meant that to be light as well, but her voice cracked.

"I'm pretty sure what we just did counts as sex. And really, we've been dating as friends for months now."

"So what are you saying?"

His grip tightened around her and she matched his gesture, wrapping her arms more snuggly around him as well.

"I don't want to assume anything here, angel."

"I don't follow."

"What do you see in your future?"

A tall, strong, kind, and noble Navy SEAL who comes and goes. But she wasn't going to admit that just yet. "I like being a real estate agent. I want to buy my own house. Find someone to share it with me." She took a deep breath, because this was where she feared their paths diverged. "Not right now, but sometime in the near future, maybe children."

It took him a long time to respond and when he did, his voice was raw. "You deserve all of that."

"It's okay if that's not what you see for yourself. It doesn't change that I want you here and now. It doesn't change anything between us."

"It kills me that another man will give you all of that happiness." The rawness of his voice shocked her, and she wanted to prop herself up on her hands and look at him, but she didn't want to risk shutting down the conversation, either.

"You're giving me the happiness I need right now," she whispered. "That's all hypothetical. All I need right now is to feel beautiful and wanted."

He stroked her hair. "I almost lost it on Saturday night when you asked me to zip up your dress." He ran his hand up her spine. "All this bare skin… God, never doubt how sexy you are to me, Cass."

She pressed a kiss to his neck. "That's all I need from you, baby. Don't worry about the rest."

———

Cassie drifted off soon after that, but Jared stayed awake long into the middle of the night.

He wanted to be the man she wanted for the rest of her life. It was crazy, totally insane, but he knew with every fiber of his being that Cassie was the one for him.

And she just wanted sex.

A small part of him tried to say that wasn't quite what she'd said, but the bigger part—the unexpectedly emotional part that he'd kept locked down good and tight until this week—felt like he'd been weighed and measured and come up wanting.

Except she wasn't rejecting him. She just wasn't asking him for anything.

Fuck, he wanted her to ask him for the moon. He didn't have the education or flight experience to be an astronaut, but he'd make it happen. He'd do anything for her. He'd die for her.

Damn it. In his late-night wallowing, he'd forgotten that *he* was the one who'd thrown up those boundaries and for good reason. Because he could die and leave her alone. And before that happened, he'd leave her alone, over and over again.

That Cassie wanted him at all was a miracle. That she'd accept he could only give her a few months was icing on top. Dawn was breaking as he finally drifted off. Cassie had rolled onto her side as she'd fallen asleep, and he wrapped himself around her again.

When he woke up, he was alone and the scent of coffee wafted from the kitchen. He made a quick pit stop in the bathroom to wash up, then found Cassie in the kitchen. She was wearing the same thing she'd slept in, a t-shirt and panties, and the sight of her tapping a spatula against her long, bare legs instantly made him hard.

"I thought I was going to make you breakfast," he growled, sweeping her up in his arms. He nipped at her ear and nuzzled her neck, relishing how she felt under his lips.

"You were sleeping so soundly." She smiled over her shoulder. "Tomorrow will be your turn."

"It's our third date. I should treat you."

She lowered her lashes and her cheeks turned pink.

"You need to tell me what you just were thinking." He loved how free and open she was with her sexuality behind closed doors. It was like a gift just for him.

"If I make you breakfast, then you can treat me by…" She trailed off and grinned. "Doing the dishes."

He tickled her waist. "That's so not what you were thinking."

She shook her head slowly. "No."

"Well?"

She turned in his arms, hooked her thumbs in her panties, and slid them to the floor. "We've got ten minutes before the frittata comes out of the oven. You could treat me to an orgasm appetizer."

He lifted her by her hips, laughing at her surprised yelp, and set her bare bottom on the edge of the counter. He dropped to his knees and kissed one thigh, then the other, nudging her legs apart with his head. "You can have two."

She leaned back, bracing herself on her hands, and he pulled her right to the edge of the counter and slid her knees over his shoulders. She was wet already, slippery and sweet, and he dived in. He'd never get enough of her taste. He kissed her deeply there, making love to her with his mouth, and when she climaxed quickly, he showered her with praise and appreciation for how amazing she was. How giving. How sexy. He gave her all the words he could, hoping they made up for the words he couldn't risk saying out loud.

When the oven timer dinged, he lowered her feet to the ground and held her in a hug for a moment before she giggled and shoved him back to the bathroom to clean up again.

After they ate, he did the world's fastest round of dishes then joined her on the couch. But even though he knew what she expected him to do—toss her over his shoulder and race to the bedroom—he couldn't. Not yet.

"I know you don't want to talk…"

She looked at him with a resigned smile on her face. "But you do?"

"Come here." He tugged her close for a kiss. "You're wonderful."

"So are you."

"I keep thinking about you in that house, wanting to fill it with kids."

She frowned. "That's not exactly what I said. And it's in the future, not right now."

"I know, but I want that for you, too."

"But not for you." Her voice was small, but strong. He knew she didn't want to talk. He knew she didn't care—right now. But he was like a dog with a bone, and he watched as if having an out-of-body experience as he dove in again.

"I can't be there for you. You deserve someone who can hold your hand through doctor's appointments and labor. Take turns doing diaper changes and rocking a fussy baby."

"Hypothetically speaking, since you won't let this go… If you were ever in that position with someone. Me, or another woman, at some point in your future…" She trailed off and gave him another frown, this one more obviously grumpy. "You'd do all of that when you're here. And when you couldn't, it would be because you're doing something just as important somewhere else."

A cold chill crawled up his spine. "I don't want that with anyone else."

She jumped up, and he stood too, but gave her space. "It's a fucking *hypothetical*, Jared. Just the same way you keep saying I'll find someone else."

"You deserve to be number one—"

"Stop telling me what I deserve, and start explaining what you're afraid of. What's got you running scared from hauling me into the bedroom and doing what I thought you were dying to do? Because it's not actually sex you're scared of. You proved over and over again yesterday that you're totally comfortable with that."

"That wasn't sex."

"Sure it was. A stupidly smart guy I know said something like, *pretty sure it counts*." She dropped her voice an octave as she mimicked him. "If you're having second thoughts, if this doesn't mean anything—"

"I didn't say it doesn't mean anything. Jesus, Cassie. You mean the world to me."

"Not enough to hang on to."

"I leave, angel. All the time. Sometimes suddenly and without any explanation." He scrubbed his face with both hands. "It's not about me wanting to hang on to you. I'd selfishly keep you to myself until the end of time. But everything that you want…that isn't me."

"Why don't you let me worry about whether or not you're what I want?"

"I don't want to hurt you."

"You're hurting me right now."

That shut him up.

"Remember last night when you told me you were done talking for the night?" She cocked one eyebrow at him. "We've had our third date. Now I want to take you back to bed. It's Christmas Eve. Let it go."

"I can't."

She laughed. "Why not?"

"Because I love you." Oh, shit. Too soon, asshole, way too soon. And also, complicating.

The laughter fell away and she just stood there.

"I do. I know it's too soon, but you lighten my day and you make me laugh and you're just so *good*. You're going to make an awesome mom and a wonderful wife and I can't stop obsessing about that because I fucking want that for myself. I want *you* all to myself. Forever." Jesus, he needed to stop talking. She was staring at him like a deer in the headlights, and he needed to put the brakes on but he couldn't. "I love you, Cassie. And it scares the shit out of me because I don't know how to be all that you need."

She pressed her hand to her mouth and made a soft noise that he couldn't read as good or bad.

"I'm sorry if that's too much information." He dropped his head and stared at the floor.

"You already are all that I need. Decent, loyal, sexy, sweet. A little dumb, maybe, since you don't know that I love you, too. But maybe I did a better job of keeping that to myself than I thought."

He jerked his head up, his heart pounding.

"It happened at IKEA. You were standing there looking at rugs and I realized you were everything I wanted. Isn't that crazy?"

"A little. I was pretty grumpy that day."

"I like grumpy."

He should have gone to her, but he was frozen in his spot. They'd barely dealt with the tip of his iceberg of fears. He kept hoping the damn thing would float away, but didn't seem to be happening. "I worry about leaving you alone."

She shook her head. "Don't worry about me. I know you think I'm fragile, but I survived infertility and the break-up of my marriage. I came out of both of those changed. Stronger. I'm not a weak woman who will cry in my cornflakes when things get tough. I can handle a boyfriend who has to go away for long stretches when his work is as important as yours."

She was strong. He knew that.

And yet...

"What?" She reached out her hand, then dropped it. "Just say it, baby."

"I don't want to leave you a single mother," he burst out. The thought of doing that to her, creating children with her and then robbing them of a father...it tore through his heart like a tungsten blade.

"Oh, Jared." She flew across the room and into his arms. "That's not it, baby. That's not it at all."

"No, I'm pretty sure that's exactly it," he said, each word a sharp confirmation of his greatest fear.

"Your kids will always have a dad. When you're away, you'll talk to them. If something happened to you, God forbid, you'll have left them a legacy of love. If we ever do something as crazy as have kids together, I promise you I'll never feel like you've abandoned me. Not ever. No matter what."

"It's so hard, angel." He buried his face in her neck and breathed in her sweet scent.

"I know," she whispered, stroking the back of his head. "It's not fair that you didn't have a dad. But you won't leave your child."

"I will, and I won't have a choice."

"That's not the same thing. Our kids are going to be proud of you. So damn proud. And so will I. But you'll never leave us for another life. We'll *be* your life. I know that in my heart."

———————

Jared picked Cassie up and cradled her against his chest. "Our kids?"

"Hypothetically speaking." She wiggled her feet. "This is becoming a regular thing, you carrying me around."

"Are you complaining?" He adjusted his hold so he could swat her naked bum.

"Nope. Are we done talking now?"

He laughed as he deposited her on the bed. "We're never going to be done talking. But the topic's shifted."

She scrambled onto her knees and pulled off her shirt.

"God, look at you." He dove at her and they rolled, with her ending up breathless and on top of him as he tugged one aching peak into his mouth, then the other. She rocked her hips, shamelessly rooting for his erection to fill her.

"I need you."

"Let me make you feel good, first."

She ached so hard for him, she was staring at feeling *good* in the rearview mirror. "You did that twice in the kitchen. Fill me up."

He stretched one long arm for the condom he'd set out on the side table and ripped the package open. His hands were shaking, but she held herself steady over him, waiting.

"How do you want me?" he muttered, nudging the tip of himself against her cleft.

She swivelled her hips. "Uh-uh. How do *you* want me?"

He flipped her onto her back.

She spread herself wide for him and he groaned appreciatively.

"Touch yourself. Show me."

She slid her fingers around her clit, then dipped lower, lifting her hips to slowly take two of her fingers inside herself. Jared groaned again. "I'm so tight for you," she whispered. "All swollen and turned on already. I'm going to come as soon as you slide in."

He huffed a laugh. "That'll make two of us."

That was totally okay by her. "I love you. Hard and fast, sweet and slow. I'm going to love how you take me, every single time." She stroked down his sheathed erection, coating him in her moisture before guiding him to where they both needed him to be.

As he entered her, he started swearing, and didn't stop until she'd wiggled her hips, seating him fully inside her. He dipped his head, pressing his mouth to her shoulder, and let out the best incomprehensible sound she'd ever heard.

"You feel amazing," she whispered.

"Holy fuck," he said in response, and she laughed.

"No laughing," he groaned, pushing himself up on his elbows and looking down at her. "I'm so close."

"Then fuck me." She grinned, pulsing her hips.

He pulled his hips back, then surged forward again, making her gasp.

"Oh God, are you okay?" He froze.

She nodded. "Do it again."

He did, more tentatively this time, but on the third thrust instinct took over, he wrapped himself around her, and lost himself in the rhythm. Cassie didn't try to follow him over the cliff—she wasn't there yet, and this was just for him.

She was pretty sure he'd want to do it again before she even cooled down a little, anyway.

He held himself inside her as he twitched though his orgasm, then reached between them to hold on to the condom as he withdrew. He didn't look at her as he sorted himself out, but he didn't go far. He pulled her to his chest, carefully avoiding her gaze the whole time, and she just waited. He'd proven over and over again he wasn't shy about talking about whatever was on his mind. Better to let him bull-in-a-china-shop his way through whatever was going through his head.

"Next time will be better," he muttered against her hair.

"It was fine," she whispered. "I can't wait to do it again."

"It might be a while before I don't lose my mind every time."

"That's okay." She smiled to herself. That was more than okay. That made her feel *awesome*. "How are you feeling?"

He reached for her hand and tugged it to his cock. "Like I want back inside you already."

She rolled onto her stomach and lifted her hips in the air. "If you take me like this, I'll come really quickly."

With the speed of a jungle cat, he'd found another condom and climbed between her legs from behind. She pressed her ass high in the air, and he rewarded her with a soft, sweet rub of his hand against her sex. "So pretty," he muttered, turning her pink again. She buried her face in the pillow, and then it was just feelings. The width of his crown pressing against her folds. The aching sweetness as he stretched her from the inside out. The slow pull and slide as he filled her, over and over again, and this time it *was* better. It was perfect. Slow and sweet, unbelievably hot, and when she cried out, he joined her, folding over her body from behind.

Later that night—after an extended nap and more lovemaking—she introduced Jared to her family as her new boyfriend. It didn't matter that her family was cold and awkward. Beside her was the warmest, sweetest, strongest man she'd ever met. And he was all hers.

EPILOGUE
18 MONTHS LATER

"ARE YOU WAITING FOR SOMEONE?"

Cassie blinked up at the nurse. She hadn't heard her come into the room. "I'm sorry?"

"Before the doctor comes in should I get anyone from the waiting room for you?"

She shook her head. She was on her own for this pregnancy.

She pressed her hand to the small round of her belly. IVF had worked on the second go-round. She'd wanted to wait after the first one didn't take because Jared had been about to leave on a long deployment, but he'd pointed out that if it worked, he'd be home for the first three months with the baby. That logic won out.

Now she was sixteen weeks along. She hadn't seen her husband since shortly after the positive pregnancy test. They were going to meet up in England for a quick visit in a week, and she didn't know how he'd react to her changing body. In clothes, she just looked chubby, totally thick through the middle. At least her boobs were full and bouncy, although he wouldn't be able to touch them, so that had limited appeal. *Except he'd be so gentle*, she thought, a shiver wracking her body.

He didn't have any privacy where he was, so the rumored Skype sex she'd heard about from other Navy wives hadn't happened yet.

He'd sent her some suggestive emails, but it turned out that her downright filthy man was pretty buttoned up when Uncle Sam was screening communications. That was okay. In the year and a half they'd been together, he'd given her a lifetime of fantasies to thrive on.

The day they closed on their little three-bedroom bungalow, he'd carried her over the threshold and they'd christened the staircase. Then the loft bedroom, with her folded over the edge of the bed and Jared palming her ass from behind. She blushed as she thought about their first time on Christmas Eve morning—or second time, rather. He'd been such a quick study, and by the end of the holidays they'd had more sex than she'd had in the entire last year of her first marriage.

Her attempt to build a life with Mitch felt like a lifetime ago. And the love that she shared with Jared cast that first marriage as pale and anemic in comparison.

Her second wedding had been an understated affair on the base, a month before his first tour. She'd promised to wait for him, but Jared was having none of that. And belonging to *him* made the deployment easier on her as well. The Navy had more resources for supporting spouses than girlfriends. None of Jared's closest friends were married yet, but one of his mentors, Drew Castle, was and came down from L.A. for the wedding with his wife Annie, who was pretty close to Cassie's age. The pretty brunette had confided that Drew missed the San Diego area, and as soon as she finished her academic studies, they'd be moving back.

In the year that had passed since they married, Jared had left the country five times. Two long deployments, including the one he was currently on, but in between there had been…training missions he called them, but they weren't all easy. Sometimes he couldn't sleep for a few days when he got back. But he always handled whatever was in his head, and before long he was back to himself. Annie and Drew had come to visit a couple of times, conveniently timing their arrivals to just after Jared left until Cassie convinced them she was fine.

And she was. But 227 days was a long time to spend apart from the man she loved. Not that she was counting or anything.

The clinic room door swung open, jarring her out of her melancholy thoughts.

"Cassie, welcome back," said her obstetrician, Dr. Canoglu. "Let's fire up the ultrasound and see how baby is doing."

———

Jared paced in the arrivals hall at Heathrow International Airport. Around him swirled a mess of sound and color, but all he focused on was the digital display in front of him. *Los Angeles - Arrived*. Any second now, Cassie would walk through those gates and he'd get to kiss her. Touch her belly and feel their baby move. Photos and video weren't the same.

He stroked his chin, wondering what she'd think of his neatly trimmed scruff. He preferred to be clean-shaven, but he had a brutal tan and was sort of scared to shave off the beard completely. Two months in the desert hadn't been kind to his skin, and even though he'd flown through Germany and had many hot showers between the sandpit and London, he knew he didn't look like the same man she'd kissed goodbye two-and–a-half months earlier.

Each long deployment he got a decent-sized chunk of time off in the middle. Last time, they'd gone to Bali. The memory of Cassie swimming naked in their private pool stirred his arousal in a way that wasn't particularly helpful in the middle of an airport concourse.

But damn, his wife was beautiful. And naughty.

For this leave he'd insisted they meet in a modern city with excellent health care. Cassie had been through so much to make this pregnancy happen, he didn't want to do anything to risk her health or the baby's.

He'd already checked into their hotel, so the only thing he carried was a massive bouquet of flowers he'd picked up from a florist down the street from the hotel. He bounced on his heels, nervous and excited to see her come through those doors. The flowers might have been a mistake—he'd just drop them when he hugged her. And that brought him full circle to wondering how big her belly was now. She didn't look big in the pictures at all, but she said she'd started to feel the baby.

His baby.

He couldn't get over how much his life had changed in the last year, or the peace that becoming a father had brought to his thoughts about his own parentage. He'd never be able to understand how a man could walk away from this responsibility, but without a doubt, he knew he never would. That was all that mattered.

In front of him a youth football team arrived, and mayhem broke out as parents and girlfriends descended on the entrance gate. It took a minute for security to get people moving again, and when the crowd broke up, there she was.

His blonde angel in a bright blue sundress, pulling a suitcase. She locked her gaze on him and smiled, a million watts of sunshine. He slid through the crowd as if no one else was there.

She dropped her suitcase when they collided—gently—and he let the flowers tumble onto it. Her hands went straight to his face, but she didn't get a chance to say anything before his lips were on hers and he was swallowing her happy sigh.

"I've missed you so much," she said with another sigh as they broke apart. She rubbed his cheek. "You're my mountain man now." Her fingers danced across the healing blisters on his cheekbones. "Were you on the sun?"

"Something like that." He cleared his throat. "I can shave in a day or a two."

"No, I might like it." She rose to her toes and kissed his jaw, and as she stretched, he felt her belly for the first time—a hard, round press against his middle. He sucked in a breath and she pulled back. "Did I hurt you?"

He shook his head and dropped to his knees, not caring that they were in the middle of an airport. Screw everyone else. He had a baby to meet.

Cassie laughed as he pressed his cheek to her slightly rounded tummy.

"It's so hard!"

"I know. Weird, huh?" She swung her small purse around, almost beaning him in the head. "Sorry. Here, I've got something for you." She pulled out a small white envelope. "Dr. Canoglu had a pretty good look between baby's legs at the last appointment. She wrote down the gender…"

He took the envelope as he stood up and pulled her close under his arm. "You don't know yet?"

She shook her head. "I thought we could open it together. But maybe not right here."

He carefully tucked the envelope back into her purse, although letting go of the paper made his fingertips tingle. He'd missed all her doctor's appointments and the first few symptoms. "Come on, we'll get a cab."

Outside, he handed over her suitcase to the driver of a classic black London cab and helped her into the spacious back seat. She settled into his side as soon as they were off, and it was like they hadn't just spent eleven weeks on opposite sides of the globe. Like he hadn't just come out of a war zone. He pressed his face into her hair and breathed in her scent. She tipped her face up to look at him and he tunnel-visioned in on her mouth.

"Kiss me," she whispered.

He complied, keeping it sweet and light, but lingering, and when they reluctantly parted he needed to shift to accommodate a new friend.

"I've missed him almost as much as you," she murmured against his ear, her hand sliding up the inside of his thigh.

"Stop looking at my cock," he muttered with a restrained grin. He wouldn't stop her if she wanted to grope him in the cab. He wouldn't have stopped her if she'd tried to have phone sex with him, either, even though he knew Big Brother was always listening. He had no limits when it came to Cassie, and he never would.

It took forever to arrive at the hotel, and when they did, he threw more pound notes than required at the driver and hustled her though the lobby and into the elevator. He waited with thinly veiled impatience for the doors to slide shut before he pressed her against the wall and took her mouth again. And this time, there was nothing sweet or light about his kiss.

"First thing we're doing inside our room is opening that envelope. Then we're getting naked and staying that way for a good long while."

"My boobs still hurt. Be gentle with them." She chased his mouth for another kiss, but the elevator car slowed and he pulled back regretfully. Their room was at the end of the hall, which would be nice for privacy, but it felt like the longest walk ever with Cassie shooting him heated looks every two steps.

She pressed into his side as he worked the swipe card—why did those damn things always take three tries to turn green?—and as soon as they were inside, she was tugging his shirt up his body. He winced as her fingers grazed a bruise on his ribcage and she stilled immediately. "What happened?"

He knew she wasn't asking for details. One of the many things that he loved about Cassie was that she implicitly understood the rules about being married to a special operative. "Got into a fight with a rock. It might have won." After a tumble down a mountainside, but he wasn't going to tell her that. "I'm fine."

———

"I worry." Cassie handed Jared the envelope again as she ducked her head around his back and kissed all his owies. It killed her not to ask about them, but she really didn't want to know what her husband did that would cause such bruises and, in at least one spot, recent scars that looked like they'd needed stitches.

He didn't seem to care, though. "Okay, ready?"

She nodded and hummed against his back, then came around his other side as he ripped into the envelope and extracted a piece of paper that he unfolded. The doctor's handwriting scrawled across the middle of the page, Congratulations, it's a boy.

"A boy?" He tossed the paper in the air and whooped, picking her up and spinning around in a circle.

She grinned at him. "A boy. Jared Junior?"

"Jason? Jasper? Jude?"

"Maybe we could consider other letters of the alphabet, too," she teased, climbing onto the bed.

He nodded at her dress. "Naked time."

She took a deep breath. Under the cute sundress lay a different body than he'd said goodbye to almost three months earlier. *Here goes nothing*, she thought. He loved her. He'd accept her in whatever shape she grew into as she gestated his baby.

Acceptance wasn't really the look on his face as he took in the totality of her nude form, though.

It was pure desire. Her heart almost exploded at the hot gaze he raked down to her toes and back up—all the way up. "You're so curvy," he groaned. "You sure I can't touch your breasts?"

All of a sudden, she wasn't sure of anything. Her nipples ached for his mouth. Her thighs were desperate for his hands. "Maybe. Just be gentle."

He stripped off his clothes in a heartbeat, then joined her on the bed, sitting on his heels. He stroked her with feather-light touches, and when she rose up to wrap her arms around his neck, he swept her onto her back and settled beside her. He kissed and licked until she was begging for him. And when he slid deep inside her body, she spurred him on—she didn't need gentle any more. She just needed him.

SECOND EPILOGUE
THE FOLLOWING CHRISTMAS

FALL AWAY

ABOUT THIS BOOK

Nothing is more awkward than waking up next to a woman whose name you can't remember... except maybe falling in love with one who'd rather not know yours.
Navy SEAL Trick Novak knows he needs to find a better cure for his insomnia, but a warm body and a pretty smile worked just fine until he met Gaby Ellis—his latest conquest's roommate. Now he's not sleeping, and he's definitely not getting laid, but that just means he's got more time to plot ways to win over the beautiful and stubborn kindergarten teacher.

CHAPTER
ONE

NOTHING IS MORE *awkward than waking up next to a woman whose name you can't remember.* Trick Novak should know—this wasn't his first time. The next five minutes would be a subtle dance of generic statements and sneaky attempts at getting her personal information—hopefully for the second time.

Although it wasn't out of the realm of possibility that he hadn't bothered to get her name the night before.

He racked his brain. He'd been dead-tired. His team had gotten home from a pretty routine extraction mission that had gone off without a hitch. The high of a job well done coupled with Dumbrowski turning twenty-seven meant that everyone had been eager to cut loose.

Before heading to The Wave, a popular bar, the other guys had racked out for a few hours.

Trick had jerked off and taken a hot shower, but sleep had eluded him, as it had for a few months now. So he went out, had a few rounds with the guys, and left with the first soft woman he could find.

He needed to find a better way to deal with insomnia than anonymously fucking his way through the female population of

Coronado Beach. It was going to bite him in the ass one of these days.

The blonde with the curvy hips and tiny red panties stirred next to him as her phone let out another quiet bleat. *Who has a fucking lamb alarm?* He squinted against the midmorning sun and peered around the room. Maybe the same person with white eyelet lace curtains and framed prints of ballerinas on the walls. Okay, so she was a good girl. That could go either way.

She sleepily patted her side table for her phone, hit the snooze button, then rolled toward him, still holding her phone in her hand.

Trick scanned her pretty face as she snuggled deep into her pillow, eyes still shut. A trickle of guilt slid through his gut. He definitely didn't know her name. And he was pretty sure that it had been her friend who had caught his eye the night before.

Damn.

As a Navy SEAL still looking at more than a decade of service—at a minimum—Trick loved one-night stands. A bit of physical release, a few laughs, a warm bedmate. Zero strings. And since he'd started struggling with sleep, that post-orgasm cuddle was better than Nyquil.

It wasn't that he was allergic to commitment, but it would take a rare girl to put up with his work schedule. And to find that kind of understanding in a woman with whom he might find the kind of sparks that lasted a lifetime?

He wasn't holding his breath. If he stumbled across love, he'd take the leap. In the meantime, he was happy with temporary hook-ups.

But he didn't like the idea that this woman hadn't had his full attention the night before. And now that he was thinking too damn much, she wasn't going to have the good kind of attention this morning, either. He needed to make a quick exit and head home.

He snagged her phone out of her hand. No password. *Oh, the innocence.* He clicked on her Facebook app. He wouldn't snoop, he just needed her name. Lila Jovan. And her friend's name was… didn't matter. Wrenching his thumb away from the screen, he clicked out of the app instead of scrolling down her list of contacts.

For whatever booze-and-fatigue-induced reasons, he'd chosen this woman last night and until he said goodbye, she was the only woman who got his attention.

He slid the phone back into her hand. With a sigh, she rolled toward him, then squeaked as her palm slide across his bare abs.

"Hi there," he said quietly.

She cleared her throat, angling her face away from his. "Hi."

"I've gotta get going, but I didn't want to sneak out." Sneaking out was never cool.

"Okay. Thanks for last night."

"I'm sure the thanks should be all mine." *No hesitation*. That was key. Set the tone as polite but finished, and she'd pick up on it. From the way she'd eased away from him, she already had.

Her alarm went off again before she could say anything else, and with a shriek, she leapt out of bed, then dropped out of sight, reappearing wearing a t-shirt from the floor. "I totally slept through my alarm, I'm so sorry. I've gotta get to work, but there's coffee in the kitchen if you want something, and the door automatically locks, so just let yourself out. My roommate is probably here, so make sure you're wearing pants."

Jesus, what kind of guys did she normally hook up with if they just wandered around her place with their junk hanging out? At least he didn't have to worry about her clinging to him like a wannabe girlfriend. He watched her gather some clothes and disappear into the bathroom, but from her frantic pace, he didn't think he could get up and out before she reappeared.

He didn't have to be anywhere until the evening, so he lay back and enjoyed the uncommon luxury of relaxing on a girlie bed covered in pillows.

Trick loved pillows, and there were only so many a dude could have on his bed before his buddies started to make fun of him. And since his roommate, Miles, had zero boundaries, he couldn't even keep a pillow collection private.

Maybe while Miles was overseas he could temporarily indulge…

He frowned.

No. While Miles and the rest of their team were overseas, he'd be concentrating on work. Doing his fucking job, supporting them however he could, and filling in where the other teams needed help.

And just like that, the good post-sex relaxation was gone.

He should be overseas with them. It was his fucking turn in the sandbox. But he wouldn't be there because he couldn't fucking sleep and couldn't keep his stupid blood pressure under control on a medical.

Panic attacks.

The medical staff had talked all the way around PTSD without actually naming it, because he'd made it clear there was no way he'd wear that label. He was *fine*. Just a bit stressed. And there were ways to deal with that and still function in the job.

So far, his commanding officer was being supportive. One tour staying behind. A training rotation, they were calling it.

Once. He'd get a free pass once. If he didn't get his head sorted out and his health under control, he knew his days as a Navy SEAL would be numbered.

That wasn't an acceptable option.

Lila started when she came running out of the bathroom, hair damp, fully dressed in what looked like a waitress uniform. "Oh, you're still here."

"I'm going, no worries."

"Uhm…" She made a face. "Okay."

"Yeah."

Fuck him. These random hook-ups had to stop.

He gave her a three-minute head start, and when the apartment sounded safely quiet, he got up, used her private bathroom to freshen up, then finished dressing and went to find his boots, which he vaguely remembered kicking off in the living room.

They weren't beside or in front of the couch. He leaned over the oversized armchair, wondering if they'd been tossed further than his vague recollection indicated.

From behind him, an unfamiliar female voice cleared her throat, then asked, "Looking for your boots?"

———

Gaby asked the question gently, but it still sounded abrupt in the quiet of the apartment. She actually hadn't realized anyone was still here.

The oversized man Lila had brought home the night before—the one with the size thirteen boots she'd tripped over this morning, and the super-fine butt she was trying really hard not to ogle—stood up with unexpected grace and turned around slowly.

"You must be the roommate," he said as he twisted. His eyebrows pulled together when he got a good look at her. "Oh. Hi."

"Uhm, hi." She smiled politely. "And you must be Lila's date from last night. I put your boots by the door earlier." *Which you can use any time now, because I have marking to do in peace and quiet.*

"Thanks." He glanced in that direction, but he didn't move. Instead, he looked at her again, frowning this time. "You were at the bar last night."

She had been, for a while, but when her friends hit the dance floor, she'd come home and gone to bed. Early and alone, as usual. If this guy hadn't slept with her roommate, she'd appreciate that he'd noticed her. But since he had… "What bar?"

"The Wave." He frowned again. "I'm sure you were there. Red t-shirt, hair in a ponytail with…" He pointed to the sides of his chiseled face. "Loose bits of hair around your face."

She could feel her face turning red as she shook her head. "You must be mistaken."

He stared at her for a second, then nodded. "Okay, my bad. Well, see you around."

She watched him cover the short distance to the door in a couple of long strides, then shove his boots on his extra-large feet, quickly check his pockets—left front, back right, back left. It looked like an unconscious routine, the way he patted himself for all his valuables. He'd probably left something behind after a one-night stand before and it had become super awkward.

Ugh. She hated the judgemental edge to that thought. And she shouldn't think about him, or his routines, or anything like that. Spinning on her heel, she practically ran to her room, trying like hell not to listen for the click of the door. Not to think about the strange man with the sharp brown eyes and extra-soft lips her roommate would probably never think about again.

Gaby didn't begrudge Lila for having fun. If Gaby was smart, she'd stop thinking so damn hard and have more fun herself.

Getting out of her head, though…easier said than done.

CHAPTER TWO

GABY LOVE-HATED THURSDAYS. She'd agreed to teach a course at San Diego State because the extra money would help her finally pay off the last bit of her student loans, but the race from work to the college meant dinner was always on the run—or skipped entirely—and then she invariably found herself starving at quarter to ten at night.

On the other hand, she was using her master's degree in education for something other than wiping sticky fingers and mediating Lego fights. She wouldn't trade her job teaching kindergarten for anything in the world, but five- and six-year-olds didn't appreciate her in-depth grasp of primary education pedagogy.

Less than two months to go, she told herself as she parked in front of Sammy's Shawarma. Six more weeks of late-night, junk-food dinners on Thursday nights. And then she'd have the summer term off, and could re-evaluate whether or not being a part-time instructor was for her.

Maybe she'd do something crazy in the summer, like actually date boys.

A group of guys was already in line, so she pulled out her phone and checked her email. She'd assigned a group project, and from the grumpy looks on her students' faces when she left, she expected to find a bunch of questions already.

She was right. *Sigh*.

"What do you mean you don't like hot sauce on your shawarma, man?" The guy right in front of her pushed his friend, who pushed him back—right into Gaby.

"Hey," she said quietly, putting her hand up to block the bump.

"Nothing says I *must* eat what you eat, Jase."

Gaby froze. She knew that rough, warm voice. *You must be the roommate*. Itchy, embarrassed heat flooded her torso and started to crawl up her neck. She ducked her head even further, curtaining her face with her hair. Maybe she should go. *No*, her stomach protested. Maybe they would order and she could keep her head down and—

"Ooof!" Gaby's phone flew out of her hand as a big, heavy, male body thudded against her, and this time she didn't see it coming. No sooner had the stunned sound been ripped from her lungs than a different male body was at her side.

"Are you okay? Sorry, we were just goofing around." The last word echoed something else he'd said, something she hadn't been able to get out of her head this week. *Loose bits of hair around your face*.

Staring at the floor, her face now flaming, she nodded roughly. She was fine. Had she been paying attention instead of hiding from the threat of this encounter, the collision wouldn't have happened at all. It was totally her own fault—on more than one level, because she would be the only one who'd think this was awkward.

"Hey," he said softly, handing over her phone. "We're sorry."

That was nice—genuinely nice—but it rubbed her the wrong way. She was *embarrassed*, not wounded. He didn't need to talk to her like she was a frightened deer.

Well, that's how you're acting.

She took a deep breath and looked up. "I'm fine."

Recognition dawned immediately, his dark eyes lifting in understanding. "And so we meet again."

"And so we do."

Behind him, the guy at the counter indicated the mens' sandwiches were ready. She cleared her throat and pointed. He glanced away, pulling out his wallet, but after handing a twenty to his friend, he slid his gaze firmly back to her face. "I still don't know your name."

She hesitated. "Gaby."

"Nice to see you again, *Gaby*." He leaned in just a hair as he said her name, his voice dropping half a register into decidedly sexy territory.

So she did the only thing that made sense. She scowled at him. He was clearly a player, and she wasn't…playing material. But from the confused look on his face, maybe he wasn't being gross. No. She re-wound his words. She was just being crazy. She offered him a weak smile that she couldn't quite make reach her eyes. She was too tired.

He laughed. "Or not. Well, I'm Trick. Hopefully the next time we see each other I'll have my boots on from the get-go, and you won't get whacked in the head, and maybe we can get past basic introductions."

"Yeah." She wiped the weird expression from her face and offered him a more reasonable, more realistic smile. "Hopefully."

From the counter, someone called for next order, and she side-stepped him, concentrating on the menu hung from the ceiling.

She could feel him behind her, hesitating.

Yes, she felt it too, something strange and heavy in the air.

But before she could absorb it, analyze the possibilities and act on the potential, it started to fade. And when she turned around, he was gone.

The roommate had a name. A pretty one, to match a pretty face that fascinated him even when she scowled. For the third time in a week, he'd only had a brief glimpse of her, but this time he'd soaked up every detail: her flushed skin, her bright eyes, her blunt bangs and heavy, dark brown, shoulder-length hair that framed her delicate, angular features perfectly.

The way she wanted nothing to do with him.

It was a problem that he'd slept with Lila. He could see it written on her face. But Trick was a US Navy SEAL. Figuring out impossible problems was kind of his thing. There was no mountain too high, no ocean too deep, no terrorist fortress too heavily protected. No woman too frosty.

And Gaby wasn't frosty toward him.

No.

She was wary, and nervous.

But not frosty.

He knew where she lived and where she got her favorite Lebanese food. It was just a matter of time before they ran into each other again.

CHAPTER
THREE

IN HINDSIGHT, it should have been obvious that he was military. The boots. The muscles. That Lila had picked him up—she loved a man in uniform—and that the hook-up had happened at The Wave. The haircut, although his hair was longer than the rest of the guys he was running with.

Gaby stared at the approaching sea of testosterone, some wearing faded green t-shirts. Others, like Trick, were gloriously stripped down.

Her heart tripped over itself in a desperate attempt to thump loud enough to grab his attention. The rest of her blushed—her standard response—and slinked lower in her beach chair.

It had been two weeks since their late-night run-in at the shawarma place. She was just past the midpoint of the school term and had come to the beach for some sunshine and fresh air while she marked the midterm assignments for her adult students.

She slipped on the hood of her sweatshirt and dug her sunglasses out of her bag. She was a warm-blooded woman and would allow herself a little gawking, as long as it was safely anonymous.

Trick was at the head of the pack as they ran past, and her eyes greedily gobbled up the front-row view of his body in action. He twisted away from her to talk to a younger man next to him, encouragement it sounded like, and his shorts dipped low on his hips, revealing a vee of muscle she'd only seen on Pinterest and in her dreams.

She bit her lip as the herd thundered past, all thighs and pumping arms, sweat glistening in all the right places. The beach had just become her favorite place—despite being a born-and-bred California girl, she normally avoided sun and sand because the combination usually required a bathing suit. And that would mean regular bikini waxes and spending a small fortune on sunscreen to cover all her skin, when clothes took care of both problems for a lot less.

But the beach in the spring, when the only people who bared skin were these men…and that one man in particular—the one with the sexy voice and the piercing gaze who was totally off-limits every-where but in her dreams—yes, a springtime beach was a very good place to be. She'd come back next weekend.

As the last few runners trailed past, she ducked her head and tried to focus on the essay in front of her, but then she heard his voice. First, it was directed at the stragglers.

"Get the fuck out of your heads, right? Mind over fucking matter." She peeked up, frowning at the harsh bark, but he was grin-ning proudly as the younger men sped away from him, their feet churning up the sand faster than before.

And then he turned, and pinned that grin on her.

Busted.

"Roommate Gaby."

She couldn't turn his name into a teasing retort, because *One-Night-Stand Trick* just sounded wrong. So did *Hook-up Trick* and… "You know, your name is really appropriate for someone who has a lot of casual sex," she blurted out. "Or inappropriate, depending on the context."

He walked over and dropped into the sand next to her. "Let's just say there's never a great context for that."

"Sorry." She was. He flustered her, but that was no excuse.

"Are you always like this with people your roommate sleeps with?"

No, you're the first I've ever thought twice about. "Again, I'm really sorry."

He waved his hand and stared out at the ocean. "I guess it's a bit awkward. I haven't seen her again, you know. I don't think—"

She didn't think she needed to hear any more on that topic. "Don't worry," she muttered as an interjection. "I think it's more that I'm awkward."

He laughed gently like she amused him. It felt warm and understanding, which threw her off-kilter a bit, but he didn't act like anything was out of order. "So last time we exchanged names. Now you know I'm in the Navy. So it's only fair that you tell me something about yourself."

"Why?"

"Because that's what people do? Exchange pieces of information in a back-and-forth fashion?"

She knew that. She taught five-year-olds to ask those basic types of questions. And yet here she was acting like a complete idiot because she couldn't understand why this guy was striking up a conversation with her. "Right. Again, I apologize. I'm working two jobs right now and my brain is a little fried. Can we go with that as my excuse?"

"You don't need an excuse, but sure. What are the two jobs?"

She found herself telling him about her teaching gigs and the freelance book editing she did in the summer when school was out —a job she liked so much more than her short-lived stint as a waitress.

"See?" He grinned. "That wasn't so hard."

She nodded in acknowledgment. "Okay, so now it's your turn again." She pointed down the beach. "Don't you have to keep up with those guys?"

"Rule number one for P.T. The guy in front can stop and talk to a pretty girl."

She swallowed hard. "That doesn't sound like a real rule."

"No, but it should be." He stood and brushed off the sand. "I'll call it the Gaby rule. I should go and catch up with them, though. Sorry."

Before she could respond, or even breathe, he'd started walking backward toward the hard-packed sand near the water.

"I'll see you around," he said with a smile, and something in her belly fluttered.

Lila's one-night-stand had just flirted with her. Gaby might be awkward and shy, but she wasn't stupid. And he'd called her pretty.

He'd slept with *Lila*, with the blonde hair and the big boobs and the non-stop smile, and then he'd flirted with *her*. Gaby, with none of the above.

Huh.

She watched, dumbfounded, as he took off at a dead sprint down the beach, and she had no doubt he'd catch his fellow sailors. Catch, pass, and then call them some names, smiling the whole time.

They'd probably love him for it.

———

Trick put two and two together, and was waiting for Gaby outside the shawarma place the next Thursday night. He went online, found the course she was teaching, added ten minutes for post-class pack-up and chatter, twenty minutes for driving, then showed up fifteen minutes early just in case.

It was the most effort he'd ever put into finding a woman who didn't seem totally into him, but he couldn't stop thinking about her. And since that first morning when he realized she was Lila's roommate, he hadn't slept with anyone else.

Which also meant he hadn't been sleeping that great.

He didn't *need* sex to sleep. He could get the same hormone release from a hot shower and jacking off. *But then your bed is still empty.*

That was the weirdest part, this new craving for a body next to him.

Trick had always liked his bed big and empty when not in active use. Now he preferred not to be in his own bed at all. That's where the nightmares had lived since the mission when a Kurdish kid had been killed right next to him.

But he wasn't a dick. He couldn't sleep with another woman when this one was on his mind.

The one who'd just climbed out of a little grey car, weariness dripping off her tired shoulders.

She slowed as she caught sight of him. "You."

He grinned. "You."

"This is becoming a routine."

"Isn't it nice?"

She pressed her lips together, but the smile escaped and lit up her face anyway.

"I was hungry, thought I might get a sandwich." He held the door open for her. "Since you're here, maybe we should grab a table."

"I have to be at work at eight in the morning."

He laughed. "I have to be at work at six."

A look of confusion rolled over her face. "And you're eating dinner now?"

He'd had dinner at five. Second dinner at seven. This was just a snack. "Gaby, I'm here because I wanted to see you again."

"Oh." Another frown, then she opened her mouth as if she was going to ask *why* again, but thought better of it. "Uhm, okay, a table. Sure."

They placed their orders, then settled into a booth along the far wall.

Then they stared at each other for a minute.

Trick didn't get nervous with women, but now he found himself unexpectedly tongue-tied. He didn't really have a clear end-game in mind. He didn't expect Gaby to invite him back to her place—not tonight, or probably ever—but he couldn't stop thinking about her.

"So…" Gaby ran her finger along her side of the table. "Trick. Is that a nickname?"

"Short for Patrick." He watched her absorb that, her lips silently saying his whole name. He didn't love his name, hence the short-form, but all of a sudden, he wanted to hear it roll off her lips. "How about Gaby?"

"Gabrielle."

He repeated it, and she shrugged. "It doesn't really suit me."

"I like it. I like Gaby, too."

"I guess you're not really a Patrick, either?" An adorable little frown formed between her eyebrows. "I mean, is that why you go by Trick?"

He could fill in the unspoken parts of the question. Patrick was a serious, mature name, heavy with tradition. Trick wasn't heavy with anything, except now he felt like his playful nickname might be loaded with a million reasons why Gaby wouldn't be interested in him.

Instead of answering, he glanced toward the counter, and seeing that their sandwiches were ready, excused himself.

A mistake, because when he came back, she had her guard up. She dug into her sandwich, politely ending the awkward-conversation part of their encounter.

Wasn't that the sum total of all of their encounters to date? What would it take to bust through to the other side?

He ate as well, because a snack was always good, and food might help him think.

Quietly they sat there, and it wasn't as awkward as talking. It was kind of nice. She kept glancing up at him, and after a few brief looks, started smiling as she slid her gaze over his face. Then she bit her lip, and his dick stirred.

Maybe silence would be their thing. He could do a lot in the quiet. He crooked a grin at her, and she laughed, a lovely, lilting sound.

Shifting in the booth, he took the excuse of having a big body and long legs to stretch out under the table, sliding his calves on either side of hers.

They sat like that, the outside of her legs pressing against the inside of his, until their sandwiches were gone.

Gaby tilted her head, first to the right, then to the left, and finally leaned across the table. "You've got a little sauce right here," she whispered, brushing her thumb against the corner of his mouth.

The innocent touch sent a bolt of desire straight to his balls. She froze, her fingers still touching him. He jerked his gaze to meet hers. Her pupils were dilated, her lips parted…she felt it, too.

Ever so slowly, she pulled her hand back, wiping her fingers on the napkin. Still she stared at him, and he stared back. Time slowed, background noises faded, and it was just the two of them.

Pretty, awkward Gaby, and the idiot who had slept with her roommate. He was going to make that a non-issue, but it wouldn't happen tonight, or any night soon. He needed to dial his lust back a billion points.

That would be easier if she stopped looking at his mouth.

Fortunately, a crowd of teenagers came in and broke the spell. Unfortunately, once it was broken, Gaby was done. "I should get going," she said quietly, grabbing her messenger bag.

"I'll walk you out to your car." He slid out of the booth and stood, waiting for her. As she adjusted her bag, he spied a bowl of plastic-wrapped mints on the counter, and sauntered over to grab two. *No particular reason,* he told himself, which was a complete lie.

If he got a chance to kiss her goodnight, he was going to take it, and he didn't want it to taste like tahini.

She took the offered candy with a small smile and popped it into her mouth.

After exiting the restaurant, they stopped just outside the door, and she stared at her car.

"This was nice," he said quietly as he brushed his arm against her shoulder. She was easily a foot shorter than him, but she didn't seem small. She had this inner strength which radiated out of her. He wanted to spend more time soaking that up. "We should do it again."

"Next week?" She kept her gaze fixed firmly ahead.

"How about Saturday night?"

"Shawarma Saturday sounds like fun."

"Are you mocking me?"

"I'm pretty sure you'd rather go to The Wave on Saturday night."

"Okay, let's do that."

She pressed her lips together, another attempt at repressing a smile. Another failure.

"No?"

"No." She laughed. "Trick, what are you doing?"

He slid his hand over the small curve of her upper arm and turned her so they faced each other. "I'm asking you out." He leaned in, curving his body over hers. "On a date."

"I'm not sure that's a good idea," she breathed, mint and doubt mingling in the air between them. The lights from the row of shops beside them reflected in her eyes as she tipped her face up to his.

God, he wanted to kiss her. He wanted to haul her hard against his body and cup her ass in his hands, kiss her until she was breathless and couldn't remember her roommate's name, let alone the fact that Trick had bumped uglies with the other woman.

But there wouldn't be any hauling, or grabbing. No, from the look on Gaby's face, he was about to be shot down.

She lifted her hands and pressed them to his chest. He flexed under her touch because he couldn't help himself, and she sucked in a breath. *Good.* At least he wasn't being rejected because she found him hideous.

"This is crazy," she whispered, biting her lip.

"That sounds like a yes," he rumbled. He was totally posturing, playing the alpha male. He didn't care. She brought it out in him—not that it was ever far from the surface. Trick liked to get his own way.

Success was the only option.

She traced the faded Avengers logo on his t-shirt before stepping back.

"Not a date," she said quietly. "But lunch, maybe?"

"A lunch date. I like it." He winked as she shook her head and laughed. He pulled his card out of his pocket, his cell phone number already scribbled on it. "Here. Text me. Or my email address is on there, too. Let me know the best way to contact you. Should I pick you up?"

Her head shook quickly. *Damn.* "I'll meet you wherever we decide to go."

"'Kay." At some point, he was going to want to pick her up. At some point, they'd have to settle that issue and put it behind them. How, though…fuck if he knew.

He dropped his gaze to her mouth. He wanted to kiss her goodnight in the worst way. She offered him another of her small smiles. Nice, but missing something. And then she licked her lips, and even though they were saying goodbye, his blood flowed to the most unhelpful of places.

"Good night, Patrick," she said, ever so quietly, and turned quickly, moving to her car.

Damn. Just like that—*pow*. She destroyed him. Maybe he liked his name after all.

He watched her drive off, then headed home.

In the shower, he thought about the way her cheeks turned pink, and the way she bit her lower lip. His cock thickened against his thigh, then crawled up his belly as he imagined Gaby perched on top of him. Naked.

Jesus Christ. He groaned and took himself in hand, slowly. He wanted this fantasy to last until he was stretched out in his bed and could imagine her curled up on top of him, rocking her wet pussy against him, whispering about how it wasn't a date. Scowling at him as he slid deep inside her, that sharp little look making him hard as nails. Her tongue licking the corner of his mouth the same way her thumb had. The way she said his name. His given name that no one else ever used. *Patrick*.

His release hovered right there, his balls tight and his primal brain taking over, but Trick made himself ease back. He needed more of Gaby. He needed her to tuck him into bed. He turned off the shower, drying himself off as he padded through his pitch-black room, crawling under the covers naked with just his towel.

He imagined her kissing up his spine. *Wishful thinking.* But the slide of her cool hand over his side, wrapping underneath his hand to stroke with him…that felt real enough in his lusty haze to do the job.

He groaned her name as he stroked himself faster, harder, right to the edge of pain. He rode the edge into the darkness, spurting into the towel as he tipped his head back, eyes pressed tightly shut.

CHAPTER
FOUR

THE NEXT MORNING, Gaby slammed the kitchen cupboard door shut a little harder than was necessary. She sloshed water into the coffee maker, glowered at the toaster, and thought seriously about calling into work sick because her mood was *not* fit for children. Or any other human beings.

Including her roommate.

"What the heck got under your skin?" Lila asked drowsily as she slowly drifted into the kitchen. "You're making enough noise to wake the dead."

Gaby didn't really want to talk about Trick surprising her at the restaurant last night, or the sleepless night she spent tossing and turning, thinking about the rub of his legs against hers and the way he stared at her mouth.

She definitely didn't want to share any of that with her roommate, lest it later be revealed as a fantasy Gaby had constructed in her mind, but in case it wasn't…now was the time to say *something* to Lila.

She sighed. "It's not what, but who."

"Oooh, boy trouble?" Lila pulled the cherry jam from the fridge and wiggled it in Gaby's direction. "You want?"

She nodded. Yes, today was definitely a cherry jam kind of day.

"It's complicated. Or maybe it's not, but it's definitely complicated in my head."

Lila popped in toast for herself and grabbed the vanilla-flavored coffee cream from the fridge.

"You're up early."

"You were being loud. You're never loud. I thought it might be important."

They weren't close friends—that made them perfect roommates, really, because they could talk about shared bills and house rules without emotion getting involved. But Lila did friendly stuff without pushing—things like waking up early when Gaby was grumpy and realizing she needed jam. Asking if there were boy troubles, but not demanding details.

Gaby sighed. "Hypothetically, if I was interested in someone you'd dated…what would you want me to do about that?"

Lila snorted. "I don't date."

Gaby blushed. "You know what I mean."

Her roommate shrugged. "I'd want you to be careful for you, but I don't get possessive over guys. If you want to hook up with someone, that's cool."

"I don't…" Gaby trailed off. This was why she dated quiet guys, guys like her. Because even though Trick had used the word date, and he'd never come out and propositioned her…maybe what he was angling for was just a one-night stand. Ugh.

"Is this a hypothetical question?" Lila tilted her head to the side. "I didn't think we had the same taste in men. But I'm sure whoever it is, I don't care. Unless he was a jerk to me. Then I'll kick him in the nuts for pawing at my roomie."

Gaby cleared her throat. "Have there been any jerks lately?"

Lila grinned. "How lately are we talking about?"

Gaby squeezed her eyes shut and fought a losing battle against the bright red embarrassment crawling into her hairline. "Last month or so?"

Amused laughter filled the kitchen. "Nope. No jerks lately." Lila sighed. "But nobody I'd call dating material, either. All nice guys, but super clear on having no-strings rules, just like me."

Gaby nodded slowly. She could be smart about this and enjoy Trick's attention as long as it lasted. *It's just flirting*, she reminded herself. And if he wanted more…well, she wasn't usually interested in casual sex, but she was twenty-six. Maybe she needed to be a little wild, just once. Try it out before ruling it out.

She definitely wanted to kiss him. So much it hurt. When he'd handed her that mint the night before, her heart had started beating at double speed, and it hadn't slowed down since. If she hadn't pulled away…

But she couldn't forget that he'd done that with Lila, too. Granted, her roommate kissed a lot of guys. And she probably hadn't done exactly *that* with Trick. Just a bunch of other similar, more naked things.

It was a lot for Gaby to wrap her head around as they silently munched their toast. She needed to be sure that her silly little crush wasn't the start of an ugly love triangle she had no hope of winning. All signs pointed to Trick and Lila not caring at all. She was the only one hung up on who'd been naked with whom.

Across the table, Lila slid out of her seat and grabbed the coffee pot. Without saying a word, she topped up Gaby's cup.

"Thank you."

"I'm not going to pry." Lila smiled. "But make sure he's worth all this heavy thinking you're doing. Because *you're* worth it."

Gaby frowned. "What if I wanted to try something more casual?"

"Do you?"

That was the million-dollar question.

———

Trick winced as he looked at the text message on his phone. One hour earlier and it would have made his day. Hell, his entire week. But just over twelve hours after he'd asked Gaby out, he was going to need to beg for a rain check.

Okay, I'm game for whatever you want to do tomorrow ~ Gaby

He clicked on the number it came from and stored her in his address book. Then he sighed again. This wasn't going to go well.

Maybe it was better to talk over the phone. He quickly tapped out a response. **Can I call you?**

Lunch is over in two minutes. Call me after four?

Crap. He was going to be on a military transport plane by midafternoon. **I need to postpone lunch. Work reason. I still really want to see you.**

A beat passed, then another. His thumb hovered over her name, ready to call her, not caring if she was surrounded by a bunch of kids. If she just heard his voice, maybe she'd believe him.

Okay, no worries. I have to go.

Damn. A thump at the door was his only warning before Lieutenant Jason Steyner stomped into the office where Trick had gone for some privacy. "Come on, Meyers is already steaming mad that we can only pull together a small extraction team. Let's not piss him off further."

"Yes, sir." Trick cleared his throat. "I was going to make a call."

"You can make it from Honolulu. Let's go."

But when they landed in Hawaii, all hell had broken lose, and by the time they got out of the briefing and had their orders, it was the middle of the night for Gaby.

He lay on his bunk and let himself slip into the mental review of what they'd do the next day. They were going to rescue a salvage boat and her mostly American crew of ocean treasure hunters, including a CIA operative who was apparently clever enough to be a spook but not clever enough to save himself from pirates. The boat had been boarded four days earlier, and yesterday they'd landed on a private island in the Pacific.

Trick's team would do a High Altitude/Low Opening jump in the cover of darkness. He visualized each step of the HALO insertion. What they'd do if the wind picked up and dumped them in the ocean or jungle instead of on the intended beach. If they were seen. Their intel didn't indicate the pirates had radar, but it was possible.

Anything was possible, but their plan would give them the best chance to take the island by surprise and hopefully save some lives.

And then he'd call Gaby, and hope she could figure out from subtext and charm that he deserved another chance at a date.

CHAPTER
FIVE

"YOU REALLY OKAY?"

Trick rolled his eyes at Chief Special Warfare Operator Nathan "Gibson" Meyers. Most of the time, the other man was his friend. They didn't usually serve on the same team, but while Trick's team was in Iraq, he was attached to Meyers' group. And right now the usually laid-back Meyers was acting like a worried mother hen. "Fuck off, Gibs. Also, a bit late, don't you think?"

Meyers laughed and looked around the V-22 Osprey aircraft they were flying in over the Pacific Ocean. "If I could have left you at home, I would have."

"I'm fine." And he was…his pulse was within normal parameters, his blood pressure was fine. He'd slept like shit last night, but that was mostly guilt over Gaby. No nightmares.

"The lieutenant says you haven't been able to connect with a girl back home?"

Steyner had a big mouth, but it was his job as part of the command group to talk to the Chief about everyone on the team. Trick got that. Didn't like it, though.

"Doesn't matter."

"She a distraction?"

"Nope."

"We do this for them, not despite them, right?"

Trick looked at his friend in surprise. "You got a girl, Chief?"

Meyers shrugged. "I got a face I see in my mind when I need to be good at my fucking job. That's all that matters."

This wasn't a new debate. Trick's teammate, Jared Sutter, had gotten married last year, and his wife was pregnant with their first child. The gentle giant didn't blink at heading to Iraq. Meyers clearly fell on the same side of the argument. Lots of other men thought the special forces teams weren't a place for married men.

Until a few weeks ago, it had only been an academic question for Trick, and he'd always leaned on the side of single being easier.

Now he wondered how dating Gaby could work if he'd failed to make their first official date. *This is why you don't date much.*

The ten-minute warning crackled through their headsets, and training swept aside his scattered thoughts. Trick checked his kit once more, slid his mask into place, and waited for his turn to step out the jump door.

The weekend dragged by, but when she hadn't heard from Trick by Monday, Gaby tried to get on with her life as it had been before he'd sauntered into it. Before she knew what it was like to be pinned down by his thinking-of-sex gaze or receive one of his knowing smiles.

It was for the best, she told herself, that it hadn't gone any further than a bit of flirtation. She'd just avoid The Wave for the rest of time, lest she accidentally see him hooking up with someone more his speed.

Or so she told herself over and over again, but none of it rang true.

At her midday break, she called Lila.

"Okay, I need to ask you an embarrassing question."

Lila laughed. "Is it awful that I'm glad you're bringing this up again, because I couldn't be nosy?"

"Yes, that's terrible," Gaby teased. "No. Okay, so the guy..." She spilled the whole story, from the boots, to the beach, to the repeated meetings at the shawarma house. "And now he's missing. I was hoping you might…"

"You know way more about him than I do." Lila sighed. "I do know a few guys in the Navy, though, I can ask around."

"Thank you. If he's just dodging me…maybe tell me he's been transferred to Alaska."

Lila must have been able to hear the tremor of doubt in Gaby's voice. "Oh, honey, I'm sorry."

"Is it weird that I want to make sure he's okay?"

"No, not weird, but…maybe a bit…what's the opposite of cynical?"

"Oh, shush. I'm not being naive." Gaby sighed.

"I didn't say that."

"No, I did. I'm trying to convince myself."

All afternoon Gaby had to force herself not to look at her phone. *Do your job, don't worry about that which you can't control.*

But after releasing the last of her charges to their parents, she kicked herself when she checked her purse and saw six unread messages.

Her heart in her throat, she swiped in and starting reading.

The first one was from Lila, something about good news, but she skipped right over it because the next three were from Trick.

Her thumb shook as she pressed on the bright screen, the pause before his messages expanded and filled the screen feeling like a lifetime.

Sorry about the radio silence, pretty girl. Got a bit busy.

What are you doing next Saturday? I'll be back tomorrow night.

And nothing can keep me away from a date with you, if that wasn't clear. Sorry, I'm a bit loopy. This is Trick.

She read the three messages over and over again, smiling so big her cheeks hurt. She didn't pick up on what he wasn't saying until the third read-through, and then she slowly sat down at her desk, her hands shaking from a completely different kind of fear.

Why was he loopy? And what had he been busy with?

She clicked on his name and pressed the call button.

He picked up on the second ring. "Hey, Gaby."

His voice sounded strained, and her heart ached. "I just got your text messages. Are you okay?"

"I'm a bit banged up, but I'll be home tomorrow."

"Where are you?"

He laughed, then wheezed. "You haven't been given the girlfriend briefing yet. You can't ask me that."

They hadn't even had a date yet—although maybe shawarma counted—and if he was hurt he was probably on narcotic pain meds, but he'd just said girlfriend. Relating to *her*. Her smile popped back into play, despite her worry. "Okay. But you're coming home?"

"I sure am." In the background someone started talking to him, and he muffled the phone receiver. "Gaby? I gotta go."

———

Trick reluctantly hung up the phone and turned his weary head toward Nathan Meyers and the military doc at the foot of his bed. He'd been there for almost an entire day, having narrowly avoided surgery on his arm. The mission had been a success, except for the part where Trick got into hand-to-hand combat with an irate pirate and came out of it with two fractures in his forearm.

At least he wasn't the other guy, broken everywhere else.

Meyers coughed and held up Trick's duffle bag—someone else had brought his ID and cell phone, but nobody had thought of clean underwear until now. "I brought you some clothes. Ready to get back on a plane?"

The doctor made noises about waiting another day to let his arm set while Meyers just grinned and nodded, knowing what Trick was going to say.

"Absolutely, brother. Let me get my gitch on and we can blow this pop stand." He made an apologetic face. "No offense, doc."

"None taken. You special forces guys are always a pain in my ass anyway." The physician signed something on a form and handed it over. "Here are your discharge papers. See an orthopedic surgeon next week."

"I'll wait outside," Meyers said, following the other man into the hall.

Trick knew he could have asked for a nurse to come in and help him—hell, one would probably come bustling in any minute, annoyed that he was yanking his boxers and pants on by himself.

But relying on others had never been his strong suit.

He was awkwardly stuffing his prescription bottles into the duffle bag with his left hand when his phone beeped with a message from Gaby.

You don't sound loopy. You sound like you need a hug.

Jesus, he needed more than a hug from her. Even medicated, his dick stirred at the thought of Gaby playing nurse for him. She could help him with his pants. Help him take them off.

That sounds perfect, he responded.

Her last message was before he boarded the plane, wishing him sweet dreams.

A hug. Sweet dreams. All her awkward nerves. He probably had no right to pursue her. Everything about her screamed Good Girl and Fragile. Everything except the look in her eyes—that was pure steel. And damn it, he wanted that hug, and those sweet dreams.

They'd have to have a talk…soon. After some kissing.

Six hours later, they landed in San Diego. The commanding officer of the team was waiting for them, and he praised Trick for coming back with the group. Like there'd even been a question of it. Even with his busted arm, he wanted no part of a cushy commercial flight.

As soon as they'd finished the pleasantries, they were swept into another debrief. They'd achieved their mission objectives: the sensitive target was rescued along with the others, maintaining his cover. Some pirates had died. Others had been secured and would be dealt with by border officials in Honolulu.

And Trick was seen, yet again, by medical staff, this time for a brief psych eval, with the same psychologist he'd seen when he came back from Iraq.

She nodded at his arm. "I won't keep you long. That must hurt."

"I've had worse." That was the thing with breaks, and she'd

know it—once stabilized and casted, it was really just inflammation that caused discomfort. Another day or two, and he'd be right as rain.

"How'd you feel being on a mission?"

"Come on, doc. You know that was a routine thing, as was this." He lifted his arm gingerly. "I'm fine. I was cleared for active duty."

"But we decided you shouldn't head back to Iraq. I just wanted to check in and make sure this wasn't a mistake."

He leaned forward and stared her straight in the eye. "I'm tired as fuck and need my bed. That normal enough for you?"

She laughed and held out an appointment card. "As long as we can have a longer talk next week?"

"Fair deal. See you then."

Meyers was waiting in the anteroom, and Trick just shrugged. They didn't talk until they were settled in the other man's pickup truck. Trick would have to come back for his SUV in the morning, but he wasn't stupid enough to fight about it now. He'd let Gibs mother-hen him a bit. Make the old man feel better.

"What are you thinking about?"

"How old you are?"

Meyers snorted. There were only two years separating them. "You're staring thirty in the face. Don't mock. Besides…chicks dig older guys. And scars. Chicks really dig scars. So any day now you'll start doing okay."

"Yeah?" Trick smirked and closed his eyes. God, he was so tired. And he only wanted one chick to dig him right now. "What time is it?"

"Almost four in the morning."

"Damn." And his phone was dead, anyway. He'd charge it and text her when he woke up. Yeah. Tomorrow…

The next thing he knew, Meyers was opening the passenger-side door and thumping him on his knee. "You need help up the stairs, there, *old man*?"

"Shut up." Trick grabbed his bag with his left hand and hoisted it over his shoulder. 'Thanks, man."

They just stared at each other for a second. They both knew Trick was thanking him more for the mission and not making a big deal about the injury, than for the ride home, but whatever. It was all good.

"Yeah. 'Kay, get some sleep, brother."

Trick let himself into his too-quiet apartment, plugged his phone in, took a painkiller, and lay down. His cast bumped his hip as he reached for his cock, and he cursed at the pain and the frustration—no jacking off while there was fucking plaster wrapped around his palm. Maybe he could cut the cast off in a couple of days.

He twisted onto his belly, carefully resting his hand on his pillow, and drifted into an uneasy sleep, wishing he had a slim, dark-haired beauty next to him.

CHAPTER
SIX

GABY KNEW she didn't have it in her to focus on anything other than when the next text message would come from Trick—where was he, *how* was he, and when the hell could she see him? So she tossed her lesson plan for the day and set up Lego and craft stations instead.

None of the kids complained.

Her principal might, if it was a regular occurrence, but Gaby could allow herself one day of worried distraction. All she could think about was Trick and the obviously not-your-regular-Navy job he had.

Not long before the dismissal bell, it dawned on her that he was probably a SEAL.

The thought made her feel kind of faint and silly for not figuring it out sooner.

He *looked* like a Navy SEAL, with his occasional scruff and slightly-longer-than-military-standard haircut. The bad-ass muscles and super-cool attitude. The way he literally ran circles around a bunch of other sailors.

The muscles.

She'd never thought of herself as being particularly affected by the male physique, but thinking about Trick's body—imagining what he looked like without a t-shirt stretched across his broad shoulders, or those jeans that cupped everything just so—that did it for her in a big way. Sitting alone in her classroom as the late afternoon sun slid through the windows, telling her to go home, she only wanted to go and find him instead. Wrap herself around him and touch him all over.

When her phone beeped, she jumped two feet in the air.

And when she saw his name on the screen, she squealed out loud without shame. His message was even better. **So, about that date…how does pizza and a movie at my place on Saturday night sound?**

It sounded like a set up for making out. She grinned. **Are you back?**

Yep.

Yep. She stared at the word, so casual on the screen. She didn't know exactly what they were doing, but she didn't want to wait until the weekend to do it. **Any reason we need to hold off until Saturday?**

You free tonight? I should warn you, I'm a bit banged up.

Right. Maybe she shouldn't leap straight to hanky-panky. Except…casual. An uncharacteristically flirty response sprang to her fingertips. **I'll bring Band-Aids.**

He fired a response back so quickly she felt a little thrill of pride at getting it right. **You've been reading my mind.**

Two hours later, after doing some shopping and going home to shower and shave her legs, she was pulling up to an apartment building a few blocks closer to the base than her place. On her passenger seat was a six-pack of beer, another of root beer in case he couldn't drink, and a box of Band-Aids to break the ice.

She climbed the exterior set of stairs to the second floor and found his apartment in the corner. He opened the door a split-second after her first knock, so her second froze in midair.

"I saw you park," he said with a blinding smile, so bright and happy she almost didn't notice the cast on his forearm.

Almost. She took a step toward him, then froze, because she didn't want to touch him lest it hurt. "Oh my God, Trick!"

"I warned you I was banged up." He shrugged and nodded his head into the apartment. "I'm fine. Come in."

He didn't move as she stepped out of the doorway and into his space, which meant she brushed against his chest. He let out a barely audible grunt.

She dropped her bags against the wall and turned carefully in the shadow of his bulkier form, tipping her face up to catch his gaze. "Just how banged up are you?"

"Some bruised ribs. The arm. Maybe a concussion." He said it with complete ease, like all of that was possibly routine for him. And none of it was as important as the two of them, standing so close they were almost touching.

"And there are rules where I can't ask you questions like what and who and why?"

One side of his mouth curled up in a wry smile. "The last one's always the same answer, pretty girl."

She swallowed hard. "What are you, some kind of superhero?"

"Nah, I'm just a guy who sometimes kicks ass for Uncle Sam."

"Okay," she whispered. "So…just so you know, that's superhero material in my book."

———

He'd meant to take it slow, but Gaby was staring up at him, eyes wide and shiny pink lips parted. She'd called him a superhero, and he wasn't, but after all the wariness and doubt because he'd slept with the wrong person at the wrong time, this felt like a moment he should grab with both hands. He should haul her against him and finally confirm that their chemistry was as off-the-charts as he suspected before she remembered he was just a regular man. An imperfect man.

Before he could do that, or greet her properly in any of the dozens of ways he'd imagined, she stepped back, breaking the spell. "Anyway. Hi. Welcome back."

She looked nervously at his cast—fucking thing, messing up his chance to get the girl.

"Hi." He reached out with his left hand, offering it to her. "I think you promised me a hug, remember?"

She exhaled, a sigh of relief maybe, and nerves too, as she closed the gap between them, twining her fingers around his. She hovered in front of him, holding her slight body an inch short of where he wanted it—plastered against him. He squeezed her hand, then lifted their hands and showed her she could touch his chest.

Like magic, her touch spread warmth through his shirt and deep into his body. He left her palm there and slid his hand to her hip, pulling her tight to his left side. No bruising there. "Hi," he whispered again, this time into her hair, and she smiled against his chest, her cheek pressing into his shirt. He wanted to feel that smile against his bare skin, but that couldn't happen until he no longer looked like he'd gone ten rounds with a Sumo wrestler.

Because he'd nearly gone ten rounds with a Sumo wrestler, pirate-style. He sighed, ignoring the aching twinge in his right side. "See? Nice. And man, did I need that."

She laughed gently. "I find that hard to believe, but yeah. Nice."

"Can I get you something to drink? Show you the place?"

"I brought some beer. And root beer, if you can't…"

"Oh, I can. Pretty much all I can't do at the moment is—" *Jerk off.* Right, he couldn't say that. He cleared his throat. "Push-ups. Bit of a challenge."

That was a lie. He could do a couple of one-handed push-ups on his left hand. Only a couple, and it would kill the ribs, but if she wanted him to…

She froze against his chest, then laughed again, this time deeper. Throatier. Jesus. Of all the sounds he'd heard Gaby make, *that* was by far the hottest. And when she glanced up at him, her tongue resting on her lower lip, all wet and shiny and *pink*… He had the feeling she knew what he'd been about to say anyway.

That feeling was more than confirmed when she drop a long, lingering look at his right hand and sighed. *Sighed*, like a sound of longing and unsatisfied desire.

"Yeah, I bet that'll suck, not being able to do…push-ups…for a few weeks. That's how long casts are on, right?"

"Usually." His damn voice caught in his throat, rough and scratchy, and suddenly his hallway was too small and lacking a soft surface for them to stretch out on. Get naked on.

Naked wasn't an option. *Bruises, dude. Ugly, scary, lady-boner-killing bruises.*

He wouldn't have thought Gaby was a lady-boner type of woman, not until that throaty laugh and her slow, deliberate tease about his masturbation problems.

Now he wasn't sure he had any clue what kind of woman Gaby was.

But he wanted to know. He wanted to know every single layer of her interesting self.

She spared him the embarrassment of continually forgetting to be a good host and turned, picking up her grocery bags. "Kitchen that way?" she asked as she headed into his living space.

She unpacked the drinks, leaving two beers on the counter and putting the rest in the fridge.

Then she held up a box of Band-Aids. "As promised…"

He laughed, which hurt, but damn, it felt good, too. "I totally wanted you to play nurse, too."

A secret smile curled up the corners of her mouth. "You said something about that." She opened the first bottle and held it out to him. "Here. Your medicine."

"I was hoping for a kiss." The truth ripped from his lips. "You know. Boo-boos and all that."

Her eyebrows shot up, but the smile stayed in place. "Any particular place?"

Damn damn damn. His cock thumped against the zipper in his jeans, claiming mortal injury, but he knew better. "My lips are awfully sore."

She opened her own beer and stepped closer, staying on his left side this time but not holding back. Good.

But she stopped again, like she'd forgotten something for a minute but her memories had thundered back into place. Trick was no relationship rocket scientist, but he'd felt these walls come up before. He knew what she was thinking about now—the last woman he'd kissed. He could honestly say he didn't really remember kissing her roommate. He remembered some things about their brief night together, but none of those fuzzy memories held a candle to holding Gaby close.

He wasn't giving that up. He'd dial it back and keep it light, but she'd gotten under his skin, and eventually he'd find a way to show her she was the only woman on his mind or anywhere near his lips.

"Maybe we should go sit," she said quietly.

"Really?" He said it warm and soft, but he said it. A little challenge because he couldn't help himself.

"I don't know," she whispered.

He cleared his throat and put on his best approximation of a smirk. "Unless you don't like kissing."

She gave him an *oh-please* face. "Of course I like kissing. But..."

He let her trail off and gave her a minute to finish the thought. She didn't, and that made his growing need for her even stronger.

"I want to kiss you. Right now, actually," he said roughly. "And I'm pretty sure you want to kiss me, too."

She didn't say anything. A million thoughts were racing through her head—he could see them in her dilated pupils, the pulsing worry he was going to hurt her.

But they needed to kiss. He felt it in his bones, that if they could just get past this awkwardness about how they met, it would all be okay.

He took their beer bottles and set them on the counter, then lowered his head, so slowly it pained him, but she needed to have time. To process this, to say no. And even that wasn't good enough. He needed her to say yes, so he froze as his lips brushed hers.

"Can I taste you, Gaby?" She parted her lips against his, and that puff of hot hair made him want to stumble into the living room, fall onto the couch, and pull her down on top of him. Instead, he rubbed a knuckle along her jaw before sliding his fingers into her hair. "Please, pretty please." He smiled, but it didn't stick. He wanted this too much. He let his voice get even rougher. Nothing wrong with showing her how much he wanted her. "Tell me yes. Tell me you want this."

———

It's just a kiss. Lips were almost *for* sharing, public space where people tested out chemistry. No big risk. And her head was swimming with how he felt, and smelled, and tasted, right there, almost kissing her. Their chemistry practically demanded to be tested.

"I think I was supposed to be the one kissing you," she said, and as she moved her lips, she did just that. When she'd look back in hindsight, she might be able to say it was an accident, but maybe that was what needed to happen to push her off the ledge.

And then he was kissing her back. Softly at first, just a firm press of his lips against hers, which was tingle-inducing enough. His lips felt strong and capable of a million fantasy-satisfying things.

When the tip of his tongue traced the swell of her lower lip, that felt even better so she opened for him. He didn't dive in. No. He took his time, and if he wasn't injured, she'd have climbed him like a tree to have more of him inside her. His breath, his tongue, his taste.

No kiss had ever been this *drugging*. Sensations zinged through her body, from her puffy, hyper-aware lips to the tips of her toes and everywhere in between, like his mouth was coaxing her into an altered state.

He eased back, his tongue slicking against hers one last time before he put a few inches of space between their faces with a groan. "I could do that all night, but we should…"

"No. I mean, yes, let's do that all night," she said, her breath sliding out of her hard and fast. She could still feel that last swipe, could still taste him, and a warm, heavy ache had settled into her muscles.

Yep, Trick was definitely a drug.

"We've got all the time in the world, Gaby. How about we move to the couch?" He nodded his head toward the living room.

He hooked his fingers through hers and she followed, snagging their bottles with her other hand. It was possible she'd follow him anywhere. That kiss had knocked down all her defenses, leaving her malleable and soft, warm and wanting more.

"This is a nice place." Her compliment came out automatically, something one should say on a first visit, but it was nice—bigger than she expected, clean and bright.

"I share it with a roommate, but he's away right now." Trick pointed to the west-facing glass doors that led to a decent-sized balcony. "Not a bad place to watch the sunset."

"I'll have to come over earlier next time." Dusk was rapidly setting in outside.

He grinned as he settled in the corner of the couch, his right arm carefully resting on the padded arm, his left arm stretching along the back. "Next time? I like the sound of that. Come here and tell me more about how you might come back."

She joined him on the couch. He was sitting on an angle, leaving just a narrow space between him and the back of the couch. It looked just her size. But if she plastered herself against him, they'd kiss again, and if they did that—while practically lying down—they wouldn't do anything else.

Like talk.

So instead of crawling right up against him, she sat on the middle cushion, curling her legs beneath her. Her hands rested casually on her knees, close enough to his knees that his jeans rubbed against the backs of her fingers as he shifted in place.

The lightest scratch of denim on her hand, and her nipples tightened up.

She was such a goner.

———

Trick watched as Gaby took a deep breath. "Why are you surprised that I say next time?"

"Hey, I didn't say I was surprised. I'm pleased that you'd be willing to put up with my company again." He let himself look at her mouth for a minute. Kissing her had been amazing. Stopping had been a challenge. He thought he'd given her a clear invitation to cuddle and kiss more, but she was sitting just out of tugging range.

God, he wanted to tug her—right into his lap. Onto his cock, if he was being honest, but he wasn't sure she'd appreciate that kind of callousness.

"Can I be honest with you, Trick?" Her voice dragged his attention out of the gutter and back to where it belonged. She was looking at him warmly, but her voice carried a touch of worry.

He nodded. There was a lot that remained unspoken between them, and it wouldn't do them any good to run scared of a bit of talking. "Of course."

"I'm the one who's surprised." She shrugged with a little smile. It looked self-deprecating, and he didn't like that. "I mean, I get that you're interested—and believe me, I like that. A lot. But I don't really get why."

"I can't stop thinking about you," he said immediately. Easily. It was true. "You're pretty and stubborn and you've got this beautiful fire in your eyes."

"Thank you," she whispered, leaning her head against the back of the couch. He liked that she didn't deny his thoughts on her value. She closed her eyes and took another deep breath. "The thing is… you're not like anyone I've dated before. And I think I'm not like anyone you've dated, but maybe I'm wrong. I don't know. This just feels…"

She wasn't wrong, but not for the reasons he suspected were on her mind. "Can I stop you there and say something that might bite me in the ass?"

She laughed. "Sure."

"This does feel different. Because it is, at least for me. It's not that you're unlike other women that I've dated…it's that I don't really date."

The laughter fell off her face. "Oh."

"I mean, I want to date *you*. That's different and new for me. But I do…I don't know what kind of boyfriend I might be—probably shitty, because I'm away a lot—but if you're willing to come back and see the sunset, and then maybe go out for brunch or something like that. Maybe we'll find that a few dates turn into dating. And I think I'd like that—with you—a lot."

"Wow." She smiled. "Okay, that was good."

She narrowed her eyes in thought and pulled the corner of her lower lip between her teeth, her hair falling over the side of her face as she tilted her head to the side. An interesting current of energy was radiating off her—like she was bursting with a million questions, but didn't know which she could ask. Hell, he'd told her most of them were off-limits. No wonder she was confused and holding back.

"Maybe we should play twenty questions." Shit, that's not what he meant. She laughed as he felt himself flushing with unexpected embarrassment. The idea of being stupid in Gaby's eyes bugged him more than he expected. "No, not the *guess the dead president with yes/no questions* kind of game. Just…"

"Learn more about each other?" Her eyes lit up at the suggestion and his feeling of being off-balance faded. "I'd like that."

"Yeah." They shared a smile, and when she leaned in, he met her halfway, kissing her softly. "Start with an easy one. What do you like on your pizza?"

"Practical, too." She laughed. "Mushrooms. Pepperoni. No green peppers. Could go either way on olives or onions."

"Love onions. Meh on olives. Can we toss spicy sausage and tomatoes on there, too?"

Once they agreed on their order, he called it in, then he circled her wrist with his fingers. "I want you closer, is that okay?"

She nodded, and he finally tugged her into the crook of his arm. They had a lot of questions to get through before their dinner arrived. "Favorite movie?"

CHAPTER
SEVEN

GABY WALKED the five blocks to Orange Ave, hoping the fresh air would calm her nerves. This was her third date with Trick and the first that might end up being an entire day.

If he wanted to spend the entire day with her—which she was pretty sure he did.

After their pizza and a movie on Tuesday night, she'd reluctantly said good night, promising to come back the next night. But Trick ended up spending Wednesday night at the base for reasons he wouldn't elaborate on—and she'd never push. Then she'd taught her third last class on Thursday, and the pre-exam questions had gone on forever afterward. So last night had been date number two.

Maybe it was because it had been a Friday night, or her expectations had been unfairly set by the magic of their first date, but something had been missing. A wow factor, and it wasn't one-sided—Trick could never disappoint her. But she worried that their second date had been…just nice. Which was totally unfair, because Trick had seemed tired during dinner, so *she'd* suggested they cut it short. And when he drove her home, she'd insisted on saying goodnight in his SUV.

She wasn't ready for him to walk her up to her door or come

inside. He'd already been in her apartment once, and that niggled, despite the fact that she *knew* it shouldn't.

But even before that, dinner had been quiet and their conversation limited. Trick talked about work in the vaguest of terms, and she'd thought to herself that it was kind of crazy he didn't get the week off to recuperate, but something told her that was his choice.

It would take time before they could talk more freely. And any expectations were too many in a week when he was recovering from a physical injury and she was swamped with the end of term.

Flicking her hair over her shoulder, she shook off the strange feeling from the night before.

It was a gorgeous spring day, and she was meeting a boy who liked her at her favorite place. A book store.

Bay Books had been Trick's suggestion, and she'd leapt at it. They'd go from there to brunch. She was wearing a dress and pretty underwear, just in case.

This was going to be a good date. She just knew it.

She found him in the military history section. He was wearing cargo pants, snug through his narrow hips and looser through the legs, and a fitted black t-shirt that stretched around his biceps and over his broad shoulders. He was leaning forward, his cast resting on a shelf above his head as he read a hardcover book. She paused at the foot of the aisle, taking a minute to absorb how the sight of him made her heart skip a beat. A few beats, actually.

He smiled slightly as she approached, even though he hadn't looked her way. "Hey, pretty girl."

"How did you know it was me?"

He tipped his face to meet her gaze, his smile spreading slow as molasses across his face. "Keen observational skills. Well-honed peripheral vision." He set the book aside and cupped the back of her neck, pulling her close so his next words were for her ears only. "And you wear the sexiest perfume."

He brushed a soft kiss across her lips. "Did you want to look around a bit?"

"Yeah. You want to stay here?"

With his casted arm, he not-so-clumsily picked up the book he'd been looking at. "I'm good. I'll bring this. You show me what you like to read."

"You sure?"

He squeezed the back of her neck. "Come here." This kiss was longer, harder, and bordered on inappropriate for a book store. She loved it. "Never think that I'd rather do my thing than your thing. 'Kay? If I want to do something, I'll tell you. And I'll find a way to make it good for both of us."

Jeez. Gaby shivered, and he laughed quietly, tipping his forehead against hers.

"I didn't mean for that to sound dirty."

"It did, though." The honest reaction slipped from her without a second thought. He'd had that kind of effect on her earlier in the week, and it had mostly been missing the night before. She grinned up at him. "And I liked it."

He wrapped his left arm around her waist and she pointed toward a stack of thriller novels.

Brunch was more of the same, little touches that felt like sparks on tinder. Looks that made her all hot and bothered, and she was pretty sure Trick was just being Trick.

When he leaned back and stretched his ridiculously long arm across the back of the chair to the left of him, and his leg stole under the table and rubbed against hers, rough cotton on bare skin, she gave him a warm glare.

"What?" he asked with a smirk.

"I think you know what." She licked her lips. "What do you want to do next?"

He didn't answer, just looked at her with sex in his eyes. If she was anyone else, she knew his answer would be something straight to the point. *You, baby.* But she'd thrown up enough roadblocks that he might not say that.

Did she want him to? *You, baby.* She imagined his eyelids dropping, the words rolling off his tongue. His mouth following that bold statement with a searing kiss and his hands...everywhere.

She was totally in over her head.

His smirk faded into a softer, more genuine smile. "How about we head back to your place?"

Not quite as explicit as she'd expected, but there it was…the next step. And she was totally going to bungle it up.

So much for her perfect date. Maybe she was the problem.

Maybe? There's no maybe about it.

With a sigh, he reached across the table and laced his fingers through hers. "Okay, the beach? Want to drive into the foothills?"

"Sure. Let's go for a drive, maybe."

Trick paid the bill, letting Gaby protest for a minute that they should split it before silencing her with a kiss. In the moment when his lips were on hers, his hand in the small of her back, almost palming her ass, it all felt right.

She needed to find a way to hang on to that feeling between embraces, because as they drove off the island and through the city, his hand constantly on her knee or around her fingers, a sweet, comfortable contentment settled in her chest. And another feeling—less sweet, more dirty, and a whole lot hotter—started to burn lower in her belly.

They parked at a canyon preserve that allowed for public hiking, and, hands entwined, they climbed the easy path to the first lookout. They were alone, as far as Gaby could tell, and Trick must have come to the same conclusion. No sooner had he wrapped his arms around her waist as they looked at the vista spread below them than he was nuzzling her neck, obviously more interested in something other than scenery.

That made two of them. His left hand was wrapped around her rib cage, his thumb so close to the bottom of her breast she thought she go crazy if he didn't shift it—up, preferably, but if not up, then down, because she couldn't think like this. Except down would be toward the hem of her dress, inching up with each nuzzle as the light fabric twisted between them. And underneath, she just had on the skimpy lace she'd worn for him—worn on purpose, and she wanted him more than she'd ever wanted anyone, ever.

But the warm fuzzies that filled her when they kissed and held hands faded to a black-and-white movie of Trick stroking his hands over Lila's body. His hands cupping Lila's breasts as he moved closer to cupping Gaby's. She wanted him, but the closer they got to being intimate, the bigger that icky feeling got.

She stiffened in his arms and he softened his grip.

"Sorry," he whispered, shifting his hips away from her bottom. She'd felt his erection, just for a second, and as he slipped back into the safe zone she'd established, hot, prickly frustration took over.

He had nothing to apologize for. This was ridiculous. She was being ridiculous, but she also couldn't help how she felt.

"It's not…" She turned in his arms. "I like you so much, Trick. You're…amazing. But—"

"But nothing." He cut her off, his brows pulling tight. "Don't say it. I'm just going to argue, and that's no way to spend a date."

"You don't know what I'm going to say."

"I can guess." He ran his fingertips over her cheekbone, then down her jaw, ending at her chin, where he held her face firmly in place as he brought his own close enough she could see the flecks in his eyes. "It's okay if you need more time."

"Stop saying the right things. That just makes this that much harder."

"This?" His voice thickened, the word coming out bigger than it should, but he didn't yell it. If anything, he was the opposite of angry. He sounded…hurt. But his eyes blazed. "Would it be so easy for you to shove me away?"

"I said it's hard," she whispered, hating how awful she felt. This felt wrong, on all levels, but she couldn't relax, either.

"Do you want me to take you home?"

"No." She should say more. Apologize and make it better, but she didn't know how.

They stared at each other for a minute, then he ducked his head and kissed her lightly. Chastely, and it felt all kinds of wrong.

"Come on, there's another lookout a little further on that's pretty cool." He slid his hand to the middle of her back and steered them back onto the path.

The rest of the date was more of the same—PG-13 touches and

warm smiles, but no more dangerously heated gazes, and his hands stayed safely away from all erogenous zones.

As they headed back to the city, Trick glanced at her a few times, his gaze hooded and unreadable. His hand found hers and he covered her fingers with his, a heavy, welcome pressure.

When he finally cleared his throat, the question that broke the silence surprised her. "How about Italian for dinner?"

"You want to go out for dinner?" It was a stupid question. He'd just asked her to do exactly that. But she'd run hot and cold, and even though he said he understood, she didn't really get how he could.

"No," he said with a quiet intensity that rippled through her. "I want to get takeout and eat naked in bed with you. But yeah, if that's not on the table, I want to take you out to a restaurant. Then maybe go to the beach after and make out."

"But what I said earlier…"

"Would time make a difference?" He said it so gently, so full of understanding that her eyes filled with tears, and she twisted to stare out the passenger-side window. "The thing is, pretty girl, I don't need time. You're the only person I see, the only person I want to hold."

Damned if that didn't just make her cry harder. "I'm sorry."

"Don't be sorry. But don't shut us down before we have a chance to see what this is between us."

She swiped her hand under her eyes furiously.

"Do you want to go home before dinner?" he asked quietly.

She shook her head.

"Can I take you back to my place? We can hang out and watch some TV."

"Sure."

It just took a few more minutes to get to his apartment complex. After parking, he came around to her side of the car, and as she stepped down to the ground, he said something under his breath and pulled her—gently—against his body.

It started as a hug, but it didn't take long for Trick to slide his hands into her hair and tip her face back so he could kiss her.

"Sorry," he whispered against her lips, and she shook her head. God, he had nothing to be sorry for. She'd ruined everything. He pressed his mouth hard to hers, making her whimper and he jerked away, but she looped her arms around his neck and pulled him back in.

After another frustrating, ache-inducing kiss, he rested his chin against the side of her head.

"I'm the one who needs to be sorry, Trick," she said quietly.

He kissed her neck, then her chin, then slowly spun her around and pointed her toward the wide exterior staircase and fell into step beside her. "Do you want me to keep kissing you?"

She took a deep breath. Just the thought of kissing made her feel better. "Yes. But—"

He grinned. "No buts. Like kissing you is a hardship or something—it's not. Consider me a willing sacrificial lamb, laying myself on the altar of your lips. We don't need to do anything you don't want."

"I didn't say I don't *want* to, I just don't think I can."

"Okay." He shook his head at her as they hit the landing on his floor.

She stopped abruptly, but he kept going. She had to lift her voice and hustle to catch up at the same time. "It's not okay for you, though."

———

She was crazy. Beautiful, sweet, and more kissable than any woman Trick had ever known, but on this point, he was starting to think she was bat-shit insane.

He laughed, as gently as possible, but he couldn't help the reaction as she trundled toward him. He opened his apartment door and ushered her inside. Her skirt swished over her bare legs and she smelled like sunshine.

Crazy sunshine.

He crossed his arms and leaned against the wall. "You think I need to have sex to survive?"

She pressed her lips together, then sighed, rolling her eyes. "Of course not. That would be ridiculous."

"My point exactly."

"But…" She trailed off.

"But what? Come on. Spit it out. Might as well put all our cards on the table."

She started pacing, traveling the length of the room three times before stopping and staring out the window. "Is this the longest you've gone without sex?"

Easy answer. "No."

She stopped and stared at him, her pretty brown eyes all too knowing. "The longest you've gone without sex while on American soil?"

Damn. "Yes."

He held her gaze until she broke the connection. He was laying himself bare. She needed to get over this hang-up.

"Trick…" She shook her head. "I'm not the girl for you. Go find someone else."

"You don't want me to do that."

She dropped her gaze to the floor, but not before he saw the flash of pain. No, she didn't. But she still didn't want to want him for herself, either.

"I don't know what to say to make this better, but there has to be something."

"You can't make it better. You had sex with Lila. I can't ever get that visual out of my head. I thought I was more mature, that it was no big deal. I was wrong."

"I've had sex with a lot of women, Gaby." She flinched, but he kept going. "And with full respect to your roommate, she just happened to be the last one. She wasn't the most memorable, or the best. I don't say that to disparage her, but to put what I did with her in some context for you."

She pressed her lips together, maybe to keep from saying something she'd regret. *Girls are crazy.* He'd heard guys say that shit all the time, but he'd never experienced this overwhelming emotion aimed at him before. Now he got it, at least in part. She had a lot of feelings: desire, jealousy, frustration. Probably more girl feelings that he wouldn't even be able to name. He couldn't identify with that, but suddenly *crazy* felt like the wrong word. Complicated, sure. Messy, definitely. Crazy, complicated, messy…however he named it, *it* didn't make him like her any less—hell, it was probably the first time that anyone had cared enough about him to be jealous.

But she already had more of him than anyone else ever had. He just needed to find a way to show her that.

CHAPTER EIGHT

THE FEELINGS inside Gaby couldn't be named with words she recognized—they were too sharp and ugly. She didn't like them. She wanted them to go away. But if she opened her mouth, they'd spill out in ways she couldn't predict. And Trick just kept going, pushing and poking and making the feelings bigger. Meaner.

"The best was this girl in high school. Do you hate her, too?"

"I don't hate Lila," she snapped. "At all. I wish I could be more relaxed like you guys about this. I know I'm a prude, okay? I know that I'm jealous and that's totally unfair because we don't have a relationship. I get in my *head* that it's just things people do with their bodies, but in my *heart*…those things are a big deal. I've only had sex with four guys, and I've thought that maybe I was in love with each of them."

Dark thunder clouds gathered across Trick's face. "First of all, we *do* have a relationship. We've had four amazing dates—"

"Three dates," she whispered, unable to hold herself back from correcting him.

"You're forgetting shawarma."

"Oh."

"And maybe last night wasn't amazing, but I was tired and my arm hurt. I'm sorry about that." He rubbed his chest.

"Are you okay?" She took a tentative step in his direction but stopped when he pinned her with a glare.

"I'm fine. You've been in love with four people?"

"Well, I *thought* I might love them."

"That's hard to compete with."

"It's not a competition." She took another slow step.

He sighed and closed his eyes. "It should be. I'm not a forever kind of guy."

"Wait, so you…what? Tell me all that stuff about other women and then just change your mind? I'm not worth it?"

"Oh for fuck's sake, Gaby!" Trick didn't yell, exactly, but he wasn't calm any longer. "You're worth the fucking moon. But if you only have relationships with guys you can see yourself sharing a white picket fence with, then I can't lead you on."

"I don't think you're that guy, Trick!" She did yell, pretty much, but calm wasn't really her forte at the best of times. She was grumpy and mercurial and hadn't been trained by the US Navy to be cool under pressure. She was toast under pressure. "I was trying to work my way up to just having a fling with you, okay?"

"A fling." He glowered at her and crossed his arms. How the hell was she supposed to understand that body language? It told her nothing.

"Like I said, I want to be more relaxed. But up in the hills today… it was too emotional." She brought her fingers to her lips and held them there for a minute. "When you kiss me…I haven't figured out how to disengage my heart from the experience yet."

He moved closer, staring at her. "I don't want you to."

"But you're not a picket fence kind of guy," she whispered.

"Yeah." A muscle twitched along his jaw. "We've got ourselves in a real pickle."

"So…."

He exhaled. "So let's get some dinner? This sounds like a problem for not right now."

Not right now, no. But soon. She nodded and he pulled a takeout menu off the fridge, giving her the option of going out or staying in.

Was there even a question?

"What do you recommend from this place?" she asked, snatching the menu.

"They have a really nice butternut squash ravioli," he said after a minute, smiling with amusement.

"Uh-huh. What about in the red meat category?"

"Their ragu with polenta is awesome."

"Sold. Do you have red wine or should we pick some up on our way to grab the food?"

"We should pick some up." He took the menu when she thrust it back at him, and eyed her warily as he dialed the number for the restaurant. "You okay?"

She shrugged. "Like you say…this is a problem for not right now."

———

They walked the long way to the restaurant and then stopped to pick up wine and a cantaloupe at the grocery store on the way back. Trick let her carry the bag of food once he had the second bag to juggle, but when they got back and she sat down to take off her sandals—sturdy, but still heels—he dropped to his knees in front of her.

"Damn, I forgot you were wearing these things. I should have realized how much walking we'd do."

"I stand on my feet all day long. It's fine." She sighed as he squeezed first one calf muscle, then the other, and then she smiled. "But thank you for the concern."

He took her ankle in his hands—sort of. He really braced it on his cast, and worked at the strap with his left hand.

"I can probably do that just as easily," she said half-heartedly, but he ignored her and she gave in. There was something quietly lovely about Trick taking off her shoes.

He ran his thumbs over the red impressions on her skin where the straps had left their mark, then stroked up her calf. His fingers awakened a million nerve endings on their slow path to the sensitive skin behind her knee, where he stopped.

"We should eat," he said quietly, but his hand stayed on her leg.

She leaned forward and brushed her fingers through his hair.

"What I said earlier—" He cut himself off. "I'm a bit out of my depth here, Gaby."

"Can I babble at you, then?" She smoothed her hand over his cheek as he gave her a go ahead nod. "This is weird for me, too. I think some of my freakout was about the intensity. You were hurt, and I needed to see you, then we talked every day, and had two back-to-back dates. It felt like…" It felt like falling in love, or that early stages of over-eager lust that you hope might be love. But she didn't want to say that, because she was pretty sure she knew Trick wasn't the man to fall in love with. "Like we were burning too bright."

"I don't want to hurt you."

Damn. How come none of the marrying kind ever said anything like that? Not smooth or practiced, just honest.

"If that was too intense…" He pressed a kiss to her right knee. "Should we dial it back?"

"Pace ourselves?"

"Something like that." He cleared his throat. "I've got a bit of experience with the…relaxed dating, I think you called it."

She laughed. "I'm not sure it's called dating."

"I'm being polite." He resumed stroking the skin behind her knee, and she squirmed. How did that feel so good? "No strings, no expectations. That what you want?"

She bit her lip. Right now, she wanted him to keep touching her and to stop talking, but yeah… "I don't know about no strings. You already know I'm the jealous type."

He made a suspiciously growl-like sound. "No other people, no matter how slow we go."

"Okay." Twisting a bit in her seat, she gave him more of her leg. "But no expectations…I like that part. We see each other when it's convenient for both of us. Like once a week? And…maybe not too much talking in between." That one pained her, because she'd liked talking and texting to him over the past week, but it ratcheted up the expectations in her heart like crazy.

His gaze was unreadable as he looked up at her. "That relaxed enough for you?"

"Is it what you want?"

He dropped his eyes, looking at her lap, and suddenly she had a very good idea of what he wanted.

"I want you however I can have you, Gaby."

"I might still need time to wipe those images out of my head, of you and—"

"We won't sleep together, then." He cut her off, his voice firm. She read between the lines—he wanted to keep the conversation positive.

She nodded her agreement. "I like kissing. I'm not…opposed to fooling around." She found his gaze and held it, heat pulsing between them. Not opposed at all, maybe. "I know I'm giving mixed messages. It's just…"

"I think I understand."

"And sex isn't off the table. Just not now."

He let out a strangled laugh. She joined him, because it was absurd, this conversation.

"I'm sorry." He tickled that spot behind her knee, and she squealed. "Uncle!" She sighed. "I really am sorry. I told you, it's not that I don't want to. I just can't, not yet."

He squeezed her leg, then glided his hand down to her ankle before slowly dragging it back up to her knee again. A few more strokes like that, and she'd be game for anything, including sex, history be damned.

"I'm going to tell you something, and I hope it comes out right." His voice had taken on a rougher-than-usual quality. It was unbelievably sexy, and her heart rate picked up. "There are some things that I haven't done with many other people. One thing in particular, I can promise I didn't do with your roommate or any other casual hookup."

He pressed another kiss to her knee, and this time, he kept his head resting on her thigh.

"What…thing?" Her question came out breathlessly, and he

grinned up at her. He liked this, the sexy, playful banter. Well, duh. Anything was better than overly emo girl-drama.

"Do you trust me?"

She nodded without hesitation.

This time, his kiss was to the inside of her thigh.

"Oh. That thing."

He chuckled as he nudged her legs apart with his chin. "Want me to stop? Because I'm hungry for you, Gaby. If you're willing."

A shudder tore through her body. "Don't stop."

He hummed appreciatively and slid his left hand lazily up her leg, under her skirt and around her hip. He tugged her forward until her ass balanced right on the end of the chair, then kissed his way up the same path, shoving her skirt to her waist as he made his way to her lace-covered, soaking wet pussy. Not a word she'd usually use about her sex, but the way he was looking at it, that was the only vocabulary that fit.

Her pulse pounded in her ears as he kissed her mound, then her thighs, breathing in deeply like he'd just discovered how turned on she was. She never wanted to forget the low grunt that tore out of his throat as he brought his head to the apex of her thighs.

She closed her eyes and tipped her head back, but at the first hot, open-mouthed kiss to her sex, she jerked her gaze back to where his head burrowed between her legs. Mother of all that was holy, nothing had ever felt as good as Trick's tongue licking her through her panties. It was hot and wet and rough, even though he was going slowly. He used his tongue, wide and flat, to work the lace against her clit, and she couldn't help but roll her hips, meeting his mouth with eager little pulses as he worked her faster than she thought possible to the edge of an orgasm.

And then he stopped.

"No," she groaned.

"I'm just getting started, don't worry." He patted her hip, urging her up so he could slide her underwear out of the way.

This time, he took his sweet time, loving her with his mouth, sucking and kissing and tracing all the intimate terrain only a handful of people had ever seen—and none of them while she was perched on the edge of a kitchen chair.

She loved it.

Seriously, having Trick go down on her was better than a candy-coated Christmas. And when he slid one thick finger into her, then added another, stretching and stroking and filling her with a delicious ache, she promised herself that nothing—no drama, no jealousy, no insecurity—would get in the way of enjoying whatever this man had to offer her.

He was magical and perfect.

When she started to shake again, her core drew tight, her breaths grew more and more shallow. She tried to fight it, but with a puff of hot air against her clit, Trick promised her all the orgasms she wanted, and she was lost. She jerked hard against his face, grinding herself to the final peak, then slumped back as he carefully licked her all over, avoiding the most sensitive parts.

As if he knew she'd need a moment to process what they'd just done, he stayed on his knees, his cheek pressed against her thigh, until she patted him on the head. Then he surged to his feet, avoiding her gaze like he was afraid she'd shut him down. But that just gave her the advantage of surprise, so when he wrapped his arms around her, she went straight for his belt buckle.

"You don't need to," he muttered, although the straining erection behind his zipper sure begged to differ.

"I want to." And right there, standing next to his kitchen table, she slid her hand behind the thick elastic waistband of his boxer briefs and started jerking him off.

"I'm close," he said with a groan after shoving his pants low on his hips.

"Do you want me…" She moved to drop to her knees, but he shook his head and tightened his grasp around her waist. He held her close as she stroked him between their bodies, his forehead pressed tight to hers as they watched together. His cock was big— thick enough her fingers didn't fully circle around it, and wider at the base. Long, too, and it felt like he was getting longer as she spread the glistening drops of pre-come with her thumb, then used them to stroke him faster. He smelled like warm, sweet skin and her mouth watered, wondering what he tasted like, but that could wait for next time.

Maybe after dinner.

She tried to match his muttered instructions, barely whispered on heavy breaths. *Faster. Harder.* More grunts, the sounds intimate and special in the quiet between their bodies, and when he came, hot and wet in her hand, she was glad he'd kept her standing, because it felt like they'd just shared something more complicated than a blow job. He pulled off his shirt, wrapping her hand in it, then kissed her with such intensity it stole her breath and probably her heart at the same time.

Watch yourself, her head warned the rest of her body.

It was good they'd just figured out some ground rules for not getting carried away, because if that's what third base in his kitchen did to her soul, sex would permanently alter her at a cellular level.

Whether for good or bad still remained to be seen.

CHAPTER
NINE

TRICK BOUNDED up the stairs to his apartment. Six and a half days had passed since he'd seen Gaby, and she was due at his place any minute. He had a new fibreglass cast on his arm—shower friendly, so that gave him a million ideas for how to have almost-sex with his almost-girlfriend—and he had a fridge full of fresh food.

He got a lot of ribbing from the guys when he fessed up the reason he'd been grinning all week, but they were all jealous.

As they should be—Gaby was fan-fucking-tastic, although some the best reasons were a complete secret. Like how fucking dirty she could be. She'd made a hand job hotter than full-on sex, and then gave him another hard-on just by eating dinner.

Her sweet little pink tongue should be illegal.

She'd stayed late, but insisted on going home when she started yawning. They held hands all the way back to her place, and had a nut-achingly sweet series of kisses outside her building before a final whispered promise to see each other again in a week.

And now that day—and hopefully night—was here.

He'd changed his sheets, bought new shower gel and towels, even grabbed a new box of condoms so if they got that far, she'd see him unwrap an unopened box. He was way over-thinking everything. When she showed up, she'd probably want to go out and do something other than getting naked. There was an outdoor concert they could go to. Sitting on a blanket together…that would be nice.

Not naked nice, but still good. Great, even, because it would be with Gaby, who only wanted to see him once a week right now because anything more was too intense.

Jesus. *Not* seeing her was making all of *his* feelings burn brighter, that was for damn sure. He'd never done this much prep for a date.

He'd only been home for ten minutes when she announced her arrival with a polite triple knock.

Her shiny dark hair was pushed back from her face by a pair of sunglasses propped on top of her head. Dressed casually, she looked ready for summer in a pale blue v-neck t-shirt and jean shorts that showed off a nice amount of creamy thigh. She wore casual canvas flat shoes today, and he was struck by how adorably short she was without her heels.

"What?" She grinned at him as he pulled her in for a kiss in greeting, making her drop her oversized canvas bag in the process.

"You're short."

She shrugged. "True story."

"I like that you're short. I could put you in my pocket."

"Sounds squishy."

"Oh, I'll squish you." He nipped at her lower lip, then kissed her again, this time deeper and longer. Hotter. In his arms, Gaby softened and arched into him, rubbing her pelvis against his rapidly hardening cock. "It's good to see you again."

"Mmmm." She smiled against his mouth, then smacked her lips against his and wiggled out of his grasp. "So, what do you want to do? I brought a change of clothes in case this is too casual."

"It's perfect, come back here." He snagged her wrist with his right hand, now neatly wrapped in the least amount of casting possible, just an inch onto his hand from his wrist and up around his thumb. It still went all the way up his forearm, but he had a lot more mobility in his fingers.

"Whoa, what's this fancy thing?" she said softly, sliding her fingertips along the dark grey outer layer of his new cast. "That's different."

"They swapped it out when they did some follow-up x-rays. This one can go in the shower."

"Nice!"

"I mean, it could go in the shower right now…"

She laughed, then slowed her giggles to a breathy sigh when she caught his gaze. "Oh! Really…."

"Now, or later today."

She sucked in a stuttering inhale. "Yes. Definitely at some point today."

"Do you want to go out?"

"I don't know. Maybe?" She laughed. "I kind of want to watch TV and make out."

He groaned and lifted her into the air with his good arm, patting her ass when she wrapped her legs around his waist. "You're my dream woman, I swear. Your wish is my command."

They didn't even bother turning on the television. As soon as Trick settled on the couch, Gaby worked off his shirt, sighing as she stroked her hands over his shoulders and across his chest. When she dipped her head to lick the tendon up the side of his neck, her sunglasses fell off and he snatched them, tossing them gently onto the ottoman. One down, five or six pieces of Gaby decoration to go until she was naked.

He let his head fall back against the couch as she peppered his neck and jaw and mouth with kisses, wriggling in his lap until she found just the right spot to rock against him.

"You feel so good," he said roughly, cupping her ass in his hands.

"But I'm so short," she teased. "Pocket-sized."

"You don't think that's hot?" He skimmed his hand under her shirt and up her back. "You make me feel all big, bad protector."

"Isn't that an oxymoron?"

Hopefully she'd never truly understand just how much big and bad was truly involved with keeping her and everyone else safe. "Don't know. Can't think. Pretty girl grinding against me."

She blushed and pushed herself up on his chest. "Am I being totally shameless?"

He nodded and rubbed his thumb at the corner of her mouth.

"It's hot, too. Everything about you is hot. The blushing. The grinding. The entire pocket-sized package." He curved his hand around her neck and pulled her closer, his lips brushing hers. "The wicked-sharp mind and wary suspicion of your big, bad protector."

"I'm not suspici—"

He cut her off with a hard kiss and she squeaked before sighing and letting him in.

When he broke away, she licked her swollen lips. "I mean…right. How can I trust you, when you're so big and bad?"

"You can't." He grinned slowly as he worked at the hooks at the back of her bra. "Can I undo this?"

"I really shouldn't let you," she said breathlessly, rolling her hips. "But I don't think I'll be able to say no."

"Because I'm so big and—"

She dissolved into giggles, falling forward to brace her elbows on his shoulders. She stroked her fingers into his hair and he rolled into her touch. "You're the opposite of bad, Trick."

"And you don't need a bodyguard, but anytime you want to role play, I'm your guy."

"'Kay. Theatrics do it for you, got it."

"*You* do it for me." How much she did scared him a bit. He shoved that thought away. "That feels good, keep doing that shoofy thing with your fingers."

"Tell me about your arm," she murmured as she raked her hands back through his hair again. Her breasts swayed in front of him, the shadow of cleavage in the v-neck shirt distracting him with the promise of soft, delicious skin. He unhooked her bra, liking the way her breath hitched. Liking the way he saw a bit more of her swells as she wiggled out of the straps before resuming her impromptu head massage.

"Not much to tell. X-rays looked good. This thing is really just a protective shield at this point."

"You're so blasé about a broken bone."

"Wasn't my first. Won't be my last."

———

He said it like he'd stubbed his toe. When she took off his shirt, she'd tried not to react badly at the yellow and purple remnants of significant bruising on his right side, but whatever happened to Trick that broke his arm wasn't *no big deal*.

She lowered her mouth to his, kissing him partly for selfish-desire reasons, partly because he deserved something sweet for being so brave. He tasted unbelievably good, like the best salty-sweet concoction, so it was like ninety-five percent selfish and barely five percent altruistic. Every brush of his lips against hers sent electric currents skittering across her skin and each slow thrust of his tongue went straight to her core. For someone who was supposed to be getting kissed, he sure took charge in a hurry.

Under her shirt, his left hand squeezed her side just a few inches below her breast. For all the intimacy they'd ended up sharing the last weekend, he hadn't made a play for her boobs again—hadn't even seen her without a shirt on yet. And it didn't seem like he was going to make that move unless she gave him the go-ahead.

She waited for the green-eyed monster to protest, but all she heard was the thump of her heart and the breathy whimper she let out as she pulled away from Trick's mouth.

"Here," she said quickly. "Let me just…"

If she'd had any doubt Trick wanted her, his groan and accompanying flex of his erection as she pulled off her shirt would have been proof enough. The way he was looking at her when she dropped the fabric and looked back at him through her flyaway hair was a cherry on top.

"Wow, I like your definition of making out." He firmly glided his hand up her fluttering midsection—could he feel her nerves? Or was that excitement?—and ever so carefully cupped her right breast, then curved his hand in a figure eight motion to stroke her left one.

"Use both hands," she urged under her breath.

"The cast is rough," he said quietly, ignoring her.

"I don't care."

"I do. Your skin is so soft. So smooth. Jesus, Gaby, I don't want to scratch you. Besides—" He lifted his thighs beneath her bottom, shifting her closer to him again. "My mouth is so much better than any hand."

He didn't go straight for the obvious goods like she expected. She had nice nipples, she thought, and only so-so boobs, but Trick seemed to like it all. The shadow between her breasts, the sensitive tissue beneath, and her puffy areolae. And when his thumb finally tweaked one now painfully erect peak at the same moment that he tugged the other deep into his mouth…that was *amazing*. Technicolor light display kind of amazing.

She gasped out loud, because how could she not, and grabbed hold of his shoulders. "More," she urged when he paused to check in, and he gave her exactly that. Overwhelmed by the rough, perfect sensations of his tongue suckling on her, she unconsciously resumed grinding, and as her body flushed from head to toe, she realized she was nearing an orgasm. From rocking against him and his mouth on her breasts.

She panted his name and he switched sides. His right arm, scratchy cast and all, banded around her butt and held her in place.

"Are you going to come like this?" He scraped her nipple ever so lightly with his teeth. "Because you should. You should come so hard for me, Gaby. You're so gorgeous, and I'm so fucking lucky to have you in my lap."

"Uhhhh," she moaned, incapable of more advanced speech, but he seemed to translate that no problem. It only took another minute of the most teasing, most delicious, most unexpected breast play ever before she was trembling her way through an orgasm that seemed to twirl on and on and on, a spiral of pleasure that started between her legs and radiated down each limb and up her neck.

Trick held her against his bare torso, his skin warm and inviting against hers. She sagged into him, relaxing as his strong arms tightened around her as if to say, *I've got you*. She lolled a bit to one side as she found a way to both lean on him and look up at him at the same time. He grinned down at her. "See? I told you. Hot."

"Yes, you are." She was slurring her words a bit, all sleepy and sated in her post-orgasmic bliss. *So this is what boneless contentment feels like*. The orgasm he'd given her the previous week had been spectacular in a different way, but their emotions had been pulled tight. Today, there was none of that. Just sweet luxuriating in a secret shared attraction.

She shifted again, wanting to burrow deeper into his warm skin stretched over hard muscles—a more perfect combination of masculine presentation she couldn't possibly imagine—when her inner thigh rolled over another hard muscle.

"Oh, you…"

He made a noncommittal noise, but fair was fair.

"Nope. It's your turn." She slid over his body and dropped between his spread legs. He sank a bit further into the couch, watching from behind half-hooded eyes as she stroked her palms up his heavily muscled thighs and hooked her fingers behind his belt. "You want to come, too, don't you?"

He choked on a laugh and reached out to cup her cheek with his big, callused hand. "That's a dirty word, pretty girl."

"You used it." She tried to keep a straight face, but the hum of electricity between them made that too difficult. He brought out the smirk in her, that was for sure.

"Yeah, I want to come for you." His voice dropped a few notes as he said it, trailing into a groan as she traced the shape of his erection through his pants. "Unzip me."

Hands shaking, she did just that, but as soon as she wrapped her hand around his straining shaft, Trick covered her fingers with his own.

"You want this, right?"

"Oh yeah," she breathed.

"Hot damn," he muttered, guiding her fist up and down his erection twice before dropping his hand to his hip.

Clear drops formed at the slit on his crown, and all of a sudden, her hand wasn't enough for her. She wanted—needed—to know how he'd react to her mouth. Wanted that power, although she already felt pretty fucking powerful when it came to him.

Gaby had never felt more beautiful or desired in her entire life. No comparison, never.

She hovered over him for a minute, loving the way he strained his hips toward her open mouth. She breathed in the scent of him there, so similar to the rest of him, but…different. He smelled like *sex*, in the best way possible. She lowered her mouth around the crown, her lips stretching wide to take him all in. There was no way she'd be able to swallow his whole length, but in a few bobs she'd worked her way down to her fist, and as she licked and sucked, getting him all wet and sloppy in the process, the up-and-down motion got easier.

And hotter.

His hands gripped her arms tightly, like he needed to hold on there to keep himself from jamming his hands on her hand and driving deep into her throat. She hummed around him at the idea of that—probably hotter in fantasy than reality, but there was no way that Trick would ever hurt her, not even for his own pleasure.

Helpless, almost angry groans and grunts spilled from his mouth and rumbled through his body as she matched his breathing and sped up. Faster, wetter, harder. She thought of the way he'd gone down on her, how he'd lapped at her like he couldn't get enough of her taste.

She knew the feeling. It was heady, having him in her mouth. Dirty, but not dirty. Right and perfect and special.

He squeezed her shoulder, which she took as an early warning. She ignored it, taking him as deep as she could. *Special.* She swallowed his release, relaxing her mouth to let his softened cock slip fully into her hand only when he was completely clean.

She snickered to herself. Clean, as in covered in her saliva. And she was soaking wet again. Giving an epic blow job apparently had that effect on her.

"How about that shower now?" Trick said, his voice thick and slow.

"Mmm-hmmm."

"In a minute, then. Just a minute." He sucked in a shaky breath, then stroked her hair. "Thank you."

She shook her head, smiling against his thigh. "It was good for me, too."

"How good?"

She bit her lip. "Good enough."

"Good enough isn't in my vocabulary." He tugged her arm, and she climbed into his lap, but he pushed her backwards with his index finger until she was flat on her back. He unsnapped her shorts, growling when he found her slippery and wet.

Two orgasms later—both hers—they stumbled into the shower, which was pretty tame in comparison, just a lot of touching and some kissing as they washed each other from tip to toe.

When they got out, Trick had to let his cast drain into the tub for five minutes, which Gaby found extra hilarious because it was more unexpected than anything.

"I don't see why it's so funny," he muttered good-naturedly as she dabbed on some vitamin E lotion he had in the cupboard in lieu of her usual moisturizer.

"It's not," she said, hiccuping, which only sent her into another fit of giggles.

He gave his cast one final shake, then wrapped it in a towel and stood, a giant, naked, man mountain beside her.

"What?"

His lips twitched in an almost-smile. "I like having you in my bathroom."

She almost-smiled back. "Okay."

"Do you need a hair dryer?"

"Sure."

He disappeared and returned a minute later with a never-before-opened box. "Here."

"Why do you have a brand-new hair dryer?"

A laugh tore out of his throat. "Because my mother is insane. She'd love nothing more than for me to settle down with a girl, so she's forever bringing me things to domestic my home."

She took the box and opened it. "When did she give this to you?"

"Last year sometime?"

And Gaby was the first woman who would use it. That did funny things to her heart. "Thanks."

He grinned and disappeared. Music came on in the other room, and when she finished drying her hair, she found him fully dressed and prepping what looked like a stir fry for dinner.

She found her clothes and pulled them on again, skipping the soaking wet panties.

"Hey," he called out from the kitchen.

"Hey what?" she yelled back, but before she could go to him, he appeared in the doorway, then steered her backwards to the couch.

"I want to ask you something," he said, settling them side-by-side after a kiss. "Stay over tonight."

"Is that a good idea?"

"We don't need to have sex."

"We *won't* be having sex. One step at a time, right?"

"Just cuddles."

She laughed. "Well, not *just* cuddles."

"Don't dismiss that as a valuable offer unto itself. I have it on good authority I'm an excellent snuggler."

"I bet."

"That was the wrong sales pitch, wasn't it?" His eyes twinkled like he knew it didn't really matter to her, and it didn't. This felt too right.

"Definitely."

"How about, I miss you when you go. It's only been a week and I've been crawling the walls for at least five days of it, hungry to see you. And I think we should extend our weekly date to the morning. Besides, I don't sleep well alone."

"That's not fair."

He grinned, a feral acknowledgement that he knew he had her. "What did it?"

She mumbled her answer under her breath. She didn't need to give him any more advantage than he already had.

"Pardon? I didn't hear you."

She winced. "You said you're hungry to see me. You said it before…you know." She made a face of defeat. "I really like it."

"Yeah, you look like you like it."

"Well, it's kind of like kryptonite. I don't think I'm supposed to like how weak it makes me."

"You haven't seen Superman, have you?"

"No. Why, did I get the reference wrong?"

He laughed. "Yes and no." He rolled her beneath him. "So when I say I'm hungry to have you in my bed…"

"So you can sleep? Because you've gone without a bedmate for weeks on end and it's so awful?" She said it archly, but her lips were twitching into a smile she couldn't hold back even before the sentence was past her lips.

"Yes on the first point. No on the second, and don't make me want to spank you. I'm still uncoordinated with my left hand." He reached out and touched her cheek. "I missed you this week, Gaby."

Leaning into his palm, she closed her eyes and admitted to herself that she'd missed him, too. But just to herself. He didn't need anything else to use against her. She took a settling breath. "We didn't talk about spanking."

"We didn't talk about it being off-limits, either." He kissed her as he stroked his palm down her hip and tapped the side of her butt. "Would it be?"

God, he was going to be the sexual death of her. "No," she whispered.

"Okay." He grinned. "One step at a time, though. I'll let you think about that while I make dinner."

GABY SIGHED and stole a look at her phone resting quietly on the edge of her desk.

It was only Tuesday. Three more days until she could call Trick and invite herself over to his place for a few rounds of "Let's See What We Can Do With Our Hands and Mouths."

A shiver racked through her at the memory of the past weekend. Their third weekend together in the new and improved Trick and Gaby 2.0. Easy, breezy, orgasm-please-y. He'd come over to her place —Lila had been gone for the weekend, taking any possible embarrassment out of the equation—and they'd driven up to the La Jolla tide pools. Then spent the night at his place before a late diner breakfast and a long, slow kiss goodbye midafternoon on Sunday.

She could so easily get addicted to him. It wasn't just that he was impossibly good-looking and had mad sex skills. He was also smart and had a closet geekiness that made her want to buy him Doctor Who boxer shorts. He asked all the right questions and listened to the answers. He cared about his job and his friends and his family and shared more than she expected about all of the above.

He was perfect.

And not a forever kind of guy.

She really needed to have that tattooed on her hand, because if she let herself slip into wanting Trick to be something other than what he was, she'd miss out on how special it was to have him in her life.

Their plan was a good one. Have fun on the weekends and not get too clingy during the week. She didn't need to weave him into every facet of her life. It would make it that much harder to move on when they were over.

She took one last look at the phone and headed for the craft area. The kids were great about cleaning up at the end of the day, but there was always some restocking and cleaning needed, plus prep for the next day.

She was almost done when a knock sounded at her classroom door. Expecting it to be one of her fellow teachers, she called out for them to come in and tried one last time to shove a sheaf of construction paper onto the top shelf before giving up.

"Need some help?"

At the sound of a rough, rumbling voice she was now intimately familiar with, she lost her grip on the paper and turned to face him as it rained down around her. "Trick!"

"Oh, shit."

She shot him an alarmed look, a natural censoring reaction when someone swore in her classroom, and he gave her an apologetic shrug as he dropped to the floor and started gathering up the red and blue and yellow and green squares. With both hands.

With extra care, she reached out and touched his right hand. "You got your cast off!"

He tugged up his long-sleeved t-shirt to reveal a black flexible brace wrapped around his forearm. "Still have to be careful, but I like this better."

She narrowed her gaze at him. "Wait...did you go to see a doctor?"

"Look at all these papers. Whatever do you get the cute children to do with them?"

"Trick..."

He winked at her. "Gaby, I think fussing about a cast falls into girlfriend territory. Leave it be."

He'd meant it as a tease, she knew that, and he was right, but it still felt sharper than she expected.

You're kidding yourself if you don't think you want that.

"Okay," she said, barely squeaking out the word.

"What?" He must have picked up on the weird vibe, and she mentally kicked herself. *He didn't mean it like that.*

"Nothing. Really. I'm just surprised to see you." She smiled. "It's a good surprise. What's up?"

"I just wanted to see you." He raised his hand. "Let's call it an exception to the agreed-upon parameters."

"Is everything okay?" She didn't know a lot about his job, but she was pretty sure he wasn't usually done at the end of the school day.

He shrugged, dropping his gaze to the papers they were still picking up.

"I'm pretty much done here, I just need to run some copies of worksheets for tomorrow. Give me ten minutes, okay?"

She kissed his cheek as she stood up, then grabbed her spelling handouts for the next day and headed to the office to make some copies.

The school receptionist, Nadia, was filing the day's attendance reports and blushed when Gaby came into view.

"Oh, so he sweet-talked his way past you, huh?"

"There aren't any kids here." Nadia stuck out her tongue. "Please don't try to tell me you didn't want that hunk of man to surprise you. Because if you didn't—"

Gaby laughed. "Oh no, I did. Thank you."

"Is it serious?"

Gaby shook her head. "It's new. And he's way out of my league, so I'm sure it won't last, but as long as it does..."

Nadia frowned. "Don't sell yourself short. Does he give you that impression?"

"No!" The retort stormed out of her, because it was the truth. "No, he's lovely."

"Military?"

She nodded. "Navy."

"Hot."

"Mmm-hmmm." They giggled together as Gaby waited for the last of her copies to spool off the printer. "Okay, I'm out of here."

"If you call in sick tomorrow, I'll cover for you!"

"I won't."

"Foolish girl." Nadia sighed and leaned against the filing cabinet. "If he has any friends. Or brothers. Or hunky acquaintances…."

"I'll be sure to point them in your direction."

Gaby wiggled her fingers and stepped into the hall—and into Trick's chest. Big, broad, hard…and shaking with laughter. She groaned and tipped her head against his shirt. "How much did you hear?"

"Hot, mmm-hmmm. And apparently I'm not sick-day worthy."

"Are you going to call in sick tomorrow?"

"Fair point." He slid his fingers through hers. "Is this okay?"

She grinned. "Sure, everyone's pretty much gone."

"For the record, you *are* sick-day worthy. There's just shit going on right now."

"Ah." That explained the visit. "So…dinner?"

"I thought I'd take you out."

"Let's swing by my place so I can get changed." She steered them back into her classroom.

Trick swung her around, pressing her back to the interior wall, so they were safely out of view if anyone glanced in the window on the door. He sucked her lower lip into his mouth as he ghosted his hands down her hips. "I like this dress, though."

"And it likes you, too." She opened for him and he thrust his tongue hungrily against hers, zooming her blood straight to the boiling point. She panted as he moved his mouth down her neck. "Maybe I just wanted a polite excuse to grab an overnight bag for your place."

He groaned. "I thought we were past niceties. And here I thought I'd have to grovel to get you in my bed in the middle of the week."

She grabbed his cheeks and pulled his head to hers. "Hey. You need some company, I want you to ask. Parameters be damned."

The look on his face made her heart melt—starkly serious, totally surprised. "Yeah?"

"Of course." She curled up on her toes, pressing her lips to his. "Now, where are you going to feed me?"

———

They settled on Mexican pretty quickly. Trick wanted to take her to a fancy place near the beach, but Gaby suggested something more casual, just off Orange Ave, and rightly pointed out that then they could have a few beers and walk back to her place.

Trick didn't ask her if Lila was home tonight. For one thing, he didn't care, and he didn't want Gaby to care or worry about why he was asking. He followed her home, then upstairs to her empty apartment. She scrawled a note on the whiteboard on the fridge and took three minutes to freshen up before they headed for the restaurant on foot.

They talked about the pros and cons of living in Coronado Beach and what Gaby's class was learning for the week. They talked about current affairs and reality television and social media, pausing only to order food. After finishing a shared skillet of queso fundido, Trick was finally feeling more comfortable with the state of his head when Gaby slid her hand over his and dragged an unexpected truth out of him.

"How was your day?"

"Rough."

She paused, eyebrows slightly raised like she'd been expecting a nothing answer. It was all he usually gave her.

He shook his head. "Sorry. That's cryptic, I know."

She tilted her head to the side. "I don't mind cryptic."

Screwing up his face against the onslaught of sound he had racing through his head—the audio recording of a SEAL fire team caught in the middle of an artillery strike—Trick looked out the window at the sidewalk of happy civilians strolling past. "I'm here, and the team I usually work with...isn't. The disconnect between what they're doing—what I usually do—and the cushy life is...."

Gaby just looked at him, her eyes soft as she waited for him to start talking again. Or not. She really looked like she'd take whatever he could share and not ask for more.

She deserved more.

Not the state secrets stuff, but…she didn't deserve a boyfriend who might be more fucked up than he thought.

"Do you have someone at work you can talk to about this stuff? Talk freely, I mean?"

He nodded. "I do. And I do talk to them. Lots of them, actually."

"So what's the deal…they tell you that you're reacting normally and you don't believe them?"

He didn't, actually. He huffed a laugh. "How'd you know?"

"Lucky guess. And a few psych classes in my undergrad." She leaned forward and held out her hand, wiggling her fingers until he took them. "So sleeping with me tonight might help?"

"Is that okay?"

She nodded. "More than okay. Thank you for asking."

They were interrupted then by the arrival of their fish taco plates, but Gaby didn't immediately let go of his hand. She smiled a polite thanks to the waiter, then slid her attention right back to him.

"Last week you said you don't sleep well alone. Is this what you meant?"

His skin prickled with discomfort. He wanted to leap up from the table and run far away, but he'd started the conversation and she wasn't wrong.

"I'm sorry. Now's not the time." She squeezed his fingers and let go, pointing at the tacos. "These look amazing."

"They do." Fresh white fish, bright cabbage, and the best salsa on the island—this had been the right call for where to go, and he told Gaby as much. She winked at him and told him to dig in.

They took their time over a shared dish of ice cream, and by the time they were walking back to her place in the unseasonably warm spring night, his tension had eased.

It threatened to come slamming back when she unlocked her apartment door and music greeted them on the other side.

"Ah, Lila's home," Gaby murmured. He couldn't see her face, but her back pulled up a little straighter than usual.

He moved closer, wrapping his arm around her waist. Leaning in, he brushed his lips against the curve of her ear. "Do you want to meet me over at my place?"

She shook her head, then twisted and kissed his jaw. "Come on."

Holding hands, they walked into the living room. Gaby's roommate was sitting on the floor, CDs spread all around her. She glanced up for half a second, smiled, then returned her attention to the case in her hand. "How was dinner?"

"Great," Gaby said. "Are you sorting or hunting for a specific album?"

"Hunting. I can't find the Jamiroquai CD, and I'm heading out to Kyra's place soon. But it's sort of turned into alphabetizing. Sorry. I'll be cleared out of here in a few minutes."

Trick wasn't sure how that was possible. Plastic cases littered the room, stacked on every available surface.

Gaby glanced up at him, then started laughing.

"What?"

"You don't think she can tidy all of this up in a flash?"

Had his doubt been that obvious? He smiled down at Gaby. "It's just that…" He shook his head at her. "You know what? I know better than to argue with the woman I'm sleeping with."

It was like he'd pressed a button and frozen time. Gaby blinked silently up at him for a moment, and then Lila started coughing and couldn't stop. Trick could feel himself turning bright read. Jesus. He'd stepped right into that one.

"Uhhhh…" He shut his mouth, because all he had were incomprehensible noises.

Gaby's eyes crinkled. She turned to her roommate. "Are you okay?"

The blonde wiped at the corners of her eyes. "Oh yeah."

Gaby turned back to him. "Are you okay?"

"Really not sure," he muttered. "Are you going to kick me out?"

She laughed. "Oh, hell no." She turned him and pointed him down the hall. "Night, Lila!" she called as she pressed her small hands into his back. "This way, Mr. Cool."

He vaguely remembered this hallway. Two bedrooms, the doors

slightly offset. He'd already been in the one on the left, so the one on the right must be Gaby's.

She steered him into the dark, then flicked a switch which controlled the two lamps on either side of the bed.

"Nice room." Filler comment, but it was true. Dark furniture, red decorations. Not quite sleek, not quite funky, just modern and perfectly Gaby.

"Nice cover." He turned and found her smirking at him, arms crossed. The door clicked shut behind her.

"Hey, I wasn't even thinking about that."

"I know." She trailed her gaze down his body and back up again. "You only had eyes for me out there."

"I only ever have eyes for you." He swallowed hard. "I'm sorry that was awkward."

She shook her head. "I'm not. That was, like, the best kind of awkward. Embarrassing. Funny. And now it's done."

Huh. How about that. She looked him up and down again, and Trick finally clued in. Notching his thumbs in his belt, he rocked on his heels. She could look her fill. He was hers to consume, with her eyes and her hands and her mouth, as much as she wanted.

She sat on the edge of the bed and took off her shoes, then moved slowly around him to put them in the closet. He watched over his shoulder as she approached him, touching his waist, then his arm, her fingertips cool like marbles as she trailed them over his skin.

Stopping in front of him again, barefoot in that pretty dress, she looked small but mighty. And never more beautiful.

"Gaby…" He settled his hands on her waist. He wanted to pick her up and toss her on the bed. Show her how much he wanted her, but she was doing something here and he had to be patient.

"We've been silly, Patrick." She tipped her head to the side and gave him a look he couldn't quite figure out. "Or maybe just me." Her voice dropped to a whisper. "I've been so, so silly."

"Never, pretty girl."

"All that fear. All that noise. When you came to see me today…it all just fell away." She ran her hands up his chest and around his neck, tugging his head down so she could kiss him. "I want you, Trick."

"You've got me."

She smiled against his lips. "No, I mean, I *want* you. Inside me."

———

Trick had been holding himself back, Gaby knew that, and she knew telling him she was ready for sex would get a reaction.

She hadn't prepared herself for how much of a reaction.

The second her words processed through his brain, he took command of their kiss. Holding her face, he tugged her lower lip between his teeth, his tongue tracing the softness just inside her mouth as he moved her backward to the bed.

Deepening the kiss, he simultaneously worked her skirt up to her waist and got her sitting on the bed, all without taking a breath. He didn't break their embrace until he dropped to his knees, whipping off his boots and shirt before sliding his hands up her thighs and tugging her panties low on her hips.

"Up," he ordered, and she fell back, lifting her hips as ordered.

As soon as they were both partially naked, he slowed down, crawling on top of her to kiss her senseless again. He carefully worked the row of buttons down the front of her dress, revealing the extra-pretty bra she'd changed into before dinner. The matching panties were now tossed on the floor somewhere, but it didn't matter—she hadn't needed to put on anything fancy.

He still gazed down at her like she was everything he'd ever wanted, just like this—rough and raw and real. She didn't need to excuse herself to put on something staged. He wanted *her*.

Her breath caught in her throat as he ever so slowly worked her breasts out of the lace cups. He circled his fingertip around one nipple, then the other, before dipping his head and suckling on her.

Her hips arched off the bed as flames of desire shot through her body, straight from his tongue to her soaking wet sex.

"Please, Patrick. Please." She wasn't above begging.

"Do you have condoms? I was tested after we started dating, but…"

"In the drawer." She was on the pill, but she'd never been tested, and fair was fair. There'd be time for that when they weren't hazy with lust.

He leaned over and grabbed one, then paused and grabbed two more. When she squeaked, he pounced back on top of her. "I've been waiting for *months* for this, Gaby. Once is not going to be enough."

"It hasn't been months," she protested, her voice eager and breathy.

"No," he said, shaking his head. "You're right. I've been waiting for you for years. I just didn't know it."

"Trick—" He cut her off with a hard kiss, all tongue and teeth and firm, strong lips that zinged her all over. Damn him, not giving her a chance to tell him she felt the same way.

But she could show him.

She wiggled her arms between them, working at his belt and his fly until she had enough play to shove his jeans down his hips. She had to reach to grab his ass, but as soon as she had a handful of him, she yanked them together.

He groaned as she rolled against him, showing him how wet she was, and for a second she thought he'd just slide right inside—and oh, how she wanted that. She wanted him to take her and make her his. He was already branded on her heart, might as well make it official.

But while he tightened his hold on her and rocked against her, he was more in control than she was. "Need this," he ground out, ripping the wrapper open.

Once sheathed, he pressed up on his elbows, watching between them as he slowly pressed his erection between the lips of her swollen, aching sex. She rocked her hips up to welcome him inside her body, but he wouldn't be hurried, and as he pressed, then pulled back before slowly thrusting again, she understood why.

She hadn't been thinking about how big he was.

"Oh my God," she whispered as he stretched her. She'd never felt so full in her life. Full to the aching point.

But she wanted even more.

On his next thrust, she tipped her hips again, and he stroked against something inside her, that same place he'd already found with his fingers, and she felt herself grow even more slick around his shaft.

He growled at the easier slide and picked up the pace, rocking in and out of her in ways that made her eyes roll back in her head and her nipples tighten to sharp little points.

"So tight." He stared down at her, his eyelids heavy and his lips wet. She reached up and wrapped her hand around his neck, holding his gaze as he thrust deep again, his eyelids fluttering almost shut. "So good."

"So good," she repeated, her breath hitching as he moved inside her. They didn't even have their clothes off, and it was off-the-charts amazing.

He shifted his weight to his right arm, sliding his left hand down her side, rumpling her dress into a narrow band of fabric around her waist. He slid his hand under her, lifting her bottom as he picked up his pace, fucking her harder and faster.

She wasn't sure what was going to happen first—orgasm or spontaneous combustion. She was okay with the latter if she got the former first. She'd never wanted that explosive release more.

"Do you need to touch yourself? Want me to—"

"No," she gasped, dragging breath into her lungs. She was so close. "That's perfect, just like that."

He surged into her again, rolling against her clit as he bottomed out, and she cried out for him to do it again.

He did, his muscles bunching under her hands as he worked hard to get them both to that blissful peak.

"Gaby…" He groaned her name, dropping his face into her neck as she locked her legs around his waist, trembling as she started to clench around him on the inside as well. "My pretty girl," he whispered, his breath coming hard and fast as he jerked roughly above her, finishing nearly at the same time.

They clung to each other, breathing hard, until Trick angled out of her and rolled to the side to ditch the condom. Then he shoved his pants all the way off and pulled her against him.

"Best thing that's ever happened to me," he whispered.

She kissed his chest, then pressed her cheek to the same spot. "You really are my superhero, you know that?"

He huffed and settled his hand on her hair.

I love you, she thought. It was blinding, the truth of her feelings now that all the boundaries had fallen away. She burrowed closer. She'd show him, again and again with her body, then hold him so he could sleep.

And hopefully one day soon he'd be ready to hear the words themselves.

He deserved them so much.

CHAPTER
ELEVEN

TWO DAYS LATER—THE first Thursday night Gaby hadn't had to work in three months—she was heading home and the sun was still up, but she was already thinking about crawling into a bed with her boyfriend at the end of the day.

Her *boyfriend*. They'd made love twice more Tuesday night, as Trick had promised, and when he'd crept out at dark o'clock for work, he'd kissed her and promised to text.

His first one had come forty-five minutes later.

By the end of the day, she'd been grinning from ear to ear, and when she left the school, he'd been waiting for her with a single red rose, leaning against her car.

She'd driven them back to his place where he'd fucked her senseless in the shower, then on his bed, and they'd eaten pizza naked when they needed fuel.

Early this morning she'd gone back to her place to get changed and pack a bag just in case tonight was a repeat at his place, but she hadn't heard from him all day.

He's only a US Navy SEAL. Jeez. Not like he might be busy or something.

She smiled as she passed the shawarma shop, then she spun around at the next intersection and double-backed.

She should surprise him with a dinner that would remind him of their first date. Or pre-date, depending on whose definition they were working under.

Twenty minutes later, she pulled up at his apartment. She didn't bother to text him. If he wasn't home, she'd call him and find out where he was, but a surprise would be fun.

She knocked playfully, wondering if there was a way to sexily present shawarma. Probably not.

When the door swung open, though, Trick had a very unsexy frown on his face. "Oh, Gaby."

"Hey!"

Instead of stepping back and letting her in, he just stood there staring at her. An uneasy worry slithered into her gut.

She gripped the bag, trying to hold at bay the frown of her own that wanted to settle between her eyebrows. "I brought some food…"

"Patrick?" a man's voice called from inside the apartment. "Who is it?"

Trick shook his head and blinked at her. "I'm sorry. Come in. It's just…my parents are here."

"Oh." She smiled. "Okay, well, no worries."

"No, I want you to come in. It's…I was just surprised. Come in."

He stepped to the side and gestured for her to enter.

She tried to think of everything he'd said about his parents. They lived in Orange County. His mom bought stuff for his apartment. His dad was an investment adviser. Not a lot to go on.

"Mom, Dad, this is my friend Gaby."

My friend. Her smile froze on her face. At least it didn't drop off. She nodded and looked for a place to dump the sandwiches. Like the garbage.

"Nice to meet you, dear." Trick's father was standing, and he stepped forward, offering his hand. She shifted the plastic bag to her other fingers and accepted the handshake.

"The pleasure is all mine, of course. Patrick has mentioned you, but I didn't know you were visiting. I'm sorry for intruding. I just brought him some dinner because I know he's been working hard and his arm…" She trailed off because she was blabbering and really, what did it matter?

His mother rose from the couch and came around to stand next to her husband. "We were just talking about going out. I'd suggest you should join us, but maybe we could order in some more food?"

Behind her, Trick groaned. "First of all, I'm not a teenager, Mom, so I've got food. I can make stuff. And really, it's not a great night for visiting, so maybe you guys should get going."

"No!" Gaby shook her head. "I've interrupted, I'm the one who should go. These are big sandwiches, there's enough there for all three of you, I'm sure. I'll just…"

She turned to leave again, but ran straight into the immovable wall that was known as Trick. The man she loved. *Her friend.* God, if she stayed a second longer, she might just start crying.

"Don't go," he said quietly.

"I have to," she whispered, staring into his shirt. "I forgot something."

She could feel his gaze, but she wasn't going to look up. He cleared his throat. "Excuse us for a minute. Gaby and I just need to have a private chat."

He walked around her, shielding her from his parents as he pressed his hand into the small of her back and moved her without any effort into his room.

"What's going on?" he demanded as soon as the door closed.

"Nothing," she said quietly, looking at the floor. "I'm being silly."

"Yes, obviously." She snapped her gaze up to meet his at the hard edge to his voice. He glared at her, but he didn't look *mad* exactly, just confused. "Is this because I called you my friend?"

Her mouth fell open, but no words came out. "Well…" she said after a moment.

"Because we are friends," he said, frowning again. "And a hell of a lot more, but we haven't talked labels, so I thought that was a safe one to start with."

"Start?"

"I don't know. Should I have assumed that I could call you my girlfriend, to my *mom*, without asking you?"

"Oh." Heat crawled up her neck and wrapped around the edge of her face. With it came the threat of tears, and damnit, she didn't want to cry. "Sorry."

He scrubbed his hand over his face and up into his hair. "No, I'm sorry. I should have assumed you'd want to come over tonight. They arrived mid-afternoon and time just got away from me."

"It's okay." She hated that little hitch in her voice.

"Gaby?" He waited until he had her full attention, then he smiled at her. "Will you be my girlfriend?"

"Jeez, Trick!" She laughed, a suspiciously watery noise that was *so* not hot. "Are you sure? I'm clearly a neurotic mess."

"Ah," he said, closing the gap between them. "But you're my neurotic mess."

"Yours?"

He wrapped his arms around her. "All mine. My girlfriend. Hmm. I like that."

"I like it too," she whispered.

"You can make this up to me later. After they leave."

"A naked apology?"

He grunted. "Nope. Can't think about that. My mom is on the other side of that door."

"Okay."

"Damn. Too late."

"What? I didn't say anything."

He shrugged and tipped her chin up so he could brush a light kiss across her lips. "I imagined you riding me, asking me if I was okay as you slid onto my dick. Instant hard-on."

"Wow." She kissed him. "Time to think of math."

"Instant teacher fantasy."

"This is hopeless, isn't it?"

"Maybe you should just stand in front of me."

————

His parents had been far too amused when they emerged from the bedroom and Trick informed them that Gaby had just agreed to be his girlfriend. Gaby had been less impressed, blushing prettily, but he'd made it up to her after they left. They took turns with the naked apologies until nearly midnight, when they fell asleep wrapped around each other.

He'd been sleeping like the dead when his cell phone went off. He sat up with a jerk, swiping into the call before the first ring ended, wanting the noise to stop before it woke up Gaby.

"Hello?"

A crackling sound had him on his feet. This wasn't a call from around the corner.

"Hey, Trick!"

"Miles. You asshole, it's the middle of the night."

"So sue me, I had a few minutes of downtime and thought you'd appreciate hearing from me. The last time you heard from me was a bit hot."

They couldn't talk much on this line, they both knew that, but Miles wasn't wrong. That audio recording had messed Trick up, even though the intel promised the fire team was fine. "Yeah. Glad that all worked out okay."

"Tell me something good, man. This place sucks."

Trick glanced at Gaby, curled up on her side. He headed for the living room. "What's new…saw Jared's wife last week, she's looking great." He opened the fridge and pulled out the carton of orange juice. "Says she's excited about flying to England to see him next month."

"Yeah, I'm heading that way for my break as well."

"No island babes for you?"

"Nah. How about you? Super lonely without me?"

Trick snorted and took a swig of juice. "Not lonely at all, in fact." He put the carton down, surprised at what he'd just realized. "Actually, I think I'm in love."

"Yeah? That's cool."

"It is cool. Her name is Gaby, and man, she's so feisty—" In the background, a buzzer sounded, and Trick knew that meant that his roommate's allotted time on the phone was up. "Anyway. Life here is good. Be safe."

He waited until the line disconnected, then crawled back into bed. Gaby murmured something incomprehensible in her sleep, and he kissed her hair.

I love you, he thought. It wasn't nearly as terrifying as he thought it might be.

It just felt right.

Saying it out loud, on the other hand…Trick shook his head at himself and slid his hand around to cup one of Gaby's breasts. He didn't know about *that*. What if she didn't say it back?

No. It was enough for now to just know she was his.

Mine. He loved the sound of that—in his head *and* out loud.

CHAPTER
TWELVE

THE ONLY THING prettier than Gaby blushing was Gaby blushing naked, but since her apartment was full of people, that probably wouldn't happen.

Not until later.

Trick handed his girlfriend a glass of champagne. "Did we do a good job surprising you?"

"We?" Lila gave him an amused look from the other side of the birthday girl, who'd officially been his girlfriend for six weeks.

He never thought he'd be the type of guy to even notice shit like that, let alone think about marking it like some sort of big-deal anniversary.

And yet here he was, proud as punch that he had a pretty necklace to give her later on.

Gaby winked at him, and he shrugged. "Okay, I did nothing for this party other than deliver you. The planning committee met via email, twice. And I missed one of those meetings because I didn't have Lila's email address on my safe list."

"Tracking you down was a nightmare. Gaby has a password on her phone."

Of course she did. His pretty girl was super smart.

"It all worked out in the end," he said quietly, staring at Gaby as her eyes crinkled. It definitely had all worked out.

"Quite clever to have a surprise party the day before my actual birthday," she murmured.

"I'm selfishly happy that your birthday falls on a Sunday this year, so the party can be tonight and I can have you all to myself tomorrow." He kissed her temple, then stepped back as her friends from the school and mutual friends she shared with Lila swarmed around her.

In the kitchen he found a group of guys he didn't know, except one.

"Nash, what the hell are you doing at my girlfriend's birthday party?"

Vince Nash was a senior chief on SEAL Team 9, a recon specialist, and last Trick had heard, he was in the sandbox with the rest of the team—Trick's team. Trick had been making himself useful on Team 11, which did extractions and short-term missions, but they didn't feel like his brothers yet, not in the same way. That would come in time—it had to, because it looked like the reassignment might be more permanent than originally planned.

His friend shrugged. "Family funeral. And it lined up with my leave, anyway, so I came home instead of going to Greece."

"Man, that sucks, I'm sorry."

"My granddad. He had Alzheimer's, so it's better that he's not suffering, but my mom and my gran..." Nash sighed. "Anyway, when Lila mentioned your name, I thought I'd come."

They shook hands, then Trick grabbed a beer and leaned against the counter. "You working something out with the commander to stay here, or are you heading back?"

"Heading back, but it looks like this might be my last tour." He made a face. "I don't want to get out, but I can't be gone for months at a time. And I need to find something that pays better at the same time. Might be an impossible task."

"You should talk to Drew Castle. He knows a guy looking for private operators. Legit guy, former Norwegian FSK."

"Yeah? You ever think about something like that?"

"Nah." Trick got up and paced to the archway into the living room, making visual on Gaby before ambling back. "Not for me. I'm good here until retirement."

Nash nodded. "Makes sense."

"You want to meet Gaby?"

"Wow."

"What?"

"You've got it bad."

Trick couldn't deny that. "She's something special."

"Yeah? Cool." Nash laughed and tipped his beer back. "Please introduce me to the woman who felled the mighty Novak."

Gaby put up with some teasing from Nash, then they introduced his friend to one of her friends, and Trick was able to settle with the birthday girl on the couch for a bit. When the more artsy guests started talking about Charades, he escaped to the kitchen again.

It wasn't until the party was over and Gaby was tucked into his side, drifting off after a quiet lovemaking session in her room, that he was reminded of his conversation with Nash.

He picked up her left hand and rubbed his thumb over her knuckles as he looked at her bare ring finger.

"What's on your mind, Trick?" She tried to hold back a yawn, but it didn't work.

He smiled at her. "Just really happy with you, that's all."

"Me too. Happy. With you."

He laughed. "You're funny when you're tired."

"And you're chatty."

"I'll shut up. Happy birthday, pretty girl."

———

Gaby had wanted to tell Trick how much she cared for him for weeks. Months, really. Her birthday party had almost been the perfect opportunity, but they didn't get a minute alone until they were both exhausted, and then the next day had been a whirlwind of planned activities.

Dating a Navy SEAL could be intense.

Turned out she liked intense. A lot, but it didn't always lend itself to sweet, quiet emotional moments.

When it finally happened, weeks later, it was when she least expected it.

The first week of May she decided she needed to add a puppet theatre to her classroom. When she told Trick she was going to Home Depot to buy power tools, he informed her he was going with.

"Do you know how to use power tools?"

He frowned at her. "Gaby, I'm a Navy SEAL. I *am* a power tool."

"Okay, first, that's not a real response. And second, I don't think that a skill saw is the same as a machine gun."

"Yes, I know how to use power tools."

"Fine, then you can be my assistant."

When they got to Home Depot, she found the major materials she needed, but as they walked down the aisle of screws and nails, she realized she didn't know where to begin.

And Trick knew it, too. He was laughing at her, damn him, and that just wasn't cool.

"If you know what screw I need, why don't you just tell me?" she demanded, whirling around and planting her hands on her hips.

Of course, that just made him laugh harder.

She rolled her eyes because it was funny. But still…

"I love that you think you can do anything, Gaby." He came closer and tugged first one hand and then the other off her hips and brought her fists to his lips. "It's one of a long list of things that I love about you."

She probably knew that already, but hearing it was something entirely different. Her heart thumped an extra beat as she let the words soak into her skin. "I love you, too," she whispered, then grinned. "Wow. You love me."

"Of course I do. I've always wanted to be with a master carpenter."

"Really? You're going to ruin this moment with teasing?"

He wrapped his arms around her, bending his knees so they were nose to nose. "Did I ruin anything?"

She shook her head. "No."

"I love you, Gaby."

"Thank you, Trick."

"You want me to pick out screws for you now, don't you?"

"Yes, please."

He kissed her, then again for good measure, which she appreciated because his kisses were yummy.

After finding every last little bit of metal she needed for the project, he did most of the work back at the school and gave her all of the credit.

Back at his place, while she cooked dinner, she tried to think of some way to thank him. Maybe tickets to Comic Con.

Unlike Trick, though, there was no way she could pull off a surprise.

"Hey," she called out after turning down the sauce she'd just made. "I have an idea…"

"But you want to run it past me because you're worried I might not like it?" Trick appeared in the doorway, an amused look on his face.

She rolled her eyes as her cheeks turned pink. "Yes, maybe."

"I'll like it."

"I don't know exactly how to do it."

Cocking one eyebrow, he leaned in with a leer. "Naked is always a good bet."

"This is in public."

"Keep the good bits covered up, then."

"Definitely." She took a deep breath. "Do you want me to get Comic Con tickets for you? And me? Would that be fun?"

A look of pure joy spread across his face. "For real? That wouldn't be too geeky for you?"

"I like geeky stuff."

"Babe, you like to geek out on shit. Like books. But the full-on fandom stuff?"

She shrugged. "I can handle full-on for a day."

"Awesome." He bounced on his heels. "You don't need to wear a sexy costume."

"Oh, yeah. No, I wasn't offering to wear anything other than regular clothes."

"I mean, if you wanted to…"

"I don't." She might see if she could find Wonder Woman lingerie to wear under a Bat Girl t-shirt. It would almost be like a girly three-way in her shirt. That would have to be good enough.

"We can work on that step for next year."

She laughed. "Won't you be overseas this time next year?"

And the happiness disappeared. She watched as his lips thinned and his gaze shuttered. "Maybe. I might stay on this team, now. But we could go anywhere at any time."

"I know."

He looked away from her, first at the floor, then at the food she was cooking. "That looks good."

"It should be. Chicken's in the oven, spinach salad's over there if you want to toss it."

She gave him a minute to do that and take it to the table, while she pulled the chicken out and poured the honey-lemon sauce over it. But as they started to eat, she nudged his foot with hers.

"Hey, do you worry that I'm not going to be able to handle your next mission, or a long tour?"

He sliced another piece of chicken before responding. "Maybe. It happens."

"But I love you."

He looked up and smiled, but it didn't go all the way to his eyes. "I know. And I love you. Really. But if you can't handle it, I'll understand."

"Poppycock."

He laughed. "What?"

"I'm sorry, let me translate into SEAL. That's fucking bullshit. If you ever break up with me, I won't *understand*. And I really don't think you'd understand if the situation was reversed. If you can so easily handle me just wafting out of your life—"

"Whoa, what?"

"Isn't that what you just said?"

He glowered at her. It did warm fuzzy things to her insides. "I was lying, silly girl. If you can't handle me being a SEAL, I'd probably stop being a SEAL. And if you left me for someone else—some teacher or banker or landscaper—I'd tear him apart limb from limb."

"That's better," she said softly. "But I never want you to worry about me, even when I tell you I hate your job. I probably will at some point, when you come back with another broken bone. But I love *you* and all that you are. I'm not afraid of what that means. When you jump out of a plane or take off to parts unknown in a submarine, yeah, that scares me. But I'm also *proud* of you. How brave and fearless you are and how you put others before yourself. I'm willing to be here, waiting for you, always. You come home with nightmares or a broken arm, I can deal with that."

He got up and stalked around the table, dropping to his knees beside her and hauling her in for a long, bruising kiss.

She thought that was the end of it, but he brought it up again at bedtime.

"There might be shit you can't deal with."

She set aside her hand lotion and flicked off the light. "Might be. Not likely."

He tugged her close, sliding his hand under her shirt to hold her boob. "Lots of SEALs get divorced."

She nodded. "I bet."

"What if that's just another side effect of my job?"

"Nightmares and broken bones aren't side effects, they're injuries. And they can be repaired. Even if you had a permanent disability, I'd still love you, because there are work-arounds. I don't know why those other relationships fail, but you're not allowed to break up with me."

"Breaking up with you is the last thing on my mind, Gaby."

"Then what *is* on your mind?" She turned slowly in the circle of his arms, kissing his neck, then his jaw, before bringing her lips to his ear. "Do you doubt that you're my superhero?"

He shook his head.

"Do you know that I love you and want you and nothing will change that?"

He nodded.

"Then shouldn't we be having crazy-hot sex instead of all this maudlin talk?"

He fisted his hand in her hair and held her still as he kissed her. "Take your shirt off, then."

They got naked in a flurry of limbs and flying t-shirts, then she settled herself on top of him, stroking his erection with one hand while she cupped his balls in her other. "Tell me again."

"I love you," he groaned, his head twisting back against the pillow as she squeezed just the way he liked it.

Rising up on her knees, she rocked her sex up the length of his cock before sliding him just inside.

"Stop teasing," he growled, eyes jerking back to her face.

"Tell me again." She was turned on like crazy, and her voice showed him how much he affected her.

He settled his hands on her hips, pressing her down. She sighed as he filled her.

"I love you, Gaby."

Now it was her turn to tip her head back and groan. "I love you, too."

He slapped her hip. "Now ride me."

"Need a minute. You're so big," she sighed. Which of course only made him bigger. Men.

When she'd fully stretched around his girth, she leaned forward, bracing herself on his shoulders as she worked herself quickly toward her first orgasm. He stroked her hips and breasts, finally settling one hand low on her pelvis as she got close, lightly rubbing around her clit as she bounced faster and faster. As soon as she exploded, he flipped her over, driving hard into her from behind.

She groaned as he pounded his hips against her bottom. When his roommate came back from overseas, she wouldn't be able to make this much noise. Such a shame.

It turned out, Gaby really liked making a lot of noise.

"I love your ass, pretty girl." She grinned into the pillow. Trick got so dirty when he was close to coming. "Almost jiggles as sweet as your breasts."

She pressed her eyes shut and tried hard not to laugh. *What?*

Well, whatever worked for him. She arched her back, pressing said jiggly bottom into his hand. He rubbed a lazy circle over her skin, then slapped her lightly. Which felt good, so she arched even more, which made Trick sink even deeper on the next thrust…

"Ahhhh," she cried out as he slapped her again. He was totally going to make her come again. By slapping her jiggling ass! The nerve.

"You like that?"

"So much," she gasped. "Do it again."

He did, a few times, until they both climaxed in spectacular fashion.

"That was really good," she said after he brought her a washcloth. She was lying flat on her back and he was tracing small circles all over her torso. "Although it's a good thing I love you, because it's generally bad form to tell a girl she jiggles."

"But I like the soft parts of you."

She grabbed his hand and kissed his fingers. "Okay."

"Next time I'll say bounce."

"I can't wait."

EPILOGUE

GABY KNEW that Hawaii was beautiful. Everyone knew that.

But to actually experience it was something totally different.

"This is paradise!" she exclaimed, twirling across the foyer of their rented condo to the floor-to-ceiling windows that overlooked a distant view of the beach and a lot of green in between. Trick had come here for work two weeks ago, and when he finished whatever he was doing, he'd called her and asked if she wanted to jump on a plane and join him for her last week of summer vacation.

"There's a pool on the other side of the lanai. It's got a great view." Trick came up behind her and wrapped his arms around her waist. "We could go skinny dipping. Totally private."

"Yeah?" She stroked the bulge of his bicep where he was holding her so securely against his body. She'd missed this, him just holding her. And all the other stuff, but while sex and talking were fun, hugs were the food of life for her. "I missed you, Trick."

"Missed you too, pretty girl." He took a deep breath, then exhaled slowly. "I've got something to tell you."

"Yeah?"

"I probably won't be home for Christmas. It looks like we're going to do something in the late fall...and we might be gone for a while. A few months."

Wow. That put their two weeks apart in brutal context. She tried to take a deep breath, tried to be brave and cool like he was, but her chest was too tight and her lungs didn't seem to work.

Trick didn't say anything. He didn't try to make it okay. He just hugged her, a solid wall of warmth and love behind her.

"Okay," she said after a minute. As she did, the tightness eased a bit. Just a bit. She still wanted to cry. But she probably wouldn't, not now. When he left…absolutely. But right now they were in paradise. Tears could wait.

"It might be less time than that. But I won't know—"

"Trick, it's really okay." She twisted in his arms so he could see her face. "God, I'm going to miss you, but maybe I'll take up scrapbooking or some other hobby. Maybe read most of the unread books on my Kindle."

"That's not why I asked you to fly out," he said, his gaze burning deep into her eyes.

"I know." She smiled. "I love you. You save the world. Try not to break anything, okay?"

"Okay." He cleared his throat. "The condo isn't the only part of the vacation I planned before I found out. I want you to know that, too."

"Sure." She wrinkled her brow in confusion. "You're being so serious."

"Yeah." His lips quirked, and she took a minute to really look at him. The day of scruff on his strong jaw. His defined cheekbones and piercing eyes. Her boyfriend was so much prettier than her, and she was totally fine with that.

"So…skinny dipping?"

"Definitely. But I don't want you to be completely naked." He stepped back and slowly dropped to one knee.

Gaby's heart bounced against her chest. They hadn't talked about this, but *oh my God*, that was a diamond ring in his hand, and *yes*, she already knew her answer.

"I'm so serious about this, Gaby. I want to marry you. I want to come home to you, and only you, for the rest of my life. I want to be there for you when you're sad and celebrate with you when you're happy. I want to read my comic books while you watch Outlander and then take you not to my bed or your bed, but our bed, in our house. I want a *house* with you. And when you're ready, maybe a baby or two. You could put them in your pocket."

She nodded, her eyes wet and her smile huge. "I want all of that. Except babies go in baby-carrier things, not pockets."

"Ours will go in pockets. They'll be extra small. Extra cute."

"Yes."

"Yes?" He stood and slid the solitaire onto her left ring finger.

She pressed her fingers against his chest. "Wow. Yes. To the marriage. Babies don't go in pockets."

"Let's agree to disagree on that point."

She laughed, and once she started, she couldn't stop. "Come here, superhero," she whispered, still giggling as she looped her other hand around his neck and pulled him close for a kiss.

He hoisted her into his arms as they kissed, two weeks of hunger lighting a fire deep in her core that she should have expected.

"Trick?"

He grunted in response.

"Is there a bed nearby? We can go swimming in a little bit, yes?"

Ten seconds later, she was flat on her back on a gorgeous king-sized bed in a probably gorgeous room. She didn't know for sure. She only had eyes for her fiancé. And it was hours before they went swimming, but when they did, all she wore was a sparkling ring.

FALL DEEP

ABOUT THIS BOOK

Navy SEAL Miles Dumbrowski is on his way back to war. He isn't supposed to fall in love.
Piper Harrington left San Diego behind, looking for adventure in Europe. The no-strings, easy-breezy kind of adventure.
Now her heart is headed to the Middle East with a man she won't see for months. But Miles seems intent on proving he's worth the wait for that second date.

CHAPTER
ONE

THREE SHIFTS into working at The Green Hedgehog, Piper Harrington had accepted this first leg of her European backpacking trip wasn't going to be the easy working vacation she had planned. That was okay by her, it wasn't work she was trying to get away from. As long as her well-meaning family stayed on the other side of the Atlantic Ocean and she got to just be Piper for a while, she'd pull pints until her arms fell off.

"Don't tell me that pubs in America don't get a crush after work." Kate White flashed a good-natured grin. Piper had lucked out two days earlier, walking past the pub just as Kate was plastering a poster in the window advertising for temporary help.

"Happy hour is more about half-priced potato skins than anything else. Don't worry—I'm not complaining, I'm just happy to find a job for the next few weeks." Piper took one last swipe at the bar with her towel and grabbed a seat next to Kate and her plate of french fries. A few patrons remained, obviously regulars, and more would join them as the evening progressed, so the break was much appreciated.

"Tell me more about San Diego. I've never been to America."

Piper shrugged. What was there to tell? Her hometown was the best place in the world, but the last place she wanted to be. She couldn't understand it herself, so explaining it to a brand-new boss seemed like a bad idea. And that wasn't really the question Kate had asked, anyway. "It's nice. Clean for a big city. Sun and surf, right?"

And over-achieving parents and siblings and pressure…

Needing a break from that drama was part of why she finally applied for a work visa. "I've lived there almost my entire life, so this trip is a big deal." Okay, that didn't sound neurotic. Good. She munched on a fry instead of saying anymore, best to quit while ahead.

Kate tilted her head, as if debating whether or not to ask more. Was it that obvious there was more to Piper's adventure? "You're not the first backpacker to come around looking for a bit of work. But you don't seem quite as carefree as most. And after an afternoon like this one, most would be looking for other work."

"Carefree isn't in my genetic code. My parents don't care what we do with our lives, as long as we work hard."

"But yet you're backpacking across Europe."

"I worked hard to plan and save for this trip. My parents are hoping I'll find inspiration for a career." Or at least stop "mooning over boys," as her mother had said. That still stung. "I guess I am, too."

She waited for Kate to probe further—not that she had any more answers she could share. Instead the pub owner turned to face the entrance as a Hedgehog regular entered. Piper recognized Sue, the slight woman with silver hair and bright blue eyes, but not the younger man she was tugging along. He was talking to her with obvious affection, head tilted to catch her response as she finished her thought and shrugged off her coat into his hands. Piper definitely hadn't seen that guy before. He was…sexy.

Down, girl. Not on the agenda, remember?

But she couldn't tear her eyes away. He was larger than life, gorgeous in a roughed-up, J. Crew-ad kind of way. He paused after hanging up Sue's coat and pulled his cell phone out of his blazer pocket. Piper's gaze measured him every which way, flickering over what looked like well-loved Doc Marten boots and dark jeans, up to his blond hair, cut short but somehow still mussed.

He was tall, broad across the shoulders, and his long torso looked lean and cut. Piper knew he would feel solid stretched out on top of her, and all her lady bits started tingling at the thought. Damn. She hadn't flown across the ocean to fall back into that old routine.

"Piper?"

She jumped, realizing she was still standing in front of the bar.

"Yes. Pardon? I'm sorry."

Kate took Piper by the shoulders and guided her around the bar. "Staring isn't polite," she whispered, then laughed as Piper pinked up.

"I wasn't…oh God, I was. I'm sorry. I was just curious…"

"Is that what Yanks call it? Curiosity?"

"What?"

"We Brits call it lust."

Piper turned beet red. She was busted. "Well, embarrassed is an international term, right? So can you go take their order while I crawl under the bar and die?"

———

Miles Dumbrowski sipped his beer and listened with half an ear as his aunt chattered on about nothing with a few friends. This wasn't his first time in The Green Hedgehog—he flew through the UK at least once a year while on leave from a tour of duty or on his way home from a mission. And, schedule permitting, he often popped down to Hastings to visit his mother's only sister.

Tonight was his last night of leave. He'd be heading back to the sandbox in the morning for three more months of deployment before returning to Coronado Beach, his permanent home as a US Navy SEAL.

This was the first tour he hadn't spent his leave time on an exotic island. His teammate Jared Sutter had flown to the UK to meet up with his pregnant wife, and Miles had thought England sounded like an excellent idea. After more than a few years of playing hard in his down time, Miles was no longer interested in a party scene. This time, he'd soaked up some culture, sat in more than a few pubs, and seen a few football games.

And mostly he'd just chilled the fuck out.

He glanced covertly at the bar again. The usual bartender seemed to be missing tonight, and in his place was the most captivating woman. Miles had been sneaking looks at her since arriving at the pub. There was a lot to appreciate. Dark hair spilled down her back in loose, hypnotic waves. Her eyes were seductive, but her easy smile was completely without guile and the rush of pink that flooded her cheeks every few minutes tended toward angelic more than anything else. She was probably a full foot shorter than him, with bouncy curves and a ton of energy. The perfect size, he realized, to crawl into his lap and watch a movie, to turn around and straddle him once they'd run out of popcorn. The perfect size to wrap his body around all night long and to make one of his t-shirts look illegal the next morning.

"Miles was in London for a meeting on Friday, and decided to stay the weekend before he headed home." His aunt dragged him back from his fantasy with a pat on the arm. She was good about not telling people what he did for a living. *A meeting*. Ha.

"Shame you couldn't stay longer," Kate tossed out as she passed by their table. "We're playing rugby next Sunday and the Whites would be happy to kick your arse again."

Miles could hold his own on the field, but he let her rib him. "I'll be back, don't worry."

Kate snorted and set her tray down at the next table before coming back to clear away their empty glasses, and as she did, she caught the fact that his gaze wasn't really on her at all. She smirked. "Have you met Piper yet? She's an American as well, just here for a few weeks. Great bartender."

Piper. He decided to go grab his next drink himself.

HE WAS LOOKING RIGHT at her. She'd been watching him, too, and there was something about him…she couldn't put her finger on it, but this was no ordinary guy. He looked like a Norse god and held himself with a certain awareness, like he might pounce out of his seat at any time.

As if he knew exactly what was on her mind, he shoved out of his chair and prowled toward the bar. Piper did the only logical thing and beetled to the far end where two regulars were arguing good-naturedly. "Would you like another?" Piper pointed to their empty glasses and flashed them a teasing smile when they paused their debate and looked at her. "At least you can agree on what to drink."

"Tell him I'm right, Poppy."

She laughed. "It's Piper, and I'm sure you're both right."

"Impossible!"

"You're both cranks and it's no wonder you're drinking with each other instead of pretty women." She winked and handed over new drinks. She loved the back-and-forth banter of tending bar. It could be awkward if she missed, but she rarely did.

"We want to know, Poppy…are you in Hastings because you lost a bet? Surely London would be more interesting."

"My parents honeymooned here, actually. My father was

working in Germany at the time, and they only had a weekend to get away. They've always talked about it fondly. Plus the hostel rates are cheaper. Win-win. And this way I get to spend time with both of you." Piper patted the bar in front of her, painfully aware the Norse god was waiting at the other end. She'd kept him waiting long enough—and when she thought about it like that, she felt silly.

Taking a deep breath, she tried to look unaffected as she moved toward him. Tried and failed, she was sure, as her stomach clenched and her heart leapt when she stopped in front of him. His eyes caught hers. Could he read her thoughts? Did he know she'd been ogling him?

"Need a refill?" she squeaked. Squeaked! Where the hell had that come from?

"Sure." He pushed his glass forward and smiled. "I'm Miles, by the way." His slow drawl rolled over her and she blushed again.

"You're not British!" Piper stammered at the harsh bite of the words. "Not that there's anything wrong with that, obviously, or that it should even be surprising, what with jet planes and all. I mean, that's how I got here too." *Shut up, Piper, and busy yourself with something other than drooling.* "I'm sorry."

His laugh was slow and warm, washing over her like a reassuring hug. He reached past his empty glass and grazed her clenched fists with the tips of his fingers. "Kate says you're an American, too."

Piper felt a current of electricity bolt up her arm, and she licked her lips. "Um." This wasn't a hard question. "Something like that." *Something like that?* "Yes. I mean, yes, I am. And tired! Obviously. I'm Piper." Her brain had turned to mush, which made thinking hard. She was pretty sure she was embarrassing herself.

She looked down at her hands, gripping the bar cloth like a lifeline, and then to Miles's still-empty glass. Shaking ever so slightly, she poured him a new pint of lager—she assumed he wanted more of what they'd ordered the first round—and slid it toward him. Her eyes lifted and stilled as his gaze caught hers once again. The air in her lungs slipped out of her body and new breath rushed in, catching at the back of her throat. *Space,* she thought, *must put some space between us*. But taking a step back only meant she could see more of him.

Miles. She rolled the name around in her mind. How strange that just a few seconds ago she didn't know his name, didn't know he was an American, didn't know what his touch felt like. *Miles*. He was staring at her, but not staring, really, because that would be rude and this was anything but rude. This was a bubble bath of attention, tingly and soft and warming to the core.

"It's nice to meet you, Piper."

"Same." She relaxed into the feelings of connection. Of interest. In the back of her head, a little voice tried to get her attention, but she told it to shut up.

The door swung open, breaking the spell, and three people made their way to stools at the middle of the bar.

"I should go do my job," Piper whispered.

"You do that," Miles smiled. "I'm not going anywhere."

———

Two hours later, he was still there, talking rugby with Kate while Piper wiped down the last of the tables. They'd had a few more exchanges, short snippets of words and long, heavy looks, but the bar had gotten busy.

Now it was almost empty. Everyone else had left a few minutes earlier, including Sue. Piper had watched Miles say a brief goodbye to his aunt and realized he planned to wait for her to finish up, warming her to her toes and scattering her thoughts.

She put a final chair in its place and headed for the bar. Miles followed. "Can I walk you to the hostel?"

Ten, nine, eight... *Try not to squeal, Piper*. "Is it on your way?"

"Close enough. We'll actually pass my aunt's house on the way, but it's just another block."

She grabbed her bag and waved goodbye to Kate.

"See you Monday. Don't do anything I would do in the interim," her boss said, winking. Piper turned quickly for the door, mortified.

Miles caught up with her a few steps outside the bar. He carefully bumped her shoulder. "Ignore Kate, she doesn't have a filter."

Piper took a deep breath and willed herself to relax. "I guess there's not very much to do at eleven o'clock at night? No 24-hour Starbucks?"

"I don't think so." Miles paused. "I don't actually live here."

Piper realized that they hadn't actually talked about much earlier, they had just stared at each other and (at least on her end) had weird tingly feelings.

"So you're just visiting?"

"Yeah."

She waited for him to elaborate. He didn't, just looked at her, which didn't feel unpleasant—just unnerving. She sucked in a breath. "That's nice. I don't have any aunts or uncles. My parents were both only children."

"I've got fourteen aunts and uncles, counting on both sides. Made for some pretty sweet Christmases growing up. But Aunt Sue's probably my favorite, and the only one in Europe."

"Fun."

"How about you? Are you an only child?"

She shook her head. "Nope, I've got a brother and a sister. And we're all close. What my family lacks in extension it makes up for in intensity."

"Good intense or bad intense?"

"Um…mostly good. Sometimes bad."

"Too close for comfort?"

"Yes. No. I don't know." She glanced over at him. She didn't know how much to share—he wasn't overly forthcoming himself, except about the size of his family. He looked genuinely interested, though, so she took a deep breath and plowed on. "We spend a lot of time together, even my brother who is married and has his own family. They're at my parents' place for dinner a couple of times a week. I love that, mostly, but I'm glad to have a break from it as well."

"So you got on an airplane and flew across the ocean?"

"Pretty much. Seeing Europe is a good excuse for some alone

time." Piper laughed. "Seriously, I'm not really running away, this is just a working holiday."

"Good way to do it." He hesitated. "I've seen a lot of the world through my job, too."

Tell me more about that, she wanted to ask. But if he'd wanted to offer more, he would have. "The idea of going to a different city every day or two doesn't appeal to me as much as staying in one place for a bit. I want a chance to sink into a community, meet people, hear their stories, discover hidden gems."

"And for that, I am grateful, because meeting you has been the highlight of my…time overseas this go round." There wasn't even a hint of smarm in what could have sounded like a line. He was genuinely charming and even though he was a total mystery to her, she trusted the authenticity in his words.

What was wrong with this guy? There had to be something… And yet even as the question flashed through her mind, Piper didn't want to find out. It didn't matter if he was perfect, or just putting on a good cover. That was the beauty of a vacation hookup, after all. Sure, she hadn't planned on ever having one, but that was before she laid eyes on six feet something of blue jeans and easy smiles.

"Maybe you could show me some of the tourist hotspots tomorrow—I don't work again until Monday."

"Hmmm." Miles slowed to a stop, his brow pulled tight.

"What? If you don't want to…"

"Oh, I promise it's not that I don't want to." He grinned and held his hand out to Piper. "I have to go to work tomorrow."

"Okay." She took his hand, his fingers warm and strong around her own. "Well, the next chance you've got."

"Why waste a perfectly good opportunity? Let's start right here. Right now."

She laughed. "Okay, I'm game. Where to?"

He winked, a dark promise in the shadowed night. "Who says we need to go anywhere? This is a pretty significant spot, I'd say."

Piper looked around at the dark, deserted street. The high street was up ahead, but there was nothing remarkable about where they stood.

"I don't get it," she whispered, but from the look on his face she wanted to get it. This sounded good. Weird, but it wouldn't be the first time Piper had fallen for weird. It would be the first time that weird could pass for Captain America.

"This spot?" He tugged her close. "This is the site of our first kiss."

CHAPTER
THREE

"THIS IS *the site of our first kiss.*"

It should have sounded like an awful line, but Piper only felt relief that he knew exactly what she wanted, and then a rush of excitement. Every bit of her hummed in anticipation, her palms itching to press into his broad chest, her hips aching to lean against his. He slid his gaze over her face—slowly, carefully. Hungrily. Was he looking for permission? Piper could taste her desire, sharpness flooding her mouth. Her lips parted, and he closed the gap. With a sharp intake of breath, he lifted his hands to her face and slid his lips over and between hers. He tasted like beer and salt. *Peanuts.* Bar snacks had never been erotic before, but Piper wanted to cover Miles's naked torso in peanuts and nibble them off one by one. She slid her tongue across his bottom lip as his hands raked into her hair. He nipped at her lower lip, eliciting a quiet groan of pleasure that doubled as his tongue moved against hers. Piper shivered, and Miles pulled back in concern.

"You're cold." He looked her up and down—she was wearing a black cotton wrap-around shirt and faded jeans, which had been fine for the walk to work at midday—and shrugged out of his blazer. "Here, put this on."

"Now you're going to be cold."

"Not a chance." He wrapped his arms around her waist under the jacket and pulled her close again, curving his upper body so their heads were close. "Where were we?"

Piper pressed her lips against his, then to his jaw and around to his ear. "Don't get me wrong, I could do this all night, but maybe we should continue this when it's not so dark and cold. I don't have any plans for tomorrow, just sayin'."

Miles took a ragged breath, pulled back slightly and kissed Piper's forehead. "I need to tell you something."

"What?" Piper slid her hands up his sides, wanting to explore all of him. She couldn't quite reach the hard planes of his back, so she smoothed her palms flat against his equally hard chest. A muscle twisted under her fingers, and she craned her head to better see his face. "Miles, what is it?"

"I'm heading back to work tomorrow afternoon. If there was any way to change my flight, I would, but…"

"You're going back to the States?"

He pressed his lips together. "No. Different direction."

She paused her hands, forgetting their original path as she frowned. "That's cryptic."

"That's my job."

"In the other direction."

"Yep."

"Are you coming back this direction any time soon?"

"I'm going to be busy for a few months."

And she'd be long gone, anyway. A few weeks here, then Paris, then Prague, and Greece… "And then?" Maybe they could meet up again.

"More work. I'm sorry."

Her fingers shook and she grabbed the bottom of Miles's t-shirt, wanting to hold on to him even as the delicious heat that had been building in her core disappeared and a cold stiffness filled her body. "So tonight… This was what?"

Miles's fingers moved again between his jacket and Piper's shirt, up and down, his thumbs rubbing from the bottom edge of her rib cage to her hips and back. "I don't know. This was the night we met."

"That's…poetic. So I'll be a bittersweet memory?"

"You're mad."

No, she had no right to be mad. He was a stranger who tasted like beer and peanuts and wrapped her in his blazer, turned her on and made her want more…but *stranger*. She sighed. "You don't think you should have mentioned you were leaving in the morning before kissing me?"

"I didn't mean to trick you, Piper. But I'm glad I didn't say anything if that was the only way I got a taste of you."

"A taste?"

"Yeah." He smiled tentatively. "Delicious taste, in fact."

As she looked at Miles's face, half in shadow, she realized he was as nervous as she was sad. She stared at him for a moment and then let her gaze drift over his shoulder to the dark building across the street. A few hours ago she wouldn't have cared. She still shouldn't. Her mother's voice rang loud in her head. *You're such a dreamer, Piper. You get swept away by hope. Success comes from good planning and hard work.* This trip might be an unusual path to success, but Piper knew she needed to find herself before she could go home. Maybe it was for the best that whatever this was between her and Miles end before it could snowball into something messy, something that would take over her life.

"Miles, I just got here. I've saved for this trip for four years, and I'm planning on traveling around Europe for the next year. Falling —" Piper cut herself off, horrified. What was about to come out of her mouth? Had she not learned anything from the first twenty-four years of her life? It was time for Piper to be her own first priority. Her only priority. Romantic delusions about Norse gods needed to be shut down. "And since your work seems to keep you busy, and our paths aren't likely to cross again, we should probably say goodnight soon and go our separate ways."

"Soon, or now?" He nuzzled her cheek, but she sensed he was holding back now. "There's no pressure here, Piper. But I think we should stop at my aunt's house, grab some warm sweaters and go sit on the beach for a bit."

She relaxed against his chest and nodded despite herself. She wasn't ready to say goodbye yet. Because beer and peanuts. He brushed a quick kiss across the top of her head and they eased into a stroll, his arm slung around her shoulders, hers tucked around his waist. He explained that Sue's house was on a side street just one block up. When they got there, Piper was reluctant to disentangle from Miles's warm, hard body, but she really didn't want to be the topic of gossip at the pub on Monday, so she let Miles go up the steps ahead of her.

"I'll wait here."

"Come on. I'm sure my aunt's in bed. The lights are all off. I'll just be a second, but you should wait inside where it's warm."

Piper tiptoed into the foyer of the narrow row house and watched as Miles climbed the stairs. The entry was lit by a small lamp, and her eyes strained to take in the details of the darkened rooms beyond. The house smelled like books and beeswax, and she could see the outline of a fireplace on the far wall, surrounded by floor-to-ceiling shelves stuffed to bursting with books. Immediately to her left in front of the window, a sofa was flanked by more piles of books, these mostly hardcovers and oversized reference books.

The floor above her creaked, and Piper jumped, but in the next second Miles reappeared on the stairs in front of her.

"Your aunt has a lot of books."

"She doesn't have a TV, never has, but she has pretty much any book you could name. She'll read anything."

"I'm the same way! I tried to get my parents to ditch their cable service a couple of times, but my brother can't live without football and my mom is addicted to the home-decorating channels."

Miles handed her a thick, oatmeal-colored wool sweater that must have been his aunt's because it was snug on Piper. He pulled on a thinner light blue cashmere sweater himself and topped it again with his blazer. Piper made a small noise of appreciation, and Miles's face reddened. She was happy to see he wasn't always totally cool.

He quietly closed the door behind them and they set out at a quick pace for the center of town, holding hands. Miles asked a few questions about her family, and Piper told him about her dad's new model-train hobby and her mom's antique shop.

"Um, what else… My brother is a contractor, and my sister is in medical school. She got the brains, he got the brawn. I'm not sure what I got. Middle-kid problems, right?" Piper shivered as they stepped on to the boardwalk, and Miles turned his body to protect her from the wind. She couldn't make out his expression exactly, but as she pressed her hand to his chest, she could feel his heartbeat pick up. "You don't really want to hear about my family, I guess."

Miles chuckled and slid his hand under Piper's shirt, warming the small of her back. "I do. Later."

They moved their faces at the same time, cold noses touching before mouths found each other and then the heat was everywhere again. Piper found Miles's skin under his shirt, and they were moving together, being inside each other's clothes because they knew it was all they could have. Miles's left palm settled at the bottom curve of Piper's breast, his other hand trailing licks of fire up and down her spine. He was being too damn gentle, Piper thought, arching toward him. She wanted to imprint all of him onto all of her, the feel of his much taller body curving around and over hers, the smell of his soap, the feel of his smooth, warm skin stretched over what felt like a very impressive set of abdominal muscles.

Stumbling, Miles backed into a wooden railing. Piper swayed against him and he groaned. He jerked them down to the ground and pulled her into his lap. "You're driving me mad."

Burying her head in his neck, she breathed in. Beneath the beer and peanuts, his skin smelled like mint and man. Miles was going to feature heavily in her fantasies over the next year, and she only had one night to fill in the details. She kissed the apex of his neck and shoulder and the tendon flexed.

"Do you like that?" Piper nipped in the same spot with her teeth, then rubbed it with the tip of her tongue.

"I like everything you do, Piper." Miles took a deep breath. "I like you way too much for having just met."

Same, she wanted to say, but what was the point?

"Hey," he said gently. "Ignore me. Tell me where you're going next on your travels."

"Paris next month."

"Nice."

"Have you been?"

"To Paris? Never."

"Where have you been?" *And where are you going?*

"My job takes me to the ugly parts of the world. I'd rather be in Paris."

"I've probably romanticized it, but I can't wait." She curled into the warmth of his torso as he stroked her arm.

"Don't go falling for a French man." He said it so quietly, she almost didn't hear it. But she did, and the impossible promise in the words was something she couldn't *un-hear*.

"I'm not planning to fall for anyone," she whispered.

He made a sound, halfway between a groan and a growl, and pulled her in for a rough, hungry kiss. "Neither was I."

CHAPTER
FOUR

"I'M NOT PLANNING *to fall for anyone.*"

"Neither was I."

Piper stilled, her face pressed into Miles's neck. Had she heard him right? What were they doing? There was no future here, and leading Miles on would be cruel if he was the type to fall hard and fast. She'd clearly read him all wrong. He looked like such an alpha male on the outside, but inside he had feelings. Which made him a great guy for dating. Totally the wrong guy to make out with.

"Miles, I…" Why did it feel like she was breaking up with him? And why did that feel wrong? *You always worry about other people, Piper. That's why you're twenty-four and have no idea what you are doing with your life. Stick to the plan.* "You're amazing. This was amazing. But it's late, and you're leaving tomorrow. We should probably cool it before we do something we'd regret."

———

Miles watched in disbelief as Piper shuttered her physical reaction and stood. He had just been dumped. One hour, that was probably a record for the world's shortest relationship. *It wasn't a relationship, dumbass, and the fact that's where your mind went is probably why Piper's running scared. You are scaring her.* He raked his hands through his hair and nodded. Pressing too hard would guarantee tonight was a one-off.

He rolled his eyes at himself as he stood to join her, shoving his hands in his pockets to keep them to himself. He'd lost sight of the truth that tonight couldn't be anything *but* a one-off. Because he was heading to Iraq for another three months.

Nodding, he gave in. "For the record, I could never regret anything with you, but you're right, it's late. Let's head back."

Relief flooded her face, and his gut pinched. What was going on in her head? This wasn't just a vacation for her—this time abroad was obviously a mission. She'd come in search of space to sort out whatever was on her mind.

But she was from San Diego. Maybe when she got back, if he wasn't overseas again…

God, that was tempting. All he needed was a connection. Something casual. He took a deep breath and offered a laidback smirk. "I've never been to Paris. Will you email me with updates on your adventure?"

She hesitated, a response frozen just behind her lips.

Hesitation was good. It wasn't a straight-up *no*, which meant there was a part of her that wanted to say yes.

He leaned in slightly. "Look, if we were back home, I'd ask for your number. This is just like that, no pressure."

"And if we lived in the same place, I'd give it to you. You're a great guy, Miles." Piper sighed and fixed her gaze on a point in the distance. "But honestly, I'm glad that's a moot point, because the last thing I want right now is a relationship. This is the year of Piper."

———

Miles pressed his lips together, like he wanted to ask a third time, but was holding himself back.

He needed to hold that line, because she was close to giving in. He was just so cute. No, not cute—he was more than that. Bigger, stronger, more noble than cute entailed. He was like a high-school quarterback, all grown up.

She took a deep breath that did nothing to quell her nerves. The last thing she wanted to do was say goodbye to Miles. But she didn't want to hook her heart on a sailing ship, either. She owed it to herself to be fully present on this adventure, not wishing for something that couldn't be. This needed to end now. Tension was rolling off Miles's body beside her, and she ached to turn and soothe him. *Not your problem, Piper.*

His voice tight, he asked what she sensed was one last question. "If we lived in the same place, you'd feel differently?"

Yes, yes, a million times yes. "No," she lied. "I shouldn't have said that. I'm not looking for a relationship right now."

Miles started talking again, but they were almost at the hostel, and he cut himself off. "Okay, I'm sorry. Look, I promise that I'm not a crazy stalker, and I'm not going to harass you, but I'd really like to get periodic updates. I'd love to see Paris through your eyes."

She couldn't say no to that. She nodded. "I'll get your email address from your aunt. But don't get your hopes up, I'm not really a computer person."

"That's okay. I don't always have Internet access at work. But when I do get online, if there was a message from you, that would make my day."

"Where the heck are you going?"

"Don't worry about it," he said quietly, stepping close and brushing his thumb against her lips. His fingertips lingered on her cheek for just a second, but it sent shivers down her spine. "I'm doing what's got to be done, and I'm fine out there."

His tone twigged something deep in her heart. Something… familiar. "Miles, are you a soldier?"

He pulled his lower lip between his lips and narrowed his eyes, looking up at the dark sky.

"You can tell me," she whispered. "I won't tell anyone."

She'd drifted closer still, and their bodies were almost touching as they stood in the shadow of the quiet building where she was staying.

He looked down at her and, with a groan, pulled her in tight for a hug. "I'm just a guy doing a job I'd rather you not think about, okay?"

It wasn't okay at all. She'd been ten kinds of selfish, and all this guy had wanted was something to look forward to at the end of whatever he was going to do.

"I'll email you," she breathed. "I promise."

He shook his head. "Don't promise anything you don't mean."

"I mean it!"

"You didn't a minute ago." He dusted a kiss across her forehead. "I want you to find me again because you want to connect with *me*. No other reason."

"But I don't want you to—"

He cut her off again, this time with a hard kiss right on the mouth. She opened for him, instantly, and whimpered when he pulled back after just a brief, bittersweet slide of lips. "It's my job. I don't need care packages and empty promises. I need you to live the life you want to live and be happy, got it?"

"Got it."

He kissed her forehead and stepped back, stopping a few feet away. "And if we ever end up in the same city, you owe me a date."

She swallowed hard and nodded. He stood there, obviously not leaving until she was safely inside, but she couldn't do it. So much for her stupid bravado about independence. One night of kisses with a stranger and her heart was leaping hard against her ribcage, desperate to be pressed against his broad, strong chest again. To feel his arms around her and his lips on hers.

Reluctantly, blindly, she stepped backwards up the steps, and opened the door. *Be safe*, she mouthed at him.

Lifting his hand, Miles waved—an acknowledgment and a goodbye wrapped in one.

She closed her eyes, and when she opened them again, he was gone.

CHAPTER
FIVE

PIPER TOSSED and turned all night, finally abandoning the effort at dawn. She pulled spandex shorts, a sports bra, a sweatshirt, and her running shoes out of her backpack. She wasn't diligent enough to train for a race, but she liked that running could happen anytime and anywhere, and it was a healthy-ish way to work shit out.

And the way her head was still spinning over Miles—the kisses, the realization that he was in the military, the *longing* she already felt for him—she needed to do some major processing.

Heading away from the quaint and historic downtown, she settled into a good pace and the restless feeling fell away. Few people were out and about so early on a Sunday morning, although she could see many having breakfast or otherwise getting ready for the day through their front windows.

Ordinary people doing ordinary things.

She thought about her family on the other side of the ocean.

Her mother always said she was the dreamer in a family of doers, although saving for a trip and taking off on an adventure felt an awful lot like *doing* to Piper. Even if it didn't have a larger goal than just seeing the world and coming back with a better understanding of herself.

Because Piper definitely didn't understand herself. She didn't get why she always felt slightly out-of-step.

Like falling for someone who she'd only known—and would only know—for just a few hours.

She needed to get over it.

Bad timing, that was all. Miles would be the hot military hero she'd tell her granddaughters about in fifty years—the one that got away.

A dull ache made her think that, if not broken, her heart was most definitely bruised. Reasonable aftereffect of being sucker punched.

She blinked back almost-tears and pumped her arms faster, driving her legs harder until her chest burned because of exertion and nothing else.

Keep telling yourself that, Harrington.

The sun was higher in the sky when she finally slowed to a walk, and the streets were getting busier, so she headed back to the hostel. As she cruised down the last block, she saw Sue step out of her row house—and then Miles was in the doorway, and Piper tripped over her feet as she jerked to a halt.

God, he was beautiful. He was wearing sweat pants and a t-shirt, but the sweats were low on his hips and the t-shirt stretched tight across his hard, chiseled chest. She could still feel the flat, strong planes of his torso under her fingers.

And more to the point, he was still there. Sue got into a waiting car. She was dressed quite formally, as if she was attending a wedding or church or something.

It only took her a split second to make up her mind. She needed to talk to him one more time. *Touch him, hold him, never let him go.* Just talk...say goodbye properly.

Her entire body tingled with adrenaline as she knocked on the bright blue door. When it swung open and Miles stepped into view, words caught in her throat. He was freshly showered, which made her all the more aware of the fact she'd just run five miles. His hair was damp, and she caught a whiff of a different soap than last night. This one was more expensive, slightly spicy, like it had a matching cologne and a designer price tag. It wouldn't normally do much for her, but on Miles it was a pheromone. A smile slashed across his face, replacing his initial surprise with obvious delight.

"Hi." Piper took a ragged breath.

"Hi." Miles reached out and slid his hands around her upper arms, guiding her inside. "You've been running?"

"Yes. I was heading past, and I saw…" She waved her hand. "You're not gone yet."

"Not yet." His hands tightened on her arms for a second, then he relaxed his grip, but he didn't let her go. "Soon."

He raked his gaze down her body, and when his eyes met hers again, they were… Dancing sounded like the wrong word. Alive. Interested.

"I wasn't sure I'd see you again," he said quietly. "And I don't want to assume too much about you showing up this morning, but…"

"You can assume," she whispered back. "Anything you want. I needed to see you."

As she talked, a frantic rush of words, his eyelids slowly dropped, hooding his gaze. Not all the way, just to half-mast. Like he was thinking hard. Holding himself back from saying things.

She felt the same way.

"Miles," she let his name whoosh out of her, half plea, half prayer. That was all it took.

Lowering his head, he slanted his mouth over hers, and she could feel the tension in his body as he held his hunger in check. She tasted his lips, his tongue—oh God, his tongue, so firm and insistent and probing—before he pulled back.

Tugging her past the foyer, he turned their bodies as one into the front sitting room, his hands sliding under her sweatshirt, hissing as he found the bare, damp skin underneath.

His mouth returned to hers, hot and demanding, and as he kissed her—although "kiss" didn't really describe the way he was consuming her from the inside out—he levered them sideways, sinking onto a soft couch.

Their legs slid together, the soft fleece of his sweat pants rubbing against her bare skin, but under that fabric she could feel strong, heavy thighs, muscles bunching as he wrapped himself around her. And when he slid a hand down to her practically naked butt and pulled her in even tighter, she felt something else.

He was huge and *hard*. For her. All of a sudden, it felt like he was practically naked, too.

Hands shaking, she squeezed his shoulders, then stroked upward to his neck. Warm, clean skin stretched taut over tight muscles. She kissed her way down the bulging tendon, licking and tasting as she went.

"Maybe this isn't a good idea," he forced out, his voice strained.

"Wait, why?" She pulled back enough for his face to slide into focus. His lips were wet, shiny from kissing her, and she wanted them to be doing that again.

He scrubbed a hand over his face, then pushed up off the couch, leaving her bouncing on her back in his wake. He muttered something she couldn't make out, then stalked into the hallway.

She wasn't positive, because all the blood had rushed out of her head and there was a dull buzzing sound between her ears, but she was pretty sure she'd just been shot down. She squeezed shut her eyes a little tighter and willed the ground to open up beneath her. When that didn't happen, and she hadn't died of embarrassment, she took a breath and decided to back out gracefully.

"Right. Of course not. You need to go. And actually, I mean, it's not... It's just that I thought you might..."

Righting herself, she avoided looking up at Miles and stumbled to the door. As she turned the knob, Miles's right hand closed over hers and his left wrapped around her waist, pulling her back into his chest. Into all of him, actually, and despite her pathetic attempt to throw herself at him followed by a complete meltdown, she could feel his erection pressing into her. He was still hard.

"Shit, I'm sorry. Don't run away. Don't run away and think for a second that I rejected you, Piper. There just isn't time right now. I absolutely want to make love to you, more than you know." His mouth pressed into her hair, his breath making the edge of her ear tingle.

She stilled inside his arms. Big, stupid man. "Who said anything about having sex? We were just making out and you put the brakes on."

He huffed a frustrated laugh in her ear.

"I was ten seconds away from ripping your shorts off. Believe me, I needed to stop."

Oh God. They could… She didn't have anything on her, but maybe if he had a condom… "Maybe we didn't need to stop."

Miles groaned, his hands moving again, grasping her waist and turning her around. He pulled her hard against his body, then up, pressing her against the door.

"Do you have protection? I don't, and we should be smart…" Miles silenced her with his mouth, kissing first her top lip, then the bottom, and harder in the middle, willing her to open for him again. As they kissed, slower and sweeter this time, he caressed her body from top to bottom, imprinting on her skin. It was goodbye all over again. She wanted to cry.

With a regretful sigh, he rocked into her pelvis, giving her a moment of bittersweet ecstasy before lowering her to the ground. "I'm sorry. God, humping you against my aunt's door wasn't what I wanted to do to you either, but I couldn't help myself. You blow me away."

Piper didn't know how to take that. "Thanks, I guess."

"Look, there's probably a lot more we could say here, but there isn't time to do this right." He dragged a breath into his lungs, then stared at her, like he was trying to find the right balance of words.

She couldn't find them, either. So she fell back to her promise. "I'll email you."

He started to say something, then cut himself off and started again. "Listen, I want you to think about something. Meeting up when I'm stateside. I'll come to you."

It was their conversation from the night before, but now she didn't want to say no.

She wasn't going to say no, but she couldn't find the words to say yes, either. She just stared at him dumbly.

"A weekend? Whatever you want, if you still want to." He

reached for her hand and lifted her wrist to his mouth. "I know that I'll still be hungry for you. I'll always be hungry for you, Piper."

CHAPTER
SIX

MILES BURIED his head deeper in the dark green linen scarf he was using as pillow and blanket and sand net. As in, *keep-the-fucking-sand-out* net.

He needed a few hours of sleep, but the wind had picked up in a big way and the blown-out building they were sheltered in didn't offer much protection. Plus the over-eager fire team they were attached to for this intelligence-gathering reconnaissance mission wouldn't shut up.

From where Jared was standing watch near the window, Miles heard a muttered instruction for everyone to be quiet, and he closed his eyes again. His buddy had his back. As soon as dark fell, they'd head out again, get what they needed, and then ditch these mother-fuckers back at the base.

He didn't normally mind working with the regular troops, but ever since coming back from England, his nerves had been on edge. This was their first time off base since returning, and last night had been good. They'd gotten a lot of pictures, and Vince Nash—the fucking ninja recon freak of SEAL Team 9—had visually confirmed that the compound was full of women and children.

Which made their job that much more difficult, but better to know.

Stop thinking about it. But if he blanked his mind, Piper snuck in. Wide eyes and a confused, wobbly smile... So fucking innocent.

He knew what she imagined he was doing here—nothing like reality.

Or maybe he didn't know, because she hadn't sent an email yet.

————

Piper sat on the edge of her bunk and stared at the folded piece of paper tucked between the pages of the paperback novel sitting beside her. She rolled her new cell phone back and forth between her hands. Kate had paid her first week's wages in cash and Piper had gone straight to the mobile shop to pick up a prepaid phone. Her first text message was to her sister-in-law, who had promptly responded with love and demands for a longer email update. Now her thumb was rolling over the screen. She'd already added his name to her address book, but she'd still hung on to the paper. **Smiles-Miles@xmail.com**. Every night for the last week, she had traced her fingers over the words and around the torn edges, reliving every detail of their few hours together. But as time slipped past, she worried that each day blurred her perception of what had really happened between them. Doubt started to creep in, making her second guess all the things she wanted to say to him.

And then there was the worry she needed to stay positive for him. Morale and all that.

She'd email him...soon. As soon as she found the right words.

Resolved, she slid her cell phone into her purse and tucked her novel under her pillow. Time to move forward. Her guide book flopped open to the pages about Paris. These words were also committed to memory, and Piper sank into them, only feeling slightly guilty at the relief that washed over her at the fantasy escape.

She'd only made it halfway through the guided walking tour of Sacre Coeur when her phone beeped. She leapt off her bed and scrambled for her purse, heart pounding, even though she knew it was ridiculous.

He doesn't have your email address, remember? It was on her to make the first move.

Instead of Miles, it was Kate. **Rugby at the park tomorrow. We need sausages and buns to grill. Can you pick them up before you come in?**

That she could do. She tucked her book away, grabbed her purse and headed for the door.

At the store, Piper piled her basket high with buns, sausages, mustard and relish. She passed on the hot dogs because they didn't look the same as at home.

All of a sudden, Miles's aunt Sue popped out from the cereal aisle. "Hello there." She cast an appraising look at the armful of meat. "Are you hungry?"

Piper laughed. "Actually, Kate invited me to a rugby game-slash-barbeque tomorrow—and tasked me with picking up some food."

"That sounds lovely. You know, I used to play, with Kate's parents, in fact. I think we'd all end up in the A&E if we tried now!"

"You're pretty spry, Sue. I think you could take the White brothers."

The older woman chuckled. "Of course. They'd never see it coming."

"How about you? You don't have a basket or a cart."

"I'm actually just getting some anti-nausea medicine. I'm leaving for a cruise on Monday."

"Oh, fun!"

"I'm looking forward to it, but I'm in a bit of a pickle, which is why I stopped you. I was hoping to ask a favor. Or maybe do you a favor? Normally my neighbor pops over to water my plants, but she's traveling to London soon because her first grandchild is due any day. I was wondering if maybe you'd like to stay at my place while I'm gone and take care of it for me. You could save the money that you're spending at the hostel, and I wouldn't come home to dead plants and missing valuables."

Piper raised her eyebrows. "Really? We just met, are you sure you trust me? I mean, I'm totally trustworthy, and if it would help you,

I'd love to do it." She worried her bottom lip as a thought occurred to her. "How long will you be gone?"

"Two weeks. Is that a problem?"

"No, not at all."

"Excellent. Thank you, dear. And hopefully it won't be too quiet and boring at my place for you."

Piper waved her hand. "Oh no, not at all. I get all the social time I need at the pub. Plus getting to read some of your books would be an added bonus."

Sue cocked her head to the side and wrinkled her brow. "How did you know... Ah, right, my nephew. Of course."

She carried on, blithely ignoring Piper's rapidly pinking cheeks. "Okay then, well, you might as well move in tomorrow morning. Come round for breakfast? Excellent."

And as quickly as she had appeared, the silver-haired elf was off again, leaving Piper alone between the freezer bins to wonder what she'd done to deserve such good luck.

———

No sooner had dusk set than the shooting started. Every ten or fifteen minutes, a few shots cracked in the night. On the horizon, a distant glow told him a house or a car was on fire. So much for getting closer to the ISIS commander's location tonight.

"We can't get involved," Jared muttered in his ear. Nothing he didn't know. They were ghosts, just gathering intel at this point.

From the darkness of the alley, Vince stepped silently into view. He shook his head. "Not us."

Not tonight, but it would be soon. This town was about to become the next front in a dangerous, unstable conflict, and Miles would be at the heart of it.

"Do we head back?"

He glanced at Sutter, then at Nash. "How much closer can we get?"

Vince shrugged. "Front-row seat if you want."

There was no question what they had to do. "Then let's pack up and go see what these assholes are doing."

CHAPTER
SEVEN

THE NEXT MORNING, Piper said goodbye to the aging hippies who ran the hostel, grabbed her supplies from the communal kitchen and trundled off like a pack mule to Sue's townhouse. The door swung open in welcome as she wobbled her way up the steps.

"Welcome! Here, let me take something." Sue held out her hand and Piper handed over her small bag of groceries from the hostel kitchen. Sue chuckled as she looked inside. "Peanut butter and crackers…hopefully we can do one better than that for a bit of breakfast. Come in, come in."

Piper found herself being herded into the front room, her rucksack slung on the bannister and her backpack propped on the floor beneath it. "Should I put these somewhere else? I wouldn't want you to trip over my bags."

"Nonsense. Everyone should live with an obstacle course from time to time, keeps you nimble. First, tea and scones."

They settled in the sun room at the back, and Piper was enchanted by the view of the narrow backyard. Someone had transformed the small space into a number of miniature gardens connected by stepping stones beneath vine covered arbors. She could see a wooden chaise lounge at the far end, peeking out from beneath a willow tree.

"Thank you again for staying here while I'm gone," Sue said as she poured them each a cup.

"Really, the pleasure is all mine." Piper smiled. "You said you're going on a cruise?"

"Yes. Truthfully, it's not my preferred method of travel, but Annie at the Travel Hut convinced me that it was too good a deal to pass up."

"Do you travel a lot?"

"As often as I can. I always have. I was a stewardess back in the day, and although we didn't get to stay very long in any of the exotic destinations, we did get to see glimpses of the entire world."

"Wow, that's amazing! This is my first time traveling by myself, but I've been on a couple of shorter trips with my mom. My favorite place so far has to be Rome. How about you? If you could pick one highlight, what would it be?"

"South Africa. There is nothing more stunning than a sunrise on a safari." Sue smiled at a private memory, and her eyes went all soft and dreamy. "That was my honeymoon."

Piper poured them both more tea, and as they sipped and ate the buttery scones, Sue shared some of her adventures to Iceland, Russia, New Zealand and Hong Kong.

"And you went to all of those places by yourself?"

"Oh heavens, no. I was lucky enough to have a husband who liked to travel, so some of those trips were with him, but he passed away almost twenty years ago. I like to go by myself now—no one else quite gets my pace, if that makes sense."

"Totally does."

"Now, I'll give you a key and show you around. I've got a Women's Auxiliary meeting this evening, but I'll be back for a late dinner. Do you have any questions?"

"I don't think so." Piper stood and followed the older woman into the kitchen, where Sue pointed out the essentials and took a spare key from a drawer. Then they headed to the front of the house, where Piper picked up her bags and climbed the narrow staircase to the small second floor.

"That's my room, there, and once I leave, if you want to change the bedding and sleep in there, you can. But tonight you'll be in here." Sue pushed open the other bedroom door, revealing a twin bed bathed in sunlight.

"I really should get a bigger bed. Miles doesn't visit that often, but when he does, he practically falls out of this thing."

Piper stood, frozen to her spot in the doorway, staring at the bed as Sue brushed past her. "I'll get you extra pillows and blankets..." Her words trailed off, but Piper wasn't really listening anyway.

Email him. Tell him that you're staying here.

Her pulse pounded in her neck. Her chest. Lower.

She flicked her gaze around the room, looking for any sign of him, and came up empty. But the room carried a faint scent that she recognized, and when she slowly stepped toward the bed, she realized it was his cologne.

"Everything okay?"

Piper jumped and spun around. "Yes! Great."

Sue smiled at her. "Thanks again."

"Yeah." Piper returned the smile.

"I'll be downstairs if you need anything. The bathroom is at the end of the hall."

When she was alone, Piper lay down on the bed and pulled out her phone. Hands shaking, heart pounding, she scrolled to his name in her contacts and pressed the envelope icon to start an email.

And this time, she was going to finish it and press send.

———

Miles headed across the common room for the computer lab.

"Hey, Dumbrowski, we've got an O Group in five, you're heading the wrong way."

"I know, I just need to check my email." It was getting a bit wishful thinking at this point. The good news was that it wouldn't take five minutes to look at an empty inbox.

But when he typed in his password to his xmail account, it wasn't empty.

Two messages. A slow smile curled up his face as he clicked on the first one.

Hi Miles,

Funny story. I'm lying on your bed. I mean, the bed that you sleep in at your aunt's place. I'm going to be house-sitting for her. And so I'm lying here, thinking of you. Feeling kind of bad for not sending this message sooner.

I wanted to. I just didn't know what to say. Hi, I guess. Let's start with that. I hope you're safe. I think about you every day.

Piper

Grinning like a fool, he clicked on the second message.

Me again. I forgot to add that the bed smells like you. In a good way. Really good. And now I'm blathering, and I know it's an email, so I could delete this, but...maybe it's better if you can see how random my thoughts are when it comes to you.

Piper

He clicked reply, already composing a response that would get past the censors but still let her know he was thinking of her, too—and how hot it was that she was sleeping in his bed, in a way.

But as his right index finger hit the H button, everything went down. The lights, the computers. His fucking good mood.

The back-up generators would kick in any second, but by the time he got logged back in, he'd have to log back out again.

Fucking war.

With a sigh, he pushed away from the desk and headed for his orders group. Hopefully he'd have time to get back to the computers before they headed back to the front.

The house was quiet when Piper returned from the picnic.

She'd opted not to play, but it had been fun to spend social time with Kate and her friends outside of the pub. If Miles had been there, she might have tried playing. The thought of Miles covered in mud and sweat, muscles flexing, tugged low in Piper's gut. She swallowed hard. *If I didn't let go of the ball, he'd have to tackle me. Pin me down to the ground, brace his legs against mine, slide his hands between the ball and my chest.*

With a giggle, she fanned herself and shoved that fantasy away for later.

Wandering into the kitchen, Piper found a note from Sue stuck to the fridge. **Made a salad for dinner, it's in the fridge. Open a bottle of wine, I'll be back soon. -S**

Wine glasses were easy to find on an open shelf, but plates were not in the cupboard above the sink or behind any other doors. One cupboard was full to bursting with cookbooks, another spices, and the last few enough dry goods to survive a prolonged natural disaster. Piper shook her head. Apparently Sue didn't follow conventional kitchen storage practices. Success was found in the first drawer she opened—colorful mismatched plates and bowls of all shapes and sizes.

Sue returned as Piper was setting the table. Over dinner, Piper prodded her to share more travel stories, and then left her to finish packing while Piper wrote to her family with a more detailed update of her first week away. Immediately after hitting send, her phone rang.

"Hello?"

"We just got your email and realized you'd still be awake. How are you? I'm so glad you got a phone!" Piper smiled at the sound of her mother's voice. "Tell me everything. Oh God, we miss you."

"Miss you too, Mom. I just told you everything in the email! And you know I love you, but I'm having a great time... Dial down the panic, okay?"

"Piper, it's my job as a mother to worry. You'll understand someday."

"Mmmm. Well, I'm only twenty-four, so let's not worry about that just yet. So, how's Dad? Anything interesting happen this week?" Piper listened as her mother filled her in on the gossip, and then the phone was passed in turns to her father and younger sister, Anna. "Are Joe and Lauren there, too?"

"Not yet." Anna covered the phone and mumbled something to their parents. "They'll be here in an hour or two. Will you still be up?"

"Probably not, I'm beat, but I sent Lauren some photos today. Ask her to share them with Mom and Dad. I'll send you some tomorrow, 'kay?"

"Okay. Miss you, Bug."

"Miss you too, Banana. Night."

On the way to the bathroom, Piper noticed that Sue's door was closed and her light was already out. No big goodnight, just quietly retiring when ready. So unlike Piper's family, but very much like Piper herself. After brushing her teeth and washing her face, Piper changed into pajamas and pulled back the covers. A warm thrill spiraled up through her body as she rolled her face into the pillow. She was acting like a teenager and she didn't care. Miles had slept on this bed, and the scent of him lingered. For the next ten days, she'd be alone in this house. Tomorrow, she was losing the pajamas.

CHAPTER
EIGHT

PIPER SHIVERED as fingers skimmed up her spine, edging her toward consciousness.

"Wake up, Piper," Miles whispered, pressing his body flush against her back as she rolled onto her side. As he teased at the side of her breast, she groaned, desperate for his thumb to swipe at her nipple, standing tight and begging for attention.

Tentatively at first, and then with more confidence, he alternated teasing strokes and rolling pinches, until Piper's breath was shallow and panting. His mouth burned hot against her neck.

"Miles," she begged.

"What do you want?"

Piper blushed. She couldn't possibly answer that question!

"Piper, do you want me to…" Miles trailed off, his fingers teasing the waistband of her pajamas.

"Mmmmmm." Piper rolled her hips toward his hand.

"Wake up, Piper."

That wasn't Miles. Piper's eyes flew open in panic. She could smell him, but she was alone. Sunlight flooded the small bedroom, and she realized the voice was Kate's, and it was coming from her bag. With a groan, she remembered programming the alarm clock on her new phone with her boss's voice after the rugby game.

"Wake up, Piper." She smacked the screen, willing it to stop, and stomped off in search of Sue's coffee maker. A Miles sex dream shouldn't be interrupted—that was her new rule.

Especially when dreams were all she had. He hadn't responded to her email yet, and he might not for a while. She had no idea what the conditions were like where he was, and so far she'd managed to resist doing an Internet search.

She snorted. What was she, her own worst enemy? She poured herself a cup, and leaned back against the counter, willing herself to think of anything other than Miles. Not the way he smelled or what his hands felt like on her skin. How he kissed her—demanding, hungry. What it would be like to have all the time in the world to explore each other's bodies…

Stop it.

Kate's voice rang out again from upstairs, and Piper admitted to herself that it was, in fact, time to go to work.

The alarm was annoying but effective.

Back in the small bedroom that smelled like the man on her mind, she skirted the bed and focused on her suitcase instead. She put on her black wrap top and soft blue jeans—the same outfit she'd worn the night she met Miles. Then she took a selfie and fired off another email to him, with a brief note saying she understood if he couldn't respond.

She headed to the pub, and promised herself not to think of him until the end of the day.

She broke that promise ten seconds later.

———

The next morning Piper didn't wake up until Miles was done with his dreamy seduction. When she waltzed into the pub, a ridiculous smile on her face, she was certain Kate would ask what was up with her mood, but her boss was busy with lunch prep and deliveries and barely noticed.

Maybe Piper didn't look like a puddle of goo after all. She didn't have any experience against which to compare this feeling. Her previous real-life relationships had never been as hot as Miles in two nights of dreams. Had her orgasm this morning really happened? Even if it had been a solo effort with a dream guy, it still had been the best of her life.

She floated through her shift and splurged on takeaway curry for dinner. Humming a random tune, she let herself into Sue's house just in time to hear the answering machine turn on.

First she heard the recorded message—Sue's happy voice encouraging the caller to try back another time because she rarely remembered to check messages anyway, and then a beep. Piper stilled as she heard Miles's voice fill the room, surrounded by crackly static.

"Hi. It's Miles. I got Piper's email, and then needed to leave for a different base. No Internet here, but I snagged a sat phone. I'll try again later."

She'd started for the phone as soon as she heard his voice, and now she dumped her dinner and purse on the counter before snatching the handset up. "Miles!"

"Piper." The rich timbre of his voice lit her up inside. "Hey."

"Hey." A big, dumb grin spread across her face. "It's so good to hear your voice."

"I don't have long." More static sounded in her ear. "It's going to be a while before I can email you back."

"I'll keep sending you little messages. They'll be waiting for you."

"That sounds real good. *You* sound good, too." He laughed. "Listen to me. First chance for a phone call in days and I lose my vocabulary."

She knew the feeling. "It's hard to squeeze everything you want to say into a few minutes."

"That's the truth. I'm looking forward to holding you again, though."

"I can't wait. You be safe, okay?"

"I gotta go," he said softly, and her heart surged into the phone line, desperate to hang on to him.

"Okay," she whispered.

She held the phone to her ear for a long while after they said their goodbyes. The cool metal made a poor substitute for Miles's warm strength. If he was here she'd wrap herself around his torso, run her hands up his chest, beneath his shirt, and find his thumping heartbeat. She wanted his arms around her like she'd never wanted anything else in her life.

Curry forgotten, Piper slithered upstairs with the half-empty leftover bottle of wine and drew herself a bath. Her sister had given her a travel-sized bottle of vanilla shower gel, and Piper decided it would suffice as bubble bath. While the tub filled, she pulled the cork and toasted herself in the mirror. "You have it bad, you know? Ignoring how much Miles makes you feel is foolish."

She slid into the scented, soapy water and let the warmth carry her away for a minute. *Seeing Miles.* She shivered in anticipation and reached over the edge of the tub to grab the wine bottle.

By the time her fingers were wrinkled, her stomach was protesting at the excess of alcohol and lack of food. She pulled the plug and wrapped herself in an oversized towel. Gripping the railing, she headed downstairs to grab the curry, her phone and a book about reconstructing Germany after the Second World War. The least romantic combination possible, but as Piper ate her dinner, wrapped in a towel on top of a bed she and Miles had both slept in, albeit at different times, she couldn't ignore the persistent ache of desire.

She'd never looked forward to sleep—and dreams—so much in her life.

———

Miles climbed into the back of the pickup truck. Out here the desert was quite beautiful. Not a bombed-out building in sight. No stench. Only a passing chance of being shot.

It was practically a vacation.

"You want one?" Vince held out a pack of cigarettes and Miles shook his head.

"I'm good." He pulled out his brew kit and fired up the tiny stove, making both of them steaming cups of instant coffee in a minute. "Here."

"Who'd you call earlier?"

Miles grinned. "A woman I met on leave."

"Shit. First Jared, then Trick, now you…everyone's dropping like flies."

"I just met her, man." He grinned again, this time a bit sillier than before. *Shit.* He could imagine Piper being the one. Maybe. "War makes you think crazy shit."

"No kidding. What's she like?"

"Pretty. God, so pretty. Curvy brunette. She's from San Diego, actually, traveling across Europe for the summer."

"That's convenient."

Miles shrugged. "She's not looking for anything serious. I didn't tell her I'm based in Coronado."

"Why not?"

He wasn't sure. "It didn't come up. We met the night before I flew back here."

"So what, you're going to call her a few times, impress her with your GI Joe-ness, then show up and whisk her off her feet in the fall?"

Sounded like a plan.

Vince snorted. "Dude, girls do *not* like to be lied to."

"I didn't lie. I barely even omitted it, it just didn't come up."

"Keep telling yourself that, brother."

"Well, maybe I'll tell her soon, then." He just needed to get back to a fucking base with fucking working wi-fi. Fucking war.

In the distance, headlights bounced toward them. Vince tapped his cigarette out. "Worry about your love life later, brother. We've got company."

CHAPTER
NINE

IT WAS another week before Miles and his team had a chance to fall back to the more permanent, better-protected base with reliable hot showers and, just as importantly, computer labs. Miles missed Afghanistan—never thought he'd say that. But on his last rotation there, the base where they'd been stationed had Internet in every room, and he'd been able to Skype with his parents and friends back home.

Now he had to read Piper's emails in a public room, and of course the only free computer was the one closest to the door. Not that she would send anything inappropriate, he was sure, but she had sent more emails and he wanted to read them in private.

And when he started clicking through them, he wanted to be alone even more, so no one would notice him just staring at the screen. Jesus, she was pretty. He loved that she'd sent a few pictures of herself just going about her day. They were small tastes of normal, and he'd cling to them.

In her most recent message, she included her mobile phone number and an apology for not thinking of giving it to him sooner.

· · ·

I'm leaving Hastings in a few weeks, heading to Paris, and I'm taking this phone with me. I don't know if calling is easier than emailing, or maybe both are impossible most of the time. But just in case, here's my number.

He hit reply.

Hi Piper,

I'm sorry it's taken me so long to respond. Been busy staying safe.

Love that you're sleeping where I've slept. Makes me think all sorts of inappropriate thoughts, I gotta admit.

I'm going to write your number in Sharpie on the inside of my brew kit. Trust me, that's a place of honor. Keep sending me pictures. I've gotta open them in a shared computer lab, so keep that in mind, but seeing your beautiful smile is the best part of my day.

Can't wait to hear about Paris. Have a crepe for me.

I'm going to hit the hay in a few. Will think about you in that bed.

Miles

———

Piper's phone vibrated in her back pocket. She looked around the pub. Everyone had a drink, and nobody new had arrived in in the last few minutes. She pulled out the phone and her heart leapt into her throat when she saw the name on the screen.

"Kate, I'm going to take five, okay?"

Her boss looked up from the liquor order sheets she'd been working on and nodded. "Sure thing. I'll cover the bar."

Piper scampered to the nook behind the kitchen. Pulse thumping, she read the message and quickly typed a response.

• • •

Maybe one day you'll tell me exactly what you think about, when you think about me in your bed.

She stared at the glowing screen after hitting send. Too much? Too forward? She buried her face in her hand. This was not her forte. A minute went by, and then another as Piper stared at a blank email, trying to compose a lighthearted follow-up message. *So anyway, how about that local sports team?* was the best she'd come up with, totally silly, so she deleted that and was about to start over when the phone vibrated, then rang in her hands. A North American number she didn't recognize flashed at her.

"Hello?"

"Hey." One syllable, and she knew it was Miles. "Is it okay that I called? Are you at work?"

"Sure. Yes, of course. I have a few minutes."

"It's an international call, I hope it isn't expensive for you. We're routed through the States."

"It's okay, I got a world-wide deal. You can call anytime." *Smooth, Piper. He'll be so impressed by your phone plan.*

He laughed. "So, about your question."

"Sorry about that. I should have said more. Or less, maybe. Are there rules about what you can get in an email?"

"No, I liked it. I just couldn't fully answer your question. Flirting is okay, though. Please, send me flirty emails every day if you want."

"Oh? I probably want to, yes." Piper blushed. She was glad nobody could see her.

"Good. So you know the deal, I've only got a couple of minutes..." He trailed off, and when he spoke again, his voice was lower, huskier than before. And quieter, so she pressed the phone hard against her ear and closed her eyes as if that might erase the thousands of miles between them. "But you in that bed... Piper, that bed doesn't do you justice."

"No?" Glee and panic pranced hand in hand through her body as she waited for what he'd say next.

"Where are you? I don't want to go past a PG-13 answer if you're with people."

She giggled. "I'm at work, but I came to the back room to email you. I'm alone."

He groaned into her ear. "That's dangerous. I can't get too worked up here."

"Aren't you going to bed soon?" She asked the question all breathy, the panic easing as she realized this was easy. And *fun*. "I mean…you're going to think about me. Can't you get a bit worked up? Won't you be able to…"

Another groan. "Not here. I'm not in a private room."

"Oh." Piper couldn't really picture what Miles's life was like there, and she realized she should probably do a better job on that front. Find out as much as she could without crossing into stalker-zone. "I'm sorry."

"It's okay. Sometimes I luck out and get some privacy. And when I do, I will do exactly what you think I'll do. And I'll have you on my mind when I do."

She made a little humming noise of appreciation.

"What are you going to do after work tonight?" She could hear him shifting around on the other end of the phone. There weren't as many crackles today as when he'd called her at Sue's house. It was a good connection, and she never wanted the conversation to end, but it would, and soon.

"Probably take a bath. I love that big tub."

Through the phone, Piper heard Miles suck in a breath and she smiled.

He groaned in her ear. "Are you trying to kill me? Please tell me there will be bubbles."

Piper giggled.

"It's not funny. It's hot as hell, actually." She heard him move again, then more background noise like people were talking close to him.

"And then you have to go to sleep in that little tiny bed."

"I don't mind it. It smells like you still, or maybe I've just imprinted that in my memory. Either way, I like it."

"At home, I've got a massive king-size bed. You'd look good on it, too. Lots of…rolling-around room." A buzzer sounded in the distance, and he swore under his breath. "That's a one-minute warning for me."

"Okay. I'm glad we were emailing at the same time. Don't worry if you can't send anything back, I know you're busy."

"We'll talk again soon. I want to tell you more about my bed. And my plans for getting you in it."

"I'm sure we'll be able to work something out. I can fly to wherever you are."

"That won't be necessary, actually. Listen—"

Piper swore as the phone line went dead. What the hell? *I guess the Army is serious about their time limits on phone calls. Jeez.*

She took a minute to sit there, replaying the conversation over and over in her head before going back to work.

Miles Dumbrowski was too good to be true. Sexy, brave, funny.

And otherwise engaged. Trying to date a real-life hero was a challenge.

CHAPTER
TEN

A BRIEF APOLOGETIC email for the cut-off conversation arrived just before Piper went to bed. From the way Miles worded it, she figured he'd written it right after they talked and it had spent some time in the bowels of the military-firewalled Internet before being delivered to her, so she sent back an equally brief response—attaching a selfie of her lying in bed—and fell asleep with echoes of his voice in her head.

They didn't talk again for almost another week, although Piper sent a daily picture anyway, sometimes with a little note about what she'd done that day, how late the pub had stayed open, that kind of thing. Each time she hit send, she closed her eyes and said a little prayer for his safety.

Miles's aunt returned from her cruise with horror stories of ship-wide gastrointestinal viruses and being stuck at a dining room table assignment with a Texan oil baron and his trophy wife. But Sue's eyes sparkled and she had three memory cards full of pictures which Piper happily flipped through on the computer, asking questions here and there. Sue was thoroughly entertaining, and Piper counted her blessings that she'd met her. She was also relieved that all house-plants had remained alive for the duration of her stewardship. She wanted to keep Sue on her good side.

When Piper made noises about moving back to the hostel, the older woman would hear none of it. "I'd love for you to stay, really. How much longer until you leave?"

Only another week. Piper's heart tugged at the thought of leaving Hastings, and the temporary home and lasting friendships she'd formed. *And the extra connection to Miles.* Which was silly, really, because her phone would work in Paris and beyond.

"I'd love to stay, then," she said, hugging Sue. Then she made tea, like a good houseguest.

The next time she heard from Miles, it was early in the morning. Dawn was breaking when her phone dinged, and his email was short, mysterious, and promising.

Do you have an xmail account? Can you make one? There's a chat feature inside the email window that I think I can use here.

Miles

P.S. You're beautiful.

Even before she got to the end of the email, she was grinning. She flipped over to the Internet browser on her phone, hoping against hope she could create a new email address without asking to use Sue's computer or going to a computer lab.

It turned out she could.

Seven minutes later, she was sending him a message from her brand-new xmail address, using the instant-messaging app her phone had helpfully suggested she download.

Modern technology for the win.

Piper: This is me.

Miles: Good morning.

Piper: Is it for you?

Miles: Morning...yes. Three hours difference. The sun is up and hot.

Piper winced. Of course it wasn't a *good* morning, not really.

Piper: This is a nice treat, being able to chat.

Miles: One of the other guys mentioned he does it with his girl.

His girl. She grinned at that.

Miles: I've got about twenty minutes, probably. Then I need to rack out.

Piper: What does that mean?

Miles: LOL — get some sleep.

Piper: Well, then we should talk about something that'll give you sweet dreams. And not get in trouble from anyone who reads this, of course.

Miles: There's a lot of things we can talk about that they don't care about, don't worry.

Piper: Like what?

Miles: Getting to know each other questions.

Piper: LOL. Okay.

Miles: What's your favorite color?

Piper: Blue. Yours?

Miles: Black.

Piper: Black isn't a color.

Miles: What?

Piper: Technically it's a shade.

Miles: We'll agree to disagree.

Piper: I don't agree to that. I like to be right.

Miles: See how much I'm learning about you already?
Piper: Ha! Okay, my turn. Um…. Hobbies?
Miles: Surfing. Skiing in the winter.
Piper: I've never been skiing.
Miles: Maybe that's what we should do when I'm back stateside. You, me, ski chalet…
Piper: Mmmm.
Miles: How about you? Favorite things to do?
Piper: Love the beach. Swimming, snorkelling. I like creative writing, too, and artsy stuff.
Miles: I don't have an artistic bone in my body, but I want to see something you've made.
Piper: Oh God, no. Maybe on like a tenth date, once I'm sure you really like me.
Miles: I promise, I really like you.

She pressed her lips together to contain an unbearably happy squeal.

Miles: Now, let's talk about swimming…bikini?
Piper: Definitely. Maybe even a skimpy one.
Miles: New plan. Beach trip on my first weekend of leave.
Piper: Deal.

They chatted for a few more minutes, but Miles had to leave just as Piper heard Sue start to move around, so she reluctantly said goodbye. But the man needed to sleep, although apparently not as much as normal people, because five hours later, as she was heading into work, her phone beeped at her.

Miles: Coffee date, 10 pm GMT tomorrow.
Piper: No question mark, so bossy. How do you know I'm not working late?

Miles: I pay attention. That he did. Wednesdays were early-close nights. She shivered at the intensity piled into those three words.

Piper: Can't wait.

———

She finished at the pub at eight o'clock the next night. When she got home and found a note from Sue saying she'd be out late, Piper drew herself a bath. Then she decided to shave her legs, and when she got out, she put on a bit of makeup to go with her yoga pants and t-shirt. It was a date, after all.

Her phone rang a few minutes before ten.

"You're early," Piper said in a rush. She really had run for the phone—she'd left it on the kitchen counter—but being breathless was just as much due to nerves.

"For what?"

"Lauren!" Piper stuttered to a stop at the sound of her sister-in-law's voice. "Uh, nothing. I was expecting a call from someone else."

"Intriguing, tell me more." God, she loved Lauren, but that teasing tone spelled disaster. Nobody could know about Miles just yet.

"I can't, gotta go. Love you!" Piper hung up and held the phone to her chest, her heart thumping wildly against it. When it rang a minute later, she took a deep breath before answering.

"Hello?"

"Hello to you, too." Miles had the best voice. She melted a little inside. "Can I buy you a coffee?"

"Yes, please. Decaf for me." Piper reached for a mug and poured a cup. Miles took a sip of something in her ear. "What are you having?"

"A latte with an extra shot of espresso. I need to go back to work later."

"In the middle of the night?"

"Cover of darkness and all that. But this is just a meeting."

"That still sounds…intense."

He laughed gently. "I guess. My frame of reference is a bit skewed. So how was your day?"

"Spent most of it looking forward to this date. How much time do we have?"

"A while. I bribed an officer to give me his phone code. No time limit."

"Sweet. Now I feel bad for not dressing up."

"You were going to dress up?" He laughed again. "In a dress?"

"Would you like that?"

"Definitely. Dresses are probably my second favorite thing for you to wear." This was silly. Happy silly. Flirting silly.

She moved to the couch and curled up against a pillow. "What's the first?"

"Nothing at all."

Her silly smile got pretty damn big at that. "Ah, is that how this date is going to go?"

"If we were on the same continent, you'd better believe it. If you want, though, I could tell you a bedtime story."

"Mmmm. No! I want to know more about you. I don't just want to hop in the virtual sack with you every time we talk. My dreams are bad enough."

He sucked in a breath. "You dream about me? I want to hear all about that."

"Um, okay. Maybe." She turned pink from head to toe.

"Piper." His voice dropped a register. "You should know that this is quite unusual for me."

"Transcontinental coffee dates?"

"Yeah, this is a first." He left the rest of his thought unsaid, but *something* hung between them on the line.

Piper swallowed hard. "First of many, hopefully."

"Damn straight. So I have a confession to make." He stretched the last few words, easing her into something.

"Oh yeah?"

"I've been holding out a key piece of information on you."

"Really." She took a sip of her coffee. "And are you going to share it now, or keep me in suspense?"

"I kind of want to give you some context first. For why I didn't tell you up front."

"Am I going to be grumpy about it?" She kept her voice light. This was a date. He'd wanted a date with her. Surely it couldn't be that bad.

"I don't think so, no. But I wasn't sure before."

"Then spill."

"You know I'm in the military. But I didn't tell you which branch."

She wasn't sure where he was going with this, so she just nodded. Which of course, he couldn't see. She cleared her throat. "Okay."

"I'm in the navy."

"Oh. Okay. Are you on a ship?" She had the distinct impression he'd gone to the Middle East, and was at a base somewhere there, but who knew how fancy boats got? She made a mental note to Google more about the navy and war.

"No, and you probably shouldn't ask me any more questions." He chuckled. "But I'm stationed in Coronado Beach when I'm home."

Oh. "Wow."

"So that weekend away…"

"Won't be so hard to organize after all." Her heart pounded in her chest. "Wow. Miles! You live near me!"

"I think so, yeah. Kate said San Diego…" He trailed off and she grinned.

"Yep. La Jolla. Holy crap!" She kicked her feet on the couch, then flopped back against the pillows. "Wow. Wow, wow, wow."

"So this isn't bad news, then." She could hear the smile in his voice.

"No, I guess not. Was I silly enough to give you the impression that would be bad news? Totally silly. Ignore any previous impressions. I'm thrilled."

They both laughed at that. The conversation wandered to movies, food, and ended up on high school experiences. He'd been his high school's valedictorian. She'd cut biology to catch a matinee of *Transformers*.

Piper could practically hear him do the math and filled in the answer. "I'm twenty-four."

"I'm thirty."

"So old," she teased, but something in her tone got lost on the phone line, because he asked her if that was really a problem.

"Oh, God no. Six years isn't that big a deal. Does it bother you that I still don't know what I want to do when I grow up?"

Miles chuckled. "Not at all. Besides, isn't that what this trip is about?"

"I don't know if I'll find my path this year or not, but for the first time it really does feel like I'm moving toward something. I can't wait to get to Paris and explore for a while, no working, no responsibilities, just ..."

"Just what?"

"You're going to think it's silly."

"Trust me." And the way he said it, of course she would.

"I want to get to know myself." She took a deep breath. "I know it's a bit romantic, the idea of Paris being a site for soul-searching and introspection, but if Stein and Hemingway could do it, I can too."

"Those are both writers, right?"

"Yeah." She might have secret writing goals, deep down in her heart. Maybe. She wasn't surprised that somehow Miles knew that about her when nobody else did. She swallowed hard and changed the subject because she wasn't ready to go there. "So can I ask when you might be back in California?"

"Our dates are always subject to change, so you need to not get too attached to this, okay?"

"Promise."

"I should be back by the beginning of August."

Then so will I, Piper silently pledged.

CHAPTER ELEVEN

OVER THE NEXT week they texted almost daily—whatever Miles had been doing, he wasn't doing it anymore, because he seemed to get to a computer frequently now—and talked on the phone a few times. Piper knew she'd need to upgrade her phone plan once she got to France. She didn't worry about Miles being a distraction from her trip anymore, though. If anything, he was her biggest cheerleader. Her family talked almost exclusively about her coming home. Miles suggested cafes guys he knew had enjoyed and helped her practice her French.

"I can't believe I'm going to the most romantic city in the world without you," she whispered into her phone late one night. He'd sent her an IM asking if she was up, and when she'd responded, he'd called right away.

"Next time we can do the midnight walk along the Seine together."

Next time. Her heart was going to explode. "That sounds perfect."

"It'll be fun to see a city that you've already gotten to know."

"You'll have to return the favor," she said, rolling onto her back. She tucked the phone between her ear and the pillow and pulled the blanket up tight around her face. "Where have you been that you want to go back to?"

"Tokyo," he said without hesitation. "You've never seen anything like their electronics district, and the food is to die for. Shopping's pretty good, too, although I don't fit into any of the clothes."

"I'm sure I wouldn't, either. My ass isn't really designed for tiny Asian clothes."

"Your ass is perfect."

Piper laughed.

"Seriously. I'm counting down the days until I can get my hands on it again." Miles lowered his voice. "My hands. My lips. My…"

"What?" she whispered breathlessly.

"I'll tell you when I see you. Not safe for Uncle Sam's virgin ears."

"You're a tease."

"I know." He cleared his throat. "I'm going to be out of comms range for a little while. I'll message when I get back to this base, okay? Don't worry."

"Pretty sure that's like *no offense* or *don't take this the wrong way*. A conversational red flag that guarantees I'm going to worry."

"Shoot. Should've gone another way with that, clearly." He laughed quietly in her ear. "Go back to sleep, gorgeous."

"Good night, my Miles." Her heart beating a mile a minute, Piper gripped the phone, wanting to hang on a bit longer. Her voice cracked as she added, "Stay safe."

"I will. I've got a date to keep."

"Hope she's hot," Piper whispered, unexpected tears sliding down her cheeks. Why was she crying now? She hadn't gotten emotional at the end of any of their other recent calls.

"Hot and cute and sweet," Miles said roughly. "Now back to bed. Go."

They whispered goodbyes again, and she buried her wet face in the pillow, breathing in the now just imaginary scent of him, regretting that she'd ever washed the linens.

Her last night in England was also her last shift at the pub. Kate's brother Daniel was also behind the bar, and before long she found herself planted on a barstool with a pint, surrounded by new friends.

"I know I was only here a short time, but this place really started to feel like home." Piper turned in a slow circle, taking in the wooden booths lined with thick red fabric, the creaky wide-plank floors, and the gleaming wood bar. The pub smelled faintly of salt and ale and wood polish, and she'd miss it.

"We have something for you," Kate said, nodding at Sue, whose eyes twinkled. They were up to something—and Piper thought she knew exactly what as soon as she opened the kraft-paper wrapping and saw the soft leather-bound notebook.

Kate grinned like the Cheshire Cat. "There's a card inside that we all signed, but the notebook is from Miles, officially."

"I acted as his secretary," Sue said with a wink.

Piper blinked her misty eyes and opened the notebook. Inside, in Sue's handwriting, was a note.

Write it all down.
   - Miles

Tucked under the first page was a card, signed by all the regulars including Sue, and Kate and her brothers. Piper swiped way her tears, laughing as everyone good-naturedly jeered a bit. She shook her head. "Happy tears, I promise!"

She circled the room, sharing a final moment with each new friend, and then sank onto a barstool and let Daniel pour her another pint.

———

The sun beat down on their vehicle as they approached the Kurdish checkpoint. Jared nodded at the guard, a man they recognized from earlier in the day, and gave the designated code phrase in Arabic. It changed every day, and today's was *Eid mīlad sa'aīd, Elmo. Happy Birthday, Elmo.* Something nobody else would say, and it made the Kurdish commander laugh, apparently. The week before the code had been *Big Bird is pretty*.

"Fucking Elmo," Vince said, dropping his sunglasses back over his eyes as they drove through the mostly quiet town. They needed to head back to the front after dark, but now it was time to hole up and get something to eat and a bit of rest.

They parked in the gated alley behind the building they were using. A local militiaman stood guard out front, and he snapped roughly to attention as the SEALs nodded on their way inside, laden down with the gear they couldn't leave in their truck.

"You want beef stew or cabbage rolls?" Vince asked once they were upstairs in the room they'd snagged. They all dumped their webbing and set their weapons on their sleeping bags. Jared grabbed the first stew, and quiet Johannson snagged the second.

Which left Miles with the cabbage rolls.

"What?" Vince asked, digging into his cold dinner. "You're Polish, you should love that shit."

"My grandparents were Polish. I'm hot dogs and french fries and fucking beef stew, all right? Cabbage is war food."

"Look out the fucking window."

"My point exactly. I don't need it literally shoved down my throat." He took the time to activate the heater bag and warm up his rations. Then he dug out a bonus condiments pack and liberally treated the entire mess with ketchup and pepper. "You think this is going to go well tonight?"

For the second night in a row, there was going to be a hard press against the insurgents to try and regain some lost ground. The night before, they'd just been observers.

Tonight, their orders were different.

Which meant they needed rest. Miles and Johannson racked out first. Three hours of sleep. Practically a luxury.

And then to war, again.

Miles counted backwards from one hundred, every ten numbers pausing to think about Piper and Paris—a world away. What was she doing right now? He couldn't wait to get back to his email and a phone line. He missed her voice something fierce.

Fatigue and thoughts of what he could be doing in France—in a bed—carried him away from the heat and the sand and the stench, and before he finished his countdown, he was drifting in an uneasy dreamland.

CHAPTER
TWELVE

I'm sorry for not sending this sooner. Mom has been sending me daily emails. I hope she hasn't been pestering you too. I've been busy exploring Paris and it's truly amazing. This city is at its best in transition, and the opportunities for spectatorship are endless. I can't think of any other city where dusk is so welcoming. The darkness doesn't chase people inside; some go home to their families or beds, but many linger in cafes, or even on the streets. I know it sounds so cliched, but Paris at midnight is amazing.

"Excusez-moi."

Piper glanced up from the letter she'd been composing to her sister-in-law on her phone. The person in the seat next to her wanted to get off the subway at the next stop.

Paris was everything she had hoped. It had rained off and on the first three days, but instead of dampening her enthusiasm, the grey skies and cool air just reinforced the city's gothic heaviness.

It was the exact opposite of southern California, and she gobbled up every detail. A hostel in Montmartre provided a perfect base for wandering on foot, and Piper was pleasantly surprised to find cheap food options at takeaway windows. She had gorged on Laotian noodles the night before. Thinking about it made her mouth water and she knew she'd be having it for dinner again.

An automated female voice announced the name of the station in quick, lilting French that Piper couldn't make out. She peered out the window as the train pulled up to the platform. Opéra. Two more stops to the museums. She moved over to the window seat to make room for another rider and turned back to her phone.

Yesterday the man at the cafe on the corner took pity on me and my pathetic attempts at French and asked me in perfect English where in America I was from. At first I was embarrassed that it was so obvious, but he said it would be obvious that he's French if the situation was reversed. True! I made him guess. He said Beverly Hills, which was pretty close. But then he admitted that California was his only guess.

He's invited me to his house for a dinner party on Friday night. His wife works late, which seems to somewhat common, so they eat late, too—he told me people will start arriving around eight.

The subway car raced around a corner and Piper braced herself against the window. Buying a metro card was a splurge. She was in no rush and it would be cheaper and healthier to walk as much as possible, but she was fascinated by the sights and sounds of the subway system. She heard fellow hostel guests complaining about the smell, but that was interesting to Piper as well—the scent of thousands of people moving quickly in all different directions. If she stopped and thought about it, she could probably pick out individually offensive notes like urine or body odor, but it was new and utterly unlike anything in San Diego so she didn't care.

I'm going to a couple of museums this afternoon, and then I'm going to find a cafe with a large window and watch day turn to night. You and Joe should come here for your ten-year anniversary. It really is crazy romantic here.

~ Piper

She saved the draft email to send once she surfaced from the metro system and tucked the phone away in her backpack. She glanced down at her oversized white buttoned down shirt, belted over black leggings and knee-high leather boots with heavy soles.

The boots had been a splurge, but her brother had sent her some early birthday money, and all the French girls were wearing them. Now Piper didn't feel so conspicuous, and sitting on a bench at a museum or with her head stuck in her notebook at a cafe, she could even slip into a fantasy about being a French student instead of an American tourist.

The subway car screeched against the rails, slowing to a stop in front of the platform. Palais Royal - Musée Louvre. She leapt into the swirl of humanity and hurried to the nearest exit.

———

It had been a week since she'd last spoken with Miles on the phone, and she'd started to worry—heck, she'd started the worry the second she knew he was going to be out of comms range.

But then yesterday there'd been an email with a tentative promise to maybe call soon. "Maybe" was music to her ears. Just the hope of talking kept all parts of Piper happy. *All parts indeed*, she thought. Awake, Piper was focused on exploring Paris and being in the moment. Asleep, she was a sex maniac and Miles was her very willing subject.

It wasn't just the fantasy or the promise of dirty stuff to come. She desperately wanted to hear Miles's… everything. She loved his self-assured laugh, his slow expulsion of breath before talking, and how he thought everything she said was sexy even though she knew it was awkward and amateur. Piper's head told her heart that she was an idiot for obsessing over a guy when she was in a world-class city on the trip of a lifetime, and her heart told her head to take off her panties.

Her breath hitched as she rounded the corner toward the hostel and ahead was a tall, built man in a uniform standing with his back to her. She sped up, her heart in her throat. It couldn't be Miles. It wasn't Miles, she knew that. Didn't stop her heart from thumping a mile a minute. *Please let it be Miles*. She was a few yards behind him when he turned and her footsteps slowed in disappointment. His profile was unfamiliar.

The Guy That Wasn't Miles smiled and tried to catch her eye as she passed, but she averted her gaze. *Sorry buddy, I just got my hopes up.*

In her dorm room, she stripped off her jacket and went to stash her backpack under her bunk when her phone vibrated.

BREAKING NEWS ALERT: American helicopter shot down on Kurdish border.

Piper numbly sat down on her bunk. *It doesn't necessarily mean anything. There are lots of troops there...* But she couldn't stop herself from scrolling to a news app and clicking on the details with shaky fingers. And as she read, she started to cry.

———

Miles couldn't believe the clusterfuck they were dealing with. Less than a hundred yards away lay the smoldering remains of a Black Hawk helicopter. The ISIS militants who shot it down were filming it and broadcasting it live to YouTube, and the rules of engagement they were currently operating under meant they couldn't go in and retake the equipment because the pilot and all but one of the troops had made it out alive. They'd carried their fallen comrade back across the front lines under cover of fire, and now they were waiting for the diplomats to try to do their jobs.

It wouldn't fucking happen.

It was the middle of the night, but they didn't yet have orders to move in.

They'd get those orders, but not until the next night. Twenty hours stretched ahead of them. Twenty hours of watching, impotently, as the enemy had their day thanks to equal-opportunity access to the World Wide Fucking Web.

Vince tapped him on the shoulder. "Spell out, man."

"Thanks." But Miles didn't step away from the observation post right away. Instead, he stood there with his friend and his fellow SEAL, and stared at the lunacy of modern warfare unfolding in front of him.

"Fucking YouTube, hey?"

Vince shook his head. "Yeah. Who would have thunk it? The people back home know more about what's going on over here than we do."

Miles frowned. "That's so wrong. You worried about your mom thinking the worst?"

His friend shook his head. "She knows better. Unless the CO and the padre show up on her doorstep, I'm A-OK."

But Piper didn't know that. Piper had no clue. And somewhere in Paris right now, the girl Miles had given his heart to in a single night was probably wondering what he'd just done to hers.

I'm right here, Piper. Be strong for me.

CHAPTER
THIRTEEN

PIPER HAD SPENT twenty-four hours glued to her phone and the television in the commons room. She needed to take a shower, but she couldn't tear herself away. *No, you need to go out and spend some time in Paris*, she could hear Miles saying in her head.

But there wasn't any chance she'd have fun when the standoff over the helicopter was being broadcast on YouTube and rehashed from every angle on BBC World and CNN International. All the footage was coming from the insurgents, and it made her sick to think that they were spinning the story to suit their own purposes.

The news reported that no further Americans had been killed, and while she'd shed more than a few silent tears for the one brave man who'd died, she was grateful it wasn't Miles.

Please stay safe, she willed.

When dawn broke in the Middle East, and the analysts said nothing else would happen until after the next round of scheduled diplomatic talks, she finally dragged herself to bed.

Sleep was elusive, but at some point between worrying about where he might be right now and imagining how good it would be to hug him when he got back to the States, she fell into an unconscious—if not restful—state, and stayed there for a few hours.

"This is fu—"

Jared shot Vince a hard look. The three of them were sitting together behind a built-up half-destroyed wall, but they weren't alone. The temporary command unit and headquarters group was within hearing distance.

Miles laughed as Vince rolled his eyes and started again. "This is futile."

"Better," Jared grumbled under his breath.

"When did you turn into such an old man?" Vince pulled out a cigarette and offered the pack to Miles, who waved him off. He didn't offer one to Jared, which only made Miles laugh harder.

"Maybe when I found out I was going to have a kid."

"Seriously, you're so square sometimes."

"I'm one hundred percent fine with that, you loser." Jared kicked at Vince's leg. "I'd like you to make it through the last few months of service without being hauled up on charges or discharged or killed."

"Pretty sure that none of those will happen if I swear in the middle of a fucking war zone."

"Whatever." Jared sighed and tipped his head back. "I don't know why I'm picking on you. This *is* fucked."

When one of the officers looked up, the SEALs all started giggling like little girls.

"Fucked indeed," Miles muttered before guffawing again. It wasn't that funny, but they'd been under intense pressure for two days. Something had to break, and apparently it was their sanity.

Just for a minute. They were the spec ops guys. They'd pull it together and do their best to save the day, but right here? Just the three of them? They could admit to each other that this was an un-winnable battle in a possibly un-winnable war. And that was, as they had definitively ascertained, *fucked.*

"What are you guys laughing about?" Johannson asked as he ambled over.

"How long it takes you take a piss," Nash drawled at him, and the other man swiped at him, but their good-natured tussling froze as a familiar *thwack thwack thwack* sounded outside.

Fucking gunshots. They all scrambled into position.

They were five hundred meters from the front. There were checkpoints and guards between them and the insurgents. Unless it wasn't a full-on attack. If it was an infiltration…

"Nash. Status report." Jared bit out the demand under his breath.

From his higher vantage point, Vince shook his head. "No visual. May have come from our twelve o'clock, two-story building. That's got a rear entrance. Guarded, but if they took those guys out…"

"Yeah." Jared pressed the speaker button on his headset. "Tango Team Leader to HQ, over."

"This is HQ comms, go ahead Tango Team Leader."

"Permission requested to move out and engage."

The voice at the other end of the line changed, and while they couldn't see the command team—HQ would have pulled back into the more fortified building behind this one—they all recognized the area commander's voice. "We don't know what we're dealing with, Tango Team Leader."

"That's precisely why we need to press forward, sir."

"Use extreme caution, Sutter. This is not our war yet."

One of the many reasons the situation was fucked. Jared nodded, even though the commander couldn't see them. "Yes, sir."

"Echo Team is moving to neutralize the technology concern." Meaning the helicopter would blow up soon and they shouldn't be surprised.

"Understood, sir."

Jared set the objective: find the shooters and neutralize the threat. Preferably without shots fired, but none of them were betting hard on that being maintained.

"Nash, you and Johannson get across to that two-story building. Dumbrowski, you cover him and stay here. If we push them out into the open, use your tear gas or shoot them. I don't really care at this point, you got it? I'm going onto the roof. Wait for my signal, then radio silence unless you're the one making the all-clear."

Miles nodded. They all did a quick re-check of their gear as Jared disappeared. Twenty seconds later, Jared told them the street was wide open, no sign of anyone at the windows—or what remained of the windows—across the way.

He closed his eyes and thought of Piper for a split second. He had a date to keep.

Swinging the door open, he tossed a brick into the middle of the street. Nothing. No scramble, no shots. "Clear, clear, clear. Go, go, go!"

With speed that always surprised him, given how much gear they were wearing and carrying, Nash and Johannson made it across the street and disappeared into the shadows. Miles swept his gaze over the street, looking for…anything. A weird movement, a too-still shadow. Any sign of something that was different than how it had been two hours earlier when they'd wearily walked back for a break, switching out their post at the front with Echo Team.

Inside the buildings to his left and right were American and other NATO forces. All hunkered down, waiting for more shots.

Nobody ever talked about the waiting game of war.

Tick. Tick. Tick.

When the explosion came, the street stayed silent for a minute, and then the fighting began—delayed reaction in the extreme. At first the fighting seemed to be closer to the front.

Miles could see, though, from his vantage point, that the good guys were in retreat, and with horror, he realized why—advancing toward them from what used to be their checkpoint was a shocking number of men, all in black.

It was the worst-case scenario.

All bets were off.

He hunkered down behind his rifle. Other NATO forces would close in behind—this wasn't going to work in the long run. The insurgents may have amassed a small army, but they were going up against pros. This would be bloody and bad, but Miles couldn't lose his cool—and he had to trust that his colleagues would act the same.

His job was to hold this building, and he'd fucking do it.

Almost too late, he saw the grenade lobbed in his direction.

"Almost" doesn't count, motherfuckers. He slammed his back

against the wall, dust and debris raining down on him as the grenade fragged the outside of the storefront. The wall shook behind him, and at first he thought he was fine—until he turned and fell over.

Ears ringing, vision bouncing around like a fucking ping-pong ball, Miles scrambled backwards to an interior doorway, taking cover deeper inside the demolished building. All around him a firefight raged full strength now and in the distance burned an actual fire. The helicopter was no more.

Deep breath. One, two, three. Another inhale, another controlled exhale. *Pull yourself together. Status assessment…* He crawled back to the front of the building and peered out the window. At least two combatants outside, close. Probably more. He listened to the return of fire. There were people at both ends of the building—between him and his team.

Nash, you asshole, you better be alive. The bastard was on his last tour.

Miles inched back up to the window. *Fuck,* his cheek burned. He didn't need to swipe it to know he was bleeding. Had some fragments come into the building? Was he hit elsewhere? He didn't feel injured but with the adrenaline pumping through his body, pain might not register.

He couldn't see for shit. Had no idea who was in the street and who'd taken cover. Where had all these guys come from?

He could retreat to the command station—he had an open sightline down the hallway to the building behind. But that would leave this storefront unprotected, and that wasn't an option. Not with Jared on the roof and Nash and Johannson still across the way. *On the other side of hell.*

Just another day at the office.

He needed his eyes to focus long enough to get a clear picture of who was outside. *Fuck it all.* He closed his eyes again and counted to ten as he pulled a tear gas canister out of his webbing and pitched it outside, making sure it skipped hard along the ground. He wanted to do two things—disorient as many of them as possible and drag some of them into the storefront.

Crab-crawling backwards, because he couldn't handle the thought of standing up just yet, he made it to the staircase just as the first fighters came through the door.

This time it was a grenade he palmed. No mercy. Just before scrambling up to the second floor, he pulled the pin and whipped it around the corner. Then he dragged himself to the landing, propped his back against the wall, and aimed his rifle down the stairwell.

Bring it on.

CHAPTER
FOURTEEN

IT WAS hard to explain the feeling of a grenade exploding beneath you. *Boom* didn't quite cover it. More of a bone-shaking thud.

Chaos followed, complete with screaming and what Miles could only assume was swearing in Arabic—his knowledge of the language didn't cover the words flowing fast and loose beneath him.

Sweat rolling down his face, his head still ringing like a bell, he tightened his grip on his rifle and waited to pick off anyone who climbed the stairs. His earpiece crackled to life.

"Well, so much for fucking radio silence," Jared drawled.

Miles just listened, waiting to see if Nash would respond. It didn't take long.

"Jesus, this is going to be a blood bath," Vince responded from across the street. "Johannson's showing off his sniper skills, though. We've got a good spot up here."

"I'm one floor up from Dumbrowski," Jared said. "I'm pretty sure he can't respond right now because he doesn't want to be heard, but I've got his back. We're going to push these motherfuckers out of this building in a minute, you ready to pick them off as they flee?"

"You know it, boss."

And then Jared was beside him, quiet like a church mouse as he crept down the stairs from the top floor.

Using sign language, Miles conveyed that he had a concussion and was having trouble walking. Jared signed that he'd go first, Miles keeping to his six.

Before they could say anything else, the first shadow stretched up the wall in front of them. Jared flattened himself against the stairwell, sliding his weapon forward until he had a clear shot. He took it. Using that downed fighter as a human shield, Jared led the way.

Miles scrambled behind his teammate, ignoring how the world tilted sideways. Three pops. Three enemy down. Jared veered right and Miles took the last two combatants down with a double tap to their center of mass. One. Two. Done.

Jared dropped his body shield and assessed the situation out the window while Miles kept a wary eye on the bodies lying in the room.

"We clear in all directions now, Nash?"

"Hells ya, brother."

Jared tapped Miles on his shoulder. "Come on, let's go."

Miles made it three feet out the door before he collapsed.

———

Five agonizing hours had passed since CNN first showed footage of an explosion of the American helicopter. The looping video ended with the English-accented spokesperson boasting that the town they were in would soon be reclaimed. The chilling end of the video showed a bleeding soldier from the unidentified checkpoint.

Terse statements from the White House Press Secretary and the Secretary of Defense didn't mean anything.

Helpless, Piper curled up on the couch in the hostel, ignoring her phone ringing every twenty minutes from her parents. Her own fault for answering once in tears. She'd told them she was fine. And if Miles would just call, she would be.

So every time it vibrated, she still looked at the screen, just in case...

"Do you know a soldier?" asked Ingrid, a backpacker from Sweden.

Piper just nodded, her lips numb and her brain too swollen to compose more of a response.

There was no reason for her to assume that Miles was there, but she just *knew* he was. *I'm gonna be out of comms range for a little while.* It was the way he'd said it, like he was trying to tell her without saying a word that he was going somewhere extra-dangerous. And from the ridiculous mess of information scrolling across the television screen, she didn't think there was anywhere hotter than that particular front right now.

"I need to take a shower," she muttered. Really what she needed was the dull roar of running water and a break from the constant stream of non-news.

She dragged her shower bag into the women's bathroom, stripped down, washed up…then stood there.

Thinking.

Trying hard not to go to the dark places in her mind.

He's big and brave and probably well-trained. She shut off the water and grabbed her towel from the bench outside the stall. As she lifted it into the air, her phone lit up beneath it.

Go away, Mom. As soon as she thought it, she regretted the rudeness, and she grabbed at the phone, swiping to accept the call. "I promise, I'm fine, stop worrying."

"Piper Harrington?" The masculine, no-nonsense voice that spilled into her ear was not her mother's. Ice-cold fear flooded her core and sluiced through her veins.

With a stupid nod he couldn't see, she answered affirmatively.

"My name is Vincent Nash. I work with Miles Dumbrowski, and he's talked about you many times over the last month. He gave me your contact information. He's currently on his way to Landstuhl Regional Medical Center in Germany…"

Wrapping her towel around her body, she snagged her shower bag and sprinted for her room.

As the man on the other end of the line kept talking, she roughly pulled on clothes and starting shoving stuff in her bags.

"Do you have any questions?"

"Just one," she said, catching her breath. "What do I have to do to see him when I get there?"

———

"You can't go in there, ma'am."

"I was summoned by one of his colleagues to meet him here, and the chaplain at the desk didn't have a problem with it. I showed my ID and—"

"I realize that, ma'am but he's—"

Naked. Miles had just shooed that same nurse out of the room so he could get changed. He chuckled to himself, ignoring the pounding in his head. Damn, it hurt to laugh. That sucked. It would probably hurt when Piper launched herself through that door any second and tumbled into his arms.

He'd have to brace himself.

Reaching for the door, he gingerly pulled it open. "I'm done getting dressed." Piper gawked at him. "Well, hell. Aren't you a sight for sore eyes."

CHAPTER
FIFTEEN

"YOU'RE OKAY," Piper breathed, her heart pounding in her throat. Four feet separated them and she was frozen to the ground. His face was bruised and he had stitches on his left temple. A grey t-shirt stretched across his broad shoulders and fluttered loose over his lean mid-section to a matching pair of nondescript grey sweatpants. As her panicked gaze randomly catalogued him, she thought he looked pretty damn good for someone injured on a battlefield. She'd expected a hospital gown—they were in a neurosurgery ward, for heaven's sake. But this was good. Better than good. He was standing and breathing and looking almost flirty.

"Okay is a relative term, but yeah." Miles winced as he lifted one shoulder, but it couldn't stop a wide grin from flashing. For the first time ever, she was seeing him with stubble. *Not the time to obsess over how sexy he is, Piper.* But he was looking her over, too, and when he spoke again, his voice was low and earnest. "And now you're here. So I'm even better."

"They told me you were going for a CT scan." She stepped closer to him, her palms itching to touch him and feel his stable, steady pulse for herself. To kiss him and hold him and—

"Had one already. Will have some more testing soon." He swayed in front of her and she was hip-checked out of the way as the nurse charged to his side. "Nope, I'm fine," he said, waving off the help. "But I think we need to sit."

Nodding dumbly, Piper followed as he turned ever so slowly, his outstretched hand always touching something for support. He gave the nurse a look and she muttered something under her breath about operators being terrible patients before closing the door and giving them some privacy.

She glanced around for a chair to pull close to the bed. There was one on the far side of the bed, squished under the window, but Miles was sitting sideways on the mattress, his back to the window, and she wasn't sure she could move it around to this side.

"What are you waiting for?" he asked gruffly, lifting his head to look at her again, the heat now undisguised.

"Um, I was just thinking of bringing that chair over here," she whispered inanely, because what she really wanted was to touch him and hold him—*and never let him go.*

"If you think I'm going to let you sit anywhere other than right here on this bed with me, you've got a surprise coming." He crooked his finger at her and she fought back tears as she shifted closer.

As soon as she was within snagging range, he wrapped his hand around her wrist, pulling her close to stand between his legs. As his fingers slid against her skin, the dam broke and her tears started falling

"No, gorgeous, don't be sad," he said against her ear.

"I'm not," she sniffled, the tears already abating now that she could feel his heart beat against her own.

She hadn't realized she'd wrapped herself around him until he groaned. With a gasp, she relaxed her grip, but he didn't let her go, just eased her back enough so they could look at each other. "It's okay. Just banged up."

"What happened?" She knew he couldn't tell her anything, really, but it seemed rude not to ask.

"Walked into a door," he said weakly, and a surprised chuckle shook her body. "No laughing, hurts too much."

"Okay." She smoothed her hands over his shoulders, ever so lightly, then trailed her fingertips up his neck and cupped his square jaw, loving the rough rasp of his five o'clock shadow under her palm. "This is a hell of a way to move up our date."

His eyes narrowed. "Not a date."

"No?" Her lips quirked at the new look of determination on his face.

"First thing—all our dates will begin with a kiss."

She leaned in and feathered her lips over his, lingering as the emotional wallop of actually kissing him hit her—because he was in a military hospital, but damn it, he was alive. He pressed his mouth more firmly against hers, soft and warm and tingle-making.

He squeezed her hip as they separated an inch, their noses still touching. "And I'm never going to wear sweatpants on a date."

"You could take them off," she said without thinking, but then he laugh-groaned and she whispered her apologies into the air between them.

He waved her off as he pressed the button to raise the head of the bed. "I like this idea of pants-free dating. I'll expect equal-opportunity bare legs, of course."

"Of course."

She stepped back as he shifted onto the bed, leaning his head back and stretching his legs out. When he patted the mattress next to him, she carefully slid in, cuddling against his side.

Even injured, he was a big, solid presence, and she closed her eyes as she lowered her head to his chest.

"I'll wear a dress," she murmured.

"I like that...technically complies with the pants-free requirement, but protects your modesty."

She giggled as he stroked her hair. "Hey, I'm supposed to be making you feel better."

"I do, a million times better—just because you're here."

When he yawned a minute later, he tried to apologize.

"Shut up. You're injured."

"It's the meds they have me on. I'm kind of loopy."

She pushed herself up a little higher so she could stroke the less-bruised parts of his face. "Go to sleep, Miles." Her voice caught on the words as her heart swelled at the contact. "I'll be right here when you wake up."

———

He drifted in and out of sleep for the better part of a few hours. In his dreams, he was still in the stifling heat, reliving the battle over and over again. If only he hadn't been so close to the wall. If only they'd fortified it so the concussion grenade and whatever else that had scrambled his brain hadn't had a chance to fuck him up. But every time he woke up, Piper was in his arms, soft and smelling a hell of a lot better than the Kurdish front lines.

He'd known Vince would call her—it was the last thing his buddy told him before Miles had been kicked out of the Middle East by a major who didn't give a shit that Miles thought he'd be fine in a few days.

He hadn't wanted to leave, but none of the doctors at the field hospital had liked his neurological responses. And when they said he was going to Germany, he stopped fighting the transport.

It was selfish, but the chance to be one small European country away from Piper? He hadn't known that she'd come, but he'd hoped.

A knock at the door announced dinner, and Piper slid off the bed to give him room. But one look at the tray in front of him had him shaking his head as soon as the orderly left. "Hell no."

"What?" Piper frowned at the salad and soup on his tray. "That doesn't look too bad."

"That's not *food*. That might be what I'd eat while waiting for food to *arrive*." He stabbed at the call button as he swung his feet off the bed, ignoring the fact that the world started spinning dangerously around him when he did that.

He was standing when the nurse popped her head in. "Yes?"

"Am I cleared to walk to the cafeteria? Because we're walking to the cafeteria."

"Not really, but as long as you've got someone with you..." The nurse shrugged as Piper looked back and forth between them with concern. "Just go slow."

He looked around for his stuff, finally finding his combat uniform in the closet. He fished his ID card out of the pocket. He vaguely remembered being stripped out of it when he arrived. He might have been in rougher shape than he wanted to admit if he couldn't completely pinpoint what happened when—his memory felt intact, but the timeline jumped around in his head.

Sliding on a pair of flip-flops, he finally held out his arm. "Shall we?"

It was a short walk to the elevator, which took longer than Miles was comfortable with. Same thing on the first floor as they headed for the dining room. But when he tried to pick up the pace, Piper slowed down.

"Hey, I'm not in any hurry to storm through our date," she said, rubbing the back of his arm.

He took a deep breath. Right.

She danced her fingers down his forearm, making his dick twitch. *Nope, don't get any ideas, buddy.* He laced their fingers together and squeezed her hand. "I can't believe you're really here."

"Of course. It's not like I was really doing the tourist thing the last few days anyway."

Heavy guilt throbbed in his gut. "I'm sorry if you saw anything on TV that stressed you out."

"Doesn't matter now." She pulsed her hand around his.

An airman was coming out of the dining room as they approached, and he held the door for them. Miles nodded in thanks. Inside he pointed her to the hot-meal counter. He'd been here twice before, once for an orthopedics consult on his knee at the end of a tour, the other time he came on his leave, visiting an injured friend.

He ordered a double serving of meatloaf and mashed potatoes with green beans, and Piper got the spätzle.

"That's basically mac and cheese," he teased as they walked to the cashier. He needed a moment after picking up the tray to orient himself. Fuck, he hated concussions.

"Yes, but it's *German* mac and cheese. With onions."

"Not really a selling point."

She laughed as they set down their trays, and he handed over his ID card.

"Sorry, it's cash only," the cashier said.

Well, shit.

"It's okay, I've got it." Piper swung her small messenger bag around to her hip and pulled out a slim wallet. "Euros?"

The cashier nodded and Piper handed over a twenty.

After she pocketed the change, she led the way to a table in the corner.

"And on a date, I'll be paying," he grumbled when she looked at him, her eyes dancing.

"So many rules for dating you. I'm not sure I'm up to the task." She winked as she tucked in to her dinner.

"Okay, change of subject. I don't want to lose the date before we even have it." And despite violating all the rules, this was still a pretty fucking awesome date. It didn't even matter that he couldn't get laid at the end of it—but maybe he could request Piper do his next sponge bath.

"Where'd you go there?" She waved her fork. "You feeling okay?"

He looked across the cafeteria table at her bright eyes, her dark, shiny hair coming loose from the clip holding some of it back, and something cracked open inside his chest. "Yep. I feel great."

"What were you just thinking about?"

He grinned. "Dirty nurse Piper fantasy."

A slow, sexy smile was all the response he needed. Not today, but hopefully before he left Germany, they'd get a chance to take their connection to the next level.

She blushed and fluttered her eyelashes against her cheeks as she dropped her gaze to her plate.

"Now you need to tell me what you're thinking of," he said under his breath, sliding his legs against hers under the table.

"Just us," she breathed, glancing up as she moistened her lips with the tip of her tongue. "Together."

His heart stuttered as the visual of that single word filled the hospital dining room. There were too many people around for him to be thinking of the two of them, naked, tangled in sheets. Piper spreading her legs for him, her breasts arching into his palms as he thrust slowly, filling her—

"Wow, okay, so another change of subject, maybe." Piper laughed, fanning her face. "But yeah, let's do whatever was in your head just then, as soon as you've got the doctor's all clear. Because I like it when you look at me like *that*."

Another grin. Jesus, this woman made him happy, even when his head throbbed and his face ached. "Yeah?"

"Yeah."

She reached across the table, wiggling her fork at his meatloaf. "Can I?"

"Sure thing. I'm not sure I need any of your noodles."

"Mmm, you're missing out." She popped the surprisingly good meatloaf in her mouth and made an appreciative noise he wanted to hear more of soon. "So… how long until you get to go home?"

"Dates haven't changed. Should be the beginning of August."

Her fork clattered to the table, and she stared at him, the colour draining from her face. "What? You're not going home from here?"

This was the hardest part about dating a civilian. "No."

"But you have recovery time…concussions are serious things."

He shook his head. "I was sent here to rule out anything catastrophic, because there's better imaging and specialists here and they needed the beds in the field hospital there. But I'm fine." He took a deep breath. "I'm a U.S. Navy SEAL, Piper. I don't sit on the sidelines."

"That's why you're not on a boat," she whispered, her eyes wide. "So that helicopter explosion that was all over the news…that was…"

He couldn't tell her anything. That was unexpectedly difficult. He squared his jaw and tried to show her that his spirit wasn't broken. Hell, it wasn't even damaged.

She bit her lower lip and shook her head slowly. "What are you trying to say, Miles?"

Yeah. This officially sucked. "As soon as I'm cleared, I'm going back."

CHAPTER
SIXTEEN

"I'M GOING BACK."

"You're serious." Piper was having a hard time thinking straight, and she knew Miles wasn't up for a fight—not that she had any right to complain about his job, but still. She wanted to yell at him and tell him how stupid it was to take the risk of going back at less than one hundred percent.

But looking back at her from across the table was the most capable man she'd ever met. Who'd had his bell rung but good by ISIS fighters and was eager to get back up and take them on again.

"Of course you are," she said, her voice softening even as her heart cracked. "I'm sorry. Right. If you're able, you go back."

"The army docs don't dick around." Miles reached across the table and picked up her hand, stroking her thumb with his. "If they don't think I'm fit, I'm not going anywhere. But if I'm fit, there's only one place I'm going, and it's where I'm needed."

Heart heavy and suddenly exhausted, she just nodded.

"But right now…" He tugged her hand towards him and lifted her knuckles to his lips. "I'm terribly unfit, and will need to stay here for a few days. So we have that."

———

Piper stayed late at the hospital until Miles's night nurse convinced her to go back to her hotel while he was sleeping. The next morning he tried to get her into family accommodations at the medical center, but as she wasn't a military dependent she wasn't eligible.

"It's okay," she told him. She still had savings, and her parents would help her out if needed, although no one in her family knew about Miles yet, which she'd thought about plenty but had done nothing to change the situation. They didn't even know she'd come to Germany.

Bad-daughter guilt gnawed at her. While they sat in the waiting room for an occupational therapy assessment a few days later, she quietly asked Miles who else other than his friend Vince knew about her.

"A handful of guys. Anyone I happened to talk to on my way to the computer lab or to the phone, probably. Your messages to me made me pretty damn happy."

Her next question was even bigger, and harder to ask. "What... exactly do they know *about* me?"

"You mean who you are to me?" She would never get enough of seeing Miles's grin up close and personal like that. He leaned in and kissed her cheek. "My girl, I guess. Girlfriend, if you're willing."

"I like the sound of that."

"Why do you ask?"

She winced. "I haven't told my parents that I've met someone. Or my sister and sister-in-law, either."

"Why not?" No judgement laced the question, just simple curiosity.

She chewed on her lip as she considered the reasons. "I worry about you enough, because this is new and unexpected and I'm not really sure what it is you do and how I should think about it. So I don't want the well-meaning concern of my mother heaped on that as well. She's the type of person to start sending everyone in your... unit? Send them all boxes of stuff they can't actually use. She'd get her bridge club involved. It would be a nightmare."

He laughed, but she had a serious point there.

"See? I don't even know what your group of guys is called!"

Less gingerly than when she first arrived, he stretched his arm out over the back of her chair, taking up an impressive amount of space. He lazily tugged on her ponytail and grinned. "I'm on a team. I do have an APO address if she wants to send me cookies."

"Miles!"

"What? I like cookies."

"Really?" She leaned in against him, glad his bruises were fading and she could be heavy against him. "I'll send you some."

He lightly grazed his lips across her forehead, and she tipped her face up to his, but before he could kiss her again, he was called in for his appointment. She pulled out a ragged old paperback she'd found in the mini library cart that made the round of the wards. At first she'd felt funny about borrowing books meant for patients, but one of his nurses reassured her they were just as much for family members.

That was stretching it, probably, but right now she was the closest person to him, at least in geographical proximity. He'd called his aunt and then his parents that morning, and it was cute watching his side of those conversations.

Her smile grew to the embarrassingly big point. Everything about Miles was cute. The way his eyes crinkled when he smiled at her. The way he called her gorgeous. The way he acted all barely restrained about wanting to have sex. She sighed to herself. They'd spent more than a month flirting long distance. Now they were close enough to touch and Miles was stuck in a hospital.

They'd done a lot of kissing. And cuddling.

Soon enough, she thought. August was just around the corner, five short weeks. Since arriving in Germany, she'd been adjusting her travel schedule in her head almost constantly. At first, she thought she'd fly straight home. Then when Miles told her he was heading back, she decided to stick with some of her original plans.

One thing was certain—she wasn't spending a year in Europe anymore. Her priorities had shifted. And if their relationship continued, there would probably be many deployments in her future. She could see Italy and Spain then. Or maybe they could travel together.

Whatever the future held, Piper knew that she'd found something special with Miles. It hadn't been what she'd flown across the ocean for, but it was more than enough motivation to return home.

She heard his laugh before Miles appeared in the doorway to the clinic space. He flashed his dimples at the OT, then again at the receptionist, but she wasn't jealous—much. Because then her golden boy zoomed in on her from across the room and his eyes lit up.

"Good news," he said in a conspiratorial whisper as she stood to join him, his head dipping down so his lips were almost brushing her hair. "She thinks the surgeon's going to discharge me tonight. Tomorrow for sure."

Piper wouldn't call it good, except in the *Miles is healthy* sense of the word. Bittersweet was more her take on him being battle-ready again. She went with the safest answer. "So all your test results must be clear? That's a relief."

He pressed his hand into the middle of her back, his hand spanning the width of her torso as he guided her into the quiet hallway. He kept his voice low. "I'm not sure you quite understand."

"I do," she said, trying to pump more enthusiasm into her voice. "You must be dying to get back to your team."

"That's not—" He cut himself off and looked around before pressing her into a recessed doorway. His body blocked her from the rest of the hospital—the rest of the world—and all she could see was Miles.

He was definitely feeling better.

"Let me try again," he murmured, his brown eyes dancing. "I've got some good news."

Piper didn't quite get what was going on, but her heartbeat picked up and an unconscious grin curled up her face. "Okay. Shoot."

"I'm going to be discharged tonight or tomorrow. And it takes twenty-four, sometimes forty-eight hours to arrange non-emergency transport."

"Oh." That *was* good news. "So you might need a hotel room to stay in for a night or two."

"I might." His thumbs stroked back and forth on her bare forearms, just below the sleeve of her t-shirt, and the touch instantly sparked a heady arousal she'd been keeping at bay while he wasn't well.

"I have one of those. A hotel room. Big bed and everything." Her words rushed out of her in a breathy stream.

"I was hoping you'd say that." He did a quick check over his shoulder before kissing her hungrily, his soft lips pressing her mouth open, his tongue not hesitating before stroking against hers. "I have big plans for that bed, Piper. You might want to take a nap."

MILES SHIFTED his rucksack on his shoulder, trying to get a better balance for the flowers in the crook of his arm and the picnic basket of random German food gripped in his hand as he raised his other hand to knock on Piper's hotel room door.

She'd wanted to stay with him until he was discharged, but as soon as his day nurse figured out they were going to have a night or two together, she urged Piper out the door. Once they had a bit of privacy, the previously tough-as-nails medical professional turned into a matchmaker in the blink of an eye. She asked a disturbing number of rapid-fire questions about what food they liked and if he needed condoms—which he did, so he tried to be cool about that one—and fed his answers into her phone.

Apparently, her German boyfriend was happy to run some errands, and even volunteered to drive Miles to the hotel.

All right then. Frank had delivered everything that Miles was now juggling, except the flowers—those they picked up on the way to the hotel.

Piper opened the door just as he lifted his fist to knock again.

"Sorry!" she said after pulling the door open. "I was having a wardrobe malfunction. Couldn't figure out what to wear, which is silly, but this is exciting." She was talking and waving him in, and it took her a minute to focus on him, so he was already inside when she gasped and pointed to the flowers. "What did you do?"

He grinned. "I told you, I've got some funny ideas about how dates should go." Setting down the picnic basket, he handed over the flowers and leaned in to kiss her cheek. "Hi."

"Hi." Her breath hitched a little as she looked at the flowers, then back up at him, and he was damn glad he'd convinced Frank to stop. "These are gorgeous."

"I'm glad you like them. Now put them down." He couldn't wait to hold her. Her hair was loose, falling in dark waves down her back. She wore a black t-shirt and a jean skirt, and her legs were bare. He wanted to touch them—he wanted to touch her all over.

She shook her head, laughing. She touched his cheek, guiding his face down to hers for a longer kiss before she nodded to the bathroom. "I'm getting water for these."

He took that twenty seconds to go through the food and put the cold stuff in the fridge, then looked around for a good place to put the condoms.

Piper chose that moment to come back into the room.

Her eyes lit up as she put the flowers, now in a vase, on the narrow desk in the corner. *Smooth, Dumbrowski.*

"I was just unpacking…"

"Good." She leisurely gave him a once-over, her gaze stopping on the box of condoms still in his hand. "So your doctors gave you the all-clear?"

Jesus, a simple question shouldn't give him a hard-on. But it totally did. "Yep." He licked his lips, suddenly thirsty for a drink of all things Piper. "I mean, we can eat first—"

He cut himself off as she launched herself in his direction. He tossed the condoms onto the bed and wrapped his arms around her, hauling her up his body.

"Food later," she whispered against his lips.

Deal. With a groan, he opened for her, letting her take her fill of his mouth as he slid his hands under her skirt, using the excuse of holding her up to palm her ass. Lord, but she felt good. Compact and curvy, she had all these secret muscles from running—strong thighs, tight butt, narrow waist that flexed and bowed under his touch.

Impatient for more of her, he tugged her shirt up, and she broke off the kiss to pull it over her head. Even better. His head was swimming a little—nothing he wasn't used to—and there wasn't a chance in the world that he'd put her down until—

"Bed," she panted.

That works, too. He swivelled and set her down, watching hungrily as she unbuttoned her skirt and shoved it to the ground. He realized it was an invitation for him to get naked, too, and stripped off his shirt before sitting on the bed to take off his boots.

Piper didn't wait. She crawled behind him and pressed herself against his spine so she could lick along his shoulder, to his neck, and then... Yep, she just nipped his ear. His dick approved, but his head needed a minute to play catch-up.

Toeing his boots off as quickly as he could, he got rid of his pants at the same time and spun around, tackling her to the bed.

"Hey there," he said, his voice unexpectedly husky as he pinned her beneath him. "What's your hurry?"

Her brows pinched together for a second, something flashing in her eyes before she dropped her eyelids a bit and smiled. "I just can't believe you're actually here."

"I am. Thirty-six hours. You're going to be sick of me when I get on that plane." Damn, that was the wrong thing to say, because the expression flickered across her face again, and this time there was no mistaking it. "Hey, no. I take that back." He braced himself on one forearm and stroked her face, pulling her gaze back to meet his. "I'm going to miss you so much. And I want to make the next two days last."

"Thirty-six hours," she whispered, her lower lip trembling. Slowly, carefully, he lowered his face to hers and swiped that lip with his tongue, soft and gentle.

"And we'll make every single one of them count." He kissed her full on the mouth, then on the corner as he pulled back a couple of inches to see her face again. They weren't going any further until they were both on the same page. "Okay, crash course in dating the uniform. Countdowns can be good and bad. It's there. It's always going to be there. Thirty-six hours until I go, five weeks until we see each other, six months to the next deployment. Sometimes ninety minutes to an unexpected mission. That's my life. I love my job. But I love being with you, too. And when I'm gone, you're with me. I take these memories we make and I hold them close when things get shitty."

"I'm sorry," she breathed, her eyes glinting bright. *Crying girl alert.* Shit.

"Don't be sorry."

"I thought I was being cool."

"You're beyond cool, Piper. My buddy calls you and tells you I'm going to the hospital, and you just hop on a train to Germany? That's fucking awesome. I derail your year-in-Europe plan and you just roll with it. I appreciate that you want to be happy-happy when we're together, but if you're *not*, inside, I want you to be honest with me, okay?"

———

Piper nodded up at Miles, blinking back the threatening tears as she took a deep breath beneath him. "Okay."

They stared at each other for a second or two, then she screwed up her face, wincing as she said the next bit. She wasn't sure she could see his reaction if he didn't take it well. "I'm scared. I know you're okay, medically, but having you where I can see you and touch you for a few days is making this saying goodbye thing so much harder a second time. I'm terrified something is going to happen to you." Her heart hurt just thinking about it. "I just *got* you, Miles. I can't lose you."

"Oh, gorgeous. Yeah. Fuck, it's hard for me, too. But you're not going to lose me. I'm coming back to you, I promise." He stroked her nose with the tip of his, then kissed her, harder this time, and when she wrapped her arms around his neck, he didn't pull away. Instead he settled his weight on top of her and kissed her over and over again, starting with her lips, then exploring her neck, down her arms, right to the tips of her fingers, and back up again.

She rolled up and into him, pushing them onto their sides, and with aching slowness they explored each other's bodies, stripping away the final small scraps of underwear they wore.

Miles stroked his hand over her bare hip as he pulled their naked bodies together, his erection hard and insistent against her belly as he squeezed her ass. His fingers trailed across the back of her thigh as he whispered for her to roll onto her back, then he teased a lazy path up the front of her leg to the sensitive valley at the edge of her sex.

Dipping his head to capture a nipple in his mouth, he nudged her thighs apart, and when she spread for him, he stroked through her wet folds.

I never want to forget this feeling, Piper thought, rocking her hips to meet his touch. He was making love to her, with her, and he'd been completely right to slow them down. She snaked her hand to where his cock lay heavy against her hip and circled her fingers around the shaft. Warm, smooth, and hard, his erection pulsed beneath her fingers and when she started stroking him, she found him wet at the tip. He groaned as she swirled her thumb over the head and she arched into him, looking for his mouth with hers.

"Kiss me," she murmured, and he grinned before he did as she asked, his eyes hot on her face until she fluttered her own eyelids shut, giving in to sensations rioting through her body.

"If you keep jerking me like that, I'm going to come all over your hip," he muttered, and she giggled as she blinked up at him again. His face was right there, all clean-cut angles and rugged planes, but his eyes were soft and his lips were swollen. *My Miles.* For the rest of the world, he was a quiet hero, a ghost in camouflage, but for her, he was this extraordinary man, unexpectedly tender and honest.

"Then you should probably get one of those condoms."

"In a minute." He shot her a wicked grin as he slid down her body, kissing her belly first, then her hip bone. She held her breath as he nosed down the crease between her leg and her pelvis—because it was possible that her heart might just explode if she missed a second of this—and started shaking as soon as he took his first leisurely lick of her aroused flesh.

"Oh my God."

"Name's Miles, actually." From between her legs, he winked at her, and just like that, all her emotions clicked back into balance.

"Oh my Miles, then," she said, rolling her hips to try and get the tip of his tongue on her clit. "Yes, right there. Ahhh!"

He made an appreciative noise as she tugged on his scruffy blond hair and kept doing what she'd just shown him she liked, a rolling loop around her most sensitive spot that quickly ramped her up to a firecracker of a first orgasm—fast sizzle, big, shuddering pop. And she wanted more.

Miles was one hundred percent on board with that plan as he circled her slippery, sensitized entrance with his fingers, but she wanted something else. She breathed his name, and when he looked up, she crooked one finger. "Come here."

He snagged the condoms on his way, shredding the box and sending plastic wrappers flying. But he caught one between his fingers, because he was just that good. He was *perfect*, and her racing heart could barely handle it. As he rolled on protection, he raked his gaze over her body, and her skin almost sizzled from the heat of his look. Slowly stroking himself, which was damn hot to watch, he teased her with just the tip of his erection, first on her clit, then between her folds, notching himself in place.

The anticipation of that first thrust made her cry out and reach for him, but nothing could prepare her for how good it actually felt as Miles worked his way into her.

His initial pump of his hips was shallow, just stretching her a bit, and she tipped her pelvis, wanting more. He gave it to her. The next thrust filled her up, and she clutched at him with her thighs. His chest brushed her nipples as he moved against her, his eyes locked on hers.

"You feel so good," he groaned, dragging his hips back. He paused there, just barely in her, then slowly entered her, all the way this time, and as he filled her, he kissed her. He tasted like summer, warm sunshine and cherry popsicles, and she never wanted to stop tasting him. His mouth, his skin. His cock, eventually. Her mouth watered at the thought of him rocking over her tongue.

Between their bodies, he cupped one breast, and with each slide of his body against hers, each thrust inside her, his thumb would drift over her nipple just *so*. Perfect. Again.

Grabbing her hand, he stretched his other arm over her head as he planted his knees more firmly on the bed, his thighs working hard. All of him, really—his arms flexed around her, muscles as far as she could see and stroke and taste with her mouth as she restlessly rolled her head from side to side.

When he lowered himself a bit more, giving her just a taste of his heaviness, she begged for more, wrapping her arms and legs around his torso. She licked across his chest and when she got to one of his tight, round little nipples, she rolled the brown tip around with her tongue.

He shuddered over her.

"Good?" she asked, her voice barely recognizable to herself.

In response he fisted her hair and held her in place so she could do it again. Then he dragged her away, only to steal her mouth with his for a blistering kiss as he arched over her.

"God, Piper, what are you doing to me?" He let out a half-laugh as she clung to him, swivelling her hips beneath him when he pulled out a bit, circling just the head of his cock with her sex.

"Making you come?"

He dropped his forehead to hers as he fucked into her again, harder, jerkier this time. "Definitely gonna do that."

"Good."

"I want it to be good for you, too," he grunted, squeezing her hip as he shifted their bodies a bit, hitting a new angle that took it from good to great in a flash.

Instead of responding, she just let herself moan, writhing beneath him as he picked up speed, thrusting faster and harder until she was making an endless stream of probably embarrassing sex noises. It didn't matter. They were both frenzied with need, moving like liquid fire now, sparking each other with every thrust and clutch.

Panting his name, Piper arched under Miles, shattering into a million pieces of love as she climaxed a few seconds before he buried himself into her one last time in a rough, ragged, and totally perfect finish.

Or maybe just the start, she thought lazily as he took a few heaving breaths while still wrapped in her body.

After all, they still had thirty-five hours.

CHAPTER
EIGHTEEN

THE TEAM WORKED QUIETLY, pulling all their gear together in their prep room. The plywood walls and metal shelves weren't much to look at, but compared to being in the field, this spec ops "office space" at Camp Orbit was swanky.

They'd spent weeks preparing for an attack on Tal Afar. They'd be inserted on the other side of enemy lines and get a visual on the ISIS commander and ensure they were minimizing civilian contact. It would be a long-ass wait for confirmation once they'd sent those images back to Ops HQ, then they'd watch as the air force did their thing, and pick off anyone who tried to escape.

Boom, motherfuckers. You aren't the only ones with balls of steel, but only the good guys get to breathe after today.

Quietly they filed onto the Chinook helicopter that would fly them in. Ten SEALs and six Rangers. Each man focused on the mission ahead of them, fueled by confidence and righteous anger. Maybe thinking of someone back home.

Miles sure was. *I'm doing this for you, Piper. Gonna do it smart and safe, then come on home to you.*

Across from him, Vince buckled himself in, the canvas straps wrapping around his gear-laden body. He couldn't actually see Vince's face in the shadow of his helmet, and a balaclava he wore under his helmet would obscure most of his face anyway. Once the man slid on his night-vision goggles for the recon, he'd be encased from head to toe in Uncle Sam's kit for the last time.

Out with a bang, man.

Above them the rotors started, and over their headsets, they heard Major Deene go through his start-up routine, talking to the flight engineer and his gunners. Then the pilot flashed a cocky grin back at the two teams. "Let's go get 'em, eh?"

Sixteen pairs of feet thudded their agreement against the metal floor of the oversized bird. *Let's go.*

————

Piper wiped her hands nervously on her skirt—again. She'd only been back in the States for six days, and in that time had found a part-time job at a bookstore, confessed to her family that she'd come home early because of a *boy*, and gone dress shopping.

She wasn't big on dresses. Skirts, jeans, shorts…those were more her style.

But it wasn't every day that she was invited to a United States Naval Base to welcome home a team of special forces operators. Miles had called her three days before—their first contact in more than a week, and she'd silently cried when she heard his voice, knowing his radio silence probably had something to do with the big air strike on an ISIS training camp that had been all over the news—and given her the details.

So she was wearing a pretty red dress, snug to the waist, flaring out into a floaty skirt, and strappy sandals that made her legs look amazing. Her hair had cooperated, falling in glossy dark waves down her back despite the humidity—thank you, silicone spray—and she'd figured out makeup that would cooperate with kissing.

There was going to be *so much kissing.* She shivered at the thought. Miles, safe and sound on American soil. They'd celebrate for days. And nights.

She'd arrived almost an hour early to make sure she could find the right building and get her visitor pass without any problems.

That had seemed smart at the time. Now she was just anxious and felt kind of awkward, and there was still fifteen minutes until the team's expected arrival.

"Is this your first homecoming ceremony?"

Piper lifted her head and found a smiling blonde woman, obviously pregnant. "Yes. Is it that obvious?"

"I recognize the nervous fidget. I was in your shoes a year ago. I'm Cassie, by the way."

"Piper." She took a deep breath and smiled. "So you're…"

"My husband is a SEAL." Cassie fanned herself with a hand-drawn sign. It was a scorching day, and the mid-morning heat was already warming up the hangar they were waiting in.

"Do you want some water or something?" Piper gestured to the refreshments table at the back. Nobody had touched the drinks yet, but for a pregnant woman, surely etiquette could take a backseat to health and safety.

Cassie shook her head. "I'm okay. I've got water in my bag. Besides, I think that might be them!" She pointed at a pair of approaching helicopters.

Bigger than Piper expected, the black machines took a while setting down, and even after they were on the tarmac, it took several long minutes for the rotors to stop turning. Finally, the doors slid open, and one by one, men climbed out. They lined up, and Piper's breath caught in her throat as she saw Miles for the first time in more than a month.

"That's my husband," Cassie whispered, pointing out the tallest of the bunch, standing one man over from Miles.

"My boyfriend is two guys to his right," Piper whispered back.

Cassie flashed her a happy grin. "So you're Miles's girl! I didn't know your name, I'm sorry. Jared doesn't get the value of gossip the same way I do. Most of our conversations are baby or house related."

Piper laughed. "Fair enough."

"But I heard you went to see him in Germany. That must have been a big relief."

Piper nodded. "I was so lucky that I was just a train ride away. That phone call was so scary."

They shared a quiet moment of understanding. It wasn't easy loving someone who lived for the fight. Piper thought about Cassie's baby. Would that make it harder, having a child together? She knew even if it was harder, it would be worth it. A tall, lean boy with blond hair and a wicked grin, or a dark-haired bouncing baby girl to twist Miles around her chubby little finger. She shivered. *Maybe someday.* Then she smiled.

The officer who'd greeted the men quietly turned and spoke to the crowd briefly, but Piper didn't really hear anything he said. All she could hear was the pounding of her heartbeat as Miles caught her gaze and held it, the corners of his mouth twitching up even at a distance.

Then they were moving toward the hangar. Around her, people waved signs, and some started to walk forward, like Cassie.

Miles picked up his pace, and she matched it, meeting him on the edge of the tarmac as he broke into a jog. He picked her up, his arms strong and true around her waist, and spun her around in a big, sweeping circle.

She wrapped her arms around his neck and squeezed him so tight he groaned, but she didn't care.

"Hey, hey, hey," he said quietly, and she realized she was sobbing, and his neck was wet with her tears.

Damn. "You're home," she said, sniffling as he set her down. She grinned up at him. "These are happy tears."

He laughed and kissed her quickly, his lips strong and sure against hers, his tongue just stealing the quickest of tastes before he set her down again. He gazed at her, brushing his fingers along her cheekbones and the bridge of her nose. "I love you."

She'd already known it, and she felt the same way, but hearing it was something special. She nodded, a tiny little wobble of her head. "I love you, too. So much. It's kind of crazy."

Grinning, he kissed her again before lacing his fingers through hers and tugging her back into the hangar, because they were in public and he was in uniform. There'd be more time to say that again, over and over, and show it as well, when they were truly alone.

He introduced her to Cassie and Jared Sutter, and Vince Nash, and a few other guys, including his roommate, Trick Novak, who used to be on his team but had been moved to another SEAL team earlier in the year. The whole time he held her close to his side, his arm banded possessively around her, his hand on her outside hip.

She nodded and smiled, but most of it went over her head, and by the time the small reception was over, she was zonked.

"How did you get here?" he murmured in her ear when they had a minute alone.

"I drove," she whispered, tipping her face up to his.

"My car is in storage." He held her gaze, the heat in his eyes promising he'd find a way to wake her up again. "Do you think you could give me a drive home?" He nodded across the hangar to where Trick was laughing with one of the Air Force pilots. "Trick's going to Gaby's tonight."

"So…" Piper took a shaky breath. "It was good that I packed an overnight bag?"

He didn't bother to glance around before lowering his face to kiss her again, and this time there wasn't anything quick or chaste about the embrace. When they came up for air, she was blushing and so was he. "Yep, good. Okay, let's get out of here before I get charged for doing inappropriate things while in uniform."

"EXCUSE ME, miss, can you show me where your travel books are?"

Piper glanced up from re-shelving and straightening mystery paperbacks and smiled at the customer standing a few feet away. "Definitely. Follow me."

"I'm going to France in the fall, and I'd like something that talks about getting around by train, if you have it…"

"As a matter of fact, I know just the book." She'd read it herself, and it had helped a lot when she'd gone to Gare de l'Est in Paris, frantically looking for the first train to Landstuhl, Germany.

"Have you been to France?"

She grinned, nodded, and asked a few questions, and soon had the middle-aged woman bundled off to the cashier with three books. Even though her own trip to Europe had been cut short, she'd learned enough in preparing for it that she was confident she'd answered the woman's questions and pointed her in the right direction.

For the last three weeks, while settling into working and seeing Miles a lot and her family a little, and generally being ridiculously happy, a little itch had niggled at the back of her neck.

She had found more in Europe than she ever would have hoped

for. But she hadn't come back with a better sense of self—she was the same old Piper, filled with wanderlust and self-doubt. Now she just had a loving boyfriend and a different set of priorities.

She still wanted to figure out what she wanted to do when she grew up.

As she returned to the mystery section, a kernel of an idea made itself known in her mind. By the time her lunch break rolled around, it had turned into a full-blown *oh-my-god-I-need-paper* plan.

It might be a decade too late to be an original idea, but Piper was going to start a blog. While she scarfed a sandwich from the shop next door, she sketched out a messy header image idea, and a schedule of blog post categories. *Miss It Mondays* would feature places people had been and wanted—ached—to go back to. *Wild Wednesdays* would be adventure travel. And on *Thankful Thursdays*, she'd help people get their travel questions answered.

The answers were already out there—on forums and social media groups, other blogs…but like the woman who'd come into the store earlier, not everyone spent their free time trolling the Internet for the cheapest way to get to Prague or how to read a Japanese address.

Piper did. And maybe that wasn't a completely useless way for her to spend her time after all.

Her phone beeped at her, reminding her she only had five minutes left in her break. She quickly searched for a web hosting company. The first one listed offered a website and a hosting package for fifty percent off for the first year.

It's a sign, said the devil on her shoulder. *Should you talk this out with someone first?* asked the angel on the other side.

She didn't need to. She already knew how that conversation would go, because the only person she'd ask was Miles, and he'd tell her to go for it. He wouldn't hesitate a beat.

She grinned, and clicked the purchase button.

———

Miles was in a weekly SITREP meeting when his phone vibrated, indicating he had a new email on his personal xmail account. Three short vibes differentiated those emails from his work ones. He kept that account pretty tight—family, Piper, and the guys he worked with were the only ones who used it regularly, although some friends he'd made over the years had it, too. Other special forces guys. So his fingers itched to check it, but before he could surreptitiously look, he was being called on to do the Latin American brief.

Before the meeting broke up, his pocket had vibrated twice again.

Three emails, all from Piper.

By the time he got to the last one, he was grinning from ear to ear. As soon as he sat down at his desk, he opened a browser window and went to the link she'd sent him. It was just a template, a place holder, with her blog title at the top and a subscribe button on the right. He clicked on it and filled in his email address.

His phone rang right away.

"Look at you, taking over the world," he answered, knowing it was Piper.

"You subscribed to my blog," she said, her voice all soft.

"Of course."

"I don't even have any posts yet. Or a header picture. But I will. I have a drawing of what I want it to look like. The drawing has a mustard stain on it, but I think that might add something special."

He laughed. "Speaking of mustard, what are you doing for dinner?"

"Hoping my boyfriend wants to cook something while I use his laptop to build my new blog so I don't have to drive all the way home."

Piper lived in the northern suburbs of San Diego, but when she'd returned from Europe, she'd gotten a job at a bookstore in Coronado Beach. Miles tried not to read too much into that, but since the only other thing in Coronado for her was him, it was a challenge.

He didn't always try hard. He was a planner—that was his nature. He knew Piper was it for him, if she could wrap her head around being a navy wife. So he watched and listened and planned —dinner on the days she worked, visits up in her neck of the woods when she didn't. More and more of her clothes were being left at his place. He didn't make a big deal about clearing out a drawer in his dresser, but as she peeled off layers at the end of a day, he put them in his laundry hamper.

If the clean clothes went into that drawer instead of a bag for her to take home…well, that was just a test balloon.

"Okay. I need to pick up some groceries because my girlfriend just invited herself for dinner, but—"

"Hey!" She giggled.

"Love you. See you in an hour or so?"

"Definitely. Love you, too."

————

Piper could hear Miles moving around the kitchen, putting dishes away. Not only had he fed her, but he'd made fancy grilled sandwiches which could be eaten with one hand so she could keep working while they ate. He read a book next to her for a bit, then went to tidy up.

She glanced in that direction, catching glimpses of his tall, swimmer's-build body. Lean compared to some of his SEAL friends, but big for anyone else, Miles moved effortlessly through his space. He'd changed into cargo pants and a white t-shirt when he came home, and every time he lifted a dish to the top shelf, his shirt pulled up and revealed a distracting slice of taut, male skin.

He looked up and caught her watching him, and heat filled her chest as he held her gaze, a slow, sexy smile curling up his handsome face. "How's it going?"

"I've got my first few blog posts scheduled, and a list of places where I want to promote it. I even have a giveaway set up!" She set the laptop on the coffee table as he came closer, and took his hand, standing to meet him. "It looks like a real blog and everything."

"Amazing." He grazed his knuckles along her jaw, sweeping her hair back before leaning in to kiss her.

"Hardly," she murmured, her words brushing against his lips.

"I. Am. Amazed," he repeated, sliding their bodies together, curving over her as he kissed her again, harder this time. "Do you have any more to do tonight?"

Slowly she shook her head, left and right, left and right, a thrill chasing through her body as he tightened his grip on her.

"Good. Take off your pants."

She laughed as he released her suddenly and reached for his belt, but he was right—that was an excellent plan. "Shirt, too?"

He wet his lips as he looked down at her. "Nope. Just the pants for now. I love you in a t-shirt and panties."

Good Lord, she should have Miles say "panties" more often. Her heart thudded hard in her chest as she complied with his request.

As soon as they were both bare-legged, he swept her backwards onto the couch and settled on top of her, a delicious weight she wanted more of.

"You drive me crazy," she said quietly, winding her arms around his neck. "One look, one word from you and I'm all turned on."

"That's how I've felt since that very first night." He flexed his hips, showing her the feeling was mutual, and they both groaned. "I looked across the bar and there you were, all curves and dark hair. I had the most inappropriate fantasy about you in a dress shirt…"

She hissed and rolled against him. "Do you even own dress shirts?"

"Clearly you haven't snooped in my closet."

"Not yet, but maybe I will."

"That would be easier if you had a key…" He trailed off, kissing wet, open-mouth marks down her neck. He tried to tug her neckline down, then got frustrated and just shoved her t-shirt up, sighing happily when he had a handful of boob.

"True, I'm a terrible cat burglar."

He laughed and squeezed her breast. "Gorgeous, that was me, offering you a key to this place."

She blinked up at him. "Really?"

"Yeah. Of course." He shook his head as he lowered his face to hers. "Well, maybe not *of course* if you didn't realize. Don't you know how much I love you?"

"Yes," she whispered, kissing him back.

"What's mine is yours." Lacing his fingers through hers, he stretched her arms over her head, holding her in place as he used his lips and his tongue to explore every inch of her mouth. He kissed her until they were both breathless and panting hard. "And *you* are mine."

"All yours."

"All?" His eyes flashed above her. "Come on."

He hauled her up, his hands all over her hips and up her shirt, groping and stroking as he tried to kiss her neck and walk her toward his bedroom at the same time.

Shivering with want, Piper swayed inside his arms, letting him move her at his own pace because the journey felt *good*. When he slid both hands up her shirt, cupping both breasts at the same time as he ground his erection into her ass, her knees almost gave out from how good it felt to be desired like that. Like he just couldn't get enough of her.

They were barely inside his room, the door still open, when his hand slid inside her panties.

"Jesus," he growled. "You're so wet for me."

"Mmm-hmmm." She rocked her hips, rolling her pelvic bone against his fingers as he explored her folds, stroking her aroused flesh in a way that was working her up, but not getting her off. "Touch my clit, Miles. Make me come."

"Bossy, bossy." He circled her nub gently, coaxing it out from under its hood, making it swollen and eager for more. "Maybe I want you to come when I'm inside you. I love how tight you squeeze me."

"Okay, that sounds good, too," she panted, leaning in vain toward the bed. He just banded his other arm beneath her boobs and held her where she was.

"What's the hurry?" His breath was hot against her ear.

"You. Are. Cruel."

He laughed as she bounced against his hand, so close to release she could taste it. Cupping her sex with one hand, he picked her up around the waist with the other arm and carried her to the bed, tugging down her panties as soon as he had her positioned on all fours.

Before she could growl at him again, he had his cock free and was stroking the head through her wetness, searching for her opening. When he found it, he eased right in, skipping the preliminary pulses he often did to fit them together.

He didn't need to—she was slick and swollen for him, completely primed.

"Mine," he grunted, his hands on her hips, holding her in place as he slammed into her. Her orgasm started on the third repeating of the possessive claim, said in time with each rough stroke inside her. As soon as she started clenching around him, he let himself go, fucking her hard and fast a few more times before climaxing with a jerk and a gasp, his fingers tightening so hard on her hips she hoped she might bruise.

"I'm so glad you've found something you're excited about," he whispered against her temple once they were cuddled up against his pillows.

"I was already excited about you, about being home and together," she said, not wanting him to think he wasn't enough.

"I know. But now you've got something to keep you busy when I'm away next."

Her heart squeezed. "You think about that? Me waiting for you?"

"Would you wait?"

"Until the end of time. You're mine, too."

EPILOGUE

"WE NEED to leave for your parents' place soon," Miles reminded Piper as he climbed into his bed—where he'd left her when he went for a run—and kissed her shoulder.

"Yep," she said distractedly, clicking away on her computer. She'd just gotten back from a travel conference in Los Angeles the day before, and her mind had been whirring with ideas ever since. He could practically see the smoke coming out her ears.

Miles knew his job was to support her—until she needed to take a break. Then his job was to make that break happen.

"What are you doing?" he asked, stroking one finger up and down her arm. "Can I distract you?"

"In ninety seconds…"

He looked at his watch. After a minute and a half of observing that in fact she was just replying to emails, clearing out her inbox and not actually mid-thought, he reached over her and closed the laptop. Leaping out of bed, he ignored her shriek of protest and stashed the laptop on top of his dresser.

"Never give a SEAL a timing you don't intend to meet, gorgeous." He prowled toward her with what he hoped was a menacing look.

She stuck her tongue out at him. "Or what?"

"Or you'll be punished with extreme prejudice."

"I don't even know what that means, you dork. Ahhh!"

He grabbed her ankle and yanked her down the bed before climbing on top of her. "It means we need to go to your parents for Thanksgiving dinner."

She laughed. "Right, dinner. It's barely mid-afternoon. And yes, spending time with my family when you've just done the big, bad wolf thing and I want to be ravished instead…that sounds like an awful punishment, one I surely don't deserve."

"Maybe I'll let you plead for leniency."

"Oooh, yes." She wiggled beneath him. "Let me! What can I do?"

"Get your cute little ass in the shower." He hauled her up and pushed her into the bathroom. "Tell me more about the travel writing workshop."

She sighed, a happy little sound that worked its way right into his heart. Now he knew what Jared and Trick meant when they said they came undone for their women. It was hard to be cold and reserved when your partner in everything melted into a puddle of goo at sappy commercials and free blogging seminars.

Piper was rubbing off on him, and he didn't mind a bit.

"I've been doing it all wrong!" She laughed as she hopped into the shower. "I mean, my blog is too basic. It's a good start, but I need to figure out more of a niche. And I was thinking that the travel writing part of it needed to wait until I actually went on a trip, but the best tip I got was to be a local travel writer. So I need a whole new section on the blog for Southern California!"

"That's genius." He stepped into the water as well and grabbed the soap. "Turn around."

"And you know I haven't used my trip to Europe yet, other than in broad strokes…" Another sigh, this one more languid as she stretched under his soapy hands. "But I think it would be a good travelogue. You'll have to read it to make sure I don't inadvertently say too much."

They'd gone over the rules so many times he doubted she'd misstep. She could talk about dating someone in the military. No pictures, no discussion of his service beyond the most generic, and no active warfare locations, ever. But Germany was fine. That there had been a medical emergency was allowed. What caused it was off-limits. "I can't wait to read it."

Back in his bedroom, they bumped into each other as they got dressed. Half her clothes were now in his closet. That one drawer he'd cleared out for her had morphed into half the dresser exploding with cute t-shirts and yoga pants. But there was a good deal of spandex and lace and cotton panties with cheeky sayings on the butt, too, so he wasn't complaining in the least.

In fact, he wanted to talk to her about that before they headed to her parents' place.

Tackling her gently, he snuggled them together on the bed.

"I thought we had to go?"

"Soon. I wanted to talk to you about something."

———

Piper wiggled closer, happy to soak up a bit of Miles's calm, warm energy before the storm that was her family during a holiday meal. Her sister and sister-in-law would grill Miles with thinly veiled questions relating to their relationship and his commitment to her. Her brother would glom on to Miles and want to talk about guy stuff —which was actually better, but still annoying. And her parents would just be intense. Either intensely approving or disapproving or both together at the same time.

That was her future. They weren't ever going to change.

But now she had Miles to suffer through it with her. Love was awesome.

"Piper, focus." He laughed, his chest shaking beneath her cheek.

"Yep. Talk."

"Trick and Gaby have bought a house." Miles's roommate was out of the country for a few months, and he'd proposed to his girl-friend before he left. "So I need to figure out what to do with this place."

Oh, he had her attention now. She'd practically moved in, but his bedroom wasn't big enough for both of them. Would it be weird to ask your boyfriend if you could be his roommate? Her clothes could live in the other room. And his boots, because those size thirteen monstrosities took up a lot of real estate.

"And I could get a new roommate, there are always new guys on the teams—" Piper's heart fell. "—but I was thinking I might be ready to buy a house. Something small, so there wouldn't be too much yard work for you when I'm gone."

Piper wasn't sure her pulse could handle the ups and downs of this conversation. The abrupt change in emotion was making her a bit dizzy. "Wait, yard work? A house?"

"What do you say? If I got a house, would you want to live with me?"

"Can you afford a house?" Coronado Beach wasn't cheap.

"I've got savings. Enough for a good down payment on a small house. In the end, it wouldn't be any bigger than this apartment, really, but maybe more conducive to cohabitation."

"Cohabitation," she repeated, grinning. "That sounds great. I kind of love the idea of living in sin with you. It'll make my dad's head explode."

He laughed and pulled her close. "I was looking at some places online. Do you want to check them out?"

"Definitely."

He reached for his laptop, perched precariously on his bedside table, and handed it to her. She twisted around so he was spooning her and set the computer on the mattress so they could look at it together. His hand tightened on her hip as the screen lit up, his last browser activity already on the screen.

"These aren't houses," Piper said softly, her heart hammering in her chest.

"Do you like them?" Miles asked, brushing his lips against the curve of her ear.

"Well, yeah." She swallowed hard around the lump in her throat. Had she just ruined a surprise? She blinked at the diamond rings glowing on the computer screen. "I mean, what girl doesn't like..." She trailed off as something smooth and cool to the touch rolled over her forearm. Her mouth dropped open as Miles dropped a ring on the blanket in front of her. She could feel his grin against her shoulder as he peeked at her. "Diamonds!"

"Will talk of weddings make Thanksgiving more or less stressful?"

She picked up the ring, a simple solitaire set in white gold. "Wow. Um, I don't think I care either way."

"I know you said you liked the idea of living in sin, but I had a different idea. Think I could change your mind?"

In a New York minute. "That sounds terribly respectable."

"We could find a way to still be scandalous. You could tell everyone that I proposed during sex."

"We're not having sex."

"We will be in a minute."

"Oh yeah?"

"Are you going to say yes?"

"Definitely."

"Yeah, then we're having sex." He rolled her onto her back, covering her with his body. "Because I've wanted you to be my wife for a long time, Piper Harrington."

"How long?"

"Maybe since the first night I saw you in Hastings."

"Maybe?"

"No. Definitely."

FALL FAST

ABOUT THIS BOOK

Navy SEAL Nathan Meyers and recent divorcee (as of an hour ago) Emme Ryan both want a night of escape from their real lives, for very different reasons. A chance meeting and a single drink at an airport bar turns into a night of unexpected fun and pleasure when a freak snow storm keeps them on the ground. But when morning comes, will they stick to the rules they set out at the start of the night?

CHAPTER
ONE
JANUARY

NATHAN MEYERS STOOD in the Terminal 2 departures hall at O'Hare Airport and groaned. He shouldn't be surprised that his flight from Chicago to San Diego was now delayed by more than two hours—a vicious winter storm was working its way toward the city. His sister had bugged him to check the flight status before he left her house, but as much as he loved Kelly and her brood—six kids, plus her husband and Polish mother-in-law—he'd been ready for some peace and quiet after three days of non-stop Uncle Nathan Fun Times.

He found a map of the terminal. It looked liked all the beer was on the other side of security, so he had two options. Head back out into the snow, or go through security early and find a burger or something.

Easy choice.

Dodging around travellers with oversized suitcases and grumpy faces, he scanned his e-ticket from his phone at the nearest available self-serve kiosk, printed his boarding pass, and headed for security.

Most of the time he flew around the world in military transport planes. But when he took detours like he had this weekend, hopping over to Chicago for some post-Christmas family time to make up for being in a South American jungle over the actual holidays, he had a simple travel routine down pat. One carry-on bag, boots unlaced in line, Navy ID visible at the top of his wallet.

The pretty redhead in front of him had the same idea, but where he carried a canvas rucksack and wore Doc Martens, she had a small wheeled suitcase and zippered boots. She wore dressy clothes for a stormy night, a slim black suit over a green t-shirt, but her iPhone case had a big No Doubt sticker on the back and when she turned around to be wanded, her shirt rode up a bit and he caught a glimpse of a navel piercing with a dangly skull resting against the slight swell of her belly. His gaze stuck on the curved waist of her dress pants, and he imagined an entire dirty-girl fantasy in the two seconds it took her to be cleared.

Damn.

When she motored ahead, her scarf slipping off her jacket and landing on the floor between them, he knew exactly how he wanted to spend the next couple of hours.

"Hey!" He snagged the cream silk from the floor and jogged after her. "Excuse me…"

Even in her heeled boots, she was small compared to him. Small and speedy. He gently tapped her elbow when he caught up, getting her attention. When he snagged her gaze, it was wary. With a smile, he stepped back and held out the scarf. "I think you dropped this."

Her eyes flared wide and her lips pulled together in a surprised O. "Thank you."

Holding out her hand, she grasped one end of the silk, but he wasn't ready to let it go, not when he'd just gotten her bright blue eyes pinned on his face. He liked them there, so he blurted out the first thing that came to mind. "My flight is delayed."

"Pardon?"

"I think they're all delayed right now."

"Yes." She tugged on the scarf and he let it go. "Thanks again."

"So I was going to get a beer and a burger, and if your flight is delayed as well, I'd be happy to buy you dinner."

"Ah. No thank you."

"No strings attached, promise. I'm flying home to San Diego

tonight, and we're under the watchful eye of the TSA. Sure I can't keep you company? I know some good knock-knock jokes."

———

Emme knew when she was being hit on in the casual, just-for-fun kind of way. In her early days as a flight attendant, she'd indulged in this game more than once. But today wasn't the day for fun. She couldn't help but smile back at the tallest, broadest, sexiest man she'd ever seen and wish she'd dropped her scarf in front of him any other day but today. And maybe that he lived a hair closer than San Diego, a city she rarely flew into.

"Well, I do like a good kids' joke, but I'm on standby for a flight that leaves in forty-five minutes, so I'll have to pass."

With a twinkle in his eye, he pointed to the display above their heads. "Not likely."

In the few minutes it had taken her to get through security, all flights had been grounded. Damn it.

She knew what this meant. Not only would she not be getting a standby flight tonight, anywhere, but she'd probably get called in to work early tomorrow. And since she hadn't fled the city fast enough, and she could use the money, she'd take the shift.

Fudgesicles. With a sigh, she turned back toward security. "That's my cue to head home to bed, then."

"Alone?"

Even though he'd obviously meant the question as a light flirtation, the question slid under her skin painfully. She glanced back at him over her shoulder, wanting to yell at *someone* for her forced period of solitary over the last year. "Yes. Alone. Not that it's any of your business."

"That's a shame." This time he said it straight up, his dark brown eyes warm with apology, but also with something she hadn't experienced in far too long—attraction aimed her way. An invitation. Like, if he wasn't heading to San Diego, maybe he might actually like to spend a night in her bed.

And since she knew he probably wouldn't be flying tonight, wouldn't that be worth exploring?

But she couldn't break her almost-two-year sex drought with someone as hot as he was. She'd need a few practice rounds before taking on a guy like… "What's your name?"

He grinned, slow and sweet, like she'd just given him the moon. That was a nice touch, but a little too practiced. She held her hand up between them before he could answer.

"No, don't tell me. Never mind." Spinning around again, not entirely sure how he'd knocked her off her course to home, she refocused on the sensible path.

Apparently he wasn't a fan of abrupt goodbyes. This time he didn't use his words to turn her around, he just reached out and slid one of his big, strong hands around her forearm. Heat radiated through her light blazer, and as soon as he had her facing him again, he let go. Persistent, but not pushy. He walked that line with care.

He narrowed his eyes in thought, then nodded. "Okay, no names. I like that, gives a bit of mystery to the next few hours. I'll call you Red, and you can—"

Emme laughed despite herself. "No. Never Red."

"Shorty."

Another giggle, and an unfamiliar warmth spread across her chest. This was weirdly fun. "Ew, no."

"Mystery Girl?"

Yeah, that would work. "You can call me M for Mystery."

"M." God, she liked the way he said her name, thinking it was just a letter. The trick jostled something inside her, spilling a drop of liquid desire in places she'd thought of as scorched earth. "And what should you call me?"

Sir. She could feel her cheeks flush at the thought, and from the way his eyes danced at her, he maybe could guess where her mind had gone. That was okay. They were flirting.

Holy crap, she wanted to do a little jig. She was flirting with a cute boy. The weight of the last week—the last year—fell away, and she cocked her head to the side. "How about we grab that dinner you mentioned and figure that out together?"

The redhead seemed to know her way around the terminal. She quickly settled them in a booth at a bar and grill, then busied herself with the menu.

Nathan let her hide for a minute before giving in to his base desire to see her eyes again. "So what else is off-limits? Can I ask where you were flying tonight?"

She blinked up at him, weighing the question for a minute before setting the menu aside. "Texas."

He laughed. "Wow, top-secret information, eh?"

"San Antonio."

"For absolutely no reason?"

"Pretty much." She leaned back against her side of the booth. "Your turn to be totally forthcoming about something."

"I'm going to San Diego."

"That's not new information."

"Because I live there."

"Neither is that." She stuck her tongue out at him, an unexpectedly playful response, and he decided to give her something.

"I'm in the navy. Originally from Chicago, hence the visit here."

"Cool." She picked up her menu again, coyly this time, and slowly slid it in front of her face. He let her get it up to her eyes before tugging at the top and shifting it to the side. "Hey, I was reading that!"

"I'm pretty sure this isn't your first or fifth time in this bar, and you know exactly what you want." He slowed his words down, teasing her a bit, because until his plane took off, he'd be happy to give her whatever it was she wanted, any way she'd take it.

"Okay." She set the menu down and crossed her hands in the middle of the table, seemingly oblivious to his double entendre. Nathan was struck with the strongest urge to touch her hands—long, slim fingers topped with neatly trimmed nails. Feminine but strong. He wanted to lace their fingers together, but he held himself back because she was so skittish. She rewarded him with a laughing grin. "I'm a flight attendant. Happy?"

"Very. If I play my cards right, maybe you'll call me up the next time you're in San Diego."

A cloud drifted over her face, and he regretted saying too much.

"Hey, it's okay. Are you… Is this a problem, us having dinner?"

She closed her eyes and shook her head. "Nope, not at all. Other than it's the first time I've done anything like this in a long time."

"That sounds like it has a heavy story behind it."

With a sigh, she blinked her eyes open, a determined look newly in place. "Not one that matters tonight. And…that's all I can handle right now—just tonight, okay?"

"Sure." He tapped the menu. "What's good?"

Two club sandwiches and a shared order of fries later, he knew his mystery woman liked tomatoes but not pickles, was addicted to hate-watching reality shows, and she was the youngest of four—something they had in common. And she was still nameless.

"Okay, M." He crumpled his napkin and tossed it onto his empty plate. "Time to nick-name me."

As she appraised him from across the booth, she pulled her lower lip between her teeth, and he found himself staring. Such a cliché, and he didn't care. She had a damn pretty mouth.

"West Coast," she started, and he frowned his disapproval, much to her obvious delight. "Big Guy. Gentle Giant. Little One."

"No. Only in the bedroom. No. And absolutely never."

"Is Sailor too obvious?" She blinked up at him as she asked, and her voice had dropped in a husky wave of words that gave him half a hard-on.

He cleared his throat, totally unnerved by how perfect the name sounded on her lips. "No, that'll do."

"So, Sailor." From the pink of her cheeks, the nickname worked just as well for her. "What do you like to do for fun?"

CHAPTER
TWO

EMME DIDN'T KNOW what had gotten into her, but she really liked the way her Navy guy kept looking at her across the table.

"I read. I like movies. I run." He shrugged. "Most of the time, I'm working, to be honest."

"Have you seen a lot of the world?"

As soon as the question was out there, she wanted to reel it back in, but it wasn't the first time he'd fielded it, clearly.

"Not the same parts you have, M."

She made a face. "I mostly see airports and hotel rooms for six hours at a time if I'm lucky."

"I mostly see military bases and cots in barracks. Six hours sounds luxurious." He winked.

"I bet." She swallowed hard. "Thank you, you know. For not sleeping a lot. And serving our country."

He just nodded, then suddenly reached across the table and covered her hand with his. "Your turn, M. Tell me something that you like."

I like you touching me. His callused fingers woke her up like nothing she'd ever experienced, as if his touch was actually electric.

"Let me guess." He dropped his voice. "You're a dog person."

"Cats."

"Long walks on the beach."

With him, sure. Anyone else… "I'm more of a camping and bonfire girl."

"I bet you look cute as hell in plaid."

She took a deep breath. "You too."

He squeezed her fingers and started to say something else when his phone vibrated on the table. He held on to her hands with one of his while he checked his messages with the other. "My flight. Says it's still just delayed, not canceled."

"Do you have to be back for work?" She could probably help him squeeze onto a Cali-bound plane if it was important. If any took off tonight.

"In theory, but if I get snowbound, they'll deal."

"I can—" She sucked in a breath as he reached across the table and pressed his index finger to her lips.

"Shhh. If I can steal another few hours with you, I'm going to do that."

"Why?" she asked against hand, breathing in the faint taste of him.

"Because you've got pretty eyes," he said, his own gorgeous gaze locked on her face. "And a sexy laugh. You travel light and have a secret punk girl hiding under your suit. But mostly because I don't want to say goodbye yet."

"Secret punk girl?" Her heart thumped eagerly in her chest.

"No Doubt sticker on your phone. Cute little skull piercing on your belly button."

She jerked her gaze down to her midsection. "Do you have x-ray vision?"

"Noticed at security." He winked. "You raised your arms."

"Oh." She held his gaze for a minute, enjoying the naked appreciation there. "It's new. Nobody else has seen it."

"Then I'm a lucky man."

She glanced over at the bar. She wanted more of this, but not here. "Come on. I've got an idea."

———

Her idea turned out to be beer that the bartender happily put in to-go cups—apparently a secret thing that made O'Hare immediately more fun in Nathan's eyes—and a bench tucked around the corner from a departure gate. In front of them was a floor-to-ceiling glass window that turned the quiet hallway into their own private airplane-geek snow globe. She pointed to the bench, handed him her beer, and promised to be right back.

While she was gone, he shot a quick email to his commanding officer, copying the clerk, advising them of his probable travel delays. If he was given an opportunity to spend another night in Chicago, he was going to take it. And maybe—hopefully—have company for breakfast.

Five minutes later she returned a completely different woman. Gone was the black suit. In its place she wore super-faded, distressed jeans, a heavy brown leather belt, and a long-sleeve thermal Henley that fit like a glove.

"Wow, you dress down nicely."

She blushed. "We need to wear business clothing when we fly standby. Since I'm not getting out of here tonight, the suit could go."

He patted the bench and held her beer out. "Come here and tell me more about the secrets of this airport."

"There's a yoga room."

"And I forgot my mat."

She laughed, her shoulder brushing his as she eased closer with each shake, and Nathan shifted his hand to the back of the bench, opening up his side for leaning if she was interested.

She was. It was tentative, but once their thighs slid together, she didn't move away. He turned his face towards her, breathing in the jasmine and vanilla scent of her shampoo, but she kept her gaze pinned straight ahead.

"Tell me something," he said quietly.

"That's the opposite of being mysterious." Her lips curled in a little smile.

"Let's make it a game, then. Two truths and a lie."

"You go first."

You make me hard. I've got condoms. I love yoga. "I'm afraid of snakes…I've never been to Disney World…I have a Betty Boop tattoo."

"No way." She spun in her spot, and he took advantage of her move to wrap his arm around her a little more tightly. Their faces were close now, close enough to kiss, but he wasn't sure they were on the same page about that.

Hell, he was ready to find the nearest bed and have her ride him. His judgement call on how fast they should move was not the measure to go by. He took a deep breath and fixed his poker face. "Well? Which one is a lie?"

"Gotta be Disney. And I'm desperate to see this tattoo."

"I'll have you know I have manly tattoos as well."

"I bet you do. And I bet they're cute. But I want to see Betty." She leaned in and touched her fingertips to his collar, tugging gently.

"Not there." His voice was rough enough for her to take notice, and she glanced up, almost bumping their faces together as she realized how close she'd gotten to him. She yanked herself back. "You've got freckles."

"Most redheads do," she said quietly.

"Hey, M. I want to kiss you right now. But I'm not sure what the deal is."

She parted her lips for a minute, then closed her eyes and screwed up her face as she if needed courage. "I want you to kiss me, too…I'm afraid of heights…I've got some issues because my divorce was finalized today."

Wow. That was some sharing. "I'm sorry."

She cracked one eyelid and peered at him, like she wanted to test his reaction. He wasn't going to make this hard for her. It sounded like she'd already been dealt more than enough of that shit.

"I mean, being scared of heights as a flight attendant—that must suck." He leaned in close, brushing a strand of hair off her cheek. "Can I kiss you now?"

"Yes, please."

He curved his hand along her jaw, savoring the softness of her skin and the sweet look on her face for a moment before he lowered his head and tasted her lips for the first time.

Vanilla lip balm and the barest touch of a warm tongue. Tentative heat and welcoming sweetness. He groaned as she breathed him in, opening for him to explore her mouth deeper. His fingers tangled in the silky straight strands of her hair as she stroked her hands up his chest and around his neck.

"Wow," she whispered when they paused for air. "That was some kiss, Sailor."

"You can probably call me N—unf!" The rest of his name was lost in her mouth as she flew into his lap, covering his mouth with hers as she straddled his legs with her own. Her fearlessness took him by surprise—and turned him on even more than before.

"Uh-uh," she said softly as she licked her way out of his mouth again. "No names."

"That's just cruel." A lie. Yeah, he wanted her name. He wanted to know everything about her. But he could handle her boundaries, no problem.

"Awww, poor baby. I'll kiss you and make it better." Her eyes crinkled up as she laughed gently. "This is fun, right?"

He palmed her ass, tugging her tighter into his lap. "Hell yeah."

This time she brought her lips to his so slowly he wasn't sure she was moving at first. But with each inch, his need for her grew, and by the time she sank her teeth gently into his lower lip, he was a goner. Rocking his hips in the cradle of her thighs, he took over the embrace, showing her with his tongue what he'd do with his cock if this wasn't such a shitty day for her.

He wouldn't—couldn't—take advantage of her. She'd been hesitant about *dinner*. No way could he play with the off-the-charts chemical reaction between their bodies just to make her forget her fragility. Because he was literally leaving on a jet plane.

Ask her how often she comes to the west coast, a voice on his shoulder said, and damned if he could tell if it was an angel or devil. *Shut up and pay attention to the only kisses you might ever get from her*, said another voice. Different. Equally conflicting.

And in his arms, a woman whose name he still didn't know swiveled her hips.

Jesus H. Murphy.

She kissed her way down his neck, and he slid one hand under her shirt. Hot, smooth skin. A dip in the middle of her back, then the rise of her vertebrae as he traced her spine north. A bra strap, and didn't that just fill his cock with all the remaining blood in his body.

Over her shoulder, out the window, snow fell in the cold, dark night. Fucking poetic as she licked the hollow at the base of his neck, and then he needed her mouth again.

He needed a hell of a lot more than that, but her mouth was what he could have.

Down boy.

His dick settled, but didn't lie down. Nathan slowed himself, pausing between kisses to tell her how good she smelled and felt and tasted. And she gave back as good as she got, whispering stuff he didn't need but still liked to hear. How big his arms were, shit like that. What he liked most was the warm string of barely restrained happiness that ran through all her murmured words.

"Is Betty hiding somewhere indecent?" she whispered against his ear, her tongue tracing the outer cartilage as he laughed against her.

"No."

She peeked down the front of his shirt, humming in an appreciative way that *he* appreciated when she saw the big tribal tattoo he had on his right pec.

"Not there," she said huskily.

"Nope."

"That's nice, though." She drew a small circle on the skin just below his collarbone with her fingertip, and he wanted to yank his shirt off and press her cool little hands all over his skin. He felt feverish and heading towards frustration, which wasn't fair. They were in a hallway in an airport. Total strangers. This had to be enough.

He swallowed hard. "Glad you approve."

"I bet it tastes good."

"Seriously, where is a private room when I need one?" He hugged her tight as she laughed. "Betty's on my back. My left shoulder blade."

"Turn around, I want to see it."

Emme traced the black-ink tat of a winking Betty Boop curled up on a motorcycle. "She's not what I was expecting."

"Better than it could have been, I suppose."

"Can I ask why…?"

His laugh rumbled beneath her hand. "Sure."

She waited a minute, filling the silence with a gratuitous feeling-up of his impressive back muscles. After outlining a long, white scar that made her wonder what part of the Navy he was in, she dove back into the conversation. "I think that was your opening to tell me more."

"But I like it when you pull the details out of me. Makes me feel better about being so curious about you."

Emme leaned forward and pressed a kiss to his back before smoothing his shirt into place. She didn't miss the shiver and faint groan. She felt it, too. Terrible timing. But she owed him an explanation, this sailor with the broad shoulders and kind eyes.

She wrapped her arms around him from the back and turned her face to the side, resting her cheek against his shoulder blade. "My ex-husband is a pilot. A big presence in my life, still, because we work together. And a philanderer, although I like the term 'cheating scumbag' better. Has a more honest ring to it."

Inside the circle of her arms, muscles tensed, ready for a fight against an unknown opponent. In that moment, she loved this stranger for his unexpected kindness.

"Were you married long?"

She shook her head. "Six very short months. The divorce took longer than the marriage lasted, for stupid reasons of money and real estate."

"Shitty deal."

"Yeah."

"Betty happened in Cabo, after surviving basic training, but not surviving a drunken celebration. I passed out—rookie mistake—and woke up as the tattooist started working."

"Against your will?"

He shrugged. "Kind of a hard thing to explain outside the moment. I didn't protest. I was young and stupid, probably."

"How old are you?"

"Come here." He tugged her around his body again, curling her into his side. "Just turned thirty-one."

"I'm twenty-seven."

"For the record, I didn't ask." He kissed her forehead. "You're still young. Gorgeous. Kiss like a killer and laugh like a princess. Shake off the ex-husband, M. He's not worthy of any space in your head."

"I've spent a lot of time over the last year thinking that I'd never have another first date. He had me investigated when we first split up, so even after my lawyer said dating was fine, I just couldn't. Not until the divorce was official, and then…when I got the decree today in the mail, it didn't even occur to me that I was free. All I could think was, now I need to sell the house I fought for for so long, because I can't actually afford it by myself. It was the hollowest of victories." As the words tore out of her, Emme started laughing. "And now I've just dumped that on you."

"Don't worry about it." He held out his hand and she laced her fingers through his. "Another round of two truths and a lie?"

CHAPTER
THREE

THEY TALKED FOR ANOTHER HOUR, pausing here and there to make out like teenagers, all eager tongues and nervous hands. He was constantly aware of the warmth of her body, drifting closer before easing back.

But he wasn't so selfish that he thought he could hold her forever. That's something he'd have done as a younger man—staying up all night for one more look from those shining blue eyes.

Now he wanted to put her first. He was beyond angry that some asshole had broken her heart and dragged her through the dirt to add insult to injury. They might just have a night, but it was going to be a good night, so she'd have the courage to do this again. Be happy again.

When she started yawning, he offered to walk her back to the security gate, but she insisted Starbucks would be a better destination.

And then she talked him into ten-minute neck massages, which proved a brilliant idea. He drew the line when she wiggled her eyebrows and pointed to the pedicure express kiosk. "My feet are just fine the way they are."

"I bet they are," she said under her breath, pressing close, and even though they were in the middle of the concourse, he pulled her tight and kissed her for slightly longer than would be considered polite. Not nearly long enough.

When his phone vibrated, he didn't want to check his messages. But when he did, he felt like he'd been handed a gift. "Looks like my flight is canceled. Re-loaded onto a different one in the morning."

"You know that could get changed a few times more?"

He shrugged. "Sure. It's not a big deal, I'll come back first thing in the morning, be pleasant to the front desk staff. I know the drill."

She gave him a brilliant smile, and despite all her flags warning she wasn't that kind of woman, he needed to ask. "Look, I was going to head back to my sister's, but if you wanted…"

"You can't come back to my place," she said in a suddenly too-small voice. "I can't…I just can't. I have this hate-love-hate thing going on with that house right now and tonight has been perfect and…"

"Sure. Hey, no worries. I've had fun, M. Thank you for showing me your secret spot." He moved closer, slow enough she could tell him to stop. This was the end of the road for them, but he wasn't going to let it end on an awkward note.

"Anytime, Sailor. Thanks for being my first date for Life 2.0." They didn't have the luxury of this happening again, but it felt good hearing her say it.

"Anytime." He echoed the lie with a rough whisper as he cupped her face with his hands. God, those eyes. They were getting bluer by the second. "M, there's no crying in baseball."

"Shut up and kiss me, Sailor."

That he could do.

With each step toward the security doors, Emme's anxiety increased. She tightened her grip on the sailor's hand, not wanting to let him go. Maybe she wanted to know his name, after all.

Maybe she didn't want to go home alone.

Or maybe she just didn't want to go home.

"Hey, your flight has been cancelled. The airline should comp you a hotel room."

"It's okay. That's for people who are truly stranded. I can head back into the city." He reached past her and pressed the door open, holding it wide for her.

"Or you could get a hotel room." She grabbed his hand, leading him to an empty spot against the wall in the crowded, chaotic departures hall.

"I'm pretty sure most of these people need those rooms more than I do."

She tugged their entwined fingers up between their bodies. He wasn't getting it. That was kind of cute, but also…man, did she have to spell it out? "Be a little selfish, Sailor." *Let me be a little selfish, too.* "There are plenty of hotel rooms to go around. Come on, I'll help smooth the way. What airline are you on?"

His eyes flared like embers reawakened with a long, slow breath. "American. Are you sure…"

"Nope." She tightened her grip on his hand. "But I don't want to be alone tonight. And something tells me I can trust you with that."

He nodded slowly, his expression solemn. He had such a ready smile, but like this, he looked like a carved Roman sculpture, all perfect lines and hard angles. Noble and worth preserving forever. "Whatever you want. Just what you want."

She pressed up on her toes, dusting a light kiss across his lips before whispering the truth. "I want a lot."

"Then let's get a room."

He didn't let her dive back into the fray to get a complimentary room voucher from the airline. As soon as she gave him the green light, he planted his hand in the small of her back, spun her around and propelled her down the main corridor toward the Hilton attached to Terminal 1. She crossed her fingers they'd have an available room.

They did. Her sailor handed over a credit card, then quietly asked if she wanted to give a copy of her own ID to the desk clerk for safety reasons. She stared up at him, wide-eyed, because not once did it occur to her that this wasn't a smart idea. Swallowing hard, she handed over her driver's license and the clerk added her to the room reservation.

Heart racing, Emme stepped onto the elevator first, glad to see it empty. She was even more glad to feel his strong arms wrap around her waist, tugging her back against his chest. He didn't say anything, just held her, and when they reached their floor he kissed her temple before pressing against the open elevator doorway and ushering her forward.

Inside the room, she found a light switch and parked her suitcase in the closet. She turned around slowly and watched him dump his bag on the chair by the window.

"I bet this isn't weird for you," she blurted out.

He slid her a slow, amused smile. "Weird isn't the word I'd use. Unusual…a bit. You won't tell me your name, for one."

"I guess I shouldn't make it about you. I just…this is weird for me. And I know that's like the least-cool thing to say after begging a guy to get a hotel room, and I'm glad you did, but—"

"Hey, M. It's okay. I didn't want to say goodbye to you tonight. I'm glad we're here, even if you sleep under the sheets and I sleep on top of them."

"We're definitely going to be under the sheets together."

He grinned, white teeth flashing in his tanned face. "Good. I get cold at night."

"This is a bit late to ask, but do you have condoms?"

He nodded slowly. "A couple."

"Okay. Good." She was twisting her hands together. Totally not cool.

"I always carry them. I don't make a habit of picking up women in airports."

"But you've done this before."

"A one-night thing?"

She nodded.

He made a face. "Do you really want me to answer that?"

"No?" She sighed. "Yes. I think so."

"Can I hug you while we talk?"

He was across the room before she finished nodding. "Hey."

She mumbled her response into his shirt.

"You're beautiful, you know that? When I saw you ahead of me in that security line, I thought, damn. Whoever gets to kiss her goodnight is a lucky son of a bitch."

Emme couldn't remember the last time Phil kissed her good night. Maybe he never had. And here she was feeling sorry for herself, when this gorgeous man just wanted to kiss her and make her happy. And she'd never see him again. Pushing away the sadness that thought welled up, she decided to embrace the freedom it gave her to be herself, nothing to lose.

"So what do you want to know? How many girls I've kissed goodnight?" He had the best voice, a rich baritone that promised he wasn't hiding anything, for better or worse.

"Do you sing?" she asked abruptly.

"Uh…yeah. A bit."

"Are you going to be nice to me tonight?"

"Absolutely."

"Are you going to give me an awful disease?"

"Nope. Like I say, I've got condoms, and I'm tested pretty regularly for work."

"I've gotten tested a couple of times over the last year. Mostly paranoia."

"No, it's smart. You weren't treated right. That would make anyone wary."

"You've got all the right answers. You sure you're not a con man?"

He laughed. "How about we dance? I heard a rumor that bad guys don't do that."

He swayed with her in his arms, and started singing under his breath. God, he was good. Too good. Too sweet.

Emme let the happiness wash over her for a minute, then took a deep breath and slung her arms around his shoulders. "How are you at poker?"

He arched an eyebrow as he glanced down at her. "You got cards, little lady?"

"I sure do." She cocked her thumb over her shoulder. "I'll get them from my bag. You raid the minibar."

They settled on the bed with the cards and a few small bottles scattered between them. Emme dealt five cards, then paused. "How are we doing this? Sips? Shots? Entire bottles?"

Her sailor took long enough in slowly sweeping his gaze from his cards up to her face that she should have known he was working on his answer. It still took her by surprise. "I thought we'd play for items of your clothing."

"Wait, what?" She could feel her cheeks burning up. "You want to play strip poker?"

Big grin. She needed to rethink her first impression that he was good as gold. Although… "Why do you think we're just playing for my clothes?"

Two card exchanges later, Emme waved her three jacks in the air and wiggled her fingers at his shirt. "Come on. Show me the whole tattoo, Sailor."

Hooding his gaze, he ever so slowly rolled the fabric up and over his head. "I'm not complaining," he drawled, tossing the shirt in her direction. "But—"

"But what? Girls can't be good at cards?"

He cleared his throat. "Of course I wouldn't say that. That would be foolish and wrong and not conducive to you taking off your shirt when I whoop your butt in the next hand."

She sweetly smiled and folded his shirt into a tiny, square trophy. "It's good to know you're not perfect, Sailor. I was getting worried there for a minute."

"Happy to oblige, M. Deal the cards."

She did, taking her time, because just two feet away was a big ol' mile of man muscles she was finding terribly distracting. And that tattoo… "Is it getting hot in here?"

Smirking, he glanced at his cards, then lowered his hand. To his crotch. "I'm good."

He was more than good. From looks of things behind his hand, he was Tony the Tiger *Grrrreeeat!* Emme's mouth watered at the brazen distraction technique which *almost* worked. She glanced at her cards. Pair of kings, the odds were in her favor. "Me too."

"Let's see 'em." Another smirk.

She lay down her cards, then bit her lower lip and blinked innocently. Two could play that game.

He waited a beat before tossing a pair of aces onto the blanket between them. He gestured politely at her chest. "No, M. Let's. See. *Them*."

Shit. She grinned. Okay, so he had a bit of luck there.

————

Nathan leaned back on one hand, giving in to the heady arousal swirling through his body. Having her greedily eat him up with her eyes had been good. Really good, and he was ready to return the hunger. But instead of taking off her shirt, his vixen stood—slowly— and turned her back on him.

Glancing over her shoulder, she winked before swaying her hips, drawing his attention to that super-fine ass of hers. Those snug jeans looked even better slipping down her hips. Underneath, she wore black cotton boy shorts, but he didn't feel ripped off at all, because her legs... Holy hell.

"Come here," he growled, not caring about the game any longer. She turned slowly, and he changed his mind. "No, turn around again. Jesus, look at you."

Her legs were long for her body, with slim and toned calves and thighs that flared in a sexy curve to meet her hips. Pale skin and sculpted muscle, sweet softness and *freckles*, a light smattering running north from her knees. And then she turned again and the round cheeks of her ass peeking from the bottom of her shorts shredded the last of his self-control.

In one fluid push he was off the bed and against her body. Like she could read his mind, she splayed her hands across his chest. He flexed under her touch because she turned him into a crowing rooster. Most of the time, his body was a machine that performed some of the worst tasks in the world. Swim in freezing cold depths.

Scramble down mountainsides. Silently disable an enemy opponent. Carry a teammate for miles.

But tonight, he had a different challenge. Simpler and infinitely more difficult at the same time, because this didn't feel like any one-night stand he'd ever had before.

And all of a sudden, he regretted the others, except without being that guy, who'd hit on a pretty woman with a lost scarf, he wouldn't be here.

"Want to keep playing?" she whispered, stroking her fingers featherlight across the tattoo that covered half his chest.

"Sure." He could play games all night long. It felt like they were immersed in a thick, erotic syrup that slowed everything down and made this foreplay dance smooth. Like all of a sudden, nothing was going to derail the attraction between them. The cards weren't tentative flirting, they were prolonged foreplay.

Aching from the need to taste her again, Nathan cupped her face and brought their lips together, open-mouthed from the start. He circled his tongue around hers, a rolling tease. They were going to do this for a while. No hurry.

He could pretend this wasn't just one night. That they weren't on a six-hour countdown to a goodbye neither would want to make.

No hurry.

Mind over matter. Mind over time.

Deeper, harder he kissed her, sucking and licking and matching his breath to hers. He tumbled them backwards, then climbed over her on the bed next to the cards.

Blindly pulling two from the scattered pile, he held one to his forehead and pressed the other to hers.

She giggled. God, he could get drunk on that sound. "What are we playing for?"

"Your shirt."

"If you win, I take it off?"

"And if you win, *I* take it off. With my teeth."

She glanced at the card on his head. "I'll see you the shirt and raise you my panties."

Wicked woman. He probably had a deuce. If there was a God, he definitely did, because she had a five. "I fold."

Peals of gorgeous laughter. "You can't fold in Indian poker."

"I fold, you win. Out of my way, woman."

She unwound her legs from around his waist and he shot down her body.

CHAPTER
FOUR

EMME'S LEGS shook as her sailor pressed his impressive shoulders between them. He paused at her belly button, circling her piercing with his finger for a moment as he stared up at her, his gaze hot and hooded. So much for getting back on the sex trolley with a mortal. They were really doing this.

He rucked her shirt a little higher, baring more of her stomach. He pressed a kiss to her side, then her hip. Sweet, hot, wet markings that blazed a trail to the waistband of her underwear, where he hooked his teeth into the fabric and tugged.

Sweet baby Jesus. Emme closed her eyes and rolled her face toward the headboard, overcome by just how *hot* that was. His hands were everywhere, too, helping bare her to his gaze, and she couldn't watch.

She wanted this, more than anything, but if there was anything he didn't like—if he expected her to be waxed or look different somehow, she couldn't bear it.

She'd had enough of *not being enough* for a lifetime.

Against her naked thigh, he groaned, and she pressed her eyes shut even tighter. *That's a good noise*, she told herself. His mouth was just above her knee now, softly sucking the skin there as his fingers spread her legs wider still.

Then nothing. And in the silence, her heart broke. Just like that. *Crack.* So fragile. Too fragile for this. Her breath, frozen in her chest, started to hurt. *Breathe.* But she couldn't.

"M," he said, and the warmth in his voice thawed her fear. She cracked an eyelid. He'd moved away to work on his belt. Taking it off. Good.

She pulled in a low, slow tug of air.

"You with me?" He shoved his pants to the ground, taking his boxer briefs with them. His hand wrapped around his erection, heavy and thick *for her.* "Just getting comfortable here. Look at what you do to me."

"I'm with you," she whispered.

"So beautiful."

"I like hearing that." *I need to hear that.* Except external validation was a fickle bitch—Emme should know better after the last year. Alarm bells sounded in the distance, but with the blood pounding in her ears, she couldn't pay any heed to the caution.

"I like saying it," he said huskily, climbing back on top of her. A scorching kiss led to another, and then he was stripping her out of her shirt. "Fuck me, M. Your tits."

Your tits. He'd said a lot of sweet things to her tonight. They were all nice. Better than anything she'd heard in a long time, maybe ever. But hearing his unguarded comment was the best—validation that her wobbly, average-sized breasts did it for him.

He ground his erection into her belly.

Really did it for him.

With a grunt, he flipped their positions, ending up on his back with her straddling his abs. Against her butt, his erection strained. Up and down her naked front his gaze raked. Up and down.

And then his hands. Big. Rough. Gentle. Deliberate.

She was going to explode just from his touch—his fingers stroking from her knees to her hips, his thumbs glancing over the sensitive creases where her thighs met her pelvis, and then her waist. He paused there, squeezing as if holding her was a joy in and of itself.

Which reminded her—she hadn't had nearly enough time

touching him. She reached back, wrapping her hands around his bent legs.

"Yeah, baby, spread yourself for me." He brought his knees higher again, making a chair out of his body for her to recline in. And because he had the world's longest arms, he still had no problem reaching his original destination.

He stroked her breasts with reverence, then cupped them both. As his thumbs circled her nipples, her hips started rocking—she couldn't hold still any longer, and the way his eyes got dark and his erection flexed behind her, he didn't mind. So she let herself go, a little bit for his gaze, but mostly for herself. For how good it felt to be turned on in a safe space. For how fun it was to be sexy.

"What are you thinking?" he asked, his voice low, so low. Dirty-low. "You just got the best look on your face."

"Thinking how sexy this is," she admitted, then laughed. Throatily, and that was sexy, too.

"Fuck yes." He dropped his hands to her ass. "Come here."

For the rest of time, those two words would instantly make her wet. She'd close her eyes and remember this night with her sailor, remember his hands on her hips, urging her closer to his face.

She'd drift into the technicolor memory and feel his tongue parting her folds. The groan of appreciation at her taste, then his fingers, holding her open as he kissed her, open mouthed and wet, lapping her up. Sucking hard as she trembled and shook, coming apart for him.

———

It had to be madness, how much Nathan wanted this woman. Sex was usually fun and lighthearted, an easy release with a willing friend. And while he'd never laughed quite so freely or so often in his entire life as he had tonight, this moment was the opposite of light. Underneath the flirting and headiness was a scary depth of feeling for two perfect strangers.

Need and desperation drove him. To make time stop and pleasure explode, to try and drive them both to satisfied exhaustion in the hopes it would feel like enough.

And every time he started to think one night might not be enough with this woman, the voice on his shoulder reminded him she didn't want him to even know her name.

But she had no problem riding his face, and from the obvious thrill it gave her—and the now-obvious fact she trusted him with her body—was a win.

It'll feel like a hollow victory in the morning.

That would have to be morning's problem.

They rolled to the side, then Nathan grabbed a condom and sheathed himself.

On the bed beneath him, she stretched like a cat, all pale skin and curves and freckles. And that sparkly fucking skull dancing against the flat of her stomach above a neatly trimmed triangle of dark red hair.

"You tasted amazing," he said roughly as he notched his cock between the swollen, slick folds of her pussy. He hissed at the warm, gripping welcome. "You feel amazing, too."

She rocked her hips up, inviting him inside. He sank an inch into her heat, and it took all of his willpower not to keep going, but she was tight and his thickness would take some getting used to. He held himself above her, reaching between them again to pull out, swirl the head of his cock around in her moisture, and slide in again, deeper this time.

"More," she breathed, circling her hips.

"You okay?"

"It's been a while, but oh my God…" She wrapped her legs around his lower back, groaning as he stretched her depths. "Please, more."

Nathan closed his eyes, giving in to the sensations as he thrust again. Slippery movement. Snug heat. All his good spots rubbing against her good spots, and the whole was most definitely better than the sum of its parts.

With each stroke, his thoughts got more fragmented and his

primal beast brain took over. She clung to him as he surged deeper, driving into her body again and again.

Around his neck, her arms tightened. Her heels dug deep into his ass. He fisted his hand in her long, silky hair and found her mouth, open and willing.

He kissed her like he fucked her, right on the edge of losing control.

Teeth and tongues. Lips, swollen and wet. God, her lips. He sucked the lower one into his mouth, loving the way she clenched around him when she did.

Fuck. He needed her nipple in his mouth.

He drove his hips hard against her, holding them together as he flipped their positions again.

On his back, he held her close, curving his body beneath hers, bringing those glorious tits to his face. Soft. Perfect.

She was making the best noises now, constantly, half words and half whimpers. He loved them all.

"Sailor," she breathed, and that fucking did it. He tugged more of her breast into his mouth, sucking hard as she rocked on top of him.

She came around him as he drove his cock deep. Hard. Too hard, probably, his hands so tight on her hips she'd probably have bruises in the morning.

He came too, with such intensity he saw stars and maybe blacked out for a second.

But when he thundered back to consciousness, all of his nerve endings firing, his first thought was that he was getting on an airplane and leaving her here. Alone, and marked by a complete stranger.

Fuck fuck fuck.

"M," he said into the quiet after his heart stopped thudding. She was glued to his chest, and that was fine—he wanted her on top of him for the rest of the night—but he needed to get rid of the condom.

She tightened her arms around his neck, burrowing her face deeper into his embrace.

"Need a minute," she whispered, and his heart cracked.

"Please tell me you don't hate me." He muttered the words ever so quietly against her hair. His voice was unsteady. He'd gone a bit crazy there at the end, but she'd been right into it.

"No hate. Never hate. That was perfect." She pressed a small kiss against his skin, then rolled to the side, wiping her eyes. "Just girl feelings, that's all."

"Hey, boys have feelings, too."

She laughed. "Have you ever cried after sex?"

"Well…no."

Another laugh. "When was the last time you cried?"

"Not the point." He got rid of the condom before tucking himself against her back, palming her ass because he could. "Shower?"

She sucked in a deep, ragged breath. "God, yes."

"Come here first." He turned her face toward his, kissing her gently. "Thank you."

"For what? Pretty sure that was a mutually beneficial thing we just did."

How to say what was on his mind without sounding creepy or emo? He rubbed his thumb over the corner of her mouth while he searched for the right words. "You're one of a kind, M. Tonight felt like a rare gift, that's all."

"Now I think I'm the one who needs to say thank you," she whispered, lifting her head to kiss him back. "And if you wash my hair, I think you'll ruin me for all men forever and ever."

"Deal." Totally selfish that he wasn't kidding, but he was okay with being selfish when it came to this woman. At some point before they said goodbye, he'd find a way to invite her to visit him out west.

CHAPTER
FIVE

AT QUARTER to four in the morning, Emme's phone went off. She rolled over to grab it but was stopped short by a heavy arm wrapped tight around her naked waist.

"Don't answer it," her sailor mumbled into her hair. "Let's run away and join a circus together."

"It'll be the overnight shift supervisor; they'll need extra staff this morning. I just need to answer this and then I can come back to bed for a bit." *And maybe we can use that last condom before I report in.*

After their shower, he'd pulled his last three condoms out of his bag and tossed them on the bedside table with a wicked grin. They'd used one before she begged him to get some sleep. Of course then she'd woken him up two hours later, rubbing her ass against his erection.

She flushed at the memory of him silently rolling her onto her stomach, hiking her hips in the air, and sliding his fingers through her folds to make sure she was ready for him.

No problem in that regard.

He'd taken her fast and hard, still silent, her face pressed into the pillow and her ass in the air.

She wanted that again.

She wanted that forever.

Damn it. No falling for the rebound guy. Not allowed.

She swallowed hard, then put on her awake-voice and answered her phone.

As she listened and responded, realizing she wasn't going to get back into bed with him, she had to tip her face to the ceiling and fight back hot, angry tears of regret.

Ten minutes later she hopped out of the shower and let herself cast a single, sad glance at the slumbering giant she was leaving behind. He really was the most beautiful man. Hard and lean, warm and safe.

This was better.

She was needed on a flight to Denver at six, and if she woke him, she'd never make it on time.

This was better.

If she climbed back into bed, even for a minute, she'd lose her heart to hopeless dreams.

Shit.

This wasn't better.

But it was what needed to be, because she needed the extra-long shift and the overtime. Because she needed to remember who she was and who she wasn't.

She found the note after she got on elevator. It was in her blazer pocket, a sheet of paper from the hotel room notepad, folded in a neat square with a capital M on the front. Her fingers shook as she opened it.

You're beautiful. Thank you. ~ Nathan
Gibson75@xmail.com

She traced over the letters in his name. *Nathan.* So her sailor had a name. A nice name. And she'd crept out while he slept. The tears threatened again, and she stared at the elevator numbers, lighting up in descending order.

She should go back up. *Nathan.* She should go back and kiss him and tell him her name.

But then what?

That would just make goodbye harder.

It would still be goodbye.

She ducked her head as she headed through the lobby toward the airport concourse, letting her hair curtain her face from the early morning travellers.

———

Nathan looked for her as he went through the check-in process for the second day in a row. He wasn't sure what airline she worked for, or what her name was, although he had at least one way of finding that out—she'd left her ID with the hotel clerk.

But he wanted her to find him. Not now. She wasn't ready.

When she was, he hoped she'd still have his notes.

There were five of them in total. One in her jacket pocket. One in her passport wallet—and it had been damn hard not to peek at her name when he was tucking that away while she slept. One in the outer pocket of her suitcase, one in her Kindle case, and the last one woven into the laces on her running shoes.

He smiled at the thought of her finding them. Hopefully she'd already found at least one.

CHAPTER SIX

FEBRUARY

DEAR NATHAN,

Emme stared at the blinking cursor on her screen. It had been six weeks. She'd thought about him every day. Replayed every minute of their night together, to the point where she wasn't sure she hadn't dreamed him up.

But the little wooden box on her bedside table held five short notes, scrawled in the dead of night, that told her Nathan was more than a fantasy and more than a one-night stand...if she could let him in.

He lives on the other side of the country.

You're broken-hearted and ill-prepared for a new relationship.

It was impossible to pretend that it would just be hooking up if she reached out to a man who lived two thousand miles away.

Wasn't there a rule about having a rebound guy before another serious relationship?

On the other hand, maybe the fact he was on the west coast would be a good thing. They couldn't rush into anything.

. . .

I'm sorry for not writing sooner. Hi. I'm Emme—pronounced M. Sorry for the little trick there.

She stared at the first line. Two apologies already. But that's how she felt, sorry for the undertow of emotional catharsis she'd drag him into if they dropped the masks and showed their real selves.

I've been thinking about you a lot. Every day, in fact, since our night together. How are you?

So weak. She growled at herself and started to erase that line, then left it. She wouldn't be able to think of anything better, and they'd already been naked together. She'd *cried* on his bare chest. The time for fancying up her words was probably long passed.

She started typing again, letting herself word vomit this time, and eight paragraphs later, she hit send before she could reconsider the action.

Shoving away from her desk, she paced across the empty master bedroom she was now using as an office. Derek had taken the master bedroom furniture, and she'd just moved her belongings into the spare bedroom rather than bringing over the mismatched furniture that didn't suit the bigger room. It had been easier on her heart to pretend that she'd eventually get nice stuff, and that this wasn't her new life—living like a college student again, suffocating under a mountain of debt she'd never asked for.

Pretend that she'd be able to afford new furniture, when she couldn't afford the house itself, not while she was still paying off a hefty legal bill. And the house had been bought on Derek's pilot's salary. It was a miracle her mortgage broker had been able to swing getting the house into her name alone.

She closed her eyes. She'd balked at the flexible mortgage he'd gently suggested, but he'd been right. She needed to rid herself of the beautiful turn-of-the-century albatross around her neck.

She'd call the real estate agent soon. And pray the market gods would smile on her.

From across the room, her computer dinged. She whirled around, her angst momentarily fleeing from her head. *An email.*

Throwing herself back into her seat, she ignored the way her knee banged against the side of the desk as she spun the wheelie chair a little too hard.

Throat dry, pulse fluttering a mile a minute in her neck, Emme clicked on the email from Nathan, her hand shaking the entire time.

M. Emme. I like it. I've had your name all this time, huh? Clever you.

I was hoping you'd email me. How many of my notes did you find? You started to wake up as I was stashing them in your luggage, or I'd have written more. I'd have written a hundred of them if I thought it would increase the odds of you actually contacting me. So don't worry about how long it's been—and I don't think six weeks and three days is that long, by the way.

Oh God, he'd counted the days. She dragged her lower lip through her teeth, the implications of his attention to detail rolling heavily through her head. But as she kept reading, he turned the conversation in a safer direction, and the pounding in her chest eased just enough to feel comfortable. It did nothing for the nervous flutter, though.

Must be freezing there. I hear you're having a wicked cold snap. Hopefully spring is early this year.

I'm going to read your email over and over again. It's great to hear from you. Nice to put a name to my memories. It sounds like you've got a lot going on—I knew that already. If writing to me about any of it helps ease that burden, feel free to flood my inbox. I'm a vault, I promise. But really...I just want to know what secret

punk girl music you're listening to, and if you managed to get away for a few days to San Antonio. Think of me as your...pen pal.

Nathan Meyers

Her heart squeezed tight. He was just as special as she'd remembered—genuinely caring about her, a complete stranger. More than anything, she needed someone in her life who she could talk to, someone who wasn't her mother or sister, who were both still disappointed that her fairy-tale marriage to the prince in the pilot uniform hadn't worked out. Or her friends from work who were so jaded about pilots they had trouble scraping up enough sympathy to hear about Emme's sadness.

And frankly, she was kind of sick of it herself.

Pen pals, she typed. **I like that. Is it weird to say I've missed you over the last six weeks? I think I have, and now that I'm typing this, I wish I hadn't taken so long to reach out.**

And I want to hear about what's going on with you, too.

Yours,

Emme Ryan

P.S. I found five notes. Still have them.

She made herself get up and go find some lunch after hitting send, but as soon as she'd assembled a ham and swiss sandwich and grabbed a Coke, she found herself settling in front of the computer again. His first response had been so quick...

But there were no new emails in her inbox. She clicked over to Facebook and worked through a dozen notifications about things she didn't really care about, then flipped back.

Still nothing.

Not liking the out-of-control roller coaster her heart was currently riding, she forced herself to finish her sandwich, then got up. She had email on her phone—she needed to get out of the house. So what if it was freezing outside?

Besides, she had three weeks left in her pre-paid gym membership. Might as well use it as much as possible before it ended.

———

Nathan felt his pocket vibrate, but right after responding to Emme's first email, he'd been pulled into an O-Group meeting with his lieutenant. They'd received an initial heads up that a sensitive subject might need to be rescued from the South Pacific. They were waiting on intel from the CIA, but they might need to pull together an urgent-extraction team. Not the type of orders group one could check their email during. He'd be torn a new asshole by the major if he pulled out his phone while he was supposed to be paying attention.

As soon as they finished up, he read Emme's message—twice, the second time with a shit-eating grin on his face—then stayed in the empty conference room to type his response.

Yep, five notes. You got 'em all.

I was in an orders group when you emailed again. You have no idea how hard it was not to check my phone when I felt it vibrate. You're going to get me in trouble.

He added a winking emoticon, then deleted it. Then typed it again. He couldn't decide if it added a playful touch, or veered into flirting too hard.

Being indecisive was a new feeling that Nathan didn't wear well. But he didn't want to fuck this up.

He could still taste her. Still heard her breathless moans as she writhed beneath him.

He could still count her freckles if he closed his eyes.

Six weeks had never felt like a lifetime before. He'd been

desperate to hear from her, but known she wasn't ready. Probably still wasn't, but her first email had dripped with loneliness.

He wanted to fly to Chicago, track her down, and hold her tight.

But if he did that, he'd never let her go.

So instead, he hit send. Winky face and all.

"Meyers, you gotta minute?" His LT's voice jerked his attention away from Chicago and back to the reality.

Nathan nodded as his team leader joined him in the empty room. "Yes, sir."

It was a knee-jerk formality that wasn't necessary with Jason Steyner, but Nathan always defaulted to a rigid command structure when they shifted into active duty. He needed to show his officer—who had less boots-on-the-ground experience, by far—in his words and deeds that the entire team would follow him straight to hell if so ordered.

And then do the impossible and come right back.

"How are you feeling about Novak doing a mission?"

Nathan put his phone away and scrubbed one hand over his face. "Yeah. He's going to be fine."

"You know him well?"

"Well enough. He'd rather be in the sandpit with Team 9. There's some guilt there." Trick Novak had been reassigned to Nathan's platoon in Team 11 after his last tour of duty, because of some concerns about possible PTSD, and his former teammates were now in the Middle East again. He was still more than capable to serve as a SEAL, but the short missions that Team 11 were currently doing were more appropriate while he was being followed by the medical team.

Steyner nodded. "Nothing wrong with shifting it up. His psych eval was fine."

Nathan gave his boss a hard look. They all knew it was possible to get the all-clear and still be a mess. "It'd be good if you underline for him how valuable he is on this mission."

"And you will…"

"Play the worried mother hen." Nathan snorted. "Probably would be more believable the other way around, if I was the hard-ass. But I've already told him to take the time he needs."

"Got it. I'll tell him time's up. Uncle Sam needs him."

As they finished up their conversation, an intelligence officer found them and Nathan excused himself to give their team a stand-by alert.

It wasn't until he threw himself into the cab of his truck, to drive home and shower and grab some sleep, that he had a quiet moment to check his email again.

That didn't mean Emme hadn't been on his mind. She'd imprinted on him that night in Chicago. He'd managed to lock that down when he woke up and found her gone. Now that she'd opened up the lines of communication, he was pretty sure that lock was permanently busted.

But he couldn't let her distract him from work—or let work distract him from her.

She deserved his whole attention when he could give it. He'd been rolling that over in his head since that flight back to California —until January, he'd had no problem limiting his dating to strictly casual connections. It was easier with his job.

It meant there was zero guilt when he couldn't look at his phone for hours, days, or weeks. When he had to leave at the last minute and couldn't say when he'd be back. When his team rotated to long tours overseas, and he packed up and didn't look back for six months or a year, because his attention had to be completely on the deadly threats ahead.

There'd be no leaving Emme behind. Hell, he already had her in his heart as they planned heading out to Honolulu to meet the underwater team. He'd see her face when he needed motivation to do the impossible.

There was a very real risk that he was over-sentimentalizing their connection. Letting his dreams of Emme fill the gaping hole in his chest.

She might break his heart.

That would have to be okay. It was hers to break.

And in the meantime, he'd do his damnedest to keep it safe for her.

CHAPTER
SEVEN
APRIL

EMAILING EMME HAD BECOME a necessary part of Nathan's day. Maybe because that was the only contact they had. Definitely because her words filled him with hope, even though she didn't give any other indication of being ready for more contact. He was waiting for an opening to ask—for a visit, a phone call, anything—but she so carefully didn't give him a chance that he told himself to be patient. And his team was in a cycle of active missions, which meant it was the wrong time to be getting wrapped up in a woman anyway. But that's exactly what was happening.

He'd fallen fast for her—months too fast—and now he was suffering for it.

Everything was out of order. When his friends got into serious relationships, they had a chance to explain to their girlfriends the ins and outs of dating a SEAL.

He wasn't dating Emme. Not yet.

Hell, he wasn't even *talking* to her.

And he sure as shit couldn't write anything out in an email.

But it was hard *not* telling her where he was going and how long he'd be gone. The day after their first round of emails back and forth, his team had flown out to Hawaii, and then beyond, to rescue a CIA operative and a crew of American ocean-treasure hunters in the South Pacific.

One of his men, Trick Novak, had ended up in the hospital with a busted arm after besting a modern-day pirate in hand-to-hand combat, which turned the planned five-day turnaround into six, and by the time they were back, Nathan was dying to see Emme's words again. Desperate to talk to her, too—he could admit that to himself. But she never offered her number and he held himself back from asking.

But when he got back, there were many emails waiting, each one soothing the ragged edges of his worry, and as soon as he replied to one, more flowed between them. He greedily soaked up all of her words like they were water flooding a desert after a drought. He sent her questions and funny pictures, anything to get another response.

Some days they sent dozens of messages back and forth, most of them short, a lot of them silly, but enough of them were raw and honest that he pieced together a pretty clear image of her life in Chicago.

Two months rolled by.

They fell into a routine of starting each day with a funny meme. **You might be cool, but you'll never be as cool as Freddie Mercury riding on Darth Vadar's shoulders**, she sent him one morning, the words spelled out in block letters on the black and white photo.

He dug around in Google and found an infographic about how many people wrote a bunch of hit songs. At the bottom was Freddie's picture next to "Bohemian Rhapsody"—he hadn't needed a team of songwriters to help him.

He was the real deal, Nathan wrote back.

Plus Brian May. Right?

. . .

Right. He stretched on his bed as he looked at his phone. She was a Queen fan. If she told him she liked *Star Wars* and *Lord of the Rings*, it would be all over and he'd die of total happiness. **You ever play guitar?**

Nope, she wrote back. **Piano when I was a kid. Then sax in high school. *Shudder*. Now I'm just a fan. You?**

He looked at the trio of guitars mounted on his wall. **Yeah, I play a bit.**

I'd like to hear that sometime.

The next night, he recorded a bit of himself playing and sent it to her. She emailed back right away with a little heart emoji.

He opened that message at least a dozen times in the days that followed. He was a lovesick puppy.

But it wasn't just flirting and fun.

She also wrote about letting go of her gym membership and cooking meals ahead so she could pull something out of the freezer when she came in late from an evening flight.

She didn't say it outright, but money was tight, and he kept flashing back to their conversation at O'Hare about the toll her divorce had taken.

She hadn't mentioned selling her house again. He resisted the urge to stalk Chicago real estate listings.

He even thought about using the excuse of visiting his sister so he'd be in the same city as Emme for a few nights, but before he could put that into action, his team was sent to South America for three weeks over Easter. When he got back, one thing came up after another, and any time he had more than a day off, Emme was working—and that meant flying all over the country, nowhere near Chicago.

And somehow, also never near California. She sent him pictures from Atlanta and Memphis and Miami.

Two complicated work schedules really interfered with getting her back in his arms.

He was more than ready to do that—he wanted to bust through the distance and the secrets. Tear down the wall between them.

This was on his mind more than usual as he locked up his comfortable little house on his quiet, pleasant street. He'd bought it two years earlier, when he'd tired of the having-a-roommate scene, and didn't want to pay rent on his own every month. Better to pour that money into equity, he could hear his father saying in his head.

What would Emme think of his place?

Would it be nice enough for her?

Why did it matter so much?

He dropped his duffel bag on his front step and grabbed his phone from his pocket. He snapped a picture of the bag, but stepped back enough to show the neat but shabby porch. He couldn't even name what it was exactly he was doing—just showing her a bit more of himself, and hoping that she didn't mind that it wasn't perfect.

That was the positive spin on it.

The truth was he was testing her. Poking a bit to find out if the feelings—big feelings—in his head were shared at all.

With a cryptic photo showing that you're going away for work again. Okay, so he wasn't great with the relationship metrics.

Before he could overthink it, he hit send.

She emailed back by the time he got to the base.

Off again?

Yep.

. . .

Is that your house? It's cute.

Hot relief coursed through his chest. **It sure is.**

When you get back, send me more pictures.

Will do.

She didn't reply right away, but when he checked his phone at the dinner break after the last O-Group, there was another email. **Maybe I should send you a care package. Is that a thing?**

He laughed as he wrote back. **Not on my current rotation, but if I ever go overseas, definitely.**

You don't want a box of cookies waiting for you when you get home?

Of course he did. **Wait, yes, send a care package. Maybe two.**

I'll need your address. She added a picture of Pinky and The Brain.

First step in taking over the world?

Something like that.

———

Emme didn't know what exactly she was going to do with Nathan's address—other than send him cookies, of course. Two batches, made with all the affection and appreciation she couldn't yet bring herself to say in actual words.

She wasn't ready to hop on a plane and just show up on his doorstep. That would be crazy. And it wouldn't change the fact that they lived on opposite ends of the country.

But his emails... Every time his name popped onto the screen of her phone, her heart did a handstand. She'd grown addicted to his written words, the sweet and funny in equal measure.

She wanted more. All the little clues he gave her had reawakened her appetite for all things Nathan, and now her dreams were filled with fantasies of being wrapped in his arms once again.

Not just at night, either—memories and imagined future scenarios were now washing over her during the day, making her smile and blush and generally be flustered. At work the triggers were strongest, because that's where they'd met.

More than once she'd pulled out her phone and started an email to him.

I just walked past the hallway where we first kissed...

But she always deleted the messages before sending them. Which was stupid, because she knew he was waiting for her to make the first move. He was holding back because she'd poured her heart out to him that night, then cried after they'd made love, and in general he knew she was a hot mess.

She should just leap, she knew that. The fact he was holding back, that he was that much of a good guy...those were reasons to go for it.

But knowing that in her head and being ready for it in her heart were two different things.

Trust was a fickle mistress.

She couldn't bring herself to accept how needy she was for him. How happy he made her, and how gutted she was when he was gone. Her airline had recently installed wi-fi on most of their planes, so provided that was working, she was never out of touch.

When Nathan was working, he was *gone*. Poof.

And dating him would mean being okay with that. Trusting that he was going to come back to her. Trusting that in the pockets of time they'd have together, they'd be able to foster a meaningful connection that wouldn't turn ugly or bitter or sad.

She was so done with sad.

One night with him had changed her, but just a bit. Not enough to make her brave.

No, she was still fragile. Still weak.

So she didn't flirt with him, because she wasn't ready to deal with the consequences. Instead, she told him about the books she was reading and funny stories about passengers on her flights. She got him to send her more clips of him playing the guitar, which amazed her, and wiggled little nuggets of gold out of him, like the fact that his favorite food was beef stroganoff and his idea of a perfect lazy Sunday was a *Die Hard* marathon.

For his part, he gave more than he asked for. She could hear him, between the lines, wondering about her house and her life post-divorce, as he asked her about to-do lists and her moods in that non-prying, just genuinely interested way of his. She'd danced around both subjects because the answers weren't fun.

Being un-fun was right up there with being sad.

She knew she could confide in him.

A big part of her wanted to.

But an even bigger parted wanted just to be happy. Full stop.

It took four months, but during a crew briefing at the end of April, she finally got a clue that the universe had been listening.

She had an early flight, which meant getting to O'Hare at four in the morning. She took the El, because it was cheaper than parking. And since being late wasn't an option, she was twenty minutes early—enough time to grab a coffee and check her email in the staff lounge. She was about to check her schedule on the airline's intranet when her friend Gina sat down next to her.

"Have you picked your flights for next month yet?" Gina pulled out a compact and checked her makeup as she talked.

They used a computerized bidding system to make their requests. It was a bit of a gamble—if you bid for a popular route as your first choice, like the international flights, and lost out to more senior staff, you could end up with your fourth or fifth choice by some cruel twist of the mysterious algorithm that nobody really understood.

Emme shook her head. "Not yet. Think I'm going to put in for Atlanta and Miami again, I like that loop."

"I'm going to put in for Singapore. You should, too."

"What?" A direct from Chicago flight to Singapore had been talked about for months, but the most recent scuttlebutt had been that it was being scrapped before it even started. "Is that a go?"

Gina sighed. "No, not direct. From San Francisco."

"Oh." Still good. Not as many flying hours, but better than the short-hop domestic flights. "What are your other bids?"

Gina rhymed off a bunch of domestics, but the look on her face said it all. She was confident she'd get the international flight.

"Why do you look like the cat who caught the canary?" Emme leaned in and lowered her voice as other crew members arrived, for their flight and other flights leaving at the same time. "If you have dirt, you share."

A lead on an easy-to-get international route was gold. The flights were easier to crew and more lucrative, because flight attendants were only paid for in-air time; and the down time between flights was way more fun in a foreign city than in same-old, same-old American cities. Most of them had signed up for the job to see the world, not yet another airport hotel surrounded by suburban outlet malls.

"Apparently they're having trouble filling that route. Last month two juniors got it when they put it first."

"You sure they weren't last minute replacements?"

"One thousand percent sure. But that's another option—put it number one, and you'll be the first person the scheduler tags when someone calls in sick."

"Wow." Emme twisted back to the computer and tabbed over to her next month's requests. "Okay, done."

"Don't get your hopes up," Gina said with a yawn.

"No, I won't." But she totally would. SFO was practically in Nathan's backyard.

She'd avoided west coast flights for reasons that sounded silly when she actually spelled them out in her head, but made sense in her gut.

Avoided. Past tense.

She was ready for the west coast and all the risk and reward it promised.

"Because you know they're going to call people based in California first. I mean, we can get the route as a commuter on the schedule, but...."

"Yeah, we're not the fill-ins they're looking for." Emme gnawed at her lower lip as she logged out of the system and gathered up her stuff.

As they made their way to their assigned aircraft and went through the crew briefing, the conversation replayed in her mind, and nervous butterflies fluttered in her stomach. She'd been a flight attendant for six years, and she was good at her job. She could pay attention to the captain and the purser and still give some of her brain power to the obvious solution: she needed to move out west.

Pronto.

Not to San Diego. That would be needy and foolish, and while she was both of those things, deep down inside, she'd pretend she wasn't.

For weeks, her real estate agent had been bugging her to drop the asking price on her house, and she'd been holding out.

It was worth more, and she needed a place to live.

Not anymore.

As soon as they'd done their seat check and were ready to accept boarding passengers, she pulled out her phone and fired off a quick text message approving a reduced listing price.

When they landed in Atlanta, she had a response. Her agent had floated the new price past two buyers who'd been through the house before but passed.

Now they both wanted to see it again.

For the first time in hours, Emme exhaled.

Then she smiled.

CHAPTER
EIGHT

JUNE

EMME TOOK a deep breath before opening her front door.

On the other side stood two big, burly men in overalls. She nodded at them and stepped back, letting them into her house.

Not your house for much longer. No more heavy mortgage burden. No more memories of a marriage doomed from the get-go.

She was totally ready for this step, but it didn't make the move any less bittersweet.

Just today. It's only bittersweet for this precise moment. After that, it would just be sweet.

Her hands shook as she thought about heading for California in a few short hours.

She hadn't gotten the Singapore route in May, but she did for June. In seventy-two, she was flying out of San Francisco for her first scheduled international flight. It was a start to a whole new phase in her life, one that was close to Nathan and far from all this failed history.

"You can begin in there," she said, pointing to the small front room she'd used as a dining room before selling that furniture. It didn't take them long to clear her neatly packed boxes out of the main rooms downstairs and onto the moving truck parallel parked on the street—a minor miracle in itself. She retreated to the second floor, but before long, she heard their footsteps on the stairs.

"In here," she called out as she did one final loop of the empty bedrooms. Everything was neatly packed up. She wasn't bringing any furniture with her.

Time for a clean slate.

"What about this?" the tall one asked as she met them in the master bedroom. He held out the small wooden box that contained Nathan's notes. Emme's heart leapt into her throat. She'd meant to put it in her purse.

"I'll take that." She snatched it away, not caring if it was rude.

That little box and the five notes inside meant the world to her.

Nathan.

He had no idea she was California-bound.

She was making this move for herself. Not him. Not any man, no matter how wonderful he might be.

Once she was settled in San Francisco—a short commuter flight down to San Diego—then maybe they could go on a date.

If it didn't work out, then she'd still have almost the entire length of a state between them and she could safely pretend she wasn't moving across the country because of a one-night stand. And five months of being pen pals, which had done just as much as their one night to bind them together.

She grinned and pressed the wooden box to her chest. He'd want to go on a date.

As she cleared out of the movers' way, she felt her phone vibrate. They'd shifted from emails to texting once she'd made her secret decision to head Nathan's way at the first opportunity, and that short double vibration still made her giddy with excitement.

She pulled out her phone and read his message: **How's your day going?**

Raining here in Chicago. What are you up to?

The screen didn't even dim before he responded. **Gorgeous and sunny here in San Diego. Year-round, so if you want to plan a reunion for our one-year anniversary, can I suggest it be here?**

She laughed. Could he sense that something was about to

change? Grinning, she nodded to the empty room she was standing in. **Okay. Maybe yeah, we should plan that.**

Okay? Shit, I should have been pushy before.

I wasn't ready before.

And now?

Now she was more than ready. All her raw edges had been worn smooth by five months of counseling and the emotional balm of being courted from afar, no strings attached. **Now I wouldn't mind a little push.**

What are you doing next weekend? I could fly out to see you.

My job is changing a bit so I'm not sure what my schedule is after this coming week, but I'll let you know.

Is everything okay?

She pressed her phone to her chest and closed her eyes for a second before responding. **More than okay. Everything is great.**

———

She got out of the cab and took a deep breath as she looked at the small one-story house, with its neatly cut lawn and spiky, tropical-looking garden running along the walk. She wasn't in Chicago anymore. A pickup truck was parked in the drive, and from the open window she could hear a slow strum of acoustic guitar.

She was really here. And on the other side of that door was Nathan.

Her heart was doing its best to pound right out of her chest.

She walked up the concrete path and across the porch she recognized from the picture he'd sent her. Raising her hand, she knocked on the screen door.

The strumming stopped, and she could hear Nathan sigh, which made her giggle. She pictured him setting down the guitar, pushing himself up off the couch or from a chair, and slowly walking to the front door.

Then he was there, a shadow on the other side of the screen, and she tipped her head to the side.

"Hi, Sailor." She raised her hand, and he just stood there staring at her for a second.

"Emme?" She watched, her breath frozen in her chest, as a slow, broad smile spread across Nathan's face. "Holy shit."

He pushed the door open, and then she was in the air—in his arms—and his mouth covered hers, hot and wet and possessive.

Perfect.

She whimpered as he kissed her, hard at first, then softer, over and over again. His hands were everywhere, shoved into her hair, then running up and down her back, and she held on to him for dear life.

"I've missed you so much," he ground out when he finally pulled away, his face less than an inch from hers, his breath puffing hot against her lips. "I was this close to flying to Chicago and walking the streets, calling out your name."

"That sounds crazy."

"You make me crazy."

"I didn't know." Her chest ached. Yes she did. She felt it too, but she couldn't handle it before. She offered him a weak, shaky smile. "But I flew to California. So maybe I do know."

"Yeah." He crushed her against his body, holding her tight as he smoothed a hand up and down her back. "How long are you here?"

"The weekend. And then..." Her voice shook as she sucked in some extra air. "I've moved, Nathan. I don't live in Chicago anymore."

"Where do you...are you here?"

She wobbled her head back and forth. "San Francisco."

"I'll take it." He kissed her again, his lips tugging at hers, his tongue eager and questing. "You taste better than I remember."

"Same."

"Come inside."

"Okay."

"I should warn you, I'm going to try to get you naked as soon as we're on the other side of that door."

"I said okay, didn't I?" She laughed as he grabbed her bag and walked backwards, holding on to her hand the whole time, and pulled her into his house. "This place is nicer than you described."

He hadn't sent her many more pictures. He'd shown her little details, a guitar on a couch or the dinner he'd cooked, but she'd never gotten a clear picture in her mind of his space.

"You have more guitars than I expected," she breathed as he hustled her down the hall. There were at least three in the living room, and she'd seen a picture of a couple in his bedroom, too.

"Uh huh." He dropped her bag on the floor and crowded her against the wall, his hands cupping her face. "Emme? It's been almost six months since I've had a taste of you. Half a year since we've had sex, and I've wanted you so badly it's hurt. So we can do the *nice place* talk after I've made you come a few times, got it?"

She'd barely had a chance to nod eagerly before he slanted his mouth across hers again. But for all the urgency she knew they both felt, he still went slowly. Making it last, making sure it was real...she wasn't sure which. Maybe both.

Her pulse pounded beneath her skin, every inch of her ready for this and nervous at the same time. When he snaked his hands down her torso and under her shirt, she wrapped her arms around his neck and lifted onto her toes, encouraging him to explore further. As he did, she pulled him hard against her body, and he spread his hands around her waist, lifting her in the air.

Wrapping her legs around his hips, she found his erection hard and ready, and rocked herself against his length.

"We need to be naked," she whispered as he ground their hips together.

A grunt of agreement made her heart sing. Rendering this man speechless was all the validation she needed that this had been the right call.

He braced one hand under her butt and the other across her back and turned them, carrying her through the kitchen—also cute, she thought in her head—to a bedroom at the back of the house.

She didn't see anything else because her t-shirt was being pulled over her head, then she was flat on her back and he was on top of her, blocking her view.

Not that she'd complain about that.

The up-close and personal view of his chiseled face—lustful eyes, a day's stubble on his cheeks, his mouth parted and slick from her kisses—was even better.

How had she gone six months without this?

She'd never make that mistake again.

"I missed you so much," she whispered as he kissed down her neck and nuzzled her breasts where they overflowed her bra. "I'm sorry it took me so long."

"Is it going to be another six months before we do this again?" He scraped his teeth along the bottom of her ribcage and she let out a small gasp.

"No."

"Then don't worry about it." He tugged open her pants, groaning as he wiggled them down her hips. Moisture flooded between her legs at the appreciative sound. "So, so pretty. Holy hell, I want to lick you up."

Now it was her turn to be reduced to helpless noises, whimpers and silent pleas for more as he tossed her legs over his shoulders and went down on her. He didn't even bother to take off her panties, he just tugged them to the side as he licked between her folds, using his fingers to hold her pussy open so he could better suck on her clit and generally drive her around the bend faster than she could imagine.

"Come on my face," he ground out, and those words worked just as well as the magic twists of his tongue against her skin. That he wanted to do this, that he'd been craving her...it all worked. Got under her skin and tugged on all the right strings to wind her up and send her flying into the stratosphere.

She twisted her hands into his blanket, fisting the fabric to keep from pulling his hair out as he lifted her hips, holding her in the air as he covered all of her secret pink skin with his mouth and gave her the best orgasm of her life. It started deep inside her body, the winding of all those strings pulling every cell in her body taut until she ached for release, then with a last almost harsh tug of his mouth around her clit, the strings snapped and she was spinning through space.

But Nathan had her.

Her legs fell wide against the bed as he peeled the rest of her clothes off, then his own, before covering her body with his.

Hot skin against hot skin.

It was too good to be true, and yet it *was* true. She arched restlessly beneath him as he found her mouth with his, as he filled his hands with her breasts. Pressing her heels into the bed, she lifted her hips again, seeking the hard length of him that kept throbbing against her thighs.

She wanted—needed—him inside her. Now.

His breath caught as she fit them together, the tip of his cock easing through her wet folds like nothing. "Emme…"

"Shhhh." She knew they needed a condom. God, but she didn't want to stop. "I'm on the pill. It's…I haven't been with anyone else, and…"

"Me too. I got tested again in the spring, and—" He cut himself off as she swivelled her hips, bringing him another inch inside her body. He rubbed his nose against hers as he searched her gaze with his own before huffing a laugh. "You. Little. Minx."

"We've waited long enough, right?" She held herself ever so still.

He hesitated a beat before nodding. He held her gaze, his own hot and piercing, as he pressed himself home in a single, filling thrust.

Their limbs tangled, her legs twisting around his and his arms twining around her shoulders, his hands roughly bracketing her head. She wasn't sure where her breath ended and his skin began. And still he held himself inside her, not yet moving.

Her chest rose and fell in an uneven, shallow pattern. She tried to find her voice. Wanted to tell him to start moving, but she couldn't.

He breathed her name, and she nodded. She was fine. Way better than fine. Lightheaded from the orgasm and filled with the most delicious feeling that she couldn't quite name, but he didn't need to wait on her account.

"Please," she finally whispered, squeezing her legs against his, her heel dragging up the back of his calf. Yes, that's what she needed to do. Running her hands down his sides, she palmed his exceptional butt. Holy Hannah, he felt good.

He got the hint. Under her fingers, his muscles flexed as he pulled out a bit, then clenched as he plunged deep again. She clung to him for the first few gasp-inducing strokes, then as their bodies found a more fluid rhythm, she let her hands roam.

They were going to do this over and over again. He was going to love her body like this as many times as she wanted. Maybe. They might run out of time and have to hit the pause button while they both went to work.

But then she'd be back.

Maybe they should talk about how often she could visit, because at that particular moment, Emme wanted to stay in Nathan's bed, naked, forever.

And maybe insist that he do the same.

She kissed the black ink decorating his chest. His skin was silky smooth there, soft and warm stretched over hard, bunching muscles. Her tongue darted out and tasted him. She couldn't get enough of that, so she arched up, tracing her tongue over his clavicle and up his neck, until the tip of her tongue caught on the barest bits of stubble.

He turned his head, capturing her mouth with his. He kissed her like he was fucking her, slow and steady, but insistent.

Possessively.

Mine, his mouth said.

Yes, her heart promised back.

As if he wasn't sure, he pulled back, casting a searching look over her face before kissing her again. He found her hands and pressed them into the mattress with his own as he picked up the pace, his teeth nipping at her lips when she didn't open fast enough for him. Her breath stuttered at the need pulsing between them. It was building fast and furiously now. She hitched her legs higher up his back, her feet digging into his ass, and the next slam of his hips made her scream.

"You okay?" he groaned, and she tried to laugh, because he didn't stop, but the only noise she could make was a long, desperate moan.

She settled for a hissing "yessss…." Which he accepted. Good. If he'd stopped, she'd have smacked him.

This was too good.

Her second orgasm was coming on fast—like a freight train and she was standing on the tracks. But nobody was yelling for her to get out of the way, and she didn't want to anyway. With each sure stroke, Nathan nudged a spot inside her that made her not care about anything beyond the here and now.

She breathed his name, barely a whisper the first time, then a heavier pant as he shifted his legs wider, digging deeper against the bed as he pistoned his hips like a machine.

"So close," he grunted. "Tell me you're—"

"Oh yeah." Her voice shook.

"God, Emme," he growled, shifting his arms to wrap tight around her, lifting her off the bed. Hauling her against him as he worked them both toward blissful release.

Little spots danced at the edge of her vision as the train got closer. The roar in her ears almost sounded like she was about to be run over by something, but the only thing to crash into her was a wave of pure pleasure.

Nathan buried himself one last time as she started to clench everywhere, from the inside out, a tingling, twitching mess of sensation that scrambled her brain.

And apparently made her do selfish things, like try to consume a delicious man. Literally.

"You bit me." Laughing, he pushed up onto his elbows.

Emme gasped. Shit, she had. A perfect circle of teeth marks marred his shoulder. "I'm so sorry."

"Don't be," he murmured roughly, brushing his lips across hers. "I don't care. It just means you're really here."

She kissed him back—gently. Although now that it was on her mind, she wouldn't mind taking a nip out of his lower lip.

"You're really here," he repeated, tugging her into his side as he rolled onto his back.

She nodded against his bare skin. She was, and it was wonderful.

CHAPTER
NINE

NATHAN BIT back a curse as the sedan in front of him slowed and put on its turning signal. And then didn't turn for three blocks.

Motherf— He was going to be late.

Emme had told him she could take a cab from the airport, but he wanted to pick her up. He'd thought he'd have lots of time, so he stopped and got flowers.

Now any second she'd text and say she was through security, and he was still ten blocks away.

It was kind of crazy how much he'd missed her this past week. They'd had two sex-filled days—and nights—together before she flew to San Francisco, then across the Pacific Ocean and back a few times. Now she had four days off and they were spending them together.

He had all the plans. He was going to teach her how to surf, and take her out for fish tacos. Hiking in the foothills and dinner at the historic Hotel Del Coronado.

Or maybe he'd get her back to his place and they'd spend the entire time in bed.

On his couch.

In his shower.

His dick swelled against the fly of his jeans and he shifted his legs apart. It wasn't helpful to think of Emme, all soapy and slick, bubbles dancing from one freckle to the next as they coursed down her pale, willowy body. Her red hair darker when wet, wrapped around his fist as he tugged her close. Her lips all pink and—

Honk. A car behind him helpfully pointed out that he'd fantasized right through the light turning green. And he hadn't even gotten to her tight, pointy nipples.

They were definitely getting naked first.

Then surfing. Maybe.

Four days wasn't enough, he groaned to himself.

His phone beeped as he took the on-ramp onto the freeway. Using his voice commands, he had Siri read him Emme's message— she was heading to the entrance—and he quickly replied that he was ten minutes out.

When he pulled up to the arrivals exit eight minutes later, he spotted her right away. Her long red hair was twisted in a thick braid that curled over her shoulder, and she was searching the parking lane for his truck.

Next to her was a guy in a pilot's uniform, and he seemed oblivious to the fact that Emme was trying hard not to talk to him.

Nathan's blood pressure shot through the roof.

There was no reason to assume that guy was her ex. Nathan took a deep breath as he parked his truck and hopped out. Didn't matter, anyway—Emme had flown here to see him. And she was a grownup. She'd expect Nathan not to pull a macho, possession-marking campaign in a two-minute airport pick-up.

The question was, would she forgive him if he couldn't help himself?

Striding around the back of the truck to greet her, Nathan kept his attention squarely on Emme. Warm eyes, bright smile, and his chest swelled at the stark relief on her face at his arrival, followed by a matching grin. He held his left arm wide in a gesture that could be a sideways wave, but was also an invitation for a one-armed hug if she wanted it.

She did.

"Welcome back," he murmured into her hair—an almost kiss—as she nestled into his side. "Your flight was okay?"

She nodded, then took a deep breath and twisted back to look at the uniformed man still loitering nearby. "Just ran into Wayne here on my way through the terminal."

Nathan held out his right hand, glad to hear the guy's name wasn't Derek. "Nathan Meyers, nice to meet you."

"Captain Wayne Fenton."

What a douche, using his title like it increased his worth. Nathan crushed the other man's hand, only offering the barest of smiles as he did it.

"I was surprised to see our Emme in San Diego. I wasn't aware she had friends down here." Fenton smarmed. Asshole. Emme wasn't his on any level—Nathan knew that without a doubt.

He wiped his hand on his cargo pants before propping it on his hip and squeezing Emme closer again. "Well, she does. Protective ones at that."

"I should have done the introductions," she interrupted nervously. "Nathan, this is Wayne. We used to crew together more often, but since the divorce, we've mostly flown on different routes, haven't we?" Her voice got stronger as she talked, sharper, and Nathan realized she was saying all of that just as much for the other man's benefit. He must be a friend of her ex, maybe his co-pilot. "And this is Nathan. My favorite part of California so far. We met in January."

Nathan knew a thing or two about diffusing a tense situation—at least he did when it didn't involve a threat to his masculinity—and he was still impressed at how Emme had spoken volumes there without making any assumptions about their relationship or betraying any confidences.

The other man gave a faint, uneasy smile.

There was something grossly unsettling about a man who got more uncomfortable the stronger a woman sounded.

Nathan picked up Emme's light carry-on suitcase and tipped his head toward the truck. "Shall we?"

She nodded politely as she turned away from her coworker, who finally got the hint and stepped back toward the terminal.

Once inside his truck, though, she started laughing. A quiet little snicker that she tried to hold back—because she was kind and lovely, and not one to laugh at anyone—but when he slid her a glance, his own amusement unrestrained, she gave up the fight for restraint. Tucking her hand into his on the center console, she tipped her head back against the headrest and filled his truck with the happiest sound ever.

"So I'm not in trouble for playing the caveman?" He dragged a last, lingering look over her beaming face before turning his attention to the traffic he was about to pull into.

In his peripheral vision, she shook her head and grinned. "You wanted to rip his head off, didn't you?"

He shrugged. "I doubt the human race would miss him."

She sighed the weakest sound of regret possible. "He's one of my ex's best friends."

"I knew there was something wrong with him." Nathan cleared his throat, stopping himself from saying anything further on that topic. "So, are you tired?"

She'd only been back in the States for ten hours, just long enough to catch a bit of sleep before hopping on a flight with some empty seats to see him. He needed to at least *check* before filling her calendar with all the things he wanted to do with her. To her. Beneath her.

Like she could read his mind, she took a long, slow breath in, then exhaled with a little breathy moan that immediately took his cock from its steady state of Emme-awareness to ready and willing.

"No, not tired," she murmured, stroking her thumb against his. When he snuck a look across the cab, she was looking down at their hands, a little smile playing across her lips. "What were you thinking?"

———

"This is unexpected," Emme hollered at him from where she was lying flat on her belly on the surfboard he'd borrowed from his friend Cassie—she was pregnant, and her husband Jared was away on deployment. Cassie had made a little joke that he could keep it for his girlfriend, because she'd bought it on sale and it didn't come with a baby seat. He couldn't do that to Jared. Instead, he promised to babysit the next time they wanted to go surfing together.

"But fun?" Nathan paddled closer.

She stuck her tongue out at him. "Yes, it's fun. I can't believe you bought me a wetsuit and everything."

"Naked surfing is frowned upon on public beaches," he said with a wink. "We can do that some other time. Besides, you look good in black neoprene."

She swiped a wet curl off her cheek and grinned. "So do you. Okay, so what do we do next?"

"Depends. Do you want to practice getting up, or just ride a few of the waves like this?" The conditions were perfect for learning: gentle rolling waves that wouldn't overwhelm her if—when—she dumped into the surf.

She made a scared face, then laughed. "Uhhhh...I'm game for anything." She patted her board and squared her shoulders. "Okay, I'll stand. We can do this, right Boardie?"

He chuckled, then described once again how they were going to pop up. He'd already shown her this on the beach, and she'd practiced it a bunch of times, but it was different on the water.

Different and way fucking cooler.

There was probably a life lesson buried in there—with greater risk comes greater reward, or something like that. But before you got the greater reward, you'd slip and fall into the ocean a half dozen times.

With a last, quick "looking at me?" glance back at Emme, Nathan paddled with the waves, and as soon as he felt the surge beneath him, he planted his hands firmly under his chest and smoothly popped up onto his feet, knees bent beneath him.

Shit, he loved that feeling. Smooth gliding. Nothing like it.

As soon as the wave dissipated, he dropped down again and got his board turned around. Paddling back out toward Emme, he watched her practice just going from paddling to getting her palms and toes propped on the board. Rinse, repeat. The whole time her pretty pink mouth was mouthing the instructions to herself.

"Remember, you can go as slowly as you need to. Get your feet planted solidly before you rise up," he said quietly as he got closer.

Staring down at her board in concentration, she nodded sharply. Then she was pushing herself up with her arms, her chest rising and falling rapidly as she breathed through the movement. Her right leg bent up beneath her body, but before she could get it settled, a wave rolled under her board and instead of tipping off, she dropped flat down again.

"Don't be afraid to fall," he laughed, and she made a face at him. "Don't believe me?"

He pushed up, deliberately off-kilter, and let his board slide out from under his feet. He slammed into the water, then under, bubbles rushing around his head as he exhaled into the salty otherness of the ocean.

Swoosh. With two strong pulls, he was above the water again, then he snagged his board and hauled himself back onto it.

Barely breathing hard, he paddled back to her side again.

"See? Nothing to it. Kind of fun, really." He winked at her as he pushed droplets of water off his face with the flat of his palm.

"Uh huh. Right up until the board beans me in the head."

"I'll nurse you back to health, don't worry."

"Sponge baths and everything?" She blushed. "Okay, I'm going for it."

The first two tries she fell off, but each time she got higher, and the third time she settled into a perfectly balanced crouch.

"Look at you!" he whooped, his heart seriously ready to explode from pride.

"Ha!" She made a fist and pumped it in the air, then quickly resumed her fingers-pointed, arms-out-for-balance position when she wobbled. "Okay, I think I'm done for today."

"Wait for a wave, M." His voice was rough, and she glanced his way. He didn't know how she knew that he said it like her nickname and not just her name, but the look in her eyes told him she did. "Trust me."

She pressed her lips together and nodded, and when the next crest rolled beneath her, she cried out. It was just a little swell, barely a foot, but it moved her forward a bit, and made her brace her legs to stay upright.

Glancing behind her, she saw another one coming, and waited for it, dropping deeper into her crouch as it approached. This one tipped her sideways, but when she came up sputtering, her face was transformed with a glittering grin. He rolled off his board and together they scrambled onto the beach, fingers linked together. He stood his board up in the sand, then took hers and did the same before pulling her close and kissing her deeply.

"I am so impressed with you," he whispered, rubbing the side of his nose against hers. She smelled like salt and sunset and happiness. "I just wanted to get out on the water, I didn't know you'd take to it like that."

"All my Pilates classes have finally paid off," she said with a gentle laugh.

"So we can do this again?"

Her eyes lit up. "Oh, heck yeah."

"Good." He pressed his lips against hers again, then hugged her tight. They were only a few blocks from his place and a hot shower. And naked time. "Let's pack up and head out."

"Can we grab some dinner on the way? I'm starving." She grabbed one of the towels he'd packed and tossed the other his way.

Okay, naked time could wait a touch longer. He rubbed the cotton over his head quickly before unzipping his suit. "Yeah, definitely." He shrugged one arm out, then the other, and shoved the suit low on his hips so he could dry off his upper body and pull on a t-shirt. "Do you feel like Mexican, or Italian, or—"

Her hands sliding over his abs shut him up real quick. He dropped the towel which had been obstructing his view, just in time to see her lean in and kiss his bare chest. "Maybe food could wait," she said huskily.

"We still have to get back to my place." His voice caught. Did they? Maybe his truck would be private enough. But then she tugged her own wetsuit open, her breasts spilling out, barely constrained by the bikini underneath, and no—they needed to be *alone* alone. "We can order in."

CHAPTER
TEN

"THANK you so much for your help with this noisy little one," the mom from seat 17B said as she stopped at the open door of their aircraft. She and her toddler were the last passengers to de-plane, because little Matty hadn't liked the landing at SFO and once they got to the gate, his frazzled mom had kept waving people past her down the aisle as she tried to soothe him.

Emme tipped her head to the side and gave him an understanding look, but he just buried his face in his mom's shoulder. She got it. Some days a rough flight made her want to cry and have an apple juice box, too.

She pressed her hand to the mother's shoulder and gave her a warm smile. "The thanks is all ours. We hope to see you on another flight soon."

"Ha," the other woman laughed weakly. "Maybe when he's twelve."

Emme watched to make sure the porter helped with the gate-checked stroller, then she headed into the aircraft to begin tidying up. She took one aisle and Gina took the other, and when they met in the galley, they shared a sigh.

"Want to get a drink once we complete our reports?" Gina yawned. "Or just have a nap together?"

Emme laughed. "I'm getting on a plane in ninety minutes."

"Again to San Diego?"

She nodded, and she knew her eyes were shining.

"He must be some guy."

"He is."

"Tell him I suggested we sleep together. That'll be a nice reward for him." Gina waggled her eyebrows.

"Oh, stop."

"No, guys like that."

"I know, but…" She blushed. "Anyway, enough about Nathan."

"Nathan. That's his name, huh?"

"*Stop*." But she smiled. She couldn't help it. "I'll see you in five days."

"Nice to get this route again, huh?"

"Seriously, right? I can't thank you enough for the heads up." Emme quickly sped through her count on the non-perishables and noted what needed restocking. They'd already done the tally on meals—there was always a discrepancy between what was ordered and what people ended up eating, because of last-minute requests which they tried to accommodate as best as possible.

As this was the last flight of the day for this aircraft, they bundled up all the blankets for laundering, did a final seat check, then checked in with their purser before heading into the airport.

The shift from staff to traveler was a weird one—in part because she was flying standby, so she was always staff. Always "on", always dressed professionally. But when she'd coded her requests for these flights to San Diego in the system, she'd flagged them as commuter flights home, not a vacation standby. Less likely to get bumped, for one thing. But it also made a difference in her own head.

So as she checked in at the gate, she started to check out a bit. She had her earbuds in and her Kindle out.

Heading home. It was crazy how in five short weeks, it had started to feel like that, even though she wasn't anywhere near ready to consider the implications.

Technically, she had a bedroom in an apartment here in San Francisco, but she'd only slept there a handful of times. She was either in a hotel room on the other side of the world, or she was in Nathan's bed. He was the world's yummiest blanket, and he made kick-ass coffee every morning.

They were still taking things slowly, which she needed—she could feel a damp anxiety crawling up her neck every time something hinting of commitment came up.

Never from Nathan—but it was crazy how as soon as you start kissing a guy, wedding shit popped up from all directions. On social media and in advertisements. In movies, TV shows, magazine articles...the entire world thought Emme Ryan was better off with a permanent mate.

The thought petrified her.

Spending time with Nathan, flying "home" to see him...that wasn't scary.

Even meeting his friends, which she was doing the next day at a BBQ, didn't scare her.

Labels, on the other hand...she wasn't ready to belong to Nathan anymore than she just *did*. She couldn't help the elemental connection they had. She'd given up trying to fight how right it felt to be together.

She just didn't want to get trapped.

The thought made her chest tight and her head pound.

She closed her eyes and turned up the music on her phone. In an hour, she'd be wrapped in his arms. An hour and a half, cuddled on his couch. Two hours, fast asleep with her head on his lap.

Nothing else mattered.

———

After surfing at dawn the next morning, and a leisurely, attentive shower together back at his place, Emme was thrilled when Nathan took her to an open-air farmer's market so they could pick up some fresh treats to take with them to the BBQ being hosted by the wife of one of his SEAL buddies.

She was more than a little concerned about maybe being the

cause of a party that might prove too much work for the hostess. A point she repeatedly told Nathan as they made their way to all his favorite vendors. "I'm just saying, if she's pregnant, we should bring stuff."

"And we are. Orange- and dark-chocolate tarts." He held up one of their shopping bags.

"More stuff."

He held up the other bag. "Fresh salsa and tortilla chips. We're being good guests."

"It's not just about making a good impression, Nathan—"

"I know," he said, laughing as he leaned in for a kiss. "You're a nice person. Don't worry, so are we. None of my teammates would take advantage of the hospitality of a pregnant woman, I promise."

When they pulled up to the cute little house—Coronado Beach was filled with them, it seemed—and Nathan parked his truck behind another truck, which was behind two SUVs, he started rhyming off names of guys that were there.

"Cade, Drew, Trick…"

She'd never remember them all. And it just got more confusing when they walked in, because a sea of over-sized, happy, good-looking guys all called out at the same time, "Gibson!"

That was followed by a rousing chorus of trash talking aimed at the Chicago Cubs and claims of losers doing the grilling.

"Is there a big game today?" Emme asked as Nathan turned to introduce her to the pretty blonde with a nice round baby bump approaching them with a resigned smile on her face.

He just laughed, which didn't answer the question. "Emme Ryan, this is the radiant Cassie Sutter. She's baking a future Navy SEAL right there."

Cassie rolled her eyes as she gave Nathan a brief hug, then pointed him to the kitchen with his shopping bags.

"I've heard so much about you," she said gleefully, waving Emme in for a so-what-if-we're-strangers hug.

"Likewise!" Emme laughed. "Thank you for inviting me."

"I'd let Nathan do the rest of the introductions, but he has work to do." Cassie linked her arm through Emme's and tugged her further into the house, pointing at the herd of testosterone as they blurred past. "Those guys are all going out to start grilling. They're Drew, Cade and Trick."

"Nathan mentioned some of them…"

"But this is Gaby," Cassie continued, clearly on a mission as she lead the way into a cozy living room where two other women sat. "And Annie. They will protect you from the horde."

———

On the kitchen counter was a list of meal prep instructions from Cassie. Nathan shook his head. The woman loved to cook, and host parties, but her husband Jared had asked her to take it easy with this BBQ and, to humor her deployed beloved, she'd agreed to let the guys do the work.

As long as she could still carefully dictate what needed to be done.

In the fridge, he found marinating steaks and chicken breasts, as well as two salads that just needed to be dressed and tossed. Someone else had brought a big-ass tub of potato salad and a veggie tray, so it looked like they were in good shape.

He took the meat outside, where Drew had the grill hot and Cade was passing around cold beer.

"Cheers." Nathan tipped the neck of his bottle against the others as they all clinked before drinking. "Sorry we were a bit late." He couldn't help but grin. He wasn't really sorry—spending time with Emme was his first priority.

Drew snorted. "Don't worry. We all get it. Even Cade, the poor single bastard."

"Gives me time to hit on your wife, man." Cade gave a slow, dirty wink to the now-retired SEAL. "Then I get to go home and play video games for hours."

"Been there, got the geek shirt. Overrated, I promise you. Better to take my wife home and play video games with her while she wears the shirt. Right, Gibson?"

Nathan shook his head and grinned. He wasn't a gamer, but the principle held true. There wasn't anything he'd rather do alone instead of finding a way to share the experience with his woman. "Took Emme surfing this morning. Might celebrate a Cubs win with her later. Sounds about right, all round."

"No fucking way do they smoke the Padres," Trick interjected, the California native nicely rising to the bait.

"Fifty bucks say they do. And loser hosts the next BBQ." Nathan chuckled as he dodged away from Trick's playful punch. It was a stupid bet, because he was the only other person in the group who had a house with a backyard—Trick shared an apartment with Miles Dumbrowski, who was overseas with Jared, Cade had an apartment of his own, and Drew and Annie lived in Los Angeles where Annie was a graduate student. They were looking to buy a place in the San Diego area when she finished her studies, but for now it wasn't so easy for them to host anything—except in hockey season, then everyone made the trip north at least once for a Kings game.

Baseball talk turned to a good-natured disagreement over grilling techniques, which somehow got the job done anyway, and before too long the steaks were underway and Nathan headed back inside to prep the rest of Cassie's planned dinner.

He checked in with Emme often, but she'd quickly lost that deer-in-the-headlights look. It turned out all four women loved to talk about travel, and their conversation flowed like water from there.

They ate inside, then moved outside for dessert and coffee and chatter about Cassie's recent trip to London, England to see Jared on his long leave mid-deployment.

"One of the most gorgeous cities, I swear," she said as she passed around her phone to show some pictures. "Crazy expensive, though. Everything was pretty much the same price, but in pounds instead of dollars. I just about had a heart attack when my credit card bill came last month."

"Oh, tell me about it!" Emme shifted on her perch on Nathan's knee. "It's always like that, though. Sydney, Tokyo, San Francisco, New York. London. The more awesome and interesting a city, the more expensive it is to experience it."

"Is that why Chicago's so cheap, Gibson?" Trick winked from across the deck.

"Hey, don't be trash talking my hometown," Emme said in her sweet but reproachful way.

"You guys are both from Chicago?" Gaby lifted her eyebrows. "That's convenient!"

Emme glanced back at Nathan over her shoulder, her eyebrows pulled together in a delicate frown. No, they didn't know that about her. They didn't know anything other than he was crazy about her. The details of her life were hers to share, not his.

"Yeah," he said quietly, his gaze locked on hers. "We met in January when I was visiting my sister."

"Oh, wow," Cassie said, the eternal romantic oblivious to the bittersweet vibe zinging between them now. "So you're the girl who Nathan's been hung up over since Christmas."

The second week in January, but who was counting?

———

Emme couldn't breathe.

Nathan knew she was reeling, but nobody else did. Around them, the conversation swirled back to travel, then one of the guys announced it was time to get watching the baseball game.

"You coming, Gibson?"

Nathan nodded, but he didn't move. His eyes didn't stray from hers, and on her hips, his grip tightened imperceptibly—to everyone else.

She felt the press of his hands like a searing brand.

Don't freak out, his gaze said.

I'm trying not to, she wordlessly promised back.

Maybe the girls could sense they needed a minute, because with a clatter of dishes and extra-loud musings about tidying up and doing some dishes, all of a sudden she was alone with Nathan on the deck.

"You okay?" he asked quietly, lifting one hand to her face. His fingers traced the edge of her jaw back to her hair, then he rubbed his thumb across her bottom lip.

"Yeah," she lied. She would be. She just needed a minute.

"It was a hard line to walk. We were emailing, and you were all I could think about, but there was this distance…I didn't know if I'd ever see you again. So I didn't keep you a secret, in the global sense that there was a woman…" He trailed off, then slowly lowered his hand to his chest. "Here. But there was."

Her own heart squeezed. "You're too good to me, Nathan."

She hadn't meant it to sound bittersweet. Hadn't meant for there to be an edge to her voice, so when he jackknifed up, almost tumbling her off his lap, she yelped and grabbed onto his shoulders.

"What?" She stared at him, at the now guarded look on his face that didn't ease until she leaned in to kiss him.

With a quiet groan, he nipped at her lips, then pressed his forehead against hers as he bore a worried gaze straight to her soul. "I don't want to scare you. There's no pressure here, you know that, right?"

She nodded. She needed to tell him that he was in her heart, too.

Nothing came out of her mouth. The truth was there, sharp and big and somehow safer locked inside.

From the living room, someone hooted his nickname, something about the Cubs not doing well in the first inning.

Emme cleared her throat and teased her fingers against the hollow at the base of his neck. She quirked her lips into a saucy pout, and the stress lines faded from his forehead as he capitulated to her more playful mood shift.

"Why Gibson?" she asked as she found the edge of his tattoo.

"Because of the guitars." He shifted against her, his arms wrapping her in warmth and safety.

"Ah. I like it." She snapped her fingers. "Your email address!"

He laughed and nodded, his eyes crinkling in genuine humor. "Yes."

"I should be embarrassed that it took me so long to figure that one out. I thought it was a random, hiding-in-plain-sight kind of thing." She climbed off his lap and stood, offering him her hand. He didn't need it, of course. More of a symbol of…something. She couldn't offer him much, but she could be present in the moment and at the very least try to be fun.

"That, too." He hooked his hand over her shoulder and tugged her close again, trailing his fingers up her neck and into her hair as she folded into his side. "You having an okay time?"

"Yes." She sighed as he brushed his lips across hers. "You want to go watch the game, don't you?"

"You want to come inside?" He glanced down at her hopefully, but Cassie and Gaby chose that moment to come back outside, with fresh cups of coffee, and Annie followed closely behind, carrying an extra cup for Emme.

"Not even a little bit." She patted his chest. "You go on. I'll be just fine. Your friends are great."

"They're acceptable," he whispered. "You're great."

She laughed quietly. "Because I don't mind being abandoned for baseball?"

"No, because you like my friends," he murmured, his voice still low and just for her. "And you make me smile. And later, you're going to put on my Cubs jersey and give me a little dance—"

"Okay, fan boy, you go watch the ball game. We can discuss the *later* plans…later."

He got a devilish glint in his eye at the censorship and leaned in again, brushing his lips against the curve of her ear. "You really don't want me to tell you now how much I'm going to enjoy perching you in my lap, wearing nothing but my favorite baseball shirt? Rubbing your clit gently as you ride me?"

She gasped and her cheeks turned pink, but she didn't stop him. She didn't want to. How did she get so lucky? "Okay," she finally whispered, her voice hitching and uneven. "That does sound great."

"Right?" He flashed a wide, white smile at her. "Now go and make small talk about babies and stuff."

"Sure…" She shook her head, like it was just that easy to get rid of the prickly, distracting desire he'd lit inside her. "And you enjoy that baseball game."

"We could leave now."

"Nope. You made your bed, you lie in it. And not the fun kind of bed, with company." She waggled her finger at him as she edged out of reach. "Let this be a lesson to you, sir."

"Sir." He nodded. "I like the sound of that. We'll file that in the *later* bin as well."

Her insides did an embarrassing warm and squirmy flip-flop as he walked backward toward the house, and her core actually clenched when he turned around at the sliding door. Damn, that man had a nice butt.

And legs. And shoulders...and heart.

With a sigh, she twisted back to the group of women who were not even trying to pretend they hadn't watched the end of her flirty teenage-esque lustfest.

"So you guys are super cute," Cassie teased.

Emme blushed and sat down, reaching for her coffee instead of answering.

"Thank you," she murmured to Annie, who winked. "That's mostly due to him. I'm a big bag of neuroses these days."

"Join the club." Gaby waved her hands in the air. "When Trick and I started dating a few months ago, I had all sorts of silly rules."

"Well, that was a bit complicated," Annie said soothingly.

Gaby scrunched her face as she looked over at Emme. "I met Trick the morning after he slept with my roommate. It was a bit awkward."

Emme laughed. "Well, I met Nathan the day I got my divorce decree. I was trying to run away to San Antonio for a weekend escape, and we got stranded at O'Hare together."

Cassie leaned in. "We didn't know that part! Tell us everything."

Emme blushed. She didn't tell them the entire story, just the bits that were safe for public consumption, but even then, by the time she finished her heart was pounding and her mouth was dry. Their connection had been intense and meaningful from the very first second.

Six months later, she still didn't have a great handle on how to deal with that.

"I'm divorced as well," Cassie said quietly.

"You are?" Emme didn't know why she was shocked. Lots of airline staff were divorced. It was the modern reality. But it felt so yucky, so *failed*, and painfully personal that few ever talked about it.

Cassie nodded. "Jared was my next door neighbor for months before we got together. I wasn't ready, either. I think it's harder to admit that you're falling for someone once you've been through a divorce."

There was that *couldn't breathe* feeling again. Emme swallowed hard.

Cassie looked at her quizzically, like she wasn't sure if she should continue.

"How did you..." Emme trailed off, her voice rough and catching. "How did you know?"

"It's different the second time. There's an edge to it at first, even when you love them." Cassie sighed. "The innocence is lost, and you'll never get that belief in happily ever after back. Not in the same way. But then, slowly, you find a different kind of faith. True trust. Not blind, not innocent. A trust so strong it bests the most jaded, cynical worldview. And it's so much better."

Emme wanted to believe this woman, who sat across from her blissfully pregnant with her new husband's baby. Then she glanced at the house. Inside was a man deserving of that trust. Who made her deliriously happy.

And still she had a sharp edge to her heart that somehow sliced all strings that attempted to attach themselves.

"It'll come," Cassie said quietly. Emme jerked her gaze up from the deck, where she'd fixated on a knot in the wood as Cassie's words sank in. The other woman just smiled at her and shrugged. "And it's okay if it doesn't for a while."

Was it okay? It didn't feel like that to Emme. It felt...unfair. Like she should have met him earlier, when she wasn't battered and bruised on the inside and crispy and defensive on the outside.

"Besides, we like you," Annie said, grinning broadly. "When I met Drew, it was Man City down here. Now I can't wait to move back, because of girls' nights and gossip and friends who get it."

"Do you guys get it?" Wow, Emme's voice was so shaky.

Cassie nodded. "We really, really do, sweetie. And I think Nathan does, too. Have faith."

CHAPTER
ELEVEN

THE CUBS LOST.

Now they were back at his place, and Emme was doing her best to make his jersey look hot as fuck to make it up to him. He loved her all the more for it. After her little freak out after dinner, though, he could hardly tell her that.

Instead, he stuck to the safe zone: private, sexy fun. Emme liked it when he unleashed his filthy side.

If his dirty talk was fueled by secret thoughts like *mine* and *forever*, that was okay. Probably.

"Come here, beautiful." He flopped back on his bed and crooked his finger, gesturing for her to climb on top of him. This felt right, having her in his house. Making her blush and peeling back the layers to find out just how many of her freckles the pink flush reached.

But tonight he wanted her to leave the jersey on. To give her a costume that kept it light and doubled as armor.

Plus the way she'd unbuttoned it, with her tits bouncing in the shadow of the open neckline…

"Come here," he repeated, his voice huskier this time. Her chest rose and fell a few times as she shimmied her way up his torso, leaning forward to kiss him first.

Her lips were wet and soft as she curved over him. His shirt rustled quietly between them, and he worked at another button. Her breast filled his palm, and they both exhaled at the same time.

So. Fucking. Right.

"I love it when you say that," she said, a hitch of hesitation telling him that the admission made her a little shy. He rocked his erection into the sweet curve of her ass. There was nothing to be embarrassed about between them.

"Why?" He nipped his way along her jaw, tasting her skin and making her gasp as he worked down her neck.

"Because…" She laughed as she wiggled further up his torso, the warm softness of her inner thighs making him throb. "It means you want…"

Hell yes, that's what it meant. "Damn straight. I love licking you like this." He palmed her bottom as she set her legs on either side of his face. He glanced up, watching as she braced her hands on the headboard. Her head dropped down so she could watch him. Her hair hung in long, sexy waves around her face, a dark curtain making this primal act even more private.

He rolled his face into her thigh. *I love you*. It vibrated through him, like he was carrying a live grenade with the pin pulled, his thumb shaky on the lever.

Above him, she rocked her hips, and he turned his head again, breathing her in. She'd never said it, but he was pretty sure he was the only man who'd ever asked her to ride his face.

Well the rest of those losers had missed out.

Emme was sensual and passionate to her very core. And all his. He just needed to keep his caveman tendencies in check until she was ready for more. At least she didn't blink when he acted them out in bed.

"You said that to me that first night," she murmured, a small gasp cutting off her last word as he traced through her folds with his index finger.

Wet. Hot. Sinfully sweet. Perfect.

"I remember," he said, groaning as she pulled her hips away from his questing tongue. "Get back here."

She giggled and drifted closer again. Her scent was driving him mad. He wanted her to come hard on his face, then he was going to pull her down his body and slam deep inside her. Punishment for being cheeky that they'd both enjoy.

"I remember, too," she whispered. Breathy sighs filled the silence that followed, because he was done talking.

Already slick and swollen, she was ready for him to dive right in, but he still took his time, because he could. That was one of the things he loved about going down on Emme—while it turned him on like whoa, he wasn't being driven out of his mind like he was when they fucked.

So he could be…precise. Controlled. Very thorough.

The view was pretty spectacular, too. Emme slowly undulating above him, the curve of her belly disappearing into his jersey, now falling off her shoulders, then the shadow of her breasts, bouncing freely above him.

Was there anything better than under-boob?

Nope.

His dick flexed as he twisted his tongue around her clit and gazed up her body.

Her eyes were closed, her mouth parted in a silent pant as he licked her, and Nathan felt like a sex superstar.

Then she slowly dropped one hand, sliding her fingers into his hair, and he stopped thinking.

Her fingertips scraped along his scalp as she urged him to cover even more of her beautiful pussy with his mouth. He obliged, flattening his tongue as he kissed her sex, swallowing everything she had to give him.

Her thighs tightened under his hands and she started shaking as he sped up, swirling his tongue faster from her silky soft opening to the hard little nub that made her moan. Over and over again he licked and sucked until she shuddered, clenching his head between her legs as she ground against him.

He kept kissing her, more gently now, as she slowly came down from her orgasm, and when her thighs relaxed, he kissed her hip. He loved every bit of her body, from the soft swell at the tops of her thighs to the dip around her belly button. He tugged gently on the ruby red barbell she wore there tonight, then explored the dusting of freckles up her torso that led straight to her amazing breasts and the ever-so-sensitive nipples that topped them.

After rolling her over and peeling off the Cubs jersey—he didn't want anything else between them now, armor be damned—he took his time moving up her body. He was torn between agony over what remained unspoken between them and fist-pumping joy over how she opened up for him.

What they had went beyond special.

It was irreplaceable.

So he'd lose himself in the act of loving her, and trust that sooner than later, she'd be ready to hear what she was already willing to feel between them.

———

Emme cried out as Nathan settled his hips between her thighs, his cock notched between her swollen folds.

She was so sensitive post-orgasm, but she wanted more of him.

"Yes," she begged, drawing him inside her with a welcoming tilt of her pelvis.

He fisted her hair as he surged into her, setting a demanding pace from the first thrust. She didn't know she needed this connection, but now that she had it, she couldn't imagine living without it. He filled her up, not just physically, but emotionally, too.

He loves you, she told herself as she wrapped her arms and legs around him. As she arched beneath him and met him stroke for stroke.

This wasn't just sex. It was something else on an elemental level, something she'd never had before. It scared the bejeezus out of her, but she wanted it even more.

So she held on to him, tight as she could.

"I want you on top of me," he said roughly. He flipped them again, his hands sure and strong against her skin. He didn't stop touching her as she settled on top of him.

"Get yourself off again," he demanded, his fingers digging into her hips. She shivered at the command and the resulting rush of moisture between her legs. He watched, eyes dark, as she reached between them. "That's one of my favorite memories of you. Watching your fingers dance over your pretty little clit as you rode me that first night. I'll never get enough of watching you make yourself come."

Breathless and more turned on than before, as impossible as that felt, she rose to her knees. A sharp breath ripped from her lungs as his heavy length slipped out of her body, stopping with just the tip inside her. Slowly, teasingly, she lowered herself onto him again, this time with her fingers sliding between her folds and around his straining cock before she settled them right where he told her to stroke.

It was her touch, but his command, and as she circled her clit, her body quickly climbed to orgasm again.

He watched with a hooded gaze as she rode him faster and faster, his own chest rising and falling erratically as his hands curved over her ass. As she started to fall apart, he took over, fucking her from below, driving up into her with grunts that destroyed her in the best way possible.

It had never been this good.

It was just getting better each time.

Tight. Desperate. Hot.

Blinding.

She cried out, eyes squeezed shut as he came inside her with a shout, and she tumbled down, her mouth finding his as she fell. His lips caught hers, his hands cushioning the rest of her, and he kissed her through the rest of her trembling climax, even as she could feel him still rocking through his own release.

It was a long time before they stopped moving, and when the stillness came, so did the worry.

"God, that was perfect," he murmured, kissing her shoulder as he tugged her back against him, spooning her body with his.

It had been. It still was.

But for how long would he think that? How long would the physical connection be enough?

CHAPTER
TWELVE
AUGUST

TIME TO RESCUE A HOSTAGE. Just a regular Monday on the job for Nathan.

The murky depths of the Pacific Ocean had provided safe shelter for their approach, but it was nearly dawn and they were about to surface from their submerged position offshore from the target island.

His eyes just above the water, waves lapping around him, Nathan watched as Trick silently ran across the beach. A hundred yards to the east, a guard stood with his back to them. He finished his twenty-second count, then sprinted to join his teammate. Lt. Steyner followed behind.

They shucked their SCUBA gear, hiding it in the scrub.

Knife drawn, Nathan ran in a zig-zag pattern, quietly closing the gap between them, the guards—seen and unseen—and the hostage beyond.

Behind him, Trick had his pistol out. He didn't need to look back to know that. But a silent takedown of this first guard would make the next step and the rest of the mission much easier.

Life was never easy.

The guard was just as well trained as they were, and he turned, sensing their presence a beat too soon.

Nathan punched first, but the other guy punched harder. Crouching to both protect his internal organs from more pummelling and to shift his center of gravity, Nathan swung his leg out, knocking his opponent off balance.

Just a hair.

It was all he needed. They tumbled together, rolling twice before Nathan was able to get his knife at the right angle.

Drawing the handle hard across his opponent's neck, he got the kill.

Breathing hard, the guy flat on the sand beneath him nodded. "You got me, motherfucker."

Nathan grinned. "Welcome to the team, Dex."

It was just a training exercise, but they still took it seriously. Leaving Hunter Dex—a recent transfer from the east coast—for dead on the beach, they carried on in their practice assault on Wake Island, a refuelling station in the middle of the Pacific Ocean.

As planned, Trick shot the next two guards in quick succession. Before the sun broke the horizon, they had their hostage and were back on the beach. Ninety seconds after radioing for transport, a Black Hawk helicopter swept in and provided covering fire as they climbed aboard the lumbering Chinook that set down right behind the gunship.

The special forces medics took over in the war games from there, treating their hostage for dehydration and broken limbs as the mini SEAL team took a breather on their way back to the aircraft carrier.

"Would have been embarrassing if Dex knocked you out, huh?" Trick grinned wickedly.

Nathan rolled his eyes. "Like that was going to happen."

Part of being a SEAL was thinking you were the best, because some days, that was half the battle. One of the reasons they trained against each other just as often as anything else.

That night, Dex came and found him in the First Class Mess Hall. The aircraft carrier was like a small floating city, complete with a coffee shop that claimed to brew Starbucks, although Pike Place never quite came out right. Dex apparently hadn't gotten that message, because he carried a paper takeout cup in his hand and had a happy bounce to his step.

Nathan winced. "Didn't anyone tell you that stuff is terrible?"

"What? I like Starbucks. Don't tell me you're one of those reverse coffee snobs who can't remember that a large is a grande?"

"Ha, no. It's just…" He shrugged. "Okay. Take a sip."

Dex sat down first. Nathan shoved the oatmeal cookie he was going to have for dessert across the table. The other man was going to need it in a minute.

"Shiiit," Hunter said, thumping the cup down after his first taste.

"Sorry."

"I was really looking forward to that."

"Their lattes aren't so bad. I think they just leave the brew on too long."

"Like six hours too long? Damn." He grabbed the cookie and Nathan laughed. "Anyway, good exercise this morning."

Nathan nodded. "You almost had me."

"You ready for tomorrow?"

Their next mission was boarding a mock pirate ship. "Yep. My bet is on the fight starting before we set up a complete security perimeter on the deck. Half the platoon will be fighting from the speedboat."

"Sounds about right." Dex yawned. "Where's Trick?"

"Went to call his girlfriend. She's flying out to meet him when we get back to Honolulu."

"You going to stick around Hawaii for some R&R?"

They had two weeks off after this large-scale set of operational exercises. No way was he spending them anywhere but next to Emme. She was back on commuter flights this month, up and down the west coast, and was home every night—that's where he was going to be as well. "Nah. I'm heading to San Francisco to see my girl."

"You guys out here are all domesticated."

Nathan winked. "Better watch out, there's something in the water."

With a laugh, Dex shoved back from the table. "Not me, man. I'm a confirmed bachelor."

"Famous last words," Nathan called out as the other man headed for the food bar. A few officers turned and looked at him, and he splayed his arms wide in a cocky non-apology. He'd saved a hostage today. He was king of the world.

The high of training going well lasted until their final night at sea, when his boss found him in his temporary quarters.

Lt. Jason Steyner gave him a big smile as he stepped inside and leaned against the small desk where Nathan had stacked some of his gear. "Normally I'd wait and talk to you about this in a scheduled career progression meeting, but since you're heading to San Francisco tomorrow…"

"Sure, no worries." Nathan stopped packing and sat down, giving the LT his full attention. "What's up?"

When his boss finished talking, Nathan was torn in two. On the one hand, the opportunity being presented to him could be perfect.

On the other hand, it would be even better six months down the road, once he and Emme were more settled.

She was still skittish. How would she take it?

He took a deep breath. "When do I need to let you know my decision? There's someone I want to talk to first."

Steyner nodded. "Take a few days."

If only it was that easy.

CHAPTER
THIRTEEN

FROM THE SECOND Nathan had landed at SFO, he'd been different.

Hungrier for physical contact, but also…restless. Like he couldn't stop moving, and he was channeling that into touching her.

As she led him up the stairs to the third-floor walkup she shared with two other girls—both thankfully gone this weekend—he was pawing at her butt, and when she stopped to put her key into the door, he buried his face in the crook of her neck.

"I missed you, too," she said, laughing.

He didn't say anything, just settled his hands on her hips.

When she pushed the door open, he ushered her inside, then slid her up against it as soon as it was closed. She wasn't opposed to getting naked in her living room, exactly, but her bed wasn't far away and it was *way* more comfortable. Plus he had to be tired.

"My room is down that—" she started to whisper, but he cut her off, his mouth crashing over hers.

His tongue stroked hard and insistent, storming right past her lips as he stole her breath. With a whimper she acquiesced as heat exploded between them. Whatever it was he needed, she wanted to give it to him.

With a rough yank, he pulled off her shirt, then ducked to kiss between her breasts where they pillowed over her new bra.

That might have been a wasted purchase, she thought idly as he did away with it with a single flick of his fingers at the clasp in the back.

Picking her up in his arms, he let her point the way to her room, where he managed to keep his hands or mouth or both on her as he set her down on the bed. Together, they stripped the rest of their clothes off.

Emme thought for sure Nathan would want to take her roughly and urgently, and get a first round out of the way to burn off the energy sizzling through his veins. But once they were pressed together, naked flesh warm against more naked flesh, he slowed down a bit—just enough to talk, anyway.

"Hi," she murmured, kissing his neck and chest as she wriggled against him. "Nice to see you again."

"So this is your new city," he said with a rough laugh.

She nodded. "It's pretty cool. What do you want to do when you're here?"

He gave her a look she didn't quite understand, beyond the familiar spark of lust. The intense chemistry no longer surprised her. "You. Over and over again."

"Nathan…" She wasn't protesting, not exactly, but something about the edge to his voice worried her.

"I'm serious. It's hard only seeing each other once or twice a month. Sexting and FaceTime isn't the same thing as…" He trailed his hand down her upper arm, dropping his fingers to her waist, then up and over the curve of her hip. Under her skin, fire licked everywhere he touched her. "As watching goosebumps rise on your skin because you know I'm going to follow that path with my tongue."

He bent over her and did just that, making her shiver as he breathed a slow, hot breath over the wet trail.

"Not the same as smelling how turned on you get, knowing I'm going to keep licking you until my head is between your legs and my tongue is buried deep inside—"

"God, Nathan."

"Don't stop me before I get to the good stuff."

"I won't," she whispered, hot tears scalding the inside of her eyelids as she pressed her eyes closed. She still didn't know how to handle the emotions he stirred in her. Heavier, more potent than anything she'd experienced in her marriage. A billion times more dangerous.

She'd come out to California. She'd done that for herself, but a little bit for him. For them. She wasn't ignorant of the fact that the long-distance thing sucked, but she'd chopped that distance by ninety percent. And half the time they couldn't see each other because of *his* job, not hers.

None of that mattered. What mattered was that when they were together, they made the most of it, and she sure as hell wasn't doing that right now.

"I won't," she repeated, clearing her throat and throwing on a brilliant, if somewhat shaky, smile. "You were saying something about your tongue?"

He narrowed his eyes at her, seeing way too much in the long seconds before he ducked his head and found the soft flesh at her waist with his mouth. His teeth grazed her side, just enough to make her gasp. Then his tongue swirled hot and wet over the same spot before he tipped her onto her back and kissed his way right to where they both needed him to be.

———

Nathan knew he needed to slow down. Even as Emme tugged on his hair and gave as good as he'd just given her—damn it, better, because he'd just about ravaged her and there was a fine line there between hot and not.

But as she squirmed under his mouth, then his fingers as he moved on top of her, he couldn't stop himself from taking. He wanted every bit of her. He wanted more. An entire future, a lifetime, and he wanted to show her they already had it.

He loved her enough for a dozen lifetimes.

He just had to show her.

Stop taking, and start giving.

"Hey," she said, breathless and flushed from her first orgasm. "Let me..."

She reached for his cock, her fingers soft and sweet as she wrapped around him.

"I want inside you, Emme." It sounded like a warning. Jesus, what was wrong with him?

He was terrified of losing her, that was the problem. It wasn't a real threat, but it wasn't a complete fabrication, either. Somewhere between *never* and *maybe* was not a comfortable spot on the scale of relationship risk. The only place he wanted to set that threat assessment was in the *hell no never* category.

Fucking her like crazy wouldn't achieve that.

"Your turn," she whispered, rubbing her lips along his jaw. Her tongue.

Fuck me. That little wet point made his dick twitch and his balls draw tight. When she traced it down his neck and across his chest, he actually growled.

She just licked him again.

He dragged in a ragged breath and nodded, rolling onto his side. She smirked at him and shoved him, hard, pushing him onto his back.

"You will be inside me," she kept teasing. "Inside my mouth, to start. You like that, right?"

He laughed harshly, which made her giggle. Why wasn't she scared of him like this? He'd mauled her and shoved her up against her door. Ripped off her clothes and carried her bodily to bed.

And she was giggling at him.

"Yeah, I like that. So fucking much, Emme." He tipped his head back and closed his eyes. "I love it." *I love you.*

"Mmmm." She hummed as she worked her way down his body, licking over the ridges of his abdomen and then the curve of muscle in front of his hips.

"Yeouch!" He snapped his eyes open as she sank her teeth into the taut skin right above his dick.

"You're...tasty." She winked. "And you're not the only one who likes to get a little rough."

"Jesus, I'm sorr—"

"Nope," she said sternly, before licking her lips. "First of all, you're not nearly as rough as you fear you are. And if I didn't like it, I'd tell you. Plus guess what? I liked it. A lot. I'll like it even more when you tell me what's going on in your head, but I think we need this first, right?"

He'd tell her. Soon.

"Soon," she echoed, like she could read his mind. "After you come in my mouth."

"Ha," he huffed. He wanted her mouth all right, hot and wet and sucking him deep, but there was only one place he wanted to spill his seed.

"You're such a caveman," she teased, still reading his mind, but he didn't care to argue because her breath was moist and soft against the head of his cock. They both watched as she stroked his length in her hand. Up. Down. Up. Down—

"Emme, put your sweet little mouth on my dick right now. Please. I'm begging you."

She grinned quickly, then swallowed him deep, using her hand to stroke the base of his cock where her lips couldn't reach.

He really did love this. And if she wanted him to come like this, that wouldn't be a bad idea. Fucking glorious, actually. But there were days for that, and days like this. When he wanted sex to be more than fun. More than a private, intimate connection.

He wanted to make love to her, hard and fast, then slow and sweet, over and over again, until he was imprinted on her soul.

In other words, he was a sappy fucking romantic, and he knew it.

She knew it too, because when he tugged her back up his body and rolled her beneath him, she kept her sass to herself and welcomed him inside her.

As she stretched around him, her slick channel slowly changing to accommodate his size, he held her gaze and soaked up the connection between them.

I love you. God, he wanted to say it out loud. And when she gasped, he wondered if maybe he had, but the only sound in the room were their ragged breaths and the squeak of her bed as he thrust in and out of her.

In. Out. Such benign words for magnificent feelings. Crazy awesome, that's what it was to be inside her. To hold her in his arms, all soft and willowy and raw, and drive his cock deep into her pussy.

In this moment, she owned him, body, mind, and spirit. There were guys he knew who talked about their energy, their *chi*, and they wouldn't have sex before a mission. Hell, some of those assholes wouldn't have sex before a big workout.

He didn't get it. What Emme did to him? What they had together? This was where energy came from. Hopefully one day this would be how they'd make a new life together.

This wasn't a threat. This was a gift.

"You're my everything," he whispered, gazing down at her as she wound herself around him. It wasn't quite what he wanted to tell her. There was a lot more. But it was a good start.

She smiled up at him, her expression soft and warm and half-drunk with desire. "I'm yours. Take me." He hadn't meant it like that. But before he could spin inside his head again, she whispered something else. "Please."

With a guttural cry, he let himself go. Giving and taking were arbitrary distinctions when she completed him like this, and it was time he trust that he did the same for her.

He just needed to dig deep and find enough of his usual cockiness to tell her the rest.

CHAPTER
FOURTEEN

TWO ORGASMS, some Thai takeout and a shower later, they were back in her bed. Emme was curled up on her side, listening to Nathan tell her how to board and disarm a ship in five minutes or less. He was always careful not to tell her anything that was classified, but she loved listening to him talk shop. He had a sharp professionalism that really did it for her—like he truly understood that what he did wasn't just macho and challenging, but also important and selfless.

"Might be the last time I do that for a year or so, though," he said quietly, his tone shifting. His voice tightened, and her nerves all stood on end.

"Why?"

"I've been given an opportunity to go to the Naval Postgraduate School."

"Oh?" That didn't sound bad. It sounded kind of cool.

"It would be a year in Monterey." He had a guarded expression on his face as he watched her. Did he think she would be anything other than ecstatic?

"Monterey, California?" She scrambled to her knees, her voice breathless and a crazy smile spreading on her face. "That's just two hours from here."

He nodded. He still didn't look as happy as she felt, though.

"What's wrong? This is fantastic, isn't it?"

"Depends." He took a deep breath and reached for her hand. Instead, she took his, and when he didn't continue, she looked down, giving him a minute to collect his thoughts. She loved his hands. His fingers were thicker than hers, blunt at the end and strong all over. She stroked her thumb over the tendon between his thumb and forefinger while she waited for him to say whatever was on his mind.

When he didn't say anything, she pulled their entwined hands up to her lips and kissed his knuckles as she looked at him softly over his hand. "Are you worried about leaving your team behind?"

He shook his head, his long, lean face all serious lines and frowning shadows.

"Then what is it? Surely this is a good opportunity. Plus…closer to me. Right?" Her voice shook at the end, which was silly. She *knew* how Nathan felt about her.

"That's the problem," he finally said, his voice strained. "I don't want to be *closer* to you. I want to be *with* you, Emme. A two-hour drive isn't any better than a one-hour flight. It's worse in some ways, because I'm not going to like that drive. I'm not going to like the feelings that come up. Worry about you if you're making the commute. Grumpiness if I'm doing it, because I'd rather you were in my bed every night."

The worry and tension radiating off him suddenly made sense. She was a grade-A asshole. The real problem? Nathan didn't know how *she* felt about *him*.

"I love you," she whispered, leaning in, wanting to be eye to eye for the first time she told him how much he meant to her. "I love you so much. Enough to be happy with you, even if it's only once or twice a month. Even if I have to fly up and down the coast to get to work. But if you're close enough that we can share a bed, I'm there. I'm in it, every night. I'm yours, Sailor."

He cupped the back of her neck and pulled her closer still, until she swore she could hear the thump of his heart beat. His eyes were dark brown granite, warm but solid as a rock. Determined. "You give me an inch here, baby, I'm going to take a mile."

"Take it," she whispered, watery tears threatening to fall again.

"Do you trust me?"

"Without a doubt."

"I'm going to love you forever, Emme. I'm not going to hurt you."

"I know." And she did. Deep down, she'd known for weeks already, but the lingering fear had been vanquished. "I can live anywhere. Monterey. Coronado Beach. Wherever you are, I can be there."

"I'm not going to want to do this half-assed, either." His lips rubbed against hers as he talked, then he kissed her, like he couldn't wait until he was done with his thought. "Okay?"

She laughed, a weird hitching sound because she was still on the edge of tears, but they felt like a happy, manic thing now. "I don't know what I'm agreeing to, but sure."

"Good." With a single, fluid twist, he rolled her onto her back. Looming over her, he was all long and lean and serious beyond measure. He took his time settling on top of her. Hip to hip. Hands to hands as he slowly tugged her arms above her head. When he trailed one finger back down her arm, slower than slow, he raised goose-bumps on her skin and made her heart swell twice its usual size.

"What, exactly, am I agreeing to?" she asked, smiling through the breathy words. She had an inkling. A wonderful, unbelievable idea had crystallized in her mind, borne of his words and that look in his eye.

"No. Half. Measures." He stroked over her collarbone and up her neck, groaning as she swallowed hard under his touch. "I wasn't planning on doing this now."

"What were you planning?"

———

"I didn't let myself get that far," Nathan admitted. Adrenaline was coursing through his body like he was about to do a HALO jump into an unknown situation.

But he had more intel now than he had when he'd told his chain of command that he'd take the courses in Monterey. Emme loved him, like he loved her. He should tell her how long he'd been keeping that inside. He should tell her what he wanted to do next. There was a lot he should tell her, and now he found himself uncharacteristically tongue-tied.

"Okay." She grinned up at him. From her sex-rumpled hair to her pale limbs tangled beneath him to her bright blue eyes, glittering happily, she was the most beautiful woman he'd ever held in his arms. Then she took it to the next level, because she was sharp as a tack and smooth like syrup at the same time. "Maybe we should plan something together. I mean, within your *full measures only* parameter, of course."

But this next step was something he was supposed to do himself. He stared down at this woman who'd stolen his heart in a single night, when he'd least expected it. Was it any surprise that the moment he would ask her to be his wife would take him by surprise as well?

He hadn't been exaggerating—every single time the idea of proposing had popped into his head, he'd shut it down. Trick had brought a diamond ring to Hawaii, because Gaby was going to visit him after their training exercise. Nathan had burned a little inside, not being sure if Emme was ready for the same conversation.

He was more than ready.

He wanted to shack up, knock her up, and keep her barefoot and pregnant forever.

After swearing his undying love and devotion in front of all their friends and family. Or just a minister. He wasn't picky.

But he didn't have a ring. He couldn't buy one for her until she gave him a clue that it was time.

Now that she had, he didn't want to wait.

Stalling for time, he kissed her hard. He even thought about going to her bedside table for her vibrator, a proven distraction.

Bedside table.

Breaking his lips away from hers, he swiveled his head to where he'd dumped his stuff. His wallet. His phone.

His dog tags.

Explaining that he'd "lost" them to the clerk would be worth it.

He leaped off the bed, grabbing his tags in one hand as he spun around in a circle. Next to her bed would have to do. Slowly, Emme followed, her eyes curving into two curious and amused half moons. Her lips were pursed together, like she was holding back a question about why he was acting so crazy.

He laughed and picked her up, holding her hard against his body before lowering her to the ground and kissing her quickly on the lips.

"What has gotten into you?" she asked, but he didn't answer. Instead, he slowly dropped to one knee, and for all his life, he'd remember the way her face slid from twinkling laughter to happy, disbelieving shock as she realized what he was doing.

"Now?" Her lips parted, flushed, and her cheeks pinked up.

"No time like the present," he muttered, shrugging.

She gave him a little, wavering smile. "We're naked."

"I think it happens this way more often than you'd think." He took a long, slow breath, wanting to stretch out the moment as long as possible. "Emme Ryan, you of the beautiful long red hair and the neat little black suit. I love the way you dance to ska music in your underwear and curl up in a ball when I'm playing guitar. I love your fearless spirit and your reasonable level-headedness. Never think that either is weakness.

Every minute I spend with you is joyful, right from the night we met. I've shared more secrets with you than anyone else, ever, and I want to keep doing that for the rest of my life.

I fell in love with you in the middle of a snowstorm. I kept that locked up tight inside me because I didn't want to scare you off. But I can't live without you any longer. I should have bought a ring. It's a long, stupid story why I didn't..."

"It's okay..." she whispered, filling in his silence. "I don't need anything."

"Oh, you do. You need everything. And I want to give you the world. We can pick out a ring together, but right now…" He trailed off again and reached for her hand, brushing his palm lightly over her bare hip first. *His*. The urge to tug her forward and bury his face in her belly was overwhelming. Wrap his arms around her thighs and never let go. In a minute.

First…

He stroked up and down each of her fingers with his left hand, then turned her hand over and pressed his dog tags into her palm, rolling her fingers around them. Holding her fist gently between both of his hands, he looked back up at her face. "Will you marry me, Emme? Will you be my wife, and have my babies, and let me give you everything you need for the rest of your life?"

She shook her head, making his heart stop for a second, then she nodded. Then she shook her head again. Tears and laughter were really interfering with him hearing the one word he needed more than his next breath, but she pulled him close, hugging his head right where he'd wanted it anyway, and then he heard it.

"Yes," she whispered, on the barest of breaths, then louder. "Yes. Not to giving me everything, you crazy man, because we need to do that together. But yes, I want to marry you. Tomorrow, if possible."

"I don't know. We'll have to look into it," he mumbled as he surged to his feet, lifting her up and carrying her back to bed, where they stayed for the rest of the night, quietly talking and making love and laughing.

No crying, though. They were all done with that.

THE SEALS UNDONE SERIES

Fall Out - Drew and Annie
Fall Hard - Jared and Cassie
Fall Away - Trick and Gaby
Fall Deep - Miles and Piper
Fall Fast - Nathan and Emme
Fall Back - Cade and Mel
Fall Dark - Vince and Larken
Fall Dirty - Hunter and Serena
Fall Quiet - Quinn and Leah
Fall Easy - Jason and Julie

Available individually and in collected volumes

www.zoeyork.com

ABOUT THE AUTHOR

Zoe York lives in London, Ontario with her young family. She's currently chugging Americanos, wiping sticky fingers, and dreaming of heroes in and out of uniform.

www.zoeyork.com

facebook.com/zoeyorkwrites
twitter.com/zoeyorkwrites
instagram.com/zoeyorkwrites
youtube.com/zoeyorkwrites